The Navel of God

The Navel of God

To Sue
a good friend &
loyal supporter —
— Mike
NOV 21, 2017

A Novel

Mike Best

New Alexandria Press
Milford

Published by New Alexandria Press
1150 Atlantic # 797
Milford, Michigan 48381
www.newalexandriapress.com

This book is a work of fiction. The names, characters, and events portrayed in this book are entirely fictitious, and are the product of the author's imagination. Any resemblance to any actual person–living, dead, or otherwise–is entirely coincidental.

Cover design ©2017 by Jeffrey Caminsky
Images for cover provided courtesy of NASA, ESA, and the Hubble Heritage Team (STscI/AURA)

Softcover Edition:
ISBN-10: 1-60915-024-2
ISBN-13: 978-1-60915-025-9

Printed in the United States of America

10 9 8 7 6 5 4 3 2 1

Acknowledgements

Few things are ever accomplished in life without the help of others, and writing a book is no exception.

I want to give thanks for the encouragement and support of my wife Kathy, Shirley Halloran, Richard Hurn, Sonia and Monte Kurtyka, Donna Lee, Pat Rensberger, Marilyn Yvon, and the late Wallace Mitchell.

Special thanks go to Jeffrey Caminsky, my friend and publisher who, being a true wordsmith, turned my prose into literature; and also to Don Harlow of the Esperanto League for North America.

Mike Best
July, 2017

To Carl Sagan....

The Navel of God

For everyone must see that the universe compels the soul to look upwards, and leads us from this world to another..

—Plato (427-347 BC)

Prologue

"DON'T PLAY WORD GAMES *with me, Zachary O. Peters. You are definitely the world's worst understater. Oh, did I just invent a word?" She tapped her spoon to her lips in a pensive manner and then pointed it at him saying, "By the way, and for the hundredth time, what does the initial O stand for? Ornery?"*

Zack was pleased that he could still distract with the best of them. "I thought I made it clear," he said without missing a beat, "that until I'm in my honeymoon or death bed–hopefully in that order–I'm not discussing the 'O' word."

"Okay, let me rephrase that...."

Zack stopped listening as he watched her pull a wisp of hair away from her eye. She turned to the window next to the table and looked outside through the white lace curtains.

Beyond the window a myriad of trees awash with a rainbow of autumn hues blanketed the rolling hills, their greenness stripped away by the photons emanating from Earth's daytime star. To the north a white steeple from the nearby village poked through the vivid fall colors.

Zack got up and moved next to her.

"You know something?" he sighed. "This is not only one of the most beautiful locations to be found anywhere, I find myself standing by one of the most beautiful women in the Orion arm of the Milky Way galaxy."

"You mean in just the one cruddy arm and not the whole Milky Way? And that's supposed to be a compliment? Harrumph."

Zack moved behind her. As their bodies touched, he slipped his arms around her waist and lowered his chin to her shoulder. He kissed the nape of her neck and whispered: "I think I am falling in love."

She turned into him to meet his kiss. "I knew you would," she smiled. "We better find Mrs. Kingswood and thank her for opening up for us."

"You're right. Without her hospitality I wouldn't have had the chance to enjoy my very first high tea."

"Sorry to break the illusion, Zack," she laughed, "but you only had a low tea." She pulled him closer to dab at a piece of torte on his chin and to adjust his tie. "One must have finger sandwiches and meats before it qualifies as a high tea."

They turned back to the doorway to take in the scenery.

"Do I have time to powder my nose?"

"Sure. I'll get our check."

Zack walked to the cash register and a kindly, gray-haired woman came into the room.

"Looks like the two of you are about to leave me."

"I'm afraid so, Mrs. Kingswood. You'll never know what all this has meant to us. We really needed a couple of hours of R & R. I wish we could have stayed for a few more days."

"You certainly would have been welcome. I've been glued to the television throughout the trial, Zack. For whatever my humble opinion is worth, you have done a superb job."

"I wish I felt that way," he smiled weakly.

Zack's lady companion came back into the room and met them at the cash register.

"I was just telling Zack what a fine job he was doing," said the innkeeper. "I'm sure the whole world is impressed with him, also. And you know something else? He's better looking in real life than on television."

"Amen to that," the younger woman laughed as she put an arm around his waist and gave it a tug. "One day he should make some lucky lady a very happy camper."

"So what's the damage, Mrs. Kingswood?" he asked.

"Don't even think about it. I opened up for you as a personal favor to the President. I don't know if she told you, but the two of us were as thick as thieves back in our university days. She and I would like you both to view this afternoon as a personal thank you."

"I hope we can come back some day and enjoy a high tea," he said.

The words caught in her throat as she said, "Yes that would be very nice if the two of you–"

The engines of the helicopter outside drowned out the rest of her words.

Zack's phone vibrated. He reached into his pocket and pulled it out. "Yes, Hayes. We're on the way."

The couple started for the door, stopping only to turn and wave to their host as they stepped outside.

"Bless you both," Anna Kingswood whispered, her eyes glistening.

They two raced hand-in-hand across the lawn as a tall, burly man beckoned them on. Nearing the helicopter, they bent forward, even though the rotors cycled a good seven feet above them. Once on board, the other crew member removed the lock-down pin from the landing gear and followed them in. The crew chief spoke briefly into his communicator, made a last visual sweep of the area, and stepped on board. Moments later, the giant helicopter began its slow climb.

Anna Kingswood locked the door and lowered the window blind, revealing the word CLOSED. *Turning off the lights, she walked to the counter, unfolded a newspaper and glanced at the headline.*

GUILTY VERDICT INEVITABLE

ODDS-MAKERS PLACE HUMAN ANNIHILATION AT 9:1

Part 1

I have loved the stars too fondly to be fearful of the night.

—Sarah Williams (1837-1868)

Chapter 1

—*1865*

ABOUT 97 TRILLION MILES from star 40 Eridani twirled Planet Earth, a rocky world third out from a yellow dwarf star in the Orion spur of the Milky Way's Cygnus-Carinae arm.

By an odd twist of fate, on April 9, 1865—the date the visitor arrived—there also took place another event, one with far less significance in the history of the universe. There, on the northern continent of the planet's Western Hemisphere, inside the McLean House at Appomattox, Virginia, another sentient being, General Robert E. Lee, stood hat-in-hand, having arrived after a one-mile journey on horseback to sign documents of surrender. Of the two, only the second event made the local newspaper headlines.

In Washington, news of the Union victory spread through the streets like a brushfire, eventually reaching a dreary building with poorly lit hallways and an exterior sign that read Elm Street Infirmary for the Indigent.

On the second floor, a nurse leaned into the doorway of Ward 2-B and exclaimed, with great excitement: "It's over! The war is over!" One of the patients, enfeebled by age and disease, managed a weak smile, thinking that if the war was truly over then her work was done. She squeezed her eyes tight in an effort to shut out the discomfort of her malignancy.

As the nurse continued down the hall, spreading the joyous news, the old patient's mind drifted back to earlier days when her dear Edward would come courting. Oh, she smiled, how she'd looked forward to those times when he would arrive in his magnificent carriage. She could still hear the sound of his horse's hooves on the cobblestones in front of her parents' home.

Though that was many years ago, through the open window beside her bed came the familiar *clop, clop, clop,* rising from horse-drawn traffic on the busy street in front of the building.

One of the carriages, drawn by a magnificent chestnut mare, came to a stop in front of the infirmary. The door opened, and the passenger stepped into the sunlight.

"Would you care for me to wait, Miss?" the driver asked.

"No but you can return for me at half-past the hour."

The driver nodded, touched the brim of his hat and pulled away, while his fare started up the crumbling steps to the front entrance. A young army officer, dressed smartly Union Blue, stepped out the doorway and came briskly to attention. He snapped a salute to address his superior and said, "Good afternoon, Colonel."

The visitor returned the salute and continued up the steps. Inside, it entered a dimly lit reception area and crossed over to an information desk where a young nurse was engrossed in paperwork.

She looked up with a start. "Oh forgive me, Reverend Father. I didn't hear you come in." She pushed her chair back and rose to her feet. Glancing at the tall grandfather clock next to the stairwell she said sadly: "I'm terribly sorry, Father, but visiting hours are over until after suppertime."

"I'm sorry," said the visitor, handing the young woman a note. "I didn't realize how late it was. But I'd consider it a personal favor if you might grant me a brief moment to see this woman on an urgent matter."

She took the paper and read the woman's name. "Well, perhaps for just a moment, Father. Mary Prosser is on the second floor in Ward B. At the top of the stairs turn to your right, then go to the last room at the far end of the hall. It will be on your left. Just let me say that Mary is one of our favorite patients. She neither complains nor makes demands on us, and always has a bright smile to offer." The young woman closed her eyes and sighed..

"It's such a shame," she said, her tone softening. "You're her very first visitor. She is such a fine and deserving soul."

"Your Miss Prosser sounds like a very special person."

"Oh yes, she is. You know, she managed a boarding house for ladies whose husbands died during the war. She would take them in, help them find employment, and often found them funds so they could return home to their families. It's really such a shame. After helping so many, she's ended up with no money left for herself. That's why she's with us, and not in a regular hospital."

The visitor glanced about the lobby. Soot smudges dotted the walls behind each lamp. A grizzled old man shuffled past, mopping the floor with half-dirty water and muttering to himself.

"Have faith, nurse," the visitor replied. "Special people receive special rewards."

"I would like to think so, Father. Good day to you."

Exhausted, her uniform soiled from tending to an array of ailments, the second floor nurse just started down the stairs to fetch some water for the patients when she saw the handsome young doctor coming up the stairs. Quickly, she swept aside a loose lock of hair from her face and stood tall against the wall to let him pass, trying, trying to show herself to her best advantage.

"Good afternoon, Doctor," she smiled cheerfully.

"I'm sure the patients appreciate all your hard work," the visitor smiled in return, continuing up the stairs. "And I know you look pretty as an angel to all of them."

At the top of the stairs, a harried head nurse shook her head. "Attendant," she said sternly, "report back to me when you're through cleaning these wards. We're short-handed again today, so we all need to pitch in and work a little harder."

Nodding, the visitor turned to the right and walked to the end of the hall. The smell of medicine and the odor of death hung in the air in the hallway.

In Ward B, a patient gazed through the half-opened window next to her bed, day-dreaming about her late husband, as a light breeze kissed her face after ruffling the torn, yellowed curtain. A dirty glass, a bottle of medicine and a spoon sat on her bed stand. As a kind-looking cleaning attendant approached, Mary Prosser turned and managed a weak smile.

Someone was in here earlier cleaning up," Mary said. "I'm doing just fine, but you might want to see if any of the ladies have needs."

Taking a seat beside the bed, the cleaning attendant leaned close and spoke in a low whisper. "I will in a moment. But first, I thought we might speak for a while."

"That would be nice although you may find I'm not very good company days."

The attendant slid the chair closer.

"There now," Mary said, smoothing her worn bed sheet with her frail hands. "What would you like to talk to me about, my dear?" She winced as a surge of pain shot through her body. Turning to the bottle on the bed stand, she gestured weakly

"If you don't mind, I'd like to take a little of that. The doctor says that it is all right for me to have it whenever I feel the need. It is opium, you know," she said, embarrassed.

The attendant poured a generous dose and gently raised Mary's head, putting the glass to her lips. Mary shuddered while swallowing the medicine.

"You may think this a strange thing to say," said Mary, "but I don't fear the thought of death. I did everything I could for as long as I could. And now, with that hateful war over, this is as good a time as any to slip away, and rejoin my dear Edward.." She closed her eyes and turned to look out the window.

"That's why I'm here to speak to you," said the visitor. "Your life does not have to end now in this manner."

Opening her eyes, Mary turned back to her guest.

"I have a proposal to offer you, one that would benefit us both. But because my proposal requires a great deal of confidentiality, I'll have to ask you to agree never to speak of it to others, no matter what your answer might be."

Intrigued, Mary nodded and her guest began to outline its plan. Once the proposal had been delivered, Mary thought for a moment and inquired, "And for my participation, you say that you could… you would...do all of that for me?"

"Oh, yes Mary. That and a great deal more."

"Then I agree," Mary smiled. "I agree with all my heart."

Unexpectedly, the head nurse stepped into the room and started walking toward Mary's bed.

"Please wait in the hall," said the attendant. "This will only take a moment, but she needs some privacy."

The supervisor backed out of the room, and the visitor turned back to the bed and took Mary's hand. A surge of warmth pulsed up the old woman's arm and, like a soft cloud, spread throughout her body. She felt healing, awareness, and a radiant glow of peace.

Mary sat up tentatively, mindful that these feelings of well-being might only be her imagination. Cautiously, she eased her legs over the side of the bed and stood up. Gingerly, she placed one foot onto the floor, followed by the other. With a sense of wonder, she soon stood erect.

"When will I speak to you again?" she asked.

"We will meet very soon, Mary. We have much to discuss."

And then the visitor was gone.

Mary bent down and reached under her bed, placing her belongings on the mattress. Removing her clothes from her tattered valise, she began to dress herself.

Only one of the patients in the room had witnessed Mary's transformation. Bed-ridden and dying, she closed her eyes and was praying.

When the head nurse returned and one a look at Mary, she covered her mouth her hand and ran out of the room. Minutes later the whole hospital staff had crowded into the ward, everyone speaking at once. In a corner of the room, by the bedside of the only patient who had seen what happened, the head nurse was on her knees, convinced she'd been present at a supernatural event.

"Please believe me," Mary said, " I am perfectly fine." Despite the distraction, she continued packing her valise.

"But how did—when did—?" a doctor stammered.

"Where are you going, Mary?" asked a nurse.

"What will you do?" asked the first floor receptionist. "Will you reopen your shelter?"

"No," Mary said quietly. She removed the last items from the small dresser beside her bed and placed them in the valise. From a tiny purse she removed two five hundred dollar promissory notes.

"I'd like you to keep these as a souvenir," she said, handing the notes to one of the doctors. "They were given to me by a widow who stayed at my shelter. Of course, in light of recent events, you probably shouldn't make any immediate plans to spend them."

The doctor read one and smiled. "Two years after the ratification of a treaty of peace between the Confederate States and the United States," he read aloud, "the Confederate States of America agrees to pay to the bearer on demand, Five Hundred Dollars. It is signed

Col. J. Stone and Treasurer H. Johnson on the 17th day of February, in the year of our Lord, 1864."

"I see what you mean, Mary," he smiled. "Rest assured that we'll hang them in a place of honor in the lobby."

"But we all thought your shelter was the most important thing in your life," said one of the nurses.

"It was, at one time," replied Mary. She smiled, closed the clasps on her valise, and made her way through the crowd, stopping at the door. Before leaving she turned, her eyes moving from one corner of the room to the next, stopping for a moment to smile at each familiar face.

"Thank you all for your love and caring," she said. "But I have a new calling now, one I sense is of much greater importance. Although I'm sad that we won't be seeing each other again, I promise that you will always be in my thoughts and prayers."

Turning, she stepped into the hallway.

The doctor glanced down and saw that Mary's timepiece was lying on the floor beside the bed. He picked it up and hurried into the hallway.

"Oh, Mary, I have your—"

But the hall was empty.

Chapter 2

—1901

THE PROSSER MANSION STOOD on the corner of Barrington Lane and Nottingham Boulevard in an aging yet elegant residential section of Arlington Heights, Virginia, a thirty-minute trolley ride from the hustle and bustle of the nation's capital. The only thing about it everyone could agree on was that it was very old, very large, and quite ostentatious.

Neither was much to be said of the old woman living there. No one recalled when she'd moved into the mansion. Some thought she was a descendent of James Leland Prosser, the scalawag cattle baron who'd had it built back in 1878. No one even knew the woman's name. She was known only as the old woman of the Prosser House.

Kitty-corner from the mansion lived Ephraim Rhoades, a mischievous boy with the neighborhood's most vivid imagination, whose his tales were typically long on intrigue and short on reliability. Ephraim couldn't remember a time when the old lady hadn't lived there. She was already old when his parents moved into the neighborhood, and the woman was seldom home. And what she did, how she got her money, or where she spent her time, no one knew. Rumor had it that she either worked at the Washington Conservatory or possibly with the government.

One bright summer afternoon ten-year old Ephraim and two of his friends walked into the alley behind the Prosser House. Deciding the old woman was not home, the boys gathered the courage to enter her backyard through the creaky gate. They crept up to the back of the house along a row of bushes that were older and taller than they were.

They tugged at one basement window after another until one of the boys found one that was open. Seconds later, the boys were inside, making their way quietly over the basement floor. They crossed over to a wooden stairway leading upstairs, guided by the sunlight peering through the windows.

Even to ten-year-olds it was clear that the basement was cleaner and more orderly than anyone's had a right to be. Let's go upstairs," Ephraim said. Reaching the first floor, they found a long hallway that ran from the front of the house to the back. When his friends saw the kitchen, hunger pangs led them to follow their instincts, and start looking about for food.

Ephraim headed in the opposite direction, toward the foyer that separated the parlor from the living room. Entering the parlor he was bewildered to see all of the furniture draped with white sheets.

"This really looks weird," he said to himself. He peeked under some sheets and guessed that the furniture had to be at least fifty years old. Glancing around, he noticed several music boxes on various tables and shelves. Satisfied that there was no adventure to be found in there, he went to rejoin his companions.

As Ephraim walked into the kitchen, one of his friends was opening and closing the cabinet doors. "There's no food in this old dump," the boy said in frustration.

"That's right," said the other boy. "The cupboards, the ice box and the pantry are all bare. Just like Old Mother Hubbard." They looked at each other and all began to laugh. From then on, they called old lady "Old Mother Hubbard."

The afternoon sun was waning, and so was the boys' spirit of adventure, and they decided to make a hasty retreat. They scampered downstairs and ran over to the basement window.

By the time Ephraim reached the window, his friends were already outside. He put his foot on a box and grabbed on to the window sill. As he was going through the window, out of the corner of his eye something caught his attention. Turning to look, he saw a closed door and what seemed to be sparkling lights around its edges. Meanwhile, not realizing that Ephraim wasn't with them, his friends were already through the gate and back into the alley.

The spellbound boy couldn't resist stepping down from the box and walking towards the door. And as he approached, the music became more distinct and the lights seemed to grow brighter. Summoning his courage, and after taking more than one deep breath, he eased the door open, and a brilliant light flooded into the basement. Too curious to stop, he raised his hand to his eyes to block the glare and stepped inside.

What he found amazed him.

Stepping into the room he found himself at the edge of a grassy glade stretching as far as he could see. The glade was filled with blossoms of every imaginable color, some as tall as himself. A pathway wound through flowers, ending at a white, wrought-iron bench next to a bubbling fountain.

Above him stretched a bright blue sky; in the sky were not one, but three suns, the largest a bright yellow-white, a smaller one tinged with blue, and the smallest a vibrant reddish-orange. Transfixed, Ephraim noticed a melodic sound, much like the eerie whine he'd heard when his Uncle Rudy played his singing saw. It all vanished from his mind the moment he felt the old woman's hand touch his shoulder.

FOUR YEARS LATER, the three boys found themselves stretched out on a grassy hill on a lazy summer afternoon, trying to think up something to do besides seeing imaginary figures in the cloud formations floating in the sky.

"Old Mother Hubbard!" cried one of the boys. Almost as one, they jumped to their feet and ran toward the Prosser Mansion, and soon the boys were standing in the alley, peeking over the back fence.

To make sure nobody was home, they decided that whoever drew the shortest straw would go to the front door and turn the bell. Minutes later, a nervous Ephraim was standing on the front porch, his outstretched hand poised in front of the door ringer, trying to ignore the goading voices of his hiding companions.

He screwed up his courage and turned the ringer. After a second turn failed to get a response, he rejoined his companions and the three of them hurried to the basement window. To their pleasant surprise, it was unlocked and ajar. His friends entered first, followed by a reluctant Ephraim. Once inside they ran across the basement and up the stairs, and saw that nothing had changed since their first visit. The furniture was still covered up with sheets, the rooms were still neat and orderly. And there wasn't a crumb of food in the house.

"Aw forget it," said one of the boys, and the adventure ended as quickly as it had begun. They ran back downstairs and over to the open basement window. For the second time Ephraim found himself the last to leave.

As he eased himself up to the window opening, a distant memory stirred him. Ephraim was tempted to turn around but didn't. Instead, he shrugged his shoulders and crawled out the window. Once he reached his chums, they laughed and jostled each other as they ran to the alley.

Back in the basement, a sparkling light shimmered to the music that wafted through the closed wooden door.

Part 2

The universe seems neither benign nor hostile, merely indifferent.

—Carl Sagan

Chapter 3

— *1978*

A RED AND WHITE ELECTRIC BUS slowed to a stop in front of the Gate of the Redeemer, one of the five original gates leading inside the thick walls of the Kremlin. The bus was one of many second-hand discards the Communist government had purchased from Detroit, Michigan, as a means of updating Moscow's streetcar system.

The eleven domes of St. Basil's Cathedral reminded most tourists of onions or artichokes. But to one elderly woman, however, they seemed reminiscent of a family of colorful Zanthee floating on a methane sea on the fourth planet out from Omicron Eridani, a star located 96 trillion miles from Earth. With an agility unusual for her advanced age, the 147-year old woman stepped from the bus and retied her babushka. Moscow was always cold in October. She glanced toward St. Basil's as its clock began to strike five. She had always been intrigued by the extremely ornate church; it reminded her of home.

On this particular afternoon, none of the domes exhibited their brilliant colors. Shrouded in metal scaffolding and gray tarpaulin, the domes were awaiting long-overdue repairs from constant terrorist attacks. In the government's grand scheme of priorities, it was of little concern that work proceeded at a snail's pace, if at all.

As the bus pulled away, the woman started across the stone

expanse of Red Square. Its name struck her as appropriate, in view of the various cruelties that had taken place there since Czarist times, when Russians were gathered in the square to be hanged, impaled, beaten to death, or simply buried alive. Once inside the gate of the 800-year-old fortress, the woman proceeded to a newsstand halfway between the Secret Garden and a statue of Lenin.

"Good day to you Comrade," said the proprietor, flashing an insincere smile. "I have those newspapers you wanted right here under my counter."

He reached down plopped a large stack of newspapers onto the counter. Without speaking, she removed a pad of paper and a pencil from her bag and wrote: "Thank you, but you may remember I requested only the front page of each, if you don't mind."

"Ah yes, I do remember now," he replied. "In the confusion of taking over this newsstand last week, I'd forgotten those instructions, and saved the entire newspapers. Believe me when I say that I am anxious to keep your generous business."

Nodding, she wrote, "I understand."

"Boy," he called out to his young nephew. "Help me separate these papers. Tear off the front pages of these newspapers and throw away the rest."

"Throw them away?"

"Yes boy, and be quick about it. We don't want to keep this fine lady waiting."

"But these are last week's newspapers," said the boy.

"Just do as you are told," he whispered sternly.

Soon, the task was complete. "Here you are, Madam," he smiled. "Please allow me a moment to calculate your bill. Let's see—we have one week of five different newspapers. With credit for your deposit, that comes to a grand total of twenty rubles."

She handed him a twenty-five ruble bill, refusing the change with a smile.

"Thank you," he said as he wrapped the papers with string. "You are extremely kind. May I expect you again next week?"

She nodded and began to take money from her purse.

"No deposit is necessary, Madam. I am pleased to be of service because..."

Before he could finish she took the bundle, stuffed it in her bag, and walked away. He shrugged and turned back to his stand.

"Excuse me, Uncle," the young lad said. "That lady bought last week's papers and still gave you a gratuity?"

"That's right, young man. Except for today's papers, the others were better suited for wrapping fish, or cleaning your backside. So, let this be a good lesson for you. Never question good fortune. Next Monday you will have them ready for her, and bundled the way I just showed you. Just the front page. Now go and help that customer."

The owner watched the woman continue into Cathedral Square. With a broad grin, he stashed the money in his vest pocket, patted it twice and turned to help a customer.

IN A POSH PART OF TOWN open only to army officers and party officials, a black 1971 Ziv drove up to an ornate building. Over the door a small metal sign with gold lettering against a black background read POTEMKIN STREET OFFICER'S CLUB. As the car glided to a stop, the two official flags flying from the front fenders drooped listlessly on their staffs. A sergeant in full dress uniform hustled to open the rear passenger door, and offered a sharp salute.

Army Colonel Pavel Aleksandrevich Federov struggled out of the back seat. Unsure whether to help, the sergeant took the less risky course and stared straight ahead.

Federov straightened, pulled at the hem of his tunic, squared his shoulders and returned a half-hearted salute. He turned to the driver and said, "Wait for me at the usual spot, Viktor."

As his car pulled away, the colonel strutted up the carpeted entrance to compensate his ungainly arrival. Once inside he removed his hat and handed it to the female sergeant attending the coatroom. She took it with a pleasant smile and handed him a claim check. He scribbled illegibly into the guest book and to the right of his signature, in a column marked guests, he wrote the number '1.'

The *maître d'* approached. "Good afternoon, Comrade Colonel. Your party has not arrived yet, but I have your usual table with a rose. Will you be taking the bar first?"

"Yes, but you can remove the rose for today."

As the colonel approached the bar, the bartender filled a crystal glass with vodka from a frosted decanter and placed it at the usual spot just as Federov took his seat.

"Good afternoon, Colonel Federov," said the bartender,

returning to his task of inspecting the stemware. He held each one up to the light of the chandelier before placing it back on the shelf.

Federov lifted the glass, stared briefly at the contents, and downed it with a slight flourish. As he did, his shoulder felt a stab of pain from an old wound, and his thoughts drifted back to a cold winter's morning in a dense forest along the Dnieper River. He shuddered at the memory of the rude intrusion of cold steel as it pierced his left shoulder, centimeters from its intended mark. Out of ammunition, a desperate German corporal had hoped to strike a blow for his Fuehrer with his bayonet. All his valor only won the young boy a bullet through the forehead from a pistol held in the right hand of an equally young and desperate Russian lieutenant.

A voice broke his reverie, "Pasha?"

Federov turned and immediately found himself locked in a bear hug with a large athletic-looking major.

"Pavel Aleksandrevich—you old rascal! Is it truly you!"

Wincing in pain, Federov soon recognized his old friend, who had a hint of garlic on his breath. Strange, Federov mused; after all those years, for the first time he remembered that the young German corporal had been eating garlic, too.

"Boris Dmitrevich," Federov responded. "You are a sight for sore eyes. What the devil are you doing in Moscow?"

"What else? I am attending boring meetings. So, how long has it been, Pasha? Four years? Five?"

"Five—it must be at least five years."

The major tapped Federov's paunch with the back of his hand. "Tell me; are you still a proud member of the Cosmonaut Corps? Or did they finally realize you were too heavy to carry to all the way to the Moon and back?"

"Borya, you know better than to speak openly of that adventure."

"Misadventure, you mean," scoffed Boris. "Pig's feet. The world is well aware that we dropped that project like a hot potato once it was apparent the Americans would beat us to the Moon. That's no secret."

"I agree, in part. But one should always exercise caution."

"Listen to you, Pasha. You sound as if the KGB was listening to us."

"It is, Borya."

The major gave a slow glance over his shoulder.

"You see, old friend," Federov whispered, "you are speaking with the KGB."

The major pulled back in surprise. "You're joking. You are joking, aren't you?"

"No. I am serious. I've been with the KGB since I left the Cosmonauts in 1973. And you know why I left?" Federov grinned. "The powers that be finally figured it would cost less to feed dogs and monkeys than to feed me all the way to the Moon."

The two men laughed.

"And that way," the colonel slapped his friend across the belly, "the Corps also ended up with a much smaller vodka bill,"

"Over here, Comrade!" Boris called to the bartender. "Two iced vodkas. Put them on my tab."

Turning to face Federov, Boris continued. "Pasha, you must come over to my table. I'm dining alone today, and want to buy you the finest beef steak in the kitchen."

"I'd like to hold you to that Boris Dmitrevich, especially when I think of all the money you've taken from me in the past playing cards. But you see I am expecting a guest."

"Ah, l'amour. And so early in the evening!" the major teased. "Perhaps she has a friend. Maybe you and I could impress them with our stories, eh? Just like in the old days."

"I am sad to say there is no lady tonight. Actually my plans are to repay an old debt. I am meeting with the son of the man who saved my life back in 1944."

"At the Dnieper River breakthrough?"

"But of course," Federov said. "Did you know Grisha Kornikov?"

"No. But everyone knew he saved your whole platoon that day on the river bank. He passed away some time ago, no?"

"Yes, he died twenty years ago. In 1958, I believe. But in a few minutes I will meet his son Mikhail for the first time. Today, I will give him a helping hand up the ladder, if you know what I mean," he winked.

"You are a good man, Pavel Aleksandrevich," Boris said, squeezing his old friend's right shoulder.

"And, later this evening," Federov added, "I must attend another meeting. It appears Fate has decided you and I will not party tonight."

"Alas, this is the price I must pay for your success, Pasha. So tell me, what do the big shots have you doing these days?"

"My dear Major," Federov whispered with a bow. "Today you are drinking with the Chief of Security for the City of Moscow."

"The whole city? Just promise you won't turn me in for my past indiscretions."

"Your many dark secrets are safe," Federov winked. "Besides, that would fly in the face of future promotions for both of us. Remember—I played a pivotal role in many of your sordid misadventures." He toasted the major and took a sip from his glass.

"I'll drink to that." said Boris. Tapping his temple a moment, a twinkle filled his eyes, "Ah—Minsk. Yes, Pasha...will you ever forget— "

Gasping, Federov put his glass back on the counter and started coughing. Boris pounded his friend on the back until the coughing fit had passed.

"Boris Dmitrevich," Federov coughed a last time to clear his throat. "Please refrain from mentioning Minsk when I'm half into my glass. And it would probably be best for both our careers if we agreed to forget that particular adventure," he added with a wolfish grin.

"I agree." Boris thought a moment. "Wasn't their father a field marshal?"

"Yes. These days you can see him standing beside our esteemed Secretary atop Lenin's tomb every May Day."

"I see what you mean. Yes...perhaps we would do well to forget Minsk and our lovely twins. But only if I have your promise we will one day begin some new adventures."

"The adventures you have in mind are for the young," Federov sighed. "We would best be content with memories of our glorious conquests. *Na zdorovye*!!"

They touched their glasses.

"And you, Borya? How do you serve Mother Russia these days?"

"These past few days, mostly by drinking. But I've been in the embassy service for five years now, most recently in Madrid. Although uneventful, it did prove a good career move. The day after tomorrow I leave on a two-year tour in the land of cold women, warm beer, and hot tea."

"Ah, London," laughed Federov. "Truly, that is a choice assignment. I am happy to see you can get along so well with the politicians, my friend. Perhaps you will be the one who wins our race for that general's star after all."

As they ordered a round for another toast, a stunning brunette in a tight-fitting black dress squeezed between them, holding a wine glass over her head with both hands. Pursing her lips, she faced Boris and whispered, "Would you please excuse me, Major?"

After passing, she turned and offered a seductive smile, before heading back to her table, where she appeared to be dining alone.

"So what do you think Pasha? Perhaps if I play my cards right—"

"Not perhaps, Boris. You will. But I suggest you make your move quickly, before one of those young stallions at the bar beat you to it. And I have two bits of advice for you. Don't take her to the ballet. And watch your wallet."

"Ha! Good-bye, old friend."

"Until next time, Boris Dmitrevich. Write and tell me how everything turned out." He watched as Boris made his way to the woman. After a few words Boris took her arm and guided her to his table.

Federov turned to the bar with a knowing smile and threw back another vodka. Glancing up, in the mirror behind the bar he saw the *maitre'd* talking to a tall and handsome Army sergeant. Stepping away from the bar, he turned and waved them both over toward him.

The young sergeant obviously felt out of place in the most prestigious officer's club in Moscow. While his manner and stride seemed casual, his eyes betrayed wonder at the room's elegance.

Federov extended his right hand and the surprised young man shook it. "Sergeant Mikhail Grigoryevich Kornikov reporting as requested, Colonel."

"Welcome to the Potemkin ,young man."

"Thank you Colonel," he said stiffly. "It is an honor to meet you. Is there something I can do for you?"

"Yes there is, Sergeant. First—please try to relax. And there is something I want you to do for me. Just as a personal favor to me, I want you to play-act by imagining yourself as an officer, and stepping up to the bar here alongside me."

Returning to the counter, Federov caught the bartender's eye. "Vodkas for my young friend and me."

Kornikov's face glowed when Federov called him friend, and shyly the young man stepped up to the bar. Taking care not to look down, he cautiously groped with his right foot until it found the brass rail. He pushed back his shoulders, trying his best to assume an air of casual confidence. When the drinks arrived, he said to Federov, "I would like to make a toast."

The Colonel nodded and the sergeant raised his glass.

"To the KGB," he said with just enough exuberance to catch the attention of some officers standing at the bar. They smiled back politely and a few raised their drinks before returning back to business.

"If it were me," Federov smiled, "I'd probably toast the beautiful women of Moscow. But no matter—let us toast the KGB."

The men touched glasses.

"Did you have any trouble finding the Potemkin?"

"Not at all Colonel. Getting here was the easy part. Getting past the corporal at the entrance was another matter."

"You say it was easy to find? That's interesting, since it doesn't have an actual address."

"Most noncommissioned officers know exactly where it is. We all like to daydream, if you understand what I mean."

"I think I do. Now tell me again. How long have you been in the service?"

"Three years," he said, tentatively. "I was one year underage when I enlisted. I know it was improper, but it's a rather common practice."

"That's a refreshing thought—and your secret is safe with me, Misha." The colonel smiled to see the young man's face brighten at the use of his diminutive. "You don't mind if I call you 'Misha,' do you? Your father and I were once very close."

"Not at all, Colonel. I would like that very much."

"Excellent. Tonight we shall have drinks, a good dinner, and discuss a business proposition I have for you. I believe you'll find it, shall we say, interesting."

Waving to summon the *maître d'*, Federov turned to the bartender, "Two more and send them over to my table."

The *maître d'* approached and bowed. "If you wish, Colonel, I can now show you to your table." he said.

The two men took seats in a discreet corner of the dining room. A few of the nearby tables had young women sitting with younger officers. Most of the tables had young women sitting with older officers. Each table had a rose in a vase; Federov's did not.

"Misha, I have been keeping an eye on you."

A waiter filled their water glasses and handed out menus. Kornikov eyes popped to see ice cubes in the water.

"We will order later," Federov said. "And now young man, I have a toast for you. To all of the women we've loved."

"And to those who turned us down," Kornikov added.

"Yes Mikhail, especially to them and their loss." They laughed while touching glasses.

"May I smoke, Colonel?"

"Of course, but try one of mine. They're English."

"That would be a treat. Thank you."

Kornikov lit the cigarette and inhaled slowly. He felt more at ease as he watched the smoke rise up to an ornate chandelier over their table. "How I envy you Colonel, being a member of this distinguished club."

"Answer me a question if you will, Misha. Have you ever entertained the idea of becoming an officer?"

"If such a dream were to come true, I would never leave the Army." He added judiciously, "Not that I ever had planned to leave the service, Colonel."

Federov handed a manila envelope to the young man. "That being so, I have something here I would like you to look at."

Kornikov opened it and pulled out what appeared to be his personnel file and a smaller, sealed envelope.

"Before you open the smaller envelope, hand me your file." Federov leafed slowly through the pages. He saw no need to tell the young sergeant about his other file---his security file, which was three times as thick, and one that Federov had personally spent the last week going over quite thoroughly.

"Very impressive, Sergeant. You've completed nearly every course offered in security. You are a marksman with pistol, rifle, and automatic weapons, and a graduate of our parachute school. I also see you're a champion wrestler, a member of the Sergeant's Chorus—and it says here you also play the balalaika. Did I miss anything?"

"I recently began taking ground school lessons. I want to fly."

"Excellent." Federov closed the file and leaned forward, his elbows on the table. "Well now, let's get on with it. You can open the envelope now."

The envelope contained a folded sheet of paper. Kornikov withdrew it and unfolded it.

"That is your commission as a First Lieutenant. You will note that it is retroactive from the date you first entered the Army."

Shaking his head, Kornikov read it twice.

"There's more, young man. I'll see that you are given your own apartment—one you won't have to share, except occasionally with a lady of your choice. And I'll arrange for you to share my brother-in-law's dacha in the country. It's less than an hour's drive from here. Just don't be too surprised if he tries to keep the holiday weekends for himself."

"Is this real? I would actually move right into First Lieutenant?"

"Yes, it is very real. Or it will be the moment I sign it. However, the offer comes with a caveat. Under normal circumstances, you would have the right to refuse a promotion. But this situation is rather unique. By offering this to you—well, let's just say I had to bend the rules a bit. For this reason, if you choose not to accept the commission, you may never speak of it to anyone. Ever."

Federov took a sip of vodka, lit a cigarette and continued. "You see, Misha, the department you would be working in has the highest security. I cannot overemphasize this point."

"I would be working in the KGB?"

"Most definitely. In fact, you would be working directly with me here in Moscow."

"Then there's no question in my mind. I accept with the greatest of pleasure."

"Excellent. Then we have a contract." He took back the paper and took out a pen from his jacket. It was black ebony with gold initials P.A.F. He signed it with a slight flourish. "There, that does it." He reached across the table and offered his hand. "Let me be the first to congratulate you, First Lieutenant Mikhail Grigoryevich Kornikov. And for good luck my boy, you may keep my pen."

Kornikov took it and then firmly shook the Colonel's hand.

"Thank you, Colonel. I can't remember having ever been so proud."

With a grave demeanor, Federov lowered his voice to a barely audible hush. "Misha, there is one last caveat that I probably should have mentioned."

"And that is, Colonel?" Kornikov frowned, his eyes widening. He suddenly realized that this offer was too good to be true, and feared he'd just been hoodwinked into something he wouldn't like.

"The next time we go drinking," Federov whispered intensely, "you are buying."

The two men laughed, and as they touched glasses the *maître d'* approached carrying a telephone. "Excuse me Colonel Federov, you have an urgent call. Do you wish to take it here or in a booth?"

"Here will do just fine. And have two more vodkas brought over for the Lieutenant and me."

The *maître d'* set the telephone down and plugged the cord into an outlet beneath their table. He glanced at Mikhail's sergeant uniform and without missing a beat responded, "Of course, Colonel, two drinks for you and the Lieutenant."

"Federov here," the colonel spoke into the phone. He visibly stiffened. "How long ago?"

Trying his best not to eavesdrop, Misha saw the colonel's eyes dart about as he listened over the phone.

"It wasn't due to go online for another two weeks" Federov said sharply. "Who did it identify and who was on duty? Have you spoken to him yet? And his response was? Was she early or on time? Hmm, you say last week too? Which areas? Are you sure it was just the lobby? That was good thinking, Captain. No, not until I arrive. About ten minutes." Federov hung up, and stared into his drink for a moment.

"There's a situation that requires my immediate attention," he said at last. "Instead of waiting until Monday, why don't you begin tonight? I want you to assist me with a problem. You and I—we would be a team. Is that agreeable?"

"I wouldn't miss it for the world."

"Well said, Misha. I'm sorry we'll be missing our dinner."

Federov stood up and snapped his finger for the *maître d'*.

"I'll need my car immediately."

"Of course, Colonel."

As they approached the coatroom, they came across a lieutenant checking his coat. The man turned and saluted.

"Young man, aren't you in my department?" asked Federov.

"Yes sir. .First Lieutenant Pessky. Vasili Ivanovich Pessky, Transportation Department, at your service."

"Well Pessky, I've heard glowing reports about your work. But right now, I need a personal favor."

"Anything, Colonel."

"That's my good man. I need you to remove your rank insignia and give it to my companion, who has just been promoted. Tomorrow, when you have it replaced, have them send the bill and any questions to my office."

"Yes sir," he said. After fumbling a moment with the snap, he handed the lieutenant's pins to Kornikov.

"Another thing, Lieutenant, should anyone complain about your missing insignia, tell them to bring their complaint to me. And let the bartender know I said to put your drinks on my tab tonight."

"Yes Colonel. Thank you very much, sir."

"Here, Lieutenant," he said, handing the rank insignia to Kornikov."

Kornikov attached it. He looked at the sergeant's stripes on his sleeve, and grinned sheepishly. "I may be starting a new fashion trend."

The corporal at the entrance saluted Federov as he opened the door to the Ziv.

"I'd suggest you start saluting my companion as well," Federov winked at the doorman. "I've heard Lieutenant Kornikov here is developing a low tolerance for noncommissioned officers who neglect protocol."

Glancing at the sergeant stripes and off-kilter lieutenant's pins, the corporal offered Kornikov a hesitant salute.

"Have a pleasant evening, sir—I mean, sirs!"

Once inside the vehicle, Federov tapped Viktor on the shoulder. "Get us to the Annex as soon as possible," said the colonel. "I'll take care of any traffic tickets."

Chapter 4

IN 1954, THE SECURITY SYSTEM of the Soviet Union underwent two innovative changes, as part of its program of de-Stalinization. First, the Party established the Komitet Gosudarstvennoy Bezopasnosti, better known as the KGB. This agency immediately became the primary intelligence and counterintelligence entity in the USSR, replacing the old Ministry for Internal Affairs—the MVD, a victim its own abuses, which quickly began a steady decline until it was finally disbanded in 1960.

The second, lesser-known innovation was the formation of a separate and highly secret entity of the KGB. Located within the Kremlin walls, and less than four miles from KGB headquarters, it was called simply the Annex. Even within the agency, its existence was more rumor than fact, and details of its operation were known only by high-ranking party officials. Fewer than three dozen people in the entire country knew its location or function.

AFTER LEAVING the newspaper kiosk with her bundle of newspapers, the old woman walked across Ivanovskaia Square, past the Tsar Bell and Archangel Cathedral and turned east into Cathedral Square. She continued to the mouth of a narrow alley between St. Vladimir Hall and the Palace of Facets.

Entering the alley, she came to a nondescript four-story building boasting a weathered, bronze sign at its entrance reading KRASNETSKY CHERNYSHEVSKY MEDICAL RECORDS BUILDING—ESTABLISHED 1933. She opened the door, and stepped inside.

The lobby was dark and dreary. Over the years, uncounted layers of paint had blurred its textured walls and resplendent ceiling. Florescent light fixtures, yellowed after years of cigarette smoke, hung in line at the far end of the lobby illuminating an open cage elevator and a marble stairwell.

The woman approached a cigar stand halfway down the hall, boasting a meager assortment of items scattered about a dusty display case. The glass countertop bent under the weight of a brass cash register and an ornate birdcage. Inside the cage was a parrot, half as old as the building.

Seated behind the counter, Sergei Bostroy had tipped back his wooden chair. He was reading the daily sports section and smoking; the cigarette's long ash hung precariously, almost defying gravity. His rumpled black suit and white shirt were badly in need of ironing.

"You startled me Comrade Maria!" he exclaimed, scrambling to his feet. "What dedication you must have coming in an hour early. Perhaps they'll promote you to this job when I retire."

He pulled out a logbook from under counter and opened it for her signature. Searching for a pen, he heard the sweet sound of wind chimes dancing in the breeze. Looking up he found himself unable to avert her gaze. A moment later he returned the unsigned log back under the counter, tipped his chair back and resumed reading.

The woman walked down the hall to the stairway leading to the lower level. One flight down was the maintenance room where she changed into work clothes. She placed the newspapers she'd purchased at the kiosk under some clean towels and pushed the cart to the elevator.

Reaching the fourth floor, she pushed the cart down the hall past a darkened office. Stenciled on the door in gold leaf were the words COLONEL P.A. FEDEROV. At the end of the hall she paused between opposing doors, each with a sign proclaiming NO UNAUTHORIZED ENTRY. One room had a red light shining over its door. She entered the other room, removed the newspapers from under the towels and scanned them into an electronic storage system, housed in a bulky computer.

Once they were copied she shredded the newspapers, and placed the residue in her cart's trash container. She removed a computer disk from her apron pocket, inserted it into a slot on the front of the computer, and entered some instructions on the control pad. Once the contents had been transferred she removed the disk.

Suddenly, she sensed a presence in the hallway outside. Outlined on the wall by her infra-red vision were images of three people. She slipped the disk in an apron pocket, took a towel from the cart, and began to dust the equipment.

The door swung open and Captain Tatyana Shlenko stepped into the room followed by two naval officers. She began speaking to the admiral and his aide.

"And in this room we have— " startled, she stopped short before recognizing the cleaning woman.

"Maria!" said the captain. "What a pleasant surprise. I hadn't expected to run into you."

Recovering from the distraction, Tatyana continued as if unfazed: "As I was saying, Comrades, this is the room where we process our data before it can be transmitted. It is scanned—that is, we create a digital image of the information—and then loaded on disks like this." She opened a drawer and held up a disk; it was identical to the one in Maria's pocket.

"And the room across the hall, Captain Shlenko?" the aide asked. "Perhaps you might show it to the Admiral before we leave."

"I'm afraid that is not allowed, Commander," she said politely. "Access to the transmitting room is highly restricted. In addition, the red light over the door indicates that a priority transmission is currently in progress."

"I understand, my dear," the Admiral said with a smile.

"We transmit from a roof top dish antenna up to the Lenin," Tatyana continued, "a satellite parked in geo-stationary orbit right over Leningrad. And now, Comrades, unless you have further questions, your car should be pulling up at our entrance right about now."

"Thank you Captain," the Admiral said. "We should return to our rooms and prepare for this evening's dinner."

"Your satellite dish," the Commander asked. "Is it movable?"

"Certainly, although its default mode aims to the Lenin, we are able to transmit to various coordinate systems—latitude longitude, altitude azimuth and right ascension declination. Wherever we want—we just aim and send."

The admiral nodded. "Just keep those transmissions going out to my—" Suddenly noticing that Maria was still in the room, he stopped.

"Don't be concerned," Tatyana said pleasantly. "If Maria didn't have a proper security rating, she wouldn't work here."

"—to my ships at sea," he finished.

"As well as under the sea," she added. "We contact your submerged submarines too."

"The walls of these rooms seem to have a different texture than the others," the aide mentioned as his hands swept the room.

"An excellent observation Commander," Tatyana replied. "They must be different, for security reasons. The walls, ceilings, and floors are constructed with sandwiched layers of composite materials that carry a live electric field. It helps keep the curious Americans ill-informed."

They all laughed good-naturedly.

"Thank you Captain," the Admiral nodded. "It's time to leave you to your duties. And my dear, I trust we will have the pleasure of your company this evening."

The lights flickered and went out, leaving the room pitch-black. Maria sensed the Admiral's right hand moving toward Tatyana's derriere and discreetly stepped between them.

"Don't be concerned gentlemen," Tatyana said, her voice soothing. "The lights will return momentarily." And as if on cue, the lights came back on.

"Why are there no emergency lights?" the aide asked.

"We have them, but for some reason they failed."

"Now to our transportation, comfortable rooms and a hot shower," the Admiral said. "Later tonight, Captain, you and I might go over some of my ideas about cementing relationships between the Navy and your facility."

"My instructions, Admiral, are to stay with you through the banquet and see that you are safely taken back to your hotel."

"Actually my dear, I have a suite at the Potemkin Officers Club."

"Of course, the Club," Tatyana said, following them out; catching Maria's gaze, she rolled her eyes and sighed.

Once they had left, Maria listened for the elevator doors to open and close before gathering her items. She glanced around the room before pushing the cart into the hallway. Seeing that the red light was off, she unlocked the transmitting room door

She was startled to hear a man's voice.

"Good evening, Comrade Maria."

Chapter 5

BY THE TIME THE ZIV was half way to the Kremlin, Federov had made two telephone calls, and explained the situation at 'A' to his new assistant.

"And that's about it," he said, leaning back in his seat. "The new system detected an intrusion."

"At the Annex?" asked Kornikov.

"Correct. But remember—never call it by that name. You should get used to referring to it as 'A,' and then only to those who you know to have clearance."

"But I thought you said the system wouldn't be active for another week or so?"

"True, but this detection was picked up during a test run."

"And the intruder is identified?"

"Yes."

Federov picked up the phone and said, "Federov here. Put me through to the lobby at A. He then turned on the speaker phone; seconds later, a man's voice answered..

"Krasnetsky Chernyshevsky, Medical Records Building. How may I help you?"

"Sergei? Colonel Federov here. Give me an exact count of who's inside now."

"Let me check the log, Colonel. Yes—there's Captain Shlenko, the admiral, his aide, myself, three guards in the barracks, and an electronics technician. Altogether that's eight."

"How about the custodian?"

"Maria? She is not due until six. That would be—let's see—about twenty minutes from now. Colonel—Captain Shlenko and her party are just stepping off the elevator now."

"Thank you, Sergei. Now put the Captain on the line."

SERGEI HELD THE PHONE up for Tatyana and whispered: 'The Colonel'. Briskly, she turned to face the Admiral.

"I'll be with you shortly," she said, and walked a short distance away.

"Yes, Colonel," she answered, loudly enough to be overheard. "The admiral and the commander are about to leave. Yes, he is very impressed. How can I help you?"

"Tatyana," said the Colonel. "Listen to me carefully, and don't repeat back anything I say. I'm en route now and will arrive in five or ten minutes. Do not tell anyone, but I have it on good authority that we had an unauthorized entry last weekend. Have you noticed anything strange? I mean, other than the Admiral?"

"I give him credit for behaving himself today," she whispered, "although I'm certain he hopes I'll be part of his entertainment package this evening. But I can get out of that without a problem. Otherwise, nothing Earth-shattering had been going on—except that the electrical power has been acting up, and your parrot has the runs. There also were a couple of short blackouts during the admiral's visit, when the back-up lights didn't kick in."

"All of Moscow is having such problems," Federov said. "I wish the Secretary would pay the electric bill."

"Oh, no, the lights are blinking again Colonel. Now they've gone out completely and once again, the emergency lights have not kicked in. Sergei—hand me a flashlight."

Tatyana sighed as she waited for the doorman to locate a working light. "Colonel, I'll stay on site until you arrive. But now I want to find Maria. The poor thing must be unnerved at being stranded in the dark."

"Wait a minute. Did you say Maria?"

"Yes sir."

"Did you see her yourself? Personally? With your own eyes?"

"Yes sir"

"Now answer me precisely: when and where did you last see her?"

"Maybe five minutes ago, in the fourth floor scanning room."

"Tatyana—listen very carefully. Your first order is to get that horny son-of-a-bitch and his slobbering aide out of my building with as little fuss as you can manage. Do you understand?"

"Yes Colonel."

"Once you've done that, I want you to go downstairs and tell the duty officer that I am declaring a Code Red, and that you are in charge until I arrive. Got it?"

"Yes sir."

"Once the Admiral's party leaves I want that facility sealed up tighter than a drum. No one comes in, and no one goes out. Not until I get there. Understand?"

"Yes sir."

"Finally— and you may find this a bit awkward—you are to place Sergei under arrest and put him in a holding cell. Then, when you locate her, do the same with Maria. But put her in a separate cell."

"Please repeat the last instruction?"

"I want Sergei and Maria arrested separately, in that order. And I want them placed in separate cells. I do not want them able to communicate with one another."

Tatyana took a deep breath. "I understand," she said quietly.

"I should be there shortly."

FEDEROV HUNG UP and tapped his driver on the shoulder. "Viktor, get us to A as fast as you can, but without warning lights or the klaxon."

Federov turned to face to young Kornikov. "In time, I plan to put you in charge of security at A. Until you settle in, you'll report to Captain Shlenko. Understood?"

"I understand, Colonel."

"We are upgrading our security with a system that provides both video and audio on stored tape."

"How does the present system operate?"

"We have only visual, with no backup storage. Right now there are only cameras in the lobby, and in the hallways on each level. I plan on having a total of five monitoring stations. Four will be in A; one in my office, one in the lobby, one at the duty officer's station and one in the barracks. The fifth will be at KGB headquarters downtown."

"Excuse me Colonel, did you mention barracks?"

“Yes. We keep three uniformed soldiers on the lower level, and a master sergeant as duty officer. They have a kitchen, sleeping quarters, and three holding cells.”

“What kind of shifts do they pull, Colonel?”

“Twenty-four hours on, and forty-eight off. One of your tasks will be to keep them on their toes. From the moment they scramble, they must be able to reach any spot in the building within ninety seconds. With our new system, we’ll continue to monitor the same areas as before plus what I consider critical locations. For your information, the call I received at the club informed me of a security breach last Saturday.”

“If I might comment, that was an inexcusable length of time before being reported to you, Colonel.”

“To tell the truth, I might never have found out were it not for an observant technician working on the system. Because the new system was still off-line, it would likely have gone unnoticed. The technician saw something odd going on with a video recording last Saturday. It showed our cleaning lady entering the lobby twice without signing in.”

“That seems odd,” Mikhail said.

“It was. The first time was at five, a full hour before her shift started. The second time she didn’t sign in was at six, her scheduled time.”

The Ziv slowed to pass through the Kremlin wall’s Redeemer Gate. A sentry recognized Federov’s identity flags and waved it through.

“May I ask what the log book shows, Colonel?"

“Now that’s good thinking, Misha. And this is precisely what we are going to find out. I didn't want to alert Sergei, our lobby guard, in case he is involved.”

“Have you found him trustworthy in the past?”

Federov chuckled. “Now, that's not such good thinking,” he said. “Would I still have him with us if he wasn’t? Besides, Sergei will be retiring soon. I can’t imagine he’d risk losing his pension after a twenty-year career.”

“I presume Sergei doesn’t suspect you know there’s a problem?”

“I don't think so, Misha. When I asked if Maria was there yet, he had to check the log. When we arrive, you’ll be meeting my top aide, Captain Shlenko. She is very competent, an excellent officer and quite attractive. Just try not falling in love too soon," he said slapping Kornikov's thigh.

"Yes sir. I mean, no sir."

"She said she'd just given an Admiral a tour of the facility. I told her to button the place up as soon as he leaves."

"An Admiral was given a tour of A?"

"Yes. The idiot is the country's third-ranking fleet admiral, so I had no option. Anyway, Shlenko said she ran into Maria, our cleaning lady, up on the fourth floor, inside a highly sensitive area."

"But why would this Maria, assuming she's the intruder, have a conversation with a potential witness?" asked Mikhail. "Wouldn't she have tried to stay out of sight?"

"Not a conventional conversation. You see, Maria is a mute and probably assumed the building was empty. And it would have been, were it not for the Admiral's party."

"Empty, except for the security guards and Sergei."

"Yes, and this is what bothers me. I've known Sergei for fifteen years and can't believe he is part of this. But, we shall find out soon enough—here we are."

INSIDE THE TRANSMITTING ROOM, the technician turned to Maria. "I'm sorry," he smiled. "I didn't mean to startle you. If it wasn't for these cursed power failures, I'd have been out of here by now and on my way home."

Maria smiled and closed the door behind her. She immediately began dusting the shelves.

"I have everything jury-rigged and functional," he said absently. "Well, at least good enough to hold together until I can return Monday with the new parts we need." He gathered up his tools and paused the door. "The bulletin board in the locker room says that you completed yet another year without a single sick day. That's commendable, Maria. Good night."

As he opened the door, the lights flickered and went out, plunging the room into darkness. The yellow emergency lights came on, followed a moment later by the regular lighting.

"There they go again," he said. "We'd better leave the floor while we can."

Maria followed him, but stopped at the door. Once he had left, she checked to make sure that her disc was in her pocket, and locked the door.

A few minutes later when the lights went out a second time, the emergency lights did not come on. Without power, the door to the hall remained locked; all she could do was sit down and wait.

THE ZIV SCREECHED TO A HALT in front of the Annex. Federov leaped out of the car, followed by Viktor and Kornikov. They found Tatyana waiting for them at the door.

"What's our situation?" Federov asked.

"Everything is as you ordered. The duty officer and I secured the building and Maria and Sergei are in separate cells, held under surveillance by two guards. Neither knows the other is being detained. Oh—and the power went off again for a few minutes."

Federov strode to the counter and scanned the log. "Any problems so far, Captain?" he asked Tatyana.

"None except while Sergei seemed quite surprised, Maria seemed almost complacent, although—"

"Although what?"

"It's probably nothing sir, but when I sent one of the men to the fourth floor to locate her, he returned saying she wasn't there. That's when I instigated a floor-by-floor search of the building. Sure enough, she was there, on the fourth floor. Locked inside the transmitting room."

"The transmitting room?

"Yes sir."

Kornikov saw the Colonel clench his jaw tightly, then take a deep breath.

"The important thing is you did find her," Federov said at last, turning his attention to the logbook. "I don't see where she signed in. What time was she due?"

"About fifteen minutes ago," Tatyana said.

"Tatyana, make sure the front entrance is secured, and have one of the men stay behind the counter. But first, have him remove his jacket, tie and cap. Better yet—Viktor, you're not in uniform. You go and stay behind the counter. But move your chair behind the pillar, so you cannot be seen from the street. The rest of you, follow me up to my office. Misha, bring the log book."

* * * * *

FEDEROV'S FOURTH FLOOR OFFICE was the most elaborately decorated room in the Annex. Its walls were covered with military maps, framed photographs, and letters and commendations. He sat behind a hand-carved, Siberian oak desk, under a portrait of the Premier. The huge desk was uncluttered; only a pen, a desk pad, a silver and glass tea mug, and a photograph of him wearing a lieutenant's uniform adorned the wooden expanse.

Tatyana and Kornikov sat to Federov's right. In front of them, Master Sergeant Sergei Bostroy stood at rigid attention with white-knuckles and fists clenched at his sides.

Federov said, "Try to relax, Sergei, before you have a stroke. Although this is serious, you are not in front of a firing squad." He turned the logbook around so Sergei could read it. "Why don't you have Maria logged in?"

"She hasn't checked in yet, Colonel." He seemed pleased at being asked a question that he had the answer for.

"I beg to differ, Sergeant. Maria was in the building, and found in the scanning room by Captain Shlenko thirty minutes before she was due to sign in." He pointed to the log and said, "As you can see, the log doesn't show her signed in once, let alone twice.

"I assure you she never came through the lobby, sir."

"Perhaps you left the back door unlocked."

"That would not have been possible, Colonel. I check all the doors when I come on duty. It was secure and can only be unlocked from the inside. I keep one key at the front desk. The only others belong to you and Captain Shlenko. May I ask what was seen on the new lobby camera?"

"The tape shows Maria coming in the front entrance, walking up to the counter, being handed a pen by you, and then walking to the stairs without signing in."

"I don't understand. Perhaps she was already in the building when I came on duty?"

"Then who is it the monitor shows coming in without logging in? There is also other evidence."

"Evidence, Colonel?"

"I haven't seen it yet, but we have a video tape from last Saturday showing you letting her into the building an hour before her scheduled check-in time."

"Last Saturday? Colonel, I assure you—I give you my word—"

Raising his voice, Federov continued, "And at that time, you didn't have her sign in! Then an hour later, at precisely the time she was scheduled to come on duty, she walked up to the counter from inside the building, apparently from the stairwell—and then, finally, let herself in."

"Colonel," Sergei stammered, "what about the electronics technician that was here earlier? Perhaps he can verify—"

"Verify what? If he didn't see her, nothing is verified. If he did see her, then you have lied."

Federov answered the phone. "Federov here. Excellent, Major, You found the technician before he got on the Metro? Good work. Now, ask him if he saw Maria, our cleaning woman, at any time during his visit here today. Yes, I'll wait."

Pleadingly, the sergeant glanced from Tatyana to Kornikov, and back again.

"He did? Good. Tell him to go about his business, and to report to me at ten o'clock Monday morning. That's correct. Say nothing more about the event, or what he saw. Goodnight, Major."

Federov hung up and turned to Sergei. "We were able to contact the electronics technician, Sergeant. He informs us that he ran into Maria while she was cleaning the transmitter room."

Federov pushed a toggle on the intercom next to his phone. A voice answered through a burst of static, "Security...—...here, Colonel."

"Come to my office and take Sergei back to his cell. Then bring Maria up. Do not let them see each other."

Releasing the switch, he turned to Tatyana "It's time we saw what is on the disk you found in Maria's pocket. Please take it down the hall and get me a print out."

WHEN TATYANA RETURNED, Maria was seated on a chair by the window. Tatyana handed Federov a disk, along with a pile of shredded paper and some printed sheets of paper. She exchanged a sad smile with Maria.

"It would appear that this garbage you brought me is nothing but Russian newspapers."

"According to the dates we can make out, Colonel, they were the front pages of last week's newspapers. In the time I had, I could only reassemble three of them, none in full. I scanned the fragments, and printed you copies." She pointed at the sheets of photocopy paper.

"Damn—I can't find my reading glasses. Tanya—which papers are these?"

"They were *Pravda*, *Trud*, and the *Moscow Times.* We also found bits of the *Leningrad Courier*, *Izvestia* and one other I don't recall. The complete images of each were on the computer disk—which are also in your print-outs."

"Is that right, Maria? This disk contains the front pages of last week's newspapers?"

Maria took the pen and wrote, "Yes."

"What were you doing with the disk in the transmitting room?" he asked.

"I beg you to forgive me," she wrote, "but I cannot answer that question."

"You can't, or you won't?" he said sternly, his tone now harsh and unforgiving. "Are you refusing to answer me? Maria, you were seen in the copy room this afternoon by the Captain. You were later by a technician in the transmitting room. Can I assume you had this disk with you, and that you transmitted data?"

"I can say no more," she wrote.

"Excuse me, Colonel," Tatyana interrupted. "We have every reason to believe that she did make a transmission."

"And why is that?"

"Because when I checked our radio dish, it wasn't pointing into space at the Lenin."

Federov responded with a blank stare.

"Because of all the power surges and temporary failures," she tried again, "we saw that dish returned to its secondary default mode, the moment it was unable to re-acquire the Lenin."

"Tanya," Federov sighed harshly, "I am a simple man. Once again—in simple words—without the technical jargon?"

"Sorry," Tatyana took a deep breath. "Whenever it is not being used for transmitting purposes, the satellite dish is programmed to point up at the Lenin satellite, which is in geo-stationary orbit above Leningrad."

"And the rest of that gobbledygook?"

"When I left the fourth floor with the Admiral, the transmitter was sending the day's final transmissions to the Lenin. Had there been a system blowout—I mean, either a power overload or a sudden drop in power— the dish would have remained aimed at the Lenin, its primary default position. By default, I mean the position the dish will move to if there is ever a problem during the time it is transmitting."

Still confused, Federov did his best to remain calm. "So, where was the dish pointing?"

"That's the problem, Colonel. It had moved to its secondary default position—in other words it was pointing straight down at the roof, the position it will take if a power problem occurs when it is not pointing at a pre-coded target."

"You are still being vague."

"Colonel, think of it as a security measure. It will bring the dish to a safe position if it receives a damaging power surge from an unauthorized target—a surge that could fry it and burn out the electronics."

"So, the implication is this was all a big accident?" Federov asked.

"Perhaps more of a coincidence," she answered. "My best guess would be that Maria had aimed the dish at a non-Soviet target and started sending a transmission just before the last power surge. When the dish software sensed the possibility of harm, the dish moved to its secondary default position—downward. The odds of that happening by chance are astronomical."

"Thank you, Tatyana. I understood half of what you said, but I am impressed with your ability to put it all together."

He turned to Maria. "This brings us back to you, Maria. Where were you transmitting to?"

Maria shook her head and pointed to what she had written.

"That is not an answer and is not acceptable. Please realize the position you have put me in. I cannot simply look past this and ask you not to do it again."

Tatyana said, "Maria, not a person in the building doesn't consider you a friend. You've not only endeared yourself to us, some think of you as a sister or a mother. Please—give us the opportunity to help you."

She didn't respond.

Kornikov spoke up saying, "Colonel? If I might make an observation."

"Go ahead. Obviously I'm making no headway with this so far."

"Looking at a worst-case scenario, let us assume Maria did send copies of our newspapers to the West. Let's even go as far as to say she sent them directly to the CIA. What damage do we suffer? What advantage would the Americans gain?"

Tatyana added, "And remember these are week-old newspapers,"

"Exactly," Kornikov continued. "Those are papers that anyone in the world can buy. Probably even in Washington. Why would Western agents not prefer current newspapers over those from the previous week?"

Federov looked first at Tatyana, then at Kornikov, and smiled. "Would it be too much to ask which side of this interrogation you two are on?"

Kornikov answered slow and politely. "What we are attempting to point out is the worst Maria can be accused of is sending worthless—"

"—and out of date—," Shlenko interrupted.

"—yes, week-old newspapers."

Federov stood up, walked to the window and stared out at the street below. "Perhaps the newspapers contained coded information," he said.

"Possibly, but any newspapers the CIA obtained locally would contain the same coded information," offered Tatyana. "I think this negates the idea that Maria could by spying for the West."

"I'm afraid I must agree with the both of you. And that takes us back to where we began," Federov said. "Why would Maria go through all this trouble to transmit material that is of no importance? What are we overlooking?" Gazing harshly at the elderly custodian, he returned to his chair.

"I'd like to ask her a question if I may, Colonel," Kornikov asked.

Federov motioned broadly. "Be my guest, Lieutenant."

"Maria, if your plan was to send secrets to the West, would you choose something other than week-old newspapers?"

She nodded and wrote, "Of course I would, if I were disloyal. But I would never do such a thing."

"Did you send state secrets to any other country?" he continued.

"No, I have not," she wrote.

"Let me be more direct, Maria," said Tatyana. "Are you spying for the Americans? A simple yes or no will do."

She shook her head and wrote, "No."

"Tatyana, I want to speak to Maria privately. Why don't you take the lieutenant downstairs and treat him to a cup of coffee. I'll call you when I want you to return."

"Are you sure?"

"I assume you've searched Maria?" Federov asked.

"Of course,"

"Well then—I have an armed guard outside my door and a pistol in my drawer. After overpowering me, she would need to walk through one of these walls and fall four stories to escape. If she can do that from my office, she can do it just as easily from a cell---except that those walls lead to dirt. But if she can do all that, she can probably tunnel through dirt, as well."

Tatyana motioned for Kornikov to follow her.

"I can't vouch for our coffee," she said, and they closed the door behind them.

When they had left, Federov looked at the old woman and shook his head. "Maria, you cannot imagine how much this situation distresses me."

She reached across his desk and touched the back of his hand gently while nodding.

"So why don't you tell me what you've been up to. If it's just a minor matter of security breaches, you won't be sentenced to more than a couple of months in a minimum security work camp. Certainly not one of our more unpleasant facilities."

He searched her face in vain for a response.

"But this facility is host to all manner of state secrets. And if it can be proved that you've somehow sent classified material to the West, you could be executed. And in that case, I could do nothing to stop it."

She didn't respond.

Federov slouched forward and shook his head. He closed his eyes, and wiped his face with his hands before adding, "Maria, please let me help you."

Imperceptibly, gentle sounds floated through the room, filling his mind with pleasant images of warm summer evenings on Lake Pzanyatzka in the Urals, reminding Federov of small wind chimes dancing with a gentle breeze.

He looked up, and was surprised to see Maria standing taller than he'd ever seen her, with the sound of the wind chimes radiating from her body as she looked into his eyes. Without averting his gaze, he took a sheet of official stationary from his drawer and began to write.

SEATED AT A WOBBLY TABLE in the building's lunchroom, Tatyana slid a mug of steaming coffee to the young lieutenant, and took a sip from her own cup.

"It seems you've had quite an unusual day," she said.

"You have a gift for understatement, Captain," Kornikov replied. "I woke up this morning as a sergeant and will go to bed as a first lieutenant. And in between—I still don't know what to make of all the in-between."

Tatyana smiled. "One bonus is you won't have to take the qualification exams. And by the way, whenever you and I are alone, you may call me 'Tanya.'"

"I will thank you. And please do the same for me."

"So your new name is also Tanya?" she grinned mischievously. Seeing the young man blush, she laughed and took pity on him. "Then Misha it shall be."

Captivated by her laugh, Kornikov couldn't help thinking that like all pretty women, she could make both time and a man's heart stand still simply by smiling.

"Tanya," he ventured, "it may be my imagination—and probably none of my business—but on more than one occasion I have felt you bordering on insubordination with the Colonel."

"I suppose you could say he and I enjoy a somewhat unusual relationship," she smirked.

Circling the outside of her cup with her finger, she seemed about to say something, but stopped and sat up straight.

"Well, I believe we've given him enough time to sort things out with Maria," she said. "Why don't you start back up to the lobby while I use the washroom?"

Reluctantly, Kornikov headed back up the stairs. Once on the main floor, he decided to read the names on the building directory next to the elevator to give himself an excuse to linger. He had just gotten half-way through when the elevator door opened and its lone occupant stepped into the lobby.

"Maria?" he said, shocked to see her.

Turning to face him, she closed her eyes and pointed a finger at the young lieutenant, emitting a low-pitched hum just as Tatyana reached the top of the stairs, and opened the door to the lobby.

"Maria—stop!" she commanded; by reflex, her pistol was already in her hand and aimed before she had time to think about what was happening.

Slowly, Maria lowered her arm and opened her eyes. Moving carefully, she took a piece of paper from her apron pocket, and handed it to Kornikov. Tatyana stepped toward them, her pistol cocked and at the ready.

Kornikov read the paper and looked up, shaking his head. "This makes no sense," he whispered. "This is a signed release by the Colonel, allowing Maria to leave the building."

"Impossible," said Tatyana, snatching the paper from his hand. After reading it twice, she placed it into her vest pocket and motioned with her pistol for Maria to walk to the counter.

"Over there, Maria—and make no sudden moves."

Tatyana stepped to the counter, her pistol aimed at the cleaning lady, and depressed the talk button on the intercom. "Colonel?" she said, her eyes never leaving her target. "This is Tatyana. I'm in the lobby. Are you all right?"

The intercom was silent.

"Colonel?"

"I—I believe so," came the reply at last.

"Sir, Mikhail and Maria are with me. Maria was trying to leave the building, and produced what appears to be a release signed by you. Was that your intention?"

"Of course not!" Federov said, now fully alert. "Bring her back up here at once."

MINUTES LATER, Maria stood in front of an angry Federov; Tatyana and Kornikov were standing behind her; Viktor was further back, guarding the door.

"You leave me no choice," the Colonel fumed. "I don't know what you were doing or how. And I have no idea how you did it. One thing, however, is certain: refusing to answer my questions has purchased yourself a free ride to KGB headquarters. There, you will be asked the same questions in a far less amiable manner by people who are not nearly as nice. If you refuse to answer their questions, you will probably be given a few chemical injections to loosen your tongue—injections that, God forbid, may very well end up turning your mind into borscht. I'll give you another thirty minutes to decide what you want to do."

Federov reached around to his credenza to switch on the intercom. When it wouldn't operate he pounded the top of it with his fist.

"Sec***ity here. Yes Col***—," a voice sputtered from the speaker.

"Maria's coming back downstairs with Viktor," Federov barked. "Place her in our own holding room—the one with the concealed camera. And patch the video through to my office. I don't want any more screw-ups in my building. But do not—I repeat, do not patch anything through to headquarters."

"Yes Col***el. Your office only and not****quarters."

"And get this God damn intercom fixed!"

"Yes sir."

Still fuming, he glared at Viktor. "Put Maria back in the holding cell," he snarled. "And if that nitwit downstairs didn't hear his orders, you make damn sure they're carried out properly."

"Yes, Colonel," Viktor saluted, and escorted Maria from the room.

The door closed, and Tatyana ran to the Colonel's file cabinet. "I'll make use of that time to run another background check on her," she suggested.

"Before you do," said Kornikov, "let's review the known facts, to see if we're missing something. We know she's sending information by line-of-sight transmission, possibly to a country that may not have spies in the Soviet Union. Or access to our mail service, for that matter."

Federov shook his head. "While I may agree with you in part Misha, it still makes no sense. I can't think of any country that fits those parameters."

"If the obvious doesn't make sense," Tatyana offered, "let's consider the obscure. Maria could be mentally unstable." She laughed. "Maybe the recipients of her messages don't reside here on Earth."

"Well, I certainly don't buy either of those possibilities," Federov sighed. "And I couldn't care less if those newspapers she's transmitting are a week or a year old. There must be more to this than meets the eye. If we can't get to the bottom of it before word leaks out, her life won't be worth five kopecks."

"Colonel, I'm afraid it's already out—at least out of this building. We have both the technician who discovered the intrusion, the calibration tapes and as you know—", she paused and nodded to his desk.

"Know what?" he asked.

"That—the release you signed. Both the security guard and Viktor saw it."

TWENTY MINUTES LATER, Tatyana and Mikhail were still going through files in Federov's office while he tinkered with the intercom.

"Have either of you two found anything useful?"

"Nothing we weren't already aware of, Uncle."

Kornikov head jerked up. "Your uncle?" he whispered, his eyebrows raised. "The Colonel is your uncle?"

Tatyana shrugged.

"Apparently," she continued, "Maria has lived alone in the same apartment for nearly twenty-three years."

"Your uncle?" he repeated.

"In fact," she winked mischievously, "she has been living there for about as long as this department has been in existence."

"That's one hell of a provocative coincidence," Federov mumbled.

"Apparently she has no family," Kornikov ventured. "Perhaps her records were misplaced or destroyed during the war."

"Also looks like that was when she became a mute," Tatyana said. "About the same time the Germans surrendered."

"And right when she started working at the conservatory," the lieutenant added.

"Yes, yes, I know all about that," the Colonel fussed. "She's worked full time there as a night custodian doing light maintenance for as long as I've known her. Her one off duty passion was botany."

"I wonder when she found any time for sleeping," Tatyana marveled.

"It would have had to have been when she wasn't working," Federov said. "But with no family or a social life, she'd have six hours a day and all weekend for that. Plenty of time, if you have nothing else to do."

"You might tell Misha about her intuitive ability, Uncle."

"I see you are on a first-name basis," Federov chuckled, rubbing and twisting his neck. "That's good. I like the thought of you two getting along. And yes, Maria is rather psychic. You might find this interesting, Misha: whenever someone loses something, she will unerringly tell where to find it."

Tatyana walked behind Federov and began massaging his shoulders.

"Thank you, my dear," he said. "Yes, Maria's been tested in the paranormal departments at both the Lenin and Moscow universities. Both concluded she has significant gifts, but is otherwise as normal as you or I."

"Normal perhaps," said Kornikov. "But I'm not a psychic."

"Don't misunderstand me," said the Colonel. "She doesn't tell fortunes in a tea room, or write some brainless column for a brainless newspaper. But she does have a gift of helping us whenever we lose things."

"And she's extremely well read," added Tatyana.

"And perceptive, too. Don't forget how she told you a while ago that there would be a significant improvement in your love life," Federov winked. Blushing, Tatyana swatted him playfully on the head.

"Yes, Mikhail, we all love her like a grandmother," sighed the Colonel." He kissed Tatyana on the cheek and crossed back over to the window. "That's why I'd give anything to have this mess cleared up in-house." Absently, his gaze fell to the video monitors on his desk. Startled, for a moment he stared in disbelief.

"What the hell is going on down there?" he shouted at last, wagging his finger at the screens.

Tatyana and Kornikov rushed to see. The left monitor screen showed Maria's cell: its door was wide open and she was sitting in a chair. Sergei and two guards were standing next to her.

"What are they—oh my God!" Tatyana screamed. One of the guards had grabbed Maria by the hair, while the other was moving an electric prod, used only for difficult interrogations, toward her mouth.

"Jesus!" Kornikov shouted.

The monitor showed Viktor filling a hypodermic syringe. Withdrawing the needle from a bottle, he pointed it upward and flicked it with his finger.

Federov turned to the intercom and threw a toggle. He slapped it twice and cursed; Tatyana and Kornikov stared dumbly at the screen.

The intercom finally began to crackle. "Viktor!" Federov screamed into the receiver, only to have it go dead again. "Damn this thing!"

"Look at Maria," shouted Kornikov. "It looks like she's glowing!"

"She's what?" Federov barked, slapping at the intercom.

"Yes," Tatyana gasped. "She's—my—my God! She's lighting up!"

"What in the hell are you two babbling about?" Federov yelled as he brushed them aside to look at the monitors. The holding cell blazed in light and both monitors went dark.

All three rushed out of Federov's office. Tatyana was the first to reach the elevator. She hit the button, paused, and began hitting it repeatedly. Glancing briefly at the floor indicator, she swore silently and darted for the stairwell, Kornikov right behind her..

Federov followed them down the stairs, dropping further behind with each passing second, and panting profusely by the time he'd reached the lower level. Opening the door to the security area, he found the room filled with smoke. He made his way to Tatyana and Kornikov, in the doorway of one of the holding cells. They were standing over two charred bodies.

"I'm sure these are—were the guards," said Kornikov. He took out a handkerchief and handed it to Tatyana.

"Maria?" she cried out. "Does anybody see Maria?" She turned around and began to cough through the handkerchief. "The heat—oh dear God, where is she?"

They could hear moaning from behind one of the security desks. Viktor was lying on the floor with severe burns. His feet jerked spasmodically.

In the cell adjoining Maria's, they found another charred body. Tatyana leaned in and said. "I think it's Sergei. He's also dead."

Federov knelt beside Viktor, and looked up at his two young companions. "What the hell happened here? Did either of you see anything? Did she have some kind of hidden explosive device?"

They shook their heads in unison.

"Tell me. Exactly what you did see?."

Tatyana took a deep breath. "I saw her open her blouse," she began, "—and—" She buried her face in Kornikov's chest and started to cry.

"We both saw it Colonel," he said, stroking Tatyana's hair. "A few seconds before the explosion, Maria unbuttoned her blouse and—"

"Spit it out man," Federov shouted. "For Christ's sake, what did you see?"

"Just before all hell broke loose, she opened her blouse—shoved her hand into her chest—and pulled out a blaze of light."

Chapter 6

HALF-WAY UP IN THE SOUTHERN SKY, a November First Quarter moon peeked through breaks in the gathering clouds, casting a creamy glow over West Virginia's Pocahontas County. Buffeted by high winds and a driving rain, trees on State Road 72 were swaying angrily, some in danger of toppling. Near the town of Green Bank, the wet pavement reflected the occasional flash of lightning overhead.

A lone car pressed on through the growing storm, following the road signs marked "NRAO," heading to the National Radio Astronomy Observatory, the largest fully steerable radio telescope in the Western Hemisphere. Under normal circumstances, the behemoth would be looking up into the heavens and studying natural radio noise emitted from planets, stars, nebulae and galaxies, searching the skies for signs of artificial radio noise—signs that would signal the presence of some form of advanced alien life, which it could detect from as far as 20,000 light years away. Today, following standard procedure to protect the telescope from storm damage, the 300-foot-wide steel mesh dish was pointed downwards.

The driver was listening to a local radio station for weather and road conditions. The announcer was saying, "—with a general clearing trend along the Mississippi River Valley. Closer to home, the Pocahontas County Weather Bureau has issued a severe thunderstorm warning until 1a.m. Deer Creek is expected to crest sometime after midnight. Due to numerous reports of power outages, residents are urged to remain clear of downed power lines and to immediately report them to Consumer Utility at 304-459-2378.

"In local news, the staff at our radio observatory had a short work day. Employees there were sent home today around noon when operations were shut down because of the high winds. The first shift is asked to report at the scheduled time tomorrow morning."

The driver turned on the car's map light, and glanced at the large photo on the front page of the morning newspaper. It showed a smiling man, with the radio telescope in the background, under a bold-faced caption reading DR. BJORN C. JOHNSEN, NRAO DIRECTOR, HONORED TODAY AT ROTARY LUNCHEON IN THE SMYTH MOTOR LODGE.

The car turned off SR 72, pulled up to the main gate's security booth at the entrance to the observatory, and rolled down the window.

A guard stepped out of his shelter and walked over to talk to the elderly lady behind the wheel, clutching his raincoat collar in vain attempt to stay dry.

"I'm sorry Ma'am," he said, "but the facility is closed for the day."

The visitor held out the newspaper, making sure that the photo was clearly visible. At the same time it read the guard's identification badge: QUINTON J. FLETCHER, SECURITY.

"Good evening, Quinton," said the driver.

Fletcher glanced at the picture, and wavered for a moment or two. Upon recovering, he smiled and said, "Good evening, Dr. Johnsen. Whatever possessed you to come out here on a night like this?"

"It seemed as good a time as any to catch up on paperwork, Quinton. By the way, who's working the main building tonight?"

"Poor old LeRoy Tittsworth pulled the night shift all week. My shift is almost over. I came in early to help lock down the telescope before the storm hit, and got to pull two hours of overtime."

Fletcher pressed a button on his hand control and the gate opened.

"Thanks, Quinton. Would you mind giving LeRoy a call to let him know I'm on the way up."

"I'll do just that. You have an exceptionally fine evening, sir."

As the car drove by, Fletcher winced at a lightning flash, closed the gate and stepped back into the booth to call his partner.

UPON REACHING the administration building, the driver took a briefcase from the passenger seat and walked up to the glass door. LeRoy was waiting inside. He pushed the door open and said, "Evenin', Dr. Johnsen."

"Good evening, LeRoy."

"You sure picked one dilly of a night to come out, sir."

"LeRoy?"

"Yes sir."

"You are getting one of your headaches. It would be best if you went to the lounge and took a rest on the couch. I'll wake you when I'm ready to leave."

"You know, I think I'm gettin' one of those danged migraines," LeRoy replied. " I think I'll head to the lounge for a spell, and take a couple of my 'bombs.' I'd surely appreciate you callin' me when you're ready to leave."

"I will, LeRoy."

The visitor walked straight to the main floor security office and took a key ring from a wooden peg on the wall. Briefly glancing at the nearby building diagram, it took the stairs to the operations area on second floor. As it passed by the window on the first landing, a lightning flash illuminated the giant telescope.

On the second floor it found double glass doors beneath a sign reading: MAIN CONTROL ROOM— NO UNAUTHORIZED ENTRY. Once inside, it switched on the room lights and walked to the master control panel next to a large window overlooking the main entrance. Outside, it saw Fletcher leave the guard booth, lock the entry gate, and drive away in his car. Once the car was out of sight, it activated the control panel, and the buttons and knobs sprang to life.

BACK IN THE LOUNGE, LeRoy opened a pill bottle and found it empty. "Dag-nab it!" He went back up to the security office to get one he'd stashed in his locker. After retrieving it he started back to the lounge. While passing the peg board for keys next to the door he noticed those for security keys were missing.

He automatically touched his belt snap. " 'Tain't there," he said "Now where in blazes...."

Slowly he recognized a familiar whirr-and-whine, coming from the other end of the building. It was a sound he knew he should never hear in this weather: the generators for the telescope were starting up.

"Oh no, not in this storm!" he yelled.

A FEW MILES DOWN THE ROAD, Quinton remembered that he'd left is wife's birthday present back at his post. He muttered, "Fletcher, if you had half a brain you'd be dangerous," he muttered. Slowing to a crawl, he turned and headed back to the observatory.

A doe bolted from the brush out onto the highway in front of him. By reflex, his foot slammed hard on the brakes, and the car slid on the wet pavement, swerving off the road and into the ditch. His heart pounding in his chest, his first thought wasn't to thank his lucky stars that he'd managed to miss the deer; he was too busy being angry at his foul luck.

"Dang—double dang!" he groaned, turning off the engine and pounding the steering wheel. After a few deep breaths, he took a flashlight from the glove box. Using an old newspaper for a makeshift umbrella, he got out to see just how bad things were. The front end of the car had cleared the ditch; but both rear wheels were stuck in the mud.

He kicked at the ground near the car, his big toe finding a large rock, sending the rock a foot or two towards the tree line and a sharp pain coursing through his foot. A few minutes later, he began hobbling down the road, heading back to the observatory.

A quarter-mile down the road, just past the first bend of his three-mile trek, his luck seemed to change, as he saw a car heading his way from the opposite direction. As it neared he stopped and began to wave; before long, through the rain could make out the unlit flashers of a police car. The car circled around and pulled up beside him. When the passenger window rolled down, through the raindrops he saw the County Sheriff, Vernon Vicksburg, and his deputy, young Tom Sanders.

"Hi there, Fletcher," said Vicksburg. "Seems you need a decent umbrella, and maybe a friendly face or two."

"Evening Sheriff—Tom You fellows sure are a sight for sore eyes."

"Looks like you found yourself a bit of car trouble."

"Sure did, Vern. Swerved to miss a doe and got myself stuck right up to my hub caps. I'm heading back up the road to call for a tow."

The sheriff motioned to the back seat. "Hop in and we'll give you a lift."

"Thanks, Vern."

"Just think of it as your tax dollars at work," the sheriff laughed. "And be sure to remember me come next election."

After sliding into the back seat, Quinton leaned forward and said, "Tom, I'd be much obliged if you'd make a quick stop at the gate so I can pick up the little woman's birthday present. I left it in the guard booth, and better not go home without it."

Chuckling, the sheriff picked up the microphone for the radio. "Base, this is Sheriff Vicksburg in Car Nine."

"Go ahead, 'Niner'," a woman's voice responded."

"Hi, Bessie. We just picked up Quinton Fletcher from the NRAO. His car's off the road on State 72 about a mile south of the observatory. I'd like you to see if you can get somebody out here tonight for a tow to a service station." He turned around. "Is that okay with you, Quinton?"

"That'll be just dandy, Vern. Oh, and you might tell Bessie the ignition key is atop the driver's side front tire."

The sheriff relayed the message. "Oh, and Bessie—Tom and I will be running Quinton home after we stop by the observatory. You might want to give his wife a jingle and let her know he's runnin' a bit late. I'll call in again after we drop him off. Over and out."

LEROY TURNED TO THE BANK of surveillance monitor screens. Seeing that they were all dark, he switched them on and waited patiently for them to sputter and stabilize. He scanned the screens of the hallways, front gate, telescope, parking lot, front and rear entrances and finally the main control room.

"Dang—double dang," he muttered, rubbing the back of his neck. and shaking his head. He bolted out the door and raced up the steps two at a time.

AS SOON AS THE SQUAD CAR stopped at the gate, Quinton jumped out and ducked his head, trying to dodge the rain and puddles. He unlocked the gate and slid it back just enough to squeeze through.

Inside the shelter was the gift, right where he'd left it. He started to leave when something caught his eye: the main building was ablaze with lights.

He figured he'd phone LeRoy to find out who was throwing the party. When there was no answer he took a walkie-talkie from its charging station

"LeRoy? It's Quinton. Do you copy?" Getting no answer, he stepped outside the shack and tried again.

"Hey. LeRoy. Listen up. It's Quinton."

Vicksburg rolled his window. "What seems to be the problem?"

"Can't figure it out, Vern. Those lights up there are blazing away like it was a holiday. I sure hope nobody's foolish enough to use the telescope tonight."

"I don't reckon anybody in their right mind would try it," Vicksburg said."

"And I can't figure out why LeRoy ain't answering."

"Probably in the can."

Quinton shook his head. "He would've taken his walkie-talkie." He put the transmitter back on his desk, locked the door and gate, and dashed back into the car with his wife's gift. "Anyway, it's his telescope and he can do what he wants with it."

As Tom turned the car around to head back to town, Vicksburg turned quickly around in his seat.

"Hold on a second," said the sheriff. "You said *his* telescope. Just who are you talking about?"

"Dr. Johnsen. It sure as hell don't belong to LeRoy."

"Dr. Johnsen? *His* telescope?"

"Vern, it's his freaking telescope. If he wants to tear it up, it ain't no skin off my nose."

"You mean the director, Dr. Johnsen"

"Yeah. Came in about an hour ago. Said he was going to work late. You thinkin' of givin' him a citation for working overtime?"

"I don't get it, Quinton," Vicksburg shook his head. "How the hell can he be working late?"

"Now don't get yourself all up in a snit. Like I said, the good professor said he was going to burn the midnight oil."

"Like hell you say!" Vicksburg snapped. "Tom—stop the car!"

Vicksburg turned to the back seat as his deputy slammed on the brakes. "Listen to me, Quinton. Something just ain't right. Johnsen was in a car wreck over in Lamb County today, after some kind of luncheon." He turned forward and picked up the hand set.

"Bessie—it's me again. You copy?"

"Loud and clear, Sheriff."

"Bessie, Professor Johnsen—from the observatory. Didn't you tell me somethin' about him being hurt? And wasn't he taken to a hospital?"

"I believe so. Wait a sec and I'll check...yes sir. He was in a car pile-up just after twelve noon today. They took him to Bi-County, I think. The report isn't clear on that."

"Do me a favor, Bessie. Call and find out when he checked in. More important, find out where is he right now? Something weird's going on out here. Call me back, quick as you can."

"Tom, take us back. And don't spare the horses."

The patrol car approached the gate, and the three men saw a bank of floodlights turned on illuminating the giant telescope.

"Holy shit!" gasped the sheriff. "Are they actually firing that puppy up?"

"Not they, Sheriff—Dr. Johnsen. LeRoy wouldn't know how."

The radio came on. "Base to Niner. That's a big Roger, Sheriff—" a burst of lightning broke up the transmission "—was his collarbone."

"You got stepped on by lightnin', Bessie. Please repeat."

"I said Dr. Johnsen is sound asleep in Bi-County Hospital with two cracked ribs and a fractured collarbone."

"That's just not possible, Vern," Fletcher insisted. "I talked to him this evening. I talked to him myself. He's up there with LeRoy right now."

The sheriff's eyes narrowed. "Bessie, I need backup pronto," he said. "How soon can you get it here?"

"Probably at least thirty minutes, Sheriff. I'll hop right on it."

"Unless it's a life or death emergency, cancel any runs and send them out here. And call old Judge Warfield. Tell him we may need some kind of writ or warrant to cover our behinds before the night is over. Niner out."

The sheriff reached under the seat, and retrieved a case; he opened it, and Quinton could see that it contained two matching pistols. The sheriff took one gun out, then closed the case and put it back under the seat.

"Quinton, you said LeRoy didn't answer any of your calls?"

"That's right."

The car slid to a halt at the front gate. The sheriff unbuckled his seat belt, checked the pistol to make sure it was loaded, and handed it to Quinton.

"Fletcher, I'm deputizin' you," he said. " As of right now, you're a deputy law man. Whatever you do, please don't screw up. Now, go open the damn gate so we can get in there."

BY THE TIME LEROY reached the top step the generators were running at full speed and all the lights in the control room were on; clearly, the telescope was going operational. The control room doors were open and his keys were in the lock. Inside, facing the control panel with her back to him stood an elderly woman.

Quietly, he made his way through the door and moved his hand to his holster: it was empty. He'd left his revolver downstairs in the security office.

Bravely as he could, he called out: "Freeze where you are! Who are you and who gave you permission to be in here? And where's Dr. Johnsen?"

The woman turned to him and morphed.

"What is all the commotion about, LeRoy?"

"Dr. Johnsen? I thought you were—I mean I just wanted to make sure you were okay. I could swear I saw a woman standing there."

"Everything is fine, LeRoy. Why don't you sit down at the table and take a nap. I'll be through here soon."

As LeRoy walked to the nearby work table, the visitor turned back to the controls and entered some commands:

Right ascension 4 hours 13 minutes —ENTER—declination minus 7.4 —ENTER—engage.

The monitor responded: **Unable—retry type r, or enter a to abort.**

As the visitor commanded the computer to retry, an alarm sounded, and a warming appeared on the monitor:

WARNING*WARNINGWARNING***Wind velocity above nominal safety parameters.**

The visitor typed **manual override code a31a**. The alarm stopped and the monitor began a countdown of five minutes.

Relaxing, the visitor took a disk from its pocket and inserted it into the panel.

DOWNSTAIRS, FLETCHER, THE SHERIFF AND TOM rushed through the front door and headed straight for the security office. When they found it empty, they scanned the bank of monitors stopping at the one for the control room.

"Who the hell is she?" asked Vern asked. "And look at LeRoy over at the table.

"What the hell, is he sleeping? Let's get up there."

Quinton was the first to reach the second floor. He glimpsed around the corner, pulled back and motioned the others to be quiet.

"This is crazy," he whispered. "Look at LeRoy. It looks like he's napping. The woman is standing at the control panel. Cover me. I'm going in."

Vicksburg whispered, "Hold on, Cowboy. You stay where you are. Tom—you go ahead. We'll cover you."

Tom crouched low and crossed to the control room door, his pistol at the ready. He took a deep breath, and stepped into the room, poised to shoot. "Stop right where you are, lady! Don't even think of moving a muscle!"

He looked at LeRoy, who stirred at the sound of his voice. "Are you okay there, buddy?"

With an effort LeRoy lifted his head. His drowsy eyes drifted from the deputy to the gun and back again. "I'm just fine, Tom. Who you planning to shoot?"

"That should seem obvious," Tom said still aiming at the visitor. "What's she doing over—over—"

Confused, Tom saw that he was aiming his gun at Dr. Johnsen.

"Doctor? I thought—aren't you in the hospital?"

"I'm perfectly fine. Holster that weapon and sit down next to LeRoy. I'll be finished here in a moment."

From their vantage point, the Sheriff and Quinton saw what was going on by the reflection in the control room window. LeRoy and Quinton sat at the table seemingly oblivious as to what was going on.

Vicksburg could barely make out the printing on the control room monitor. It read: **WARNING*WARNING**WARNING***Wind velocity above nominal safety parameters—Do you wish to disengage?**

The visitor typed NO.

Quinton whispered, "How long before our backup arrives?"

"No matter," the Sheriff said. "We can't wait no longer." Stepping out into the doorway, he said grimly: "This is the Pocahontas Sheriff's Department. You are trespassing on government property. Stop what you are doing and step out into the hall with your hands behind your head."

The visitor said to Tom and LeRoy: "You must keep those intruders from interfering with our work."

"This is the last time I'm going to say this," Vicksburg said. "Come into the hall with your hands behind your head. Do it now!" When the visitor failed to respond he said, "Fletcher, we have to make our move before the storm tears up the telescope or our guys get injured. No one can accuse us of not giving the intruder a fair shake. On the count of three, we move into the hall. You fire a warning shot over her head. Mind you now, just a warning shot. If that don't stop her I'll take her out. We go on the count of three. One..."

They both drew with their side arms.

On the monitor, the countdown continued:

"...6...5...4—"

Vicksburg said, "two"

"—3...2...1...

"target acquisition," read the monitor

Vicksburg said, "three."

They moved into the hallway and Quinton fired his warning shot. When it became apparent the intruder had no intention of stopping, Vicksburg issued a final warning, and took his shot. The visitor stiffened, depressed a key and slumped to the floor.

Inside, a groggy Tom fired two wild shots in the general direction of the hallway. Then he turned to see the visitor sitting on the floor. It morphed from Dr. Johnsen to an elderly woman.

"Quinton," she gasped, her eyes starting to glaze, "you and LeRoy must leave this room immediately if you want to save yourselves."

Slowly, she began unbuttoning her blouse.

As Vicksburg stared in disbelief, the intruder began to glow brighter and brighter. "Everybody, get the hell out," he ordered. "Move it! Move it!"

Only LeRoy glanced over his shoulder as the four raced for the door. He shouted, "Holy shit, she's on fire. She's burning up!"

OUTSIDE, THE TELESCOPE MOUNTINGS strained against the wind. When they reached their stress limit, one of the four gusset flange plates snapped loudly and the huge dish began a slow-motion descent to the ground.

Vicksburg glanced out the window and yelled, "It's going down!" Pointing over his shoulder at the visitor, he hollered: "She's a-goin' too. Everybody—into the stairwell."

The control room filled with a blinding light and the men shielded their eyes and braced for an explosion. Instead, they heard only silence. As the luminescence subsided, Quinton went back to the control room door. "She's gone," he marveled. "There's nothing left of her."

Vicksburg followed him in and grunted. "We need to have a serious talk."

"Forget it Vern," LeRoy said. "I'm out of here."

"I'm with you," added Tom "I need a drink."

"Hold your horses everyone," the sheriff said sternly. "Nobody's going nowhere until we agree on what the hell happened here, and just how we're going to report it. Hear those sirens? We've got less than five minutes before company arrives. You can be damn sure we'll each end up sitting in front some board of inquiry, asked a bunch of questions we'll never be able to answer---why shots were fired, who this woman was, how she got in here, and where the hell she disappeared to—not to mention how she lit up like a roman candle."

"Who shot at who?" Tom asked.

"One of you dimwits shot at him and me!" snarled Quinton.

"Bull crap."

"Don't forget about the telescope," added LeRoy.

"Shut up you fools, and listen to me," Vicksburg snapped. "God damn it—I vote we keep things simple. How about this? There was a hell of a lot of confusion during the storm. It looked like there'd been a break-in at the facility—and somebody looked to be fiddling with the controls. We tried to track down the intruder, and in the middle of everything—with the storm and all---the telescope collapsed in the wind. And any intruder—if there ever was one—simply vanished."

"That really ain't stretching the truth much," Tom said. "Just leaving out a bit."

"What are we gonna say about that woman and Dr. Johnsen?" asked LeRoy.

"What woman?" Vicksburg replied with a blank look. "Who the devil are you talking about? I didn't see any woman. Did anyone here see a woman? Or the Doc, for that matter?"

They all shook their heads.

"Now you boys are getting the picture," said the sheriff. "There was nobody here but us—and maybe some intruder, who must've gotten clean away. And I'm telling you right now, gentlemen, if this plays out any other way, we'll find ourselves locked up tighter than a drum in the state prison or a loony bin. Maybe both!"

"Can we get away with it?" asked LeRoy.

"We better," Quinton said. "Except for Tom, the rest of us are too old to start looking for another line of work."

"Okay," LeRoy said. "I'm with the sheriff."

Everyone nodded.

"Then it's settled," sighed Vicksburg. "And as the saying goes, speak now or forever hold your piece, cuz our back-up just arrived."

Chapter 7

— 2004

"YOU'D BEST BUNDLE UP, FOLKS," the lobby guard told passengers exiting one of the Federal Security Building's elevators. "It's cold out there for this time of year."

He touched the brim of his hat to the ladies adding, "Would you believe it's going to be Thanksgiving in another month? Be careful everyone. Hey—look out!"

The warning came too late for Zack Peters, who had been paying a little too much attention to the attractive new agent in the Central Intelligence Agency's midtown Cryptography Department, cleverly hidden inside the 12th Floor suite marked: ARCHIVES AND RECORDS DIVISION, DEPARTMENT OF HOMELAND SECURITY. Not looking where he was going, he bumped into a custodian. The old woman staggered, and Zack caught her arm; his newspaper, briefcase and overcoat dropped to the floor, and tipped over the woman's rolling travel bag.

"Are you okay, Mary?"

"I'm just fine, Dr. Peters. But your newspaper could use some rearranging."

"I should watch where I'm going."

"It's perfectly understandable. Lise Danfers is a striking young lady."

The guard came over and helped put the newspaper back together while Zack picked up his briefcase and brushed off his coat.

"Good night, Mary," he said over his shoulder as he entered the building's revolving door. As he stepped outside, into the rush-hour crowd, he realized he really had been ogling the pretty girl Mary had mentioned.

"Now there goes one fine young man," the guard said to Mary. "If I was any judge of character, I'd say he has a promising future ahead of him."

"Oh, he does, Sam. You can bet your next pay check on that. By the way, how is that shoulder of yours?"

"You know, I was just about to mention how I haven't had any trouble with it since you gave me that massage the other day. You sure do have a gift. Magic hands, I'd call it. If I could bottle your talent, I could make us both rich."

"Now wouldn't that be nice," she said. "Good night, Sam."

"Good night, Mary. Stay warm."

Mary passed through the revolving door, walking by that nice Dr. Peters and the young lady who caused the mishap by the elevator.

"Yes, I just started work here the day before yesterday," she overheard the young woman telling Zack. "It's nice to meet you. My name is Lise Danfers."

Mary continued down the street to the corner newsstand.

"And a very good evening to you, Mrs. Prosser!" the proprietor beamed. "How is my favorite customer?" He stood on tip toes to reach for a small stack of tied papers on the far side of his kiosk. "Here are those front pages you wanted. Sad to say I'm missing one *L.A. Tribune* and two *Detroit Journals*. But I adjusted your bill for them."

"Don't fret," she smiled, and handed him his money. Thanking him for his kindness, she put them in her bag and continued down the street.

The proprietor turned to his other customer and shook his head. "If I had more customers like her I'd only have to work a couple of days a week," he sighed.

"Why is that?"

"She just wants the front pages of six national dailies from the past week. She stops by each Friday and pays me full price—plus a generous tip. All for old newspapers. Unbelievable."

*****

TWO BLOCKS UP THE STREET, Mary stopped at the door of an upscale jewelry store and waited until there were no customers before entering. Judging her to be a woman of limited means, the proprietor turned his attention to his interior decorating magazine, trying his best to ignore her until Mary walked up to the counter and stared at him.

"Is there something I could show you?" he sighed.

"I have a diamond to sell," she replied. She took a handkerchief from her purse and unfolded it. Inside was a large diamond.

"Let me take a closer look," said the jeweler. After a careful examination, he sat up in his chair and set his eyepiece to one side. "This is a very nice stone," he observed "I'd say three carats, more or less."

"It is exactly three carats," Mary replied. "And being a perfect blue white, you can buy it from me for only $3,000. You can easily resell it for twice that."

In an effort to hide his enthusiasm, he said, "Yes, I believe I can take this off your hands. I'll just need your name, address and a piece of identification with your picture."

She looked directly into his eyes; silently, her lips formed the words: "You are one of my best customers. None of that will be necessary. If you will wait here, I'll get your money."

The man repeated the phrase verbatim, and went to the back of the store. He returned with an envelope containing three thousand dollars. Once again her lips moved silently: "I won't remember this conversation or that you were here this evening. I will have another three thousand dollars ready for you when you return next Friday."

He repeated the words exactly, took the diamond, and handed her the envelope.

"Thank you so very much," she said, putting the money in her purse. Once outside, she crossed to a bus stop and sat down on a bench to wait for the Arlington Heights bus.

When it arrived, the driver tipped his hat. "Good evening, Mrs. Prosser," he smiled. She returned his greeting, showed him a bus identification card and sat down in the first row across the aisle from him.

"Aren't you a much too young to have a senior citizen's pass?" he winked. "By rights I should charge you full fare."

"Thank you, Mr. Newman. You certainly are a charmer."

The door whooshed to a close as the bus pulled away.

"I was watching TV the other evening," said the driver. "Looks like that conservatory of yours just opened a new wing. Maybe now your bosses will give you some extra help on your night shift, so you won't have to do everything all by yourself."

"I'm sure they'd be willing. But I really don't need any help. I like working alone."

"I have to hand it to those skinflints—getting one person to take care of the whole place. Must save a ton of money. Hey—is there any truth to the rumor that some philanthropist donated ten million dollars for a new wing? Rhoades was his name, I think."

"Yes, I understand that's what happened."

"I can't imagine being that rich. Say—maybe I'll take my new lady friend to the conservatory this weekend. What do you think?"

"That would be very nice. If you like, I'll see that there are two passes waiting for you at the ticket desk."

"I'd really appreciate that! She just may start thinking I'm a classy guy. One with connections. Which area do you think she'd enjoy? I hear the desert area is nice."

"We're proud of that section. It's one of the finest in the country."

The bus pulled up to let three sailors and their dates off. At the same time two teen-aged toughs boarded and strutted to the back. Before the bus had pulled away, they were talking loudly.

Mary glanced over her shoulder. "I think I know one of those young men. I'll go back and say hello."

"I don't think that's a good idea, Mrs. Prosser."

"Don't worry. I'll be fine." She moved to the back, sat down facing the boys, and opened her purse.

"Now I want you both to listen very carefully to me, and not make a commotion," she said. "Just take out your knives and the handgun, and put them in my purse."

"What knives? What gun?" one of them asked while bopping his head to imaginary music.

"That .25 millimeter Moser you have in your belt under your shirt, Charles. Serial number M12470."

His companion stiffened in his seat.

"Hey lady—how come you know all that shit—knowin' my name

and all?" Charles smirked. "Hey, Snake—does this old lady look like an antique gun collector, or just an antique busybody?"

"I don't know, man. But just for kicks, why don't you check out the serial number."

"Lady, you ain't taking nothin' from me or Snake," sneered Charles. "But I'm gonna make you a one-time offer. Call it the Bus Ride Special. You take your money out of that ugly purse and put it on the seat next to me, and I won't use my knife on you—you know, the one you seem to know all about."

"Chuck, I wouldn't do this. She gives me the creeps."

"Do what, Snake? Like what am I doin' that's so upsetting?"

"Take out your piece, dude, and check the damn numbers."

"No way, man. I'd rather free up some currency from old nosey pants. Maybe do the same with our chauffeur up front."

As Charles rose from his seat, she grabbed his wrist and eased him back into the seat. His head drooped and came to rest against the window. His eyes, still wide open, were dull and lifeless.

"Check his pulse, Mr. Snake. You'll find his heart has stopped. If you don't cooperate he'll have permanent brain damage in four minutes. In six minutes he'll be dead."

Snake felt for a pulse—first on Charles' wrist, then on his throat.

"Holy shit, lady! Start him up. Here, take my knife. Here's his stuff." He pulled the knife out of the Charles' pocket and the hand gun from his belt.

"There, that's all of it. For Christ sake lady—you gotta start my buddy up! Please!" He put the knives in Mary's purse, and checked the gun's serial number. His eyes widened, and he looked at her in amazement..

"That's impossible lady. How do you do that?"

Without answering, she took the gun. Sighing deeply, she placed her hand on Snake's chest. Instantly he sat up, gasping for breath.

"Is everything all right back there Mrs. Prosser?"

"We're just fine, Mr. Newman."

She turned to Snake. "Your friend will feel light-headed for a while. For now, just sit here quietly. When I head back to the front, pull the cord for the next stop. When the door opens, leave the bus, and don't cause any more trouble. At least not today."

"Yes Ma'am," he said.

When she returned to her seat, the driver asked, "What was going on back there? I was afraid they were going to start something."

"The boys were fine. But as it turned out, I didn't know them after all."

Snake pulled the signal cord. When the bus stopped, the two boys left by the rear door.

"I still think they were up to no good, Mrs. Prosser," Newman said. Mary just smiled.

A short time later the bus arrived at Nottingham Road. Newman opened thc door and grinned. "There you are young lady, all safe and sound. Have a pleasant evening."

"I wish the same to you, Mr. Newman. Oh—and when you and Anne Marie visit the conservatory, you might treat her to lunch and a glass of wine in our dining room."

"That's a great idea. She'd like that. And if you happen to be working next Saturday, maybe the three of us can get together on one of your breaks."

"That would that be nice, except that I don't begin my shift until late that evening. Well after closing. But it's always nice seeing you."

Mary entered her home, locked the front door, and headed upstairs with her newspapers, gliding past bedrooms furnished with outdated and unused furniture that were covered with sheets. She entered the bathroom and turned on the light. Stopping to check herself in the mirror, she stepped into the tub fully clothed and pushed both hot and cold water handles towards the wall. A hidden door opened into a windowless room filled with electronic devices. Walking to one of the devices, she scanned the newspapers and transferred them to a data base. This done, she stepped to the small rectangular device resting on a wooden table by the west wall, and pressed the orange button.

A widow's walk wrapped around a large wooden cupola on the flat roof of her home. It housed a parabolic dish antenna that was always pointed at the Fifth Langrangian point of the Moon. That position, known as L-5, was one of five locations in space forming an equilateral triangle made up of the Moon, Earth and L-5; each side of the triangle was 238,000 miles long. Objects there are held permanently in place by the gravitational inter-attraction of the two orbiting bodies.

Hidden among the timeless debris in the Moon's L-5 spot was a device of alien origin. One of its two antennae pointed permanently at Earth, the other was aimed at the dwarf planet Ceres, a small world 580 miles wide, one of billions of rocks orbiting the Sun in the asteroid belt between Mars and Jupiter.

A half-second after Mary pressed the orange button, a generator beneath the parabolic dish raised its output just enough to startle some pigeons resting comfortably on the gutters of the cupola. The silent vibrations ruffled their feathers sufficiently to send them flying off in a huff, in search of more serene surroundings.

One and a half seconds later, Mary's data reached the Moon's L-5 position. There, an interstellar transformer frozen into position gave the transmission a much more powerful boost than the small rooftop generator could manage, given the primitive electrical system of the host planet, and the information packet embarked on its second leg of its journey: a trip of 96 trillion miles to the star 40 Eridani.

Under the most advanced laws of physics understood by the technological novices inhabiting Planet Earth, the journey should have taken almost sixteen years to reach the 40 Eridani.

Under the rudimentary laws of physics taught to children of the more advanced civilizations for the past few millenia, the data arrived a tenth of a second after being rerouted through the transformer.

Once the transmission was completed, Mary walked to her basement and opened the wooden door behind the furnace. Sparkling light seeped out from around its loosely fitted frame. Stepping inside, she was greeted by daylight and a magnificent garden of exotic flowers.

Soft, otherworldly music floated through the air as she continued to a white bench in the center of the garden. She sat down and removed her clothing, folding it neatly and placing it on the bench beside her. She tipped her head back to bask in the warmth of three Suns shining overhead, her toes slowly lengthening into long tendrils that flowed down into the nutrient-rich soil.

THAT EVENING, in a house kitty-corner from the Prosser Mansion, an aging Ephraim Rhoades slouched in the chair beside his fireplace. The crackling fire bathed him in warmth, and the vials on the table next to him were lined up like toy soldiers at muster. But the medicine that clouded his once razor-sharp mind gave only passing relief from the disease that had gnawed at his insides for the past five years, and the growing pain that was now a daily companion.

He found comfort staring into the flames dancing among birch logs. Their hypnotic dance helped him to smile, reflecting a lifetime that had been very kind to him.

Thanks to a gifted mind and generous heart, prosperity had never been a stranger, and Rhoades had used much of his fortune to enhance the lives of many people less fortunate than he. In a dying burst of generosity, he'd largely underwritten the costs of restoring the Washington National Conservatory to its former glory. His breathing grew labored, and he drifted off into a stuporous twilight, dreaming a young boy who'd once gone on splendid adventures with his two best friends. Exploring the eerie basement of an old house, he remembered an old wooden door cloaking lights that peeked through its cracks and around its edges. His mind opened the door, and he looked to see an immense garden of exotic flowers and plants that seemed more exotic than anything he could imagine.

Suddenly pain returned with a vengeance, jerking him back to the present, reminding him that for all his past generosity, he was facing his future alone. Trying as best he could, he tried blocking the pain with the most joyful memories he could muster, but try as he might, he couldn't block out the thought that every moment that passed could be his final ones on Earth.

He found himself unable to imagine finding the courage to make it through another night, or to hope that his health would ever return.

Unable, that is, until an old woman's hand touched his shoulder.

Part 3

It pays to keep an open mind, but not so open that your brains fall out.

—Carl Sagan

Chapter 8

Universal Associated Press Friday, Oct. 8, 1702 UT

Today, White House Press Secretary George Lily announced a change in venue for next week's signing of the North American Acid Rain Accord. Originally slated for Ottawa, the leaders of Canada, Mexico, and the United States will now meet in Windsor, Ontario to conclude eight years of efforts to solve the growing problem of acid rain in North America.

Following a video-phone conference, leaders of all three nations agreed to defer to the wishes of Great Britain's Prince of Wales. A co-author of the NAARA, the Prince requested the change when it was brought to his attention that the signing ceremony would come within days of the 65th anniversary of the Royal Visit to Windsor by his great-grandparents King George VI and Queen Elizabeth in 1939.

End. UP: Fri., 10-08-09, 1704 UT.

Embargo: none.

See 6.2-inch side bar: Will Wild Willie Win Wimbledon?

WITH A BRIEFCASE IN ONE HAND, an umbrella in the other, a trench coat draped over one arm, a newspaper pressed to his side by the other, and a bag filled with coffee and a prune Danish clenched in his teeth, Zack Peters contorted himself just enough to turn the key to his sixth floor office in the Old Secret Service Building and open the door.

Stepping carefully around the books and papers littering the floor, he managed to unload his cargo without making a mess, his first successful effort of the day. Grunting with satisfaction, he hung up his overcoat and umbrella, and made his way across his small office to open the window. He stared for a moment at the brick wall across the alley and shook his head. Leaning out the window, he glanced to his left; leaning just a bit more, he was finally able to make out the westernmost sliver of the Capitol dome.

"One heck of a view, Mr. Farholm," he whispered. "Thank you very much." He closed the window and removed his brown lunch bag from his briefcase, carefully placing it on the radiator, just below the window ledge. The radiator hadn't worked in twenty years; neither, he mused, had half the staff.

The door opened and Tim, the annoyingly cheerful mail boy, stepped into the office. "Good morning, Dr. Peters," he grinned. "I have a ton of mail here for you. You'll need to sign for this big one. And here's your copy of the basketball pool. Looks like you won again."

"Thanks, Tim."

"I'll catch you on my three o'clock run."

Zack closed the door, sorting through the mail as he crossed over to his desk. The envelope he'd signed for—marked SECRET—caught his eye. He removed a set of orders as well as a smaller sealed envelope marked PERSONAL & CONFIDENTIAL. He read the orders first.

DEPARTMENT OF HOMELAND SECURITY
Archives and Records Division

Order 284-27 11 October

To: Zachary O. Peters
From: E. Douglas Farholm, Asst. Chief, AGPAC
Re: Operation Trident

1. On Thursday, 16 Oct, you and three operatives of your choice will proceed to Windsor, Ontario by commercial air transportation, coach class. Rooms

will be held for you at the Prince Andrew Hotel, downtown Windsor.

2. Upon arrival you will implement backup security measures for President Tomlinson. He will arrive by helicopter at the Windsor waterfront on Friday, 17 Oct.

3. Following the treaty signing the following day, you will monitor the President's departure by helicopter for Detroit Metropolitan International Airport.

4. Although security considerations for Prime Minister Montreau and President Diaz do not come under the jurisdiction of this office, you are still authorized to implement protection to those parties as long as such procedures do not jeopardize your primary responsibility to President Tomlinson.

E. Douglas Farholm, Asst. Chief, AGPAC

Zack set the orders down, sipped his coffee, and opened the smaller envelope. It contained a bumper sticker that read LIFE IS UNCERTAIN—EAT YOUR DESSERT FIRST, along with a hand written letter.

Zack—

Just a brief note of thanks for your hard work putting together the NAARA operation. I know you aren't pleased at the switch to Windsor, but hey—shit happens. I hope you can see that the Prince's efforts to facilitate the treaty entitle him to leeway for some idiosyncratic (my word-of-the-day on my desk calendar) behavior. But if not for him, our three countries would probably still be screaming at each other.

There's also a bright side to my authorizing four agents in Ottawa instead of the eight you requested. With the move to Windsor, you can still take three with you and stay within budget. That's because I can now arrange for temporary assignment of four more agents from our Detroit office. With Windsor just across the river, they won't have per diem expenses, or nearly the transportation costs. All we'll be out will be popping for one lunch, and one dinner.

Looks like you'll be using the hydrofoil or one of the tunnels. It's anyone's guess as to when the bomb damage to the Ambassador Bridge will be repaired.

You have my OK to treat everyone to lunch and dinner on Sunday. I assume you still want Stan Ranier and Phil Macaulay. I wish you'd reconsider taking Lise along, for reasons we've discussed before—but it's your call. I can almost see your dad's reaction, rest his soul, at the thought of today's agents kissing, etc. He didn't have female agents when he was with the company. And as Lise has been saying: "The department that plays together stays together?"

Whatever, I don't need to know. And I'll make you a deal—marry the girl, let me be your best man, and I'll get you a bigger office with a real view. What can I say? I'm just a hopeless romantic.

Break a leg,
Doug.

A FEW DAYS LATER, Zack entered the Prince Andrew Hotel in Windsor just as its lobby grandfather clock struck noon with Canterbury chimes.

"May I help you sir?" asked the desk clerk.

"I believe you're holding four reservations under the name of Peters, from Washington."

"Ahh—Dr. Peters? We're holding a single room for you, and three more for your party. You'll be in Room 609 with a nice view of the river. I see you plan to stay with us for one night with a late departure set for tomorrow, Sunday. Is that correct?"

"Would there be a problem if I decide to stay over an additional night?"

The clerk checked his computer. "Not if it would just be the one room," he replied. "If you need more than that...."

"Just mine," Zack smiled. "Have any of the other members of my party arrived?"

"Just one," the clerk said quietly. "She requested the room next to yours and moved the other two gentlemen to the third floor. Apparently, they both have a problem with heights. She left this for you."

Zack took the note and his cardkey. He pointed out his bags to the bellman, picked up a complementary *Windsor Daily Globe* at the front desk, and followed the bellman to the elevator. On the way to his floor he opened the note.

> *Hi! Gone shopping. (Who'd have thunk it?) Be back by noon. Don't snack so we can have lunch together. Hugs, C.*

After showering and unpacking, Zack sprawled on the bed in a plush robe offered for sale by the hotel. He was reading about various theories regarding the recent rash of terrorist bombings when the inside door to the adjoining room opened, and Lise Danfers peeked inside. An attractive brunette in her mid-30s, she'd captivated Zack the moment they'd met four years earlier. She closed the door quietly, and hid in the shadows.

"Hotel security, Dr. Peters," she cooed. "We require you to kindly remove any and all females you may have hidden in or under your bed and replace them with—!"

Laughing, she burst into the room, jumped on the bed ,and poked him in the ribs. "Is this your first night in town sailor?"

Without missing a beat, Zack lowered the newspaper and turned down the TV volume, and pulled his glasses down the bridge of his nose. "I take it you're working her way through college?"

"You got it, handsome. And if you play your cards right—." She began to purr and draw slow circles on his chest.

Zack's cell phone rang.

"Let it ring," she pouted. "I'm psychic, you know. I can tell that's a wrong number."

Zack looked at the number, and pressed the button to answer the call. "Hi, Doug."

"Tell Farholm we've eloped," she whispered, flopping back on the bed, and pulling a pillow over her face.

"Actually, Lise and I were just talking about you."

She lifted one corner of the pillow. "Hey Doug," she shouted. "I'm getting pregnant and taking maternity leave here in Windsor. Send my paychecks to the Prince Andrew Hotel."

"He says congratulations. Oh, and you're fired." In mid-laugh, Zack's face turned serious.

"You've got to be kidding!" he protested. "How bad? No—no problem on this end. Same game plan? Right—we're all meeting at Detroit's Old Westin this afternoon. Yeah, I will—yup— right. Thanks, Doug. Bye."

Lise sat up, and brushed her hair off to one side. She sensed that their playtime had just disappeared.

"What did he say?"

"President Tomlinson was injured in a bomb blast in New York about an hour ago."

"Oh my God!"

"Right in front of the U.N. building. Just as he was going in to address the General Assembly."

"Is he all right?"

"He has minor burns on his face and arms, and some temporary hearing loss. The Veep. will stand in for him tomorrow. Other than that the game plan stays the same."

She gave him a kiss on the cheek and slid to the edge of the bed. "So much for romance," she shrugged. "Okay, Peters—grab your coat. I'll let you buy me lunch at the floating restaurant I found on Riverside Drive."

Zack laughed. "I presume it's a nicer place than Stan or Phil would choose."

"Well...the hired help all keeps their clothes on, if that's what you mean."

Zack opened the door, and followed Lise into the hallway. The plush carpeting felt soft against his feet, and he marveled at the artwork hanging from the walls.

"Just so the food is good."

"Speaking of Stan— "

Zack shook his head.

"Nothing's changed?"

"Nope. Twelve months. Eighteen, at the outside."

"He doesn't look it."

"No—and I'm not going to be the one to tell the rest of the guys. Not unless he brings it up himself."

"Looks like he means to go out with a bang."

"That he does. He's even talking about taking up skydiving."

The elevator opened, and the two of them stepped inside. The ride down was more somber than either of them expected.

* * * * *

IT WAS SIX O'CLOCK by the time Zack, his Washington agents, and the four from the Detroit office were wrapping up their meeting in the Eagle's Nest conference room at the top of the Westin Hotel. Phil Macaulay hunted through the local papers, anxious for the news about events in New York. Stan Ranier walked to the window looking across the river to Windsor. The city lights sparkled on the water, and downstream an ore freighter was nearing the Ambassador Bridge.

"I still can't get over the President canceling out at the last minute."

"Stan," chided Lise, "I think the White House was probably more worried over his injuries than about disappointing you."

Zack, seated at a large oak conference table, was still poring over the reports that the Home Office had sent him. Impatient, and not wanting to admit to herself that she was worried, Lise poked him in the shoulder.

"So," she shrugged, "in the end all we have to do is to babysit the Vice President?"

"Right," Zack nodded, looking up from his briefing papers. "Nothing else changes. Not the positioning, not the assignments. She's the only VIP we need to keep an eye on."

Phil Macaulay glanced up from a newspaper. "It says here that four perps were involved in the assassination attempt. It seems they shot fifteen or twenty rounds into the Presidential limo before the bomb went off."

Zack shook his head. "Not according to Doug. The report he sent says there were just two attackers, and only six rounds fired. Everything else is media hype. And all the guns did was scratch the windows. It was the bomb that caused the damage."

"I'll bet that cleared his sinuses, Princess," Ranier winked at Lise.

"Or worse," she smirked.

"One more thing," Zack said. He looked over the group, wondering how they'd take this next bit of news.

"Doug also says we'll have a second no-show at the party—the Prince of Wales."

"You have got to be kidding!" snapped Phil. "That's the reason they moved everything to Windsor in the first place!"

"I couldn't agree with you more, Phil," Zack sad. "But this is a legitimate deal. Farholm says that the Prince had an emergency appendectomy last night."

"An emergency appendectomy," scoffed Lise. "I haven't heard that one in years."

"Well—is that going to change our game plan?" Stan asked.

"The Mayor may make some minor changes to the speakers list, but that won't concern us. Remember, the Mounties are heading up this entire operation. They'll have fifty of them in dress uniform and ten more in civilian clothes, blending in with the rabble."

"Agent Peters," ventured one of the locals, "do you know what the RCMP priorities would be in the event that a Level Five disruption arises?"

"You mean, if all hell breaks loose?"

"Well...."

"In that event, it won't matter much what the Mounties do," said Zack. "Our observer status will end, and we will do whatever it takes to get the job done."

Zack looked around the room. "Okay—one more time around on positioning and we'll call it a day. Phil?"

"I'm on the hotel roof maintaining visual and radio contact with Stan on the Coast Guard cutter as well as each of you on the ground."

"Stan?"

"I'm on the cutter, listening in with a P-6 and ear-mike and trying not to get seasick."

"Stan, if you'd rather hang over the roof, we can always switch places," Macaulay said with a smirk.

"And Stan, be sure to check out an automatic rifle from this officc and keep it under wraps until you're aboard the cutter," Zack said. "And I don't want anyone mentioning the rifle to the Mounties, okay? We don't want to make them nervous. Yes Lise."

"I'm glued to Eagle Two along with the sexiest man in town?"

"But I thought I was assigned to the cutter?" Stan quipped.

"In your dreams, Stan. Zack and I will pack P7s, leaving our hands free for a beer or a hot dog."

"Let me guess, Stan joked. She's pregnant or going to the chair."

"No food, no booze," Zack added. "We're keeping this a class act. Fred?"

"My three guys are in casual mufti and packing P-6s. Two of us will mingle with the crowd and two will be up front behind the barriers."

"Perfect," Zack said. "And Fred, be sure to introduce yourself to the senior Mountie. He's expecting you but won't be able to recognize you. Are there any last questions or comments?"

"When do we officially wrap up this here gig, Zack?" a Detroit agent asked.

"Once the mayor introduces local dignitaries to the three VIPs, there will be some short speeches. Then, once the treaty is signed, the VIPs will all depart by helicopter around 1500 Hours to their respective airports. At that point we are done."

Zack took a deep breath. "All right," he said, letting his gaze wander around the room once more, looking each member of the team directly in the eye before letting his gaze move on to the next. "Any more questions?" He smiled to see nothing but shaking heads and averted glances.

"Then that should do it."

As everyone began to rise, Zack chuckled to himself. "One last thing, he added. "Doug's agreed to pick up everyone's dinner tab tonight but you'll put tomorrow's lunch on expense accounts. Send them on to Doug or me back in Washington."

"All right!" one of the Detroit agents said enthusiastically. "Now I just happen to know a very expensive eatery next to the casino…"

Zack laughed. "I'm sure that'll be okay with Doug—and as far as I'm concerned, the sky's the limit. Just remember, no booze after seven."

As the rest of the group departed, Zack motioned for Stan and Phil to remain. "Why don't you two have dinner with Lise and me?" he asked, when the others had left.

"I really wish you would," nodded Lise. "We found a place in Windsor so classy and expensive you'll that you'll get a chance to hear me give my order in French."

"No thanks, Princess," Stan shook his head. "I have philosophical objections to eating food I can't pronounce."

"Besides," said Phil, "we decided we'd improve our minds at the downtown library."

"Right," Lise smirked. "The closest thing to reading material you'll see will be name tags on the thongs of some scantily clad dancer."

"My dear lady," Stan moaned, clutching at his heart, "you cut me to the quick. We're just clean-cut Washington boys alone in the Big City, who'll probably end up in bed by ten o'clock reading Shakespeare."

"Really guys," coaxed Zack. "You're more than welcome to join us."

"Thanks, but no thanks," Stan sighed. "We'll see you both in a couple of hours."

"Yeah, goodnight," added Phil.

"I expect you two to be looking sharp and down in the lobby at 9," Zack called loudly as the two stepped off to hail a cab. Stan laughed and waved; Lise and Zack watched as the two of the rode off.

Lise leaned her head against Zack's shoulder. "Does Phil know about Stan?"

"I think so. Stan said he would be up-front with everybody."

"Then they aren't really going prowling tonight?"

"Actually, I think they're headed for the Essex Scottish Armory to listen to a bag pipe rehearsal."

"That reminds me," she said. "What's the real definition of a gentleman?"

"I give up," he said.

"Someone who knows how to play the bag pipes, but doesn't." Laughing, the two of them walked arm in arm down the street.

THE WAITER in Chefs de Paris, the hotel's five-star restaurant, lost much of his enthusiasm when Lise began to order.

"Bon soir, garçon," she began. "Nous voudrons—"

The waiter offered a brief smile before turning to see if Zack would place the order. Zack shook his head and nodded to Lise. She gave their order without missing a beat, oblivious to the rebuff of the waiter, who smiled blandly and left without a word.

After dinner, Zack topped off Lise's wine. Curious, he asked, "So where did you learn to *parlais en Français*?"

"Two years of high school, and three years in the Army. And I was stationed in Paris, so when my hitch was up I stayed there. Even studied for two years at the Sorbonne. Then I married a chiropractor and stayed there for a few more years."

"I suppose you've heard the one about a French chiropractor that married a high wire artist?"

"Obviously that's the main reason I married one."

"It's a great joke even if it took a while to catch the punch line. So then what happened?"

"After we divorced I returned to the States, joined the Company, and graduated from Bainbridge. Four years ago I transferred to DC and met you."

"Well—to be serious for a moment—when Doug called this morning he told me that this will be the last assignment that we can work together."

"Pardon my French, but where the Hell does he get off saying something like that?"

"Let's see," Zack mused, "I think it was something about Section Two, Paragraph Two; "Assignments with a substantial risk factor will preclude co-assignments of two or more family members'."

"What the heck does that have to do with the price of eggs? Wait a minute, you—oh God!" She covered her mouth. "Zachary O. Peters, did you just ask me to marry you."

"Depends on your answer."

"Yes. No. I mean—yes. Wait. Let me think." She stood up, and turned to face the window.

"You're joking," he said.

Turning around to face him, she sat down. A moment later she stood up, then sat down again. "Well, I—I guess I want to have more time to relish being courted. I'm afraid that if I accept too fast I'll just be another old, engaged person. I want to really feel special."

"You already are special, Lise," he said taking her hand.

"Can I sleep on it?"

"Your hand?"

"Funny. Assuming I say yes, we can celebrate by staying over an extra night. We'll let Stan and Phil head home without us."

"I already told the desk we might stay."

"Aha!" she chided. "See—you're already taking me for granted."

"I promise never to do that."

"Actually, I told the desk clerk the same thing, myself. After the Vice President leaves tomorrow, I want you all to myself."

"Sounds like a plan. Still want to go for a walk?"

"As long as you keep me out of the casino and shops," she smiled.

Moments later, they found themselves standing outside, under the hotel canopy staring out at a sudden downpour.

"I propose scrubbing our leisurely stroll," said Zack.

BACK AT THE HOTEL, Lise slipped her plastic key card into the door lock and pushed it open. She turned and gave him a polite kiss on the cheek.

"That's it?" Zack winced.

"Now that you're making an honest woman of me I want a night of celibacy to luxuriate in my happiness."

"Sheesh."

"Good night, Boss." She kissed him on the other cheek.

"Good night, Lise. I love you."

"Love you too."

Returning to his room, Zack thought about catching the late news, but decided to get ready for bed. He was surprised to find his eyes drooping as he finished brushing his teeth. He was sound asleep within minutes of his head hitting the pillow.

Soon, he could feel himself floating in the darkness. As the light gradually returned he seemed to be gliding through a room filled with flowers. He looked around, and saw he wasn't in a florist shop. Things appeared slightly out of focus as he found himself drifting towards a closed casket beneath a blanket of roses.

He came to a stop and noticed a leather identification wallet propped open among the flowers. He strained to make out the wording. When he saw the man in the photo was him, a chill flooded through him. He awoke abruptly, drenched in sweat, his heart pounding furiously.

"Oh, hell," he muttered at last. "I'm hungry."

Tossing on whatever clothes he could find, he took the elevator down to the first floor lobby. When he walked into the coffee shop, he was surprised to find Lise seated at the counter.

"Mind if I join you?" he smiled.

"I didn't know I was coming apart," she laughed. "You having trouble sleeping, too?"

"It was easy falling asleep," he said. "I just didn't like my dreams."

A waitress came over. "Can I get you something, sir?"

He nodded at Lise's cup and said, "I'll have whatever she's having."

"So, about the dreams—by any chance did they include vivacious women chasing you through a swamp with venomous snakes drooping down from moss-covered trees"

"You have quite a vivid imagination there. You should have been a novelist?"

The waitress returned with a cup of hot water.

"You're having hot water?"

"Yes."

"Hot water?"

"It starts out that way," Lise explained, adding some cream and sugar to his cup. "There, now you have silver tea."

"Silver tea?"

"It not only helps you sleep, it's good for you. My mother-in-law introduced me to it. The cream makes it look like tea; the sugar gives it taste."

He took a sip, pursed his lips, and gave a shrug. "You do know what they say about mothers-in-law?" he grimaced.

*****

THIRTY MINUTES LATER they stood outside the hotel, looking at the landing pad where the helicopters would arrive later that morning. A hundred feet to the left workers were attaching flags and bunting to a reviewing platform. Downriver, through the fog, they could make out construction lights on the bridge between Windsor and Detroit.

"Do you know how long the repairs are supposed to take?" she asked.

"According to the news, it will take at least three more weeks. A bomb blew a hole through the roadway. Fortunately nobody was hurt."

"The world is getting ridiculous, Zack. Not a day goes by that there aren't killings or bombings somewhere. Nowadays it seems like everybody's angry with everybody else."

"As a boy, I'd hear about these sorts of bombings, but they only happened a few times a year. And never here. Now, there's so much hate in the world that crazy seems to be a way of life."

Holding hands, they walked to the platform and sat on the steps. Lise pointed up at a steel tower in front of them that anchored the Canadian end of the nearly complete Can-Am Skyway.

"That would be the perfect spot to cover tomorrow's action," she said. " Just put me in that gondola with a few hot dogs and I could handle the whole show myself."

"You'd have to get in line behind Doug. He suggested the same thing. It's a great idea—except the Skyway won't be operational for another two weeks."

"Better yet---tell Stan you've decided to have him swaying up there in the gondola instead of on the cutter. With his fear of heights— "

"You're a mean woman, Danfers. Seems I'm stuck with a crew infected with all sorts of phobia."

"We're the best darn team in the department."

"I agree." Zack stood and stretched, and offered his hand to help her up. "I believe that silver tea is starting to kick in."

"You're getting sleepy?"

"I have to pee," he laughed. "Let's head on back."

When they stepped into of the elevator, Zack patted his pockets.

"Crap---I left my key card in my room. I'll go to the front desk and get another one."

"Come stay in my room."

"I still have to get my pajamas."

"You're expecting a fire drill?"

Chapter 9

THE FOLLOWING MORNING, Zack's team was in place well before the crowds began to gather.

"Your chariot awaits, my Lord," Lise said, bowing to Stan with an exaggerated sweep of her arm toward the Coast Guard Utility Boat *Marlin*, bobbing in the swells next to the dock.

"Thank you, fair maiden," he grinned nervously. "And may I say that you look resplendent in basic black. The color well-suited to my anticipated demise from sea sickness."

"Guess I'm just a chic chick. Please note my red scarf, splashing impudently across my modestly endowed blouse. It's supposed to herald my confidence, though I may just use it for a napkin."

"The only thing I'm confident about," Stan said, trying his best to be heard over the roar of the cutter's engines, "is that my heroic effort in boarding such a tiny boat in that big Detroit River should guarantee my receiving hazardous duty pay. Isn't that right, Zack?"

Zack was too intent on listening to a radio transmission through an ear bud to pay attention.

"Forget it—see you later, Princess. How about a kiss for luck?"

Lise offered the back of her hand and a curtsy. Stan gingerly boarded the boat with help from a crewmember. The tiny waves from passing pleasure boats made him nervous.

"Wait, Stan!" Lise called out. "I almost forgot the present I wanted to give you." Holding onto a piling, she leaned out over the water to hand him a barf bag.

"It's from my flight to Detroit."

"Thanks. I'll try to bring it back to you intact. And full."

"How far out from shore do you plan to be?" Zack asked the Marlin's skipper, a tall, reed-thin lieutenant commander with a stunning tan. "There must be a couple of hundred pleasure boats out there."

"I'm shooting for five-hundred feet," the handsome young officer replied. "But I'll be content with half of that." He pointed toward the roof of the hotel. "Is that one of your people up there?"

"Yes. That's Phil Macaulay, just to the left of the flagpole. He just radioed down to wish everyone a bon voyage."

"Well, off we go. Good luck, Zack. Don't forget our date at the yacht club after the festivities. I want to buy drinks and dinner for your team."

The Coast Guard boat started to cast off; Zack tossed a crewman the last bow line. "We're looking forward to it."

Lise shouted, "Don't forget, Skipper—I get your dinner receipt for my expense account!"

Suddenly, the radio crackled; it was Phil, chiming in with an update.

"Zack, Eagle Two's chopper is due any moment. Montreau and Diaz just lifted off from Windsor Airport. Their ETA is eight minutes."

"Sounds like a decent separation, Phil."

"Everyone copy that?" Macaulay asked.

"Stan here, that's a Roger."

"We Roger that also," a Detroit agent said.

"Zack, here comes Eagle Two up the river," Phil said. "And over there to my right—yes, that's the Prime Minister and Diaz."

From somewhere in the crowd a dozen or so loud reports were heard followed by some screaming. Lise dropped into a crouch and reached for her service pistol.

"Firecrackers," Phil said. "Just firecrackers—some kids in the crowd. The Mounties are on it already."

"That sure cleared my sinuses," Lise radioed as she holstered her piece. "Oh, rats. I spilled my coffee. And it was just the right temperature."

"Kill the chatter, people," Zack ordered.

"Zack? It's Phil. I just gave the co-pilot of Eagle Two a go for touchdown as soon as it's above the pad in about a minute."

"Roger that, Phil. Everybody—look sharp. Lise, you're with me. I'll take the starboard door. Once she's down, you cover the nose."

"Check." The wind flattened her hair. "So much for trying to look glamorous," she groused.

"Zack? Phil here. From the looks of that cross wind, it might be a tad sticky down there. Wait a second. Hold on. It sounds like a change coming up."

"Roger."

"Zack, the *charge d'affaires* wants Eagle Two to remain on board so that the Prime Minister and Diaz can go over to greet her."

"Crap. Okay, Phil—I'll hold her here until they arrive."

The helicopter touched down with a last-minute sway from a sudden rush of wind off the river. When Zack approached the hatch, Lise moved in front and began scanning the area. The forward hatch opened and a spit-and-polish Marine sergeant in full dress blues dropped to the ground with an armload of paraphernalia. He placed safety pins in both landing gear and bracketed the tires with wheel chocks, then ran to the front of the craft and offered a smile before giving the pilot a thumbs-up. Dashing back to the starboard hatch, he pulled down the internal stairs and snapped to attention. A gust of wind sent his dress hat cart-wheeling across the landing pad.

Zack stepped to the door and pointed to the identification badge on his jacket. The sergeant nodded and let him board the helicopter.

Looking around, Zack instantly spotted their VIP.

"Welcome to Windsor, Madam Vice President," he shouted to make himself heard above the din of the helicopter's engines.

"Thank you. You must be Jack Peters?"

"Yes. But it's Zack with a Z."

"Sorry we're late. There was a bomb threat at Metro Airport."

Zack pointed up to the helicopter coming into view a mile or so up river. "Would you mind remaining on board for a few minutes? The Prime Minister and President Diaz would like to walk over and greet you as you deplane. Afterwards we'll proceed to the reviewing stand, escorted by two of the RCMP's finest. Will that be all right?"

She fanned her face with a brief case she said, "That'll be fine, Agent Peters. I only wish we could get some fresh air in here."

He poked his head out of the hatch and spoke into his communicator. "Lise? Phil? How's it looking out there?"

"Everything's cool, especially this yummy Marine," Lise said as she walked over to where she could catch Zack's eye. She moved her lips to form the words "I love you."

"We're clean and green old buddy," Phil said. "The two choppers are on approach."

"Roger that," Zack answered. He turned to the pilot and gave the shutdown sign by moving his index finger across his throat. The pilot cut his engines and the blades began decelerating.

"Sorry we couldn't offer you some sunshine, Ma'am," Zack said. "But at least it's stopped raining."

She nodded while placing a handkerchief over her face to block the fumes.

"Any word about Prince William?" she asked.

"Just that he had appendicitis."

"Well, it doesn't look good. I'm told he's not snapping back as fast as they'd like."

"We hadn't heard that. Most of us assume appendicitis is pretty much a non-event these days."

The Vice President looked out the window and caught sight of Lise. "Why don't you introduce me to your charming companion?" she smiled.

Zack tapped his communicator. "Lise, come over to the hatch please."

Lise approached the door; the first thing she noticed was that she and the vice president were wearing identical outfits.

"Good afternoon, Vice President Brandstadt ," Lise said offering her hand and a big smile. "I'm Lise Danfers. It's a pleasure to meet you."

"And I'm pleased to meet you, Miss Danfers. May I call you Lise? I might add that you have excellent taste in clothes and supervisors." She turned to Zack, and added, "These fumes are getting horrendous. I've got to step outside for some air."

Zack got out first, turned and offered the Vice President his hand as Lise started back to the front of the aircraft. She stopped half way, removed her sunglasses and cocked her head to one side as she looked up at the Sky Way gondola. She began to walk backwards towards the helicopter muttering something and then picked up her pace as she called out to Zack, "Boss," she said pointing up with her sunglasses. "The gondola windows; they were closed five minutes ago!"

Zack looked up just as two men appeared in one of them. Without hesitation he pushed the Vice President roughly towards the bottom of the stairs. Lise was withdrawing her weapon as one of the two men up above brandished an automatic weapon.

Up on the hotel rooftop Phil noticed Zack and Lise's erratic movements. "What's going on down there guys?" Then he heard the chattering of an automatic weapon from the gondola.

Cement chips danced around Lise's feet. She managed to get off two shots before she was hit. The gun slipped from her hand and clattered to the ground. She dropped unceremoniously to her knees, and turned to Zack. Apologetically she said, "Sorry about this Boss. I seem to have caught some incoming."

Zack shoved the vice-president unceremoniously up the steps into the helicopter. "Phil, Lise is down," he barked into his radio. "Wave-off Diaz and the P.M.—now!"

A second burst of gunfire tore sheet metal off the hatch inches above Zack's head. The Marine guard brought his hands halfway to his bloody face before dropping to the ground, dead.

The windshield of the helicopter shattered and the front tires blew out. Immediately, Phil radioed: "May Day! May Day! May Day! Incoming flights, abort landing! I say again abort landing! We are under attack. We are under attack."

The helicopters veered sharply and began flying a zigzag pattern towards Detroit. Out on the river, the commander of the *Marlin* was standing outside the wheelhouse oblivious to the events unfolding on shore. He had just loaned his binoculars to Stan and found it amusing to watch him maintain his footing on the rolling deck, scan the shoreline and grasp the railing all at the same time. His amusement was short lived when the binoculars slipped out of Stan's hand, bounced off the railing and fell into the river. When he saw Stan's panicked look, his pointing frantically towards shore, he rushed to the wheelhouse, turned on the siren, and ordered the helmsman to return to shore.

"Full ahead!" he growled. "Punch it man. Punch it!"

"Zack? Phil here. The *Marlin*'s alerted and moving in fast. Get that mother airborne!"

His charge safely inside the helicopter, Zack could feel the pandemonium gripping the river front. Screams filled his ears, and he could see people scurrying up the grass embankment to Waterfront Drive.

As the *Marlin* neared the shore, Stan started firing on the gondola. Zack stepped off the ladder and knelt beside Lise, grasping her hand. He picked up her gun and eased her into a standing position so they could dash for the boarding ladder.

"Talk to me Phil," he radioed. "Can you see what the hell is going on?"

"Looks to be two shooters in the gondola. Get your butts on board and get the hell out of there!"

As the *Marlin* circled underneath the gondola, Stan and a coast guardsman were firing up into it. The few spectators who weren't running away were cowering behind cover, some kneeling with their arms wrapped around their children.

Phil saw two Detroit agents move out from the crowd and head for the helicopter. They stopped when automatic fire forced them back.

Ignoring the emergency startup procedures, the pilot forced the engines back to life. Smoke and bursts of flame belched from the exhaust ports creating an unexpected but welcome smoke screen. The crew chief shook his head, thinking of the engine overhaul needed after this improper start-up.

Zack helped Lise step around the sergeant's body and up the ladder. Inside the helicopter they both collapsed on the floor. As the engines roared up to full power he shouted to the pilot: "Take it up now. Go!"

The rear of the helicopter began to lift off slowly followed by the nose. Brandstadt slid to the floor, cradling Lise in her arms. She saw blood on Zack's pant leg. "You're hurt, too," she cried.

"Zack," Phil called over the radio, "those idiots must be out of their minds if they think—Oh no!"

A handheld rocket launcher appeared in the gondola window. Its missile wobbled in flight as it flew towards the helicopter. Exploding on impact, it broke the chopper in half. Its rotors spinning out of control, the two sections of fuselage plopped onto the ground simultaneously.

"Oh my God," Phil whispered as flames and smoke poured from the wreckage. He could see three figures staggering out of the forward hatch: Brandstadt, Lise and Zack. They stumbled towards a small auxiliary power unit parked forty feet away, and crouched behind it. Lise looked badly wounded.

Phil turned his attention to the helicopter, where two crew members were trying to pull themselves clear of the debris. A sudden explosion consumed the wreckage in a ball of flame.

With the Vice President out of their line of fire, the men in the gondola began shooting at the *Marlin.*

"Zack?" Phil radioed. "Nothing we do is affecting those bastards. They must have shielding. Wait a minute—what the hell?"

"What the hell—what?" demanded Zack.

"It's the *Marlin.* She's moving back out into the river. One of the TV news choppers is positioning itself over it."

"Screw the chopper Phil. We need medics ASAP. I don't know how long we can hold out here. Now listen up, everyone. This is Zack Peters. As of this moment I am turning operational command over to Phil Macaulay, who has eyes on the bad guys."

"Roger that," said one of the locals. "Phil, we're pinned down, here. We've pumped everything we have into the gondola but it's not doing any good."

"I copy, Fred. Do whatever it takes to get medics to Zack. They're behind the APU. Lise is wounded."

"We have two medics with a rolling gurney, but they're hesitating before making a run—at least until things lighten up."

"Keep those medics safe," said Zack. "We can hang in here for a while longer."

Phil turned his binoculars back to the *Marlin.* "Zack—Stan just hoisted himself onto a landing skid of one of those news choppers, and is climbing up into the cockpit."

Lise looked up and whispered, "You go, big guy."

"It looks like—well, now the pilot's dropping into the river," Phil continued. "I can't tell if he jumped or if Stan pushed him. But, Stan's flying that puppy all by himself, now. He's peeling away and headed towards you."

"Tell Zack to monitor B-channel," Fred chimed in. "The Coast Guard is up-river chasing a speed boat that's heading our way."

"Zack, did you copy that?"

"Yes. I'm tuning in now."

"... on board have weapons. Repeating; this is the Belle Isle Coast Guard Station. Our utility boat *Barracuda* is moving down river at flank speed to assist in the fire fight. A high-speed powerboat with three armed men has just passed the *Barracuda* and is also headed down river. It's dragging personnel pick-up lines. Repeating; this is the Belle Isle Coast Guard—"

"Phil? It's Zack. Listen up: it looks like those gondola bastards plan to get picked up by the powerboat. Do whatever it takes to make sure they can't."

"Zack—Stan, here."

"Stan—what the hell do you think you're—?"

"Zack, I can see that speed boat screaming down the river. That *Barracuda* is on its tail but doesn't have a rat's-ass chance of catching up. I sure hope those perps in the gondola don't get away clean and green."

"Stan, my man: you're now our spy in the sky. We're proud of you."

"Listen up good buddy," Stan replied. We're running out of time and have some tough decisions to make. Here's my proposition."

"I don't do propositions Stan," Zack said. "If you were any dumber I'd have to water you twice a week."

"Here's the deal. Just promise me that you'll take care of our princess; I'll take care of things up here. Gotta go now. Life's about to get dicey. I love you all."

"Stan! Don't you even think about it! There is still time—"

Once the men in the gondola saw Stan's helicopter closing on them, they turned their fire power on it. As the chopper rammed into them, a giant fireball flamed in the air, leaving the debris to fall into the river.

"My God, Zack," Phil radioed. "Stan, he's—he's gone." After a moment to gather his composure he added, "I can make out those two medics and a gurney headed your way. I'll try to get you another."

Lise used her good arm to adjust her disheveled hair and to brush the blood from her jacket. She spoke softly to Zack with forced calmness. "Zack, listen to me---you and the Veep have to move now towards Fred's team, in case—"

Zack interrupted. "First, Stan was giving me orders and now you are. Last time I checked, I was still calling the shots. I—we are not leaving you," he said firmly.

Lise raised her voice for emphasis. "—in case, there are any more deviates lurking around here."

His voice cracked. "I need to be here with you—period!"

"Excuse the insubordination, but just shut up! A first-year med student could see I can't walk. Now reload my piece and get going. When you get back here I expect you to bring two hot dogs—heavy on the onions, no mustard."

"Some silver tea too?" he smiled weakly.

Lise winced. "No, I'm going to need caffeine. Make it strong."

Counting out his remaining rounds, he took two and slid them into her clip. He slapped it in place and placed it in firmly in her hand. He dabbed dirt from her cheek with the back of his hand, kissed her and glanced around before helping the Vice President to her feet.

Brandstadt leaned down and caressed Lise's cheek. "I promise we'll be back for you." She and Zack crouched low and began working their way toward the crowd.

The medics with the gurney approached the vice president. She pointed for them to continue on to Lise. They nodded and kept going.

"Let me catch my breath," said Brandstadt. Fred and a local agent hurried over to help.

"You two are a sight for sore eyes," said Zack. Fred took his arm to steady him as his partner helped the vice president to her feet.

The gurney bearers stopped half-way to Lise; the taller one lifted a blanket to reveal two semi-automatic rifles. Both men grabbed one and turned to aim at Brandstadt.

Phil saw what was happening from the top of the hotel. "Code Red!" he screamed into the radio. "Behind you!"

Zack and the others turned.

One of the weapons had jammed. The attacker holding it cursed while the other opened fire. Brandstadt was the first one hit, grasping her right leg and hip as she dropped to the ground. Fred's partner dove to shield her and was hit three times, dying as he covered the vice president with his body. Fred fired off three rounds before a bullet shattered his skull; Zack was hit in his arm and leg and dropped to one knee.

Lise, struggling to stay conscious, lifted her weapon, calmly aimed, and fired off her last two rounds before slouching wearily, her arm drooping listlessly as her weapon dangled from her trigger finger, her first shot scattering an attacker's brain over his accomplice's face; her second shot caught the second attacker between the shoulders. He dropped his jammed weapon and fell to the ground, then turned and glared hatefully at the woman who had shot him.

The wounded gunman kicked his useless weapon aside. He glanced first at Lise and then at the Vice President, marking the distance to each. Turning back to face Lise, he took a long knife from an ankle scabbard and began crawling towards her, hatred twisting his face into a contemptuous sneer.

"Zack," Phil radioed. "He's going for Lise!"

Zack began limping toward the attacker but with no great urgency. There was more than enough time to dispatch him with his last round.

Phil said calmly, "Go for it, Zack. The bastard has a knife."

Lise glanced first at her empty pistol and then the gunman. She realized her options were played out, except one. She gave the man her most defiant glare and spat at him. Then her dismay began to ebb because Zack was catching up to him. Her relief was short-lived, as three more attackers broke from the crowd and started running at Brandstadt.

Three Mounties also saw them, opening fire as soon as they had a clear shot. Two of the gunmen fell immediately; the third took cover behind a towering maple tree, reloading his gun and screaming in a foreign language.

At once Lise could see everything playing out. She keyed her radio for Zack. He had heard the firing and turned away from Lise. He answered and turned but her voice was barely intelligible. She shook her head firmly, held up the palm of her hand for him to stop and then jabbed a finger towards Brandstadt.

"Save… her!" she said.

When Zack saw who she was pointing at, he stopped short and made a decision that would haunt him the rest of his life. Brandstadt was struggling to free herself from under the fallen Detroit agent as the third attacker leveled his gun and took aim at her. He was shielded from the Mounties, but Zack had a clear shot.

Zack aimed and fired at the attacker, who spun around and dropped, blood pouring from his chest.

He turned back to Lise but it was too late. The assailant's dagger had found its mark—over and over again. The Mounties fired at him and he fell lifeless across her body, then raced over to where

Lise lay bleeding. One felt for her pulse and turned to Zack, shaking his head.

Zack looked to the river, and saw the wreckage of both the gondola and Stan's helicopter smoldering and bobbing in the waves. The *Barracuda* and *Marlin* were bracketing the speedboat, which was drifting in the water, its occupants standing with their hands clasped behind their heads as the Coast Guard crew climbed aboard.

Wincing, the vice president sat up just in time to see one of the Mounties remove his bright red jacket and place it over Lise's body. Lying back down onto the bloody pavement, she began to cry.

* * * * *

A WEEK LATER a black sedan with government plates pulled up in front of the Harrison Funeral Home in Alexandria, Virginia. Phil McCauley stepped out of the car, went around to the trunk, and removed a wheelchair. He brought it up to the front passenger door and leaned forward to set the brakes. Zack, his arm in a sling, slid off the seat and into the chair.

Inside, they were met by an attendant. "May I direct you gentlemen?" she asked, her voice pleasant but restrained.

Zack tried to reply, but his voice cracked; Phil answered for him. "Lise Danfers, please."

"Of course," the attendant replied. "If you'll just follow me."

She led them down the hall to a room with closed doors. "You are the first to arrive but you may go right in."

Zack turned to Phil. "If you don't mind I'd like to—"

"I'll wait out here for a while," Phil nodded. "Look, big guy—there'll never be a good time to mention this, but now is as good as any. The last time I spoke to Lise by radio at the end just before—well, she made me promise to tell you that her answer was 'yes'. I think I know what the question was. And I'm sorry."

Zack nodded, but said nothing. He wheeled himself inside and rolled to a stop in front of the casket. For the first time in his life he knew the full meaning of déjà vu: the room, the setting—it was all hauntingly familiar. Just like his dream, everything was slightly out of focus, but now he knew why. He was looking at everything through his own tears.

Thank God the casket was closed, he thought. He wouldn't have been able to bear it otherwise. He took out his identification wallet and placed it on the casket among the flowers. He wheeled back a few feet, turned and glided back to the doorway where Phil and Doug Farholm were standing.

"Zack," Doug stammered, "I can't—tell you how badly I—we all feel. If there's anything at all you ever need—"

"Actually, there is," Zack said. "My badge is inside with Lise, but you can have these." He reached into his jacket and handed Doug his P7 revolver and clip-on holster. His two friends stepped aside, and Zack wheeled himself out the door, and into a gently falling rain.

Part 4

Do there exist many worlds, or is there but a single world? This is one of the most noble and exalted questions in the study of nature.

—Albertus Magnus (1193-1280)

Chapter 10

"YOU KNOW SOMETHING, MUFFINS?" Zack said as he peered at his bedroom mirror. "I never noticed it before, but that nose is way too long."

The beige-and-white Shih-Tzu lying at his feet looked up and cocked her head to one side before lowering it to her paws with a sigh.

"No, not yours, mine."

Zack walked out on his balcony in stocking feet, an undershirt and black trousers with white suspenders dangling from the waist. The high-rise condominium had a clear view of the Capitol Golf and Country Club's eighth tee. Six miles further he easily made out the white dome of the Capitol. To his right a passenger jet was on its final approach to Reagan National Airport.

Calling Muffins outside to share the sunset, he removed the dust cover from a modest refracting telescope and pointed the slender tube toward a brilliant object above the western horizon. Peering through the eyepiece, he tweaked the focus knob.

"Now that's a beautiful sight, girl," he smiled. "Would you like to take a look at Venus?"

Trying her best not to appear disinterested, Muffins wagged her tail before lying down and placing her head on her paws.

After spending a few minutes gazing at Venus, Zack covered up his telescope and went back inside. He took his dress shirt from the bed, uncovering a theater ticket that read: WASHINGTON SYMPHONY ORCHESTRA, Oct. 8, Aisle B, Row 11, seat 12. He placed his shirt next to the shirt studs.

"I guess I've put this off long enough, girl," he nodded. "The problem is I can't remember how I did this last time. Do I put the studs in first and pull the shirt over my head, or put it on and then add the studs?" He chose the former. After tucking in the shirttails and pulling up the suspenders, he started attaching his clip-on bow tie, only to snap off one of the metal clasps. He dropped it into the wastebasket and reached into his garment bag for his real bow tie. The one he bought the clip-on to replace.

"Close your ears, girl," he sighed. "You shouldn't be exposed to the language I'll be using for the next few minutes."

Muffins turned and walked into the living room, circling twice before flopping onto a throw rug.

The bow tie was going poorly until he remembered the trick Phil Macaulay taught him when they worked at the AGCAP. He went to the closet, took out a shoe, closed the door and revealed a full-length mirror.

"Now watch the master at work," Zack winked. He put the heel of the shoe under his chin, lowered his head until the shoe was tight against his chest, then closed his eyes and tied the shoe lace. After raising his chin so the shoe would drop, he took the ends of the bow tie dangling around his neck and duplicated the motion.

"Perfect. Phil, wherever you are, I owe you one."

Muffins returned to the bedroom carrying her leash and dropped it at his feet. Zack shook his head.

"Sorry, girl. You wouldn't like the finale of the 1812 Overture. Especially the cannon in B-flat."

Muffins walked away, her ears drooping and her tail lowered. Zack followed her into the living room and sat down, coaxing her onto his lap. As he stroked her ears, his eyes drifted to a framed photograph on the desk across the room. Though too far away to see details, the photo had long since been burned into his memory: Phil Macaulay, Stan Ranier, and Zack were all standing side-by-side in front of the Lincoln Memorial. Their outstretched arms held a lithesome Lise Danfers, who was lying horizontally in her version of a Hollywood glamour pose. Her arms held a beige and white puppy.

"I miss them too. Well...I've got to get cracking, or I'll be late."

She jumped from the chair as he rose to take his dinner jacket from the couch.

"Good night, girl. Be good. I'll see you later." He left the light on his end table glowing, and headed into his attached garage.

Zack smiled proudly as the garage lights came on to shine on the lone extravagance he allowed into his otherwise Spartan lifestyle: a shiny, pre-owned Pan-Sony Excalibur Rainbow V. His particular model year had been very hard to find, and cost more than half a year's salary. It took nearly as long to get used to its unique shade of metallic red.

By no stretch of the imagination could Zack Peters ever be referred to as a fashion plate. His standard attire consisted of khaki pants, plaid shirt, loafers, a sport coat draped over one shoulder and a pair of sunglasses often held together with a paper clip.

Under duress he could be talked into a loosely knotted tie, but only after he recounted to anyone who'd listen, the origin of neckties and his personal disdain for self-garroting. As he recalled, after some long-forgotten British admiral died during a naval battle, the crew mourned his passing by wearing black ribbons tied loosely around the neck. Unfortunately the idea spread, ultimately metastasizing into the modern necktie. Zack could never figure out why they didn't just toast the old boy with a mugful of rum and be done with it.

He pressed his key ring sequencer and the window on the driver's door lowered before the door rolled underneath the chassis. Concerned with what would happen if the battery failed, he had installed an aftermarket torsion spring that could lower and raise the door once without power.

"I have to admit getting dressed up and sliding behind the wheel of a fine automobile was good for the soul," he murmured while placing his thumb on a memory pad that unlocked the engine starter.

A synthesized voice emanating from dashboard speakers greeted him. "Good evening, Dr. Peters. A systems check finds me to be within operating parameters. However, within the next hundred kilometers or one month, whichever occurs first, an oil change will be required. In addition, my two front tires are deficient in air pressure."

"I'll make note of that, Charlie. But for now, let's just get on with it so we can get to the theater sometime tonight."

A red light on the dash turned green and the engine started. Not that Charlie was a major annoyance, but somehow it never remembered that Zack always kept the tires at less than the recommended pressure; he preferred the softer ride.

"The garage door is closed and secured," Charlie said as he pulled into the street.

"Any messages?"

"You have neither messages nor unanswered calls, Dr. Peters," replied Charlie.

"Charlie, we've been over this before. When you say neither, it must be followed by nor. And when you say either, it must be followed by or. They are not interchangeable. You really must work on your grammar. "

"Yes, sir."

Zack was quick to admit to his own faults. Besides his not being a snappy dresser, he only badgered his dashboard computer; never people, even though Charlie's grammar was obviously the fault of a poor high school English teacher, or an engineering school that thought grammar was an obsolete operating system. He was famous for being tardy to a function, and hoped it meant he'd be late for his own funeral. But not tonight: to ensure he'd get to the performance on time he allowed an extra half-hour to get into the city. He decided to double-check the on-board audio road map for traffic conditions.

"Dr. Peters," his computerized sidekick ventured, "there are numerous traffic delays on I-95 from McMillan Road through most of the midtown exits. May I suggest taking State Road 498 as an alternate route even though we will arrive twenty minutes later?"

"That will be fine Charlie," Zack shook his head. "So much for good intentions."

Along the way it began raining hard, but bad weather or not, there was never an excuse for a former or active agent to be unaware when he was being followed. Whoever they were, Zack thought, they were good at their job. Every so often the car tailing him would turn off and be replaced by another.

When he arrived there was a long line of vehicles waiting for valet parking. He drove into the parking structure himself where, to his surprise, he found a convenient space on the second level. Filing the intelligence report on concert parking away for future use, he pulled into the parking spot and punched in the security activation program.

"Sir, how long shall I remain inactive?

"Hmmmm," Zack pondered. "Let's say four hours."

"Dr. Peters, I am now immobilized. Enjoy your evening."

Entering the lobby, Zack went straight to one of the portable bars and ordered a glass of champagne. The lady bartender gave it to him in a plastic champagne glass with a flimsy snap on stem. He wondered aloud to the bartender how odd it was we could send people to Mars but couldn't manage a more elegant way to serve champagne, before reaching into his pocket.

"So what's the damage, Miss?"

"Eight dollars," she replied.

Rolling his eyes, he handed her a ten dollar coin and told her to keep the change. She turned away without so much as a smile.

"You're welcome," he said, loud enough for her to hear. He looked at his watch; there were still a few minutes left before show time. Plenty of time to lean back against one of the ornate marble columns and do some people watching. While the ladies appeared to outnumber the men, he was pretty sure he would end up flying solo tonight. He'd bought season tickets, if only to have an excuse to break out of his normal evening routine: sitting alone at home, and reading. Besides, he was starting to think he might be spending too much time at the local watering holes.

Be that as it may, tonight was the opening of the symphony season—a bold first step in his most recent self-improvement program, forcing him to branch out and do new things. He smiled at the thought that popped into his mind, from a handwritten note he'd found across the top of his doctoral thesis back in his Ann Arbor, from his professor, mentor and close friend, Dr. Bertram Powel: "Those who live in a small world remain small-world people. Those who live in a cosmic world become cosmic people."

His thesis was about the search for extraterrestrial intelligence; it seemed like a lifetime ago. He finished the champagne and returned for another.

"What would you like?" asked the bar maid, whom he mentally dubbed Miss Disinterested.

"If I buy a second glass of champagne, is there a discount by using my old glass?"

She pointed to a sign with the pricing.

That cinched it, he smiled to himself; no tip for her this time.

With a new glass in hand he turned away from the bar and bumped into a woman.

"Jeesus!" he exclaimed. It wasn't so much the eight dollars of champagne launching over the rim that troubled him. Worse was the fact that the contents had slipped down the top of a strapless black gown worn by a stunningly beautiful woman.

Her eyes widened, and she took a deep breath.

Zack gasped and turned the bartender.

"A towel—napkin—anything! But quickly!"

Grudgingly, the bartender handed him a towel. "I'll need that back," she said, sternly.

"Please forgive me," Zack said as he turned; but she was gone.

"Damn," he mumbled under his breath. He dropped the towel on the bar and began searching the crowded lobby in hopes of finding her. But the dimming lights silently proclaimed that patrons should take their seats in the auditorium. By the time he reached his aisle, the adrenaline rush had subsided, but he could tell that his mystery lady wouldn't be leaving his mind any time soon. Silly it might be, but he found himself quite smitten.

He scanned the audience as the usher led him down the aisle, hoping to spot her. Upon reaching his row the usher gave him a program and directed him to the empty space ten seats from the aisle. Offering a few pardons to those whose feet he was inconveniencing, he stumbled to his seat and sat down.

He kept looking for his mystery maiden, hoping he hadn't damaged her dress enough to make her leave. And unless she also had season tickets, he knew he might never get another chance to meet her.

The musicians came on stage, sat down and began warming up. Soon the lights dimmed and the oboe sounded its tuning note. Before long, the audience applauded politely, as the conductor made his entrance onto the stage. Zack was about to give up his quest when he saw his mystery lady coming down the aisle with an usher, looking none the worse for wear. They stopped two rows in front of his; she took the second seat in and placed an evening wrap on the aisle seat.

The conductor raised his baton, but Zack found he couldn't concentrate on the music. Instead, his mind began racing through a half-dozen ways to speak to her. The obvious one had to do with the empty seat next to her. He figured the soonest he would be able to approach her would be during the intermission.

He fidgeted through the closing bars of the Beethoven, and when the house lights came on to signal Intermission, most of the audience began standing to leave the auditorium. Rising at the same time as the man sitting next to him, Zack managed to step on the man's foot. By the time he finished apologizing, the mystery lady had left her seat and was heading into the lobby.

As he had no idea where to begin searching, he went to the scene of the mishap—the bar. Striking out there, he began wandering through the lobby, eventually camping out near one of the ladies' rest rooms. Discouraged, he went back to the bar.

"Zack?" called a man's voice behind him.

Looking up, Zack saw someone he recognized immediately, approaching through the crowd leading a lady on his arm.

"My God, it's Phil Macaulay—you old hound dog!"

The two men shook hands and hugged.

"Zack, you haven't changed one iota—except you finally shaved off the cheesy mustache! How long has it been?"

"Five or six years. At least. Not since you transferred to Texas!"

"How are you?" they asked in unison.

Macaulay laughed. "Tell me how you've been, Buddy. Gosh, how I've thought about the team—you in particular. You sure don't appear any the worse for wear."

"I'm just fine, living the high life in the suburbs with Muffins. And you should know," he said, highlighting his bow tie with both his hands, "I tied this all by myself thanks to your great instructions."

Macaulay inspected and adjusted the tie. "Well, it's good to know you still have Muffins. How old is she now?" He suddenly turned to the woman beside him. "Excuse me, honey. This is Zack Peters."

"As if I couldn't guess," she said, extending her hand. "I'm Betty and I feel I already know you after all the stories Phil's told me. You know, we moved back to Washington as soon the minute the EPA issued a 'thumbs up' on the city's air quality, after it had returned acceptable limits."

Zack pressed her hand warmly. "I'm happy to meet you, Betty."

"Hey, Zack," Phil interjected. "I hear that you ended up with Doug Farholm's old job after he got promoted."

"Well, while doing battle with myself about going back, it didn't take long to see I lacked the credentials for any other decent job. So I accepted."

"Well...the full pension and medical benefits probably didn't hurt, either. But you deserve every cent of it. Never forget that you saved the vice-president's life while putting yours on the line too." Macaulay gave him a playful jab.

"Last year I ran into Stan's wife Clara," he continued. "She's remarried—and quite successfully from what I hear. Her new hubby is a mid-level diplomat billeted here in Washington and fairly well off."

"Good for her. And how about...."

"Yes—Betty and I tied the knot four years ago," Macaulay said, putting his arm around her.

"How about you Zack? Are you…?"

"Well," he said sheepishly, "actually, I met—well, kind of ran into this incredible woman just before the concert. I've been wandering around looking for her so I could introduce myself."

"Zack, the debonair ladies' man," laughed Macaulay.

"How long were in Texas?"

"Stayed about a year, then we transferred to Socorro."

Zack's eyes widened.

"Transferred, my foot!" Betty exclaimed. pulling on her husband's arm. "Phil was promoted to security chief for all New Mexico and stationed at the Very Large Array. That's where the huge astronomy radio telescope facility is—in Socorro."

Macaulay shook his head and laughed. "And you'll be interested to know, Mr. PhD in Astronomical Physics, that I can now converse fluently in astronomy. Well, as long as nothing gets too technical. On a quieter note, have you ever gone back to see…?"

"No," Zack replied, more sharply than he intended. "I've been really busy," he added, with a tepid lift in his voice. "Here, let me buy you both a drink."

"No, thanks," Phil smiled. "I think we'll pass on drinks, tonight. Betty's parents are here with us tonight and we kind of deserted them. We really should get back."

"It was great seeing you again, Phil—and a pleasure meeting you, Betty."

Phil scribbled on the back of his business card. "Here's our unlisted number," he said, pressing it into Zack's hands. "The in-laws are leaving on Sunday. If you don't call by dinner time on Monday, I'll send out the hounds. It'll be fun. We'll rehash the good old days. It'll be good for you. Heck, it'll be good for both of us."

Zack watched as Phil and his wife walked away. For a split second the crowd opened and Zack saw her standing by one of the doors leading into the auditorium. She was looking straight at him.

As the lobby lights dimmed, she turned away and went inside. By the time he'd caught up, she was already in her seat, so he walked up to her row. Leaning over the aisle seat he screwed up his courage and asked, "So what do you think of my inventive way to meet a beautiful woman?"

She answered with a disinterested glare.

Plodding along through the muck of what remained of his confidence, he continued, "I want to apologize. Will you forgive me? Perhaps I could take this seat for a moment?"

"Yes to the first," she said, turning to look ahead. "No to the second."

"No doubt about it," Zack whispered to the man in the next row, who was eavesdropping on their conversation. "She's crazy about me."

Retreating to the safety of his seat, he noticed that the man whose foot he had stepped on earlier had been watching the conversation as well.

"You know, she's really quite taken with me," Zack said.

"Now you just have to convince her," the man sneered.

The lights faded and the crowd hushed as the conductor came on stage. He accepted the applause with a slight bow and stepped on the podium.

Zack was beaming: he had now heard her voice, and it was lovely. He'd even spoken with her, sort of. All was right with the world. More or less; all things considered.

The final selection for the evening, *Capriccio Español*, was on his short list of favorites. He enjoyed its drawn-out conclusion, and often said it was a crime when a great piece of music ended too abruptly.

As the piece ended, the audience rose with a resounding applause. And as the auditorium cleared he looked for his mystery woman, who had faded into the crowd. After hanging about the lobby hoping for a miracle, and giving the traffic jam in the parking structure a chance to clear, he glumly admitted defeat and sulked his way back to the garage.

Nearing his car, Zack used his remote voice command to unlock the driver's door, lower the window, and open the door. He checked for messages and, finding none, triggered the security sequencer.

"Good evening, Dr. Peters. I've made a search of my systems and find all within acceptable parameters. I would remind you that I will need an oil change in 73 kilometers and…"

"Yes, I know that each of your tires is deficient in air," Zack interrupted. "Charlie, we've got to find you a new memory chip or a better script writer."

Zack started the engine, and the headlights in the grill and fenders swung out and turned on, the grille light matching the maneuvers of the front wheels. He backed out of his parking space, and the headlights revealed a woman a few cars down, in obvious distress. The hood of her car was raised and she was leaning into the engine well of a sports car, painted in a vivid glen plaid. She straightened and covered her eyes with one hand as he pulled up.

Zack felt adrenaline surging through his system. Impossible as it seemed, he had found his woman in black.

And maybe—just maybe—if his God's Gift to Women approach had fallen flat, maybe Zack the Tool Man would have better luck.

Chapter 11

ZACK GAVE A VOICE COMMAND to lower the passenger side window.

The mystery lady spoke first "Perhaps you know of an ingenious technique to start this motor?"

"Yes I do...if you'll first allow me to apologize again."

Her response was the same stare she'd given him in the auditorium, but it soon softened to a smile.

"It would seem that bearing a grudge would not be in my best interests this evening."

He pulled into the nearest parking space and walked back, well aware that car engines were one of the three things in the world he knew absolutely nothing about. The second was women. The third escaped his mind when she turned away from him and leaned deep into the engine well.

"Oh my," he whispered. His eyes widened in horror at the realization that he'd said it out loud.

"Pardon me?" she said straightening up.

"I said how—how long have you had this problem?"

She wiped her hands with a rag. "This is the first time."

"It seems the local deities have intervened so we could meet."

"I wasn't aware you'd been praying," she sighed, stepping aside to clear his way to the engine compartment.

Zack handed her a handkerchief and pointed to the grease smudge on her cheek. It pained him to discover himself unable to think of a graceful way to work her captivating fragrance into the conversation.

"I appreciate the gesture, but it may leave a permanent stain."

"It's old. Just one of many I keep for ladies in need."

Taking it she returned her first genuine smile of the evening.

He leaned into the engine well, grunting for effect as he wiggled a few wires before straightening up. "I think your alter-winder pluggie cable is shorting out the thing-a-ma-bob on the left side of that black thingy," he concluded grimly.

"What?"

"I haven't the slightest idea what's wrong," he shrugged, pointing a finger at the engine. "To be perfectly honest, I only know that this thing makes the car go."

"An honest man," she smiled through pursed lips. "In this day and age I find that refreshing."

"What I actually can do is to call for a tow truck."

"No thank you. I can leave it here and have my mechanic pick it up in the morning. But I would appreciate it if you could take me someplace where I might find a taxi. With all of the taxi robberies recently I have heard the companies prefer not to take phone requests at night."

"Why don't you let me drive you to where you are going?"

"That would be very nice. I'm staying at a friend's apartment about three miles from here."

Savoring the sudden turn of miraculous good fortune, Zack won his internal struggle not to scream in triumph. "I'll be happy to take you there," he nodded instead.

She closed the hood and engaged an electronic theft control. As they approached his car, Zack gave a voice command and the two doors swung out and underneath the car.

"I have never seen that before," she said. "This should be interesting."

Because the seats of his car were lower than most, she hiked her skirt before dropping into the passenger seat. He closed her door walked around to the other. It wasn't as though he hadn't seen legs before, he mused; but those legs were amazing.

After he'd turned onto the street and traveled a few blocks, Zack felt an awkward silence and tried frantically to come up with a neutral topic. "Would you like to stop for a drink or something to eat?" he said at last, having given up as hopeless the attempt to sound interesting.

"No thanks. I have an early day tomorrow and I just want to get to bed. I suppose I should introduce myself. My name is Li-Hwa Zaranova."

"And I'm Zack Peters, Lee."

"I prefer being called Li-Hwa."

"Of course," he said; strike one, he thought. ". Where do you work, Miss Zavarona?"

"It's Zaranova, pronounced zah-rah-NO-vah, Mr. Peters."

Strike two, Zack grimaced.

"Please call me Zack."

"I'm employed with Aeroflot, the Russian National Airline."

"I travel quite a bit but haven't had the opportunity to fly Aeroflot. Are you in ticket sales or in reservations?"

"I am a flight crew member," she replied stiffly.

"Excellent. Then that will be my incentive to fly Aeroflot. And should I ever have the good fortune to meet you on a flight, I'll be asking for a perfect vodka martini—with no ice. And I won't embarrass you by offering a gratuity. I know you're not allowed to accept them. But I promise to give you one of my captivating smiles."

She turned abruptly to the window. "I am not a flight attendant," she said icily. "I am a flight officer." She turned back to him saying, "What is it with men? Do you all share a gene that has you assume women are secretaries, nurses or flight attendants, rather than office managers, doctors or pilots?" She turned back to the window and folded her arms.

Strike three, he thought. "Sorry, Lee." When she turned to him with 'that look' he added, "I mean, Li-Hwa. Look, I apologize, and am just trying to impress you. I confess—I'm attracted to you and am tripping over my mouth trying to avoid making blunders. You say you're a commercial airlines pilot. That's quite an accomplishment. Your parents must really be proud of you."

"Failure is frowned upon in Chinese culture," she replied. " I had to work hard to obtain a pilot's ticket on single and twin propeller aircraft as well as second officer on three, four and six-engine jets." She paused for a moment.

"Zack, it is your turn to forgive me," she continued. "I become infuriated with male chauvinism in this country. In other countries a woman performs a man's work and receives a man's wages—all without the imputed loss of her femininity."

"I can say in all sincerity that you're about as feminine a woman as I've ever had the pleasure of displeasing. It is Miss, isn't it?"

"Yes. And you?"

"Me? I'm single also."

"I was referring to your profession, not your marital status."

"I'm an astronomer—of sorts."

"So you tell fortunes?"

"Not an astrologer, an astronomer. We study the universe. And for what it's worth I have the same reaction to being cast as a fortune teller as you have being seen as a flight attendant."

"I was teasing," she smiled. "Please turn left at the next light."

After a moment he asked, "How do you spell Li-Hwa?"

"Using my alphabet, or yours?"

Zack gave her a blank stare; Li-Hwa laughed and shook her head. "Capital L, small i, hyphen, capital H, small w, small a."

"Zaranova. I would guess it's Russian."

"Yes. My father is Russian. Oh, you can turn left here. There it is, the second building on the right. The one with the green and white awning running out to the curb."

Zack pulled over, and hit a button to open the car door. "May I see you the next time you're in Washington," he asked.

Seeing his downcast face as she rattled off her litany of woes with delayed and erratic flights, scheduling snafus, and jet lag, she took pity on him. "Why not give me your business card," she smiled. "Perhaps I can call you the next I am in town."

Zack rummaged through his pockets eagerly, trying to keep from telling himself that the odds of hearing from her were close to non-existent. He didn't notice the car that drove past them; it was one of the three that had followed him since leaving the symphony hall.

"I can't find one," he said at last. "Let me write my mobile number on the back of a parking receipt. I hope you'll let me make amends for our little champagne disaster."

"We'll see, Zack. It was very kind of you to drop me off. Thank you."

Zack noticed two uniformed police officers stood inside the lobby of her building, and pointed them out.

"Yes, I see them," Li-Hwa said. "If you don't mind waiting, perhaps I could wave to you after I find out everything is alright."

She thanked him again and walked to the entrance. She returned to the car with widened eyes, and shaking her head.

"Someone was murdered there tonight," she said. "They will not let anyone in or out until all of the occupants have been questioned. That could take forever."

"What did they tell you to do?"

"One officer offered to escort me to the apartment to let me gather some items so I can spend the night elsewhere. Would you mind waiting a while longer, and then perhaps drop me off at a hotel?"

"Take all the time you need."

Returning to the entrance, she spoke with an officer, who walked her to an elevator. While she was gone, Zack checked his phone for messages. There was only one, from an agitated woman..

"Zack, it's Priscilla. Why in blazes aren't you answering your calls? Call me as soon as you get this. The boss needs to speak to you---like an hour ago!"

He returned the call, to find the agitated woman on the other end.

"It's me, Miss Golightly. What's up?"

"Where in hell have you been? Excuse my French—but where the hell have you been? I've been going crazy trying to reach you."

"I was at the symphony and had my pager turned off. I thought it would be nice to get through an entire evening without getting dragged into a crisis. Please don't tell me I have to go out of town."

"My readout shows you're in your car."

"Does it tell you how dashing I look in evening clothes?"

"I'm sure you do. Now turn your scrambler on. This is important."

"My scrambler isn't working."

"Then we can't talk right now, Zack! How soon do you plan on getting home?"

"It will either be in an hour or tomorrow morning, depending on whether I get lucky or not."

"Then I'll expect a call in about forty-five minutes. And yes, you guessed right, so start packing as soon as you get home. You're flying out tomorrow at 0700."

"Crap! How long will I be gone this time, Priss?"

"I'm told two days. Four at the most. It's concerning F.S."

"Then it's a crisis. I'll pack for five."

"Sorry if I sounded sharp, Zack. Good luck on tonight's conquest. And get your scrambler fixed."

As the call ended Li-Hwa came out of the apartment building wearing a white knit dress. She was pulling a small rolling suitcase, and a garment bag was draped over her other arm. She went to the rear of the car.

"Sorry, this car's engine is in the rear. Bring those things up here." He released the hood and got out to help.

"I thought you were tugging my foot," she said.

"I believe you mean pulling my leg."

"Yes, thank you; pulling my leg."

As they drove off she asked, "Do you know a place downtown that is relatively safe? I prefer to avoid airport hotels."

"What time do you need to check in tomorrow morning?"

"The crew checks in at 0600."

"Well, it's almost midnight," Zack said, trying his best not to sound too eager. "By the time we find you a downtown hotel and get you settled in, you won't get much sleep. My condo is half-way between here and the airport. Since I have to catch a flight at tomorrow morning at 0700. Why don't you stay there, and I can drive you to the airport myself tomorrow morning?"

"I appreciate your offer but that seems inappropriate, having just met."

"Be practical. I'll even lend you my attack dog to sleep at the foot of your bed. Plus, the bedroom has an inside lock. I'll sleep in the living room."

"Then I accept," she smiled. "And what is the name of my brave guard dog?"

"Muffins."

She started laughing, and nearly choked in the process.

"No. It really is Muffins. Of course, the only thing she attacks is her food dish."

"Such a sweet name. How did she come by it?"

"Her biggest weakness is eating blueberry muffins. She loves them."

"Perhaps that's the secret to courting a woman, Zack. You simply have to discover what her 'muffin' is."

She slipped off her shoes and slid her feet back and forth on the carpet. "Luxurious carpeting is one of my muffins."

"Guess I'm in trouble then."

"Why is that?"

"My place has hard wood floors."

"Ooh—you must be wealthy."

"Not really," Zack chuckled. "Wood was my second extravagance; my first being this car. I spent a year eating kelp burgers and grilled cheese sandwiches to pay for it." He tenderly patted the dashboard. "But then, we only go around once."

"I take it you don't believe in reincarnation?"

"One time around is plenty for me."

"I imagine that once you've found your soul mate, one time would not be enough. May I use your phone to call about my car?"

He passed it to her and said, "It's a little old fashioned. You have to tap 'U' to unlock it, then 'F' to bypass the Fax and then slowly speak the number."

While it was connecting she said, "I do believe the perfect woman would make your reincarnation very..." She raised a finger to interrupt him, and began speaking in Russian.

"I'm sorry about that, Zack," she sighed, handing him back the phone. "They don't speak English very well."

"My Russian isn't very good either," he said, looking straight ahead. "I think you were mentioning something about the symphony, some kind of a connection and someone was to speak to the person in charge. How did I do?"

She looked surprised. "You did very, very well. I asked that someone pick the car up tomorrow and deliver it to the apartment."

"And if your friend isn't there when they deliver it?" Zack smirked.

"I feel I should clarify things," she said primly. "I wasn't sure that I wanted to see you again. I led you to believe it was a friend's apartment. Actually it's mine."

"That was the smart thing to do."

"But now I know I do want to see you, Zack. Do you still want to see me?"

"You can be sure of that. So tell me, Li-Hwa, are there English words for your name? I only know a handful of Japanese."

She frowned. "Don't you remember that my father was Chinese?

How does that vulgar American adage go—you slant-eyes all look alike? ”

“Wait just one second Li-Hwa. Granted I may not have a degree in world cultures, linguistics or anthropology, but I’m getting a little tired of choosing my words for phrases that won’t offend you.”

She was quiet for a moment and then said, “You are right again. Please forgive me. The last few days have been hectic. Last night I was in Honolulu, and tonight I am in Washington. Let us blame it on jet lag. I grant the distinction between Chinese and Japanese may be subtle to most people. To make things even more complicated, my heritage is Asian and European.”

“So let’s both forgive and forget, Li-Hwa.”

“Tell me all about my guard dog,” she asked, after a long pause.

“She’s a nine-year-old female, beige and white Shih Tzu.”

“That’s a coincidence. I have a five-year-old Shih Tzu that I call Su-Shi.”

“Sounds like raw fish—which, by the way is one of my favorite dishes.”

“That's it exactly!” she touched his arm. “You and she both love sushi. I chose to call her Su-Shi using Chinese phonetics.” She squeezed his arm gently before placing her head against the window and dozing off.

Unfortunately, the reality of Li-Hwa being both shapely and lovely worked against him. After years of participating in covert operations, he should have detected the three vehicles that were taking turns following him. He didn’t.

Pulling into his driveway, Zack activated the garage door

“Garage door and residence are secure,” Charlie announced, startling Li-Hwa. “An oil change will be required within the next one hundred kilometers and...”

Zack joined the chorus, “…each tire is deficient in pressure by two kilograms.”

Li-Hwa looked at him quizzically.

“It's a private joke,” he said.

ONCE INSIDE THE HOUSE, Zack was encouraged to see Li-Hwa and Muffins hitting it off so well. Feeling brave, he offered her a cocktail.

“No thanks...just show me my room before I fall asleep on the floor here with Muffins.”

"I put clean sheets on this morning and you'll find towels and washcloths in the bathroom closet," said Zack, ushering her to the bedroom. "I'll give you a call at five because we're only a few minutes from the airport."

"Do you need to get any night clothes?"

Zack shook his head. "Just my bathrobe," he said, picking up his robe from the floor, where he'd dropped it that morning. "I sleep in my shorts."

"Well...goodnight and thank you for your kindness."

After she'd closed the door, he went into the den to use the phone.

"It's me, Priss. We're scrambled."

"Good. Are you alone?" she asked.

"No. I have a friend staying over."

"Anyone I know?"

"Not unless you know some Aeroflot flight officers."

"Are you crazy it? Aeroflot? The boss will have your skin. That guest could be a spy!"

"Should I wake her up and ask?"

"A woman? That's even worse. You better hope you don't talk in your sleep," Priss scolded. "But back to business. I have a recorded message for you from the President. Are you using your ear bud?"

"Of course," Zack lied.

"Here it comes."

"Zack, we have reason to believe that the Russians are highly agitated and ready to move up to their version of our DEFCON 2. We believe they are suspicious of F. S., and for that reason I need you to fly to Bermuda tomorrow morning. Pricilla has made your flight arrangements and booked a room at the Bermudiana Princess. Someone from M-6 will meet you at the airport. You are scheduled to meet director J. Winthrop Winstanly at the hotel at noon. He'll have some priority documents for you. Look them over and have copies made, and bring them to me when you return.

"When I spoke to him earlier today he preferred not discussing anything over the phone, no matter how secure we thought the line might be. He did allude to the idea that the Brits becoming increasingly uneasy with their commitment to the U.S. and F. S. This is obviously a touchy assignment, so I need you on your toes and your best behavior. Please be diplomatic—and of course scramble me if anything needs my immediate attention."

When the line cleared, Priscilla asked, "Zack? Did you copy that okay?"

"Loud and clear Priss. I assume I'm on the Atlantic flight at 0700. And Julius will meet me at the hotel?"

"Damn it Zack! Excuse my French, but don't ever call him Julius. He hates that. You'll restart the Revolutionary War again---or at least set Anglo-American relations back ten years."

"I'm just yanking your chain. Win and I have been tennis buddies for years."

Zack heard a harsh sigh over the phone. "Yes, you are on Atlantic 101 departing DCA at 0700 with a full breakfast. The ticket's in your name, and you can pick it up at the will-call desk. I left your return flight open. You'll find $1,000 waiting for you at the hotel."

"Thanks, Priss. Why don't you take a couple of days off and meet me there? Just be sure to bring along your polka dot bikini."

"Bermuda is not ready for me in a bikini."

"But you must know the department that plays together stays together."

"You're a letch, Peters—a loveable letch, but still a letch. Lucky for you I love it. Goodnight!"

The bedroom door opened and Li-Hwa stepped out in white silk pajamas.

"Excuse me, Zack, but I heard you on the phone and knew you were still up. Do you have some aspirin?"

"Of course I do," Zack said, springing to his feet. He walked to the bar, leaned over the front and came up with a small bottle.

"Thank you."

She returned to the bedroom and closed the door. Muffins went over and started whimpering. A few minutes later, Li-Hwa opened the door and peeked out.

"Is it alright if she sleeps with me?"

"She'd love it. And don't worry. She won't need to pee until morning."

* * * * *

ZACK AWOKE to the aroma of coffee and bacon.

Tossing on his bathrobe, he shuffled into the kitchen where Li-Hwa greeted him with a cheery smile.

"Good morning, Doctor Peters."

She had on black slacks with freshly ironed pleats and a white uniform shirt with button-down pockets and epaulets. A black tie hung loose from the collar, and she wore low-heel black shoes. Her hair was pulled back into a tight bun.

"You didn't mention you were a professor," she said, pressing the button to start the microwave. "I saw two doctorate degrees on the wall. I'm very impressed."

"They're just for decoration. I never speak of them and in your case I don't want you to think of me as a stuffy professor."

"But I think that is what I like about you," she said handing him coffee. "I couldn't find any milk or cream so you'll have to do without."

"I keep them right here," he said opening a cabinet door. He removed a small bowl filled with beige cubes. Dropping one in his coffee changed the color from black to a medium brown.

"It's a quirky idea someone came up with," he explained. Sugar and cream mixed into a single dry cube. Tastes pretty decent, too. What I like most is that the fat's taken out of the cream, and there's no danger it'll go bad in the fridge."

The fridge?"

"Refrigerator," he answered pointing to it.

She took two plates from the microwave filled with eggs, bacon, and toast and set them on the table next to marmalade, orange juice, and napkins.

"I could get used to this," Zack nodded. "I rarely take time for this kind of a breakfast. It's easier to grab two cups of coffee and a sweet roll somewhere."

"That's not nutritious. So why do you have these items in your...fridge?"

"It's what I cook for dinner. Simple and fast."

She sat down, and spread her napkin on her lap. "It appears that you need a woman around here full time," she said firmly. "Now please try a little of this."

Dutifully, Zack started eating.

"Do you mind if I use your phone?" she asked. "Mine needs

recharging. I'm packed and ready to go in case you need to use my bathroom."

He nodded toward the phone, and sipped at his coffee. Listening unobtrusively, he noticed she was again speaking Russian, but he couldn't make out what she was saying.

"Good news," she said, returning to the table. "My flight is on time. We have another thirty minutes before we need to leave."

She sat down, replaced her napkin and daintily sipped her coffee; Zack wolfed down his food.

"Li-Hwa, it's easy to picture you in a fashion magazine," he said, leaning back in his chair. "But I can't bring myself to seeing you slaving away in a man's kitchen."

"That is a sweet thing to say. But mother kept reminding me that my good looks would eventually leave me. However, if I could please my man in the kitchen, she said he would never leave me."

"My dear Miss Zaranova, you needn't concern yourself with losing men."

He took his coffee into the living room and stopped at a wall television.

"If you want to look at the morning paper, just push power and it will appear on the screen. Scroll up and down with this hand control and if you prefer a hard copy, just select the page and press this button."

"Would you mind showing me?"

"Sure." He punched in commands and the first page of the newspaper fed out below the screen. "Just touch 'off' when this light flashes green."

As Li-Hwa watched the morning news Zack took Muffins down the hall, and thanked a neighbor profusely for agreeing to dog-sit for a few days.

THE DRIVE to Reagan International was pleasant. Li-Hwa dozed with her head on his shoulder. He thought about the subtle change he'd noticed in her voice and mannerism since the night before. It was if she was gradually losing her accent, and to some extent her innocence and naivety. She stirred when he mentioned they were arriving at the Aeroflot terminal.

"Good morning, sleepy head. So what strange and exotic

destinations are you going to visit today?" He smiled to see her stretching as she awoke; she reminded him of a cat.

"Today it's a Washington to London to Cairo flight. Tomorrow we fly Cairo to Paris to San Francisco. The day after that we continue on to Bermuda for a two-day layover."

"That's perfect, Li-Hwa. I'm heading for Bermuda today to what I've been promised to be a short meeting. Then I can take a few days off to relax. It will be fantastic opportunity for us to meet again and have time together."

"I'd like that very much," she said leaning over the seat back to gather her luggage. "Where are you staying?"

"At the Bermudiana Princess."

"That's just a few minutes from one of my uncle's homes. I'll call you from the airport after I arrive or go directly to the Bermudiana."

Zack slowed to a stop and double parked. "Here we are."

"Thank you. Can I ask another favor? It's important that we give the appearance of being professional in case we run into my flight crew."

"I understand," he said. He walked around to her side, lifted the door and helped her out. "I liked the skirt better," he whispered.

She nodded and offered a perceptive smile. As he was placing her items on the curb a taxi pulled up directly behind them. Her flight crew emerged; they all recognized Li-Hwa, and gave her a wave.

"There's my crew." She extended her arm and shook his hand firmly. She raised her voice enough to make sure her crew could hear her. "I want to thank you again for the ride, Dr. Peters. Be sure to say goodbye to your charming *wife*," she said, emphasizing the last word.

"I'll be sure to do that, Miss Zaranova. Have a pleasant trip."

"You are going to love the way I cook," she whispered as she picked up her bag. With a perky smile she strode off in a strong and deliberate pace.

Zack got back into the car, and a Deputy County Sheriff strolled over to the open passenger window. "Let's be moving this vehicle, young man," he grinned. "You know, I could write you a citation for what you were thinking as that pretty young thing walked away."

Zack released the parking brake and dropped into first gear. He replied, "Deputy, if you knew what I was thinking, you'd lock me up and throw away the key."

As he pulled away the Deputy's expression changed from pleasant to gravely serious. Taking the phone from his belt, he keyed in a number and began to speak in Russian.

Chapter 12

ZACK STEPPED OFF THE ENCLOSED WALKWAY and into the terminal just as he heard his name being paged.

"Atlantic Airways arriving passenger Dr. Zachary Peters, pick up any white courtesy telephone."

He was passing one and he did. "This is Zack Peters. I believe you have a message for me."

"Yes, Mr. Peters. You have a party waiting for you in customs control in baggage concourse 3-A."

"Is that where I pick up my luggage from Atlantic 101 from Washington?"

"Yes, in 3-A."

He walked across the arrivals lobby and took an escalator to the baggage concourse. As he walked towards carousel 3-A, he was approached by a man wearing a white suit, shirt, socks and shoes. He reminded Zack of an ice cream vendor.

"Dr. Peters, welcome to Bermuda," the man said holding credentials in one hand and extending the other. "Gregory Ashleigh, British Consulate Office."

"Thanks for meeting me Mr. Ashleigh. Is Director Winstanly with you?"

"I'm afraid not. He got himself shot up a bit. Bad show and all that. But not to worry. He's tip-top and eager to meet you at the hotel."

"Shot? What happened?"

"I prefer to let him fill you in on the details, Dr. Peters."

Zack caught sight of his bag coming around the bend. "There's my bag. And please call me Zack."

"Right you are," Ashleigh smiled blandly. "And so Zack it is. Give your valise a yank and we'll head directly outside. I've cleared you through customs so we'll just pop out to our lift. And do call me Ash, if you would. Everyone else does." He turned and started ushering Zack toward the door.

"But do try to be careful with the pronunciation, if you catch my drift," he added with a wink.

AFTER A SHORT RIDE, the limo pulled up in front of the hotel. "Here we are gentlemen," the driver announced, scurrying to the trunk to unload the luggage. "The Bermudiana Princess. Enjoy your stay on our beautiful island. Please take one of my cards, and remember that my name is Thomas. I provide private tours in my own vehicle so you can see the very best sights in Bermuda—some that are not included in the more expensive tours."

Ashleigh escorted Zack up the walkway leading to the main entrance. Marble columns framed the entrance, and Zack could see a magnificent view of the beach through the French doors on the other side of the lobby.

Ashleigh said, "I'm afraid I must abandon you here and pop off to a pressing engagement. It was awfully nice meeting you," Ashleigh said pleasantly, extending his hand. "Here's my card. And don't get it mixed up with the drivers. I wrote my home number on the back. Ring me up if you cannot reach me at the consulate."

Ashleigh approached the doorman. "I've made reservations for Dr. Peters," he said. "So be a good fellow and see that he gets safely to Suite 110-B."

Ashleigh was quite generous with the gratuity; Zack figured it would be buried somewhere in his expense account.

"Now remember, Zack—I'm at your beck and call. Ring me up if I can be of any service. You should find Winstanly in the suite. Here's your key-card. You won't find the room number on it for security reasons so you will need to remember it; 110-B." Ashleigh walked back to the limo and waved farewell as it pulled away.

When Zack got to the room, he knocked twice; hearing now answer, he slid his card key through the lock and opened the door.

"Hello? Win? Is anybody home?"

J. Winthrop Winstanly, director of the United Kingdom M-6 Intelligence Agency had been napping in a wing back leather chair. Groggily rising to his feet, he stifled a yawn.

"Come in my fine fellow."

Tall and slender, balding and sporting a red mustache, he approached Zack with an outstretched hand. Zack thought that Winstanly—the second-ranking member of Britain's external intelligence agency—would be the logical choice for any TV show or movie needing a character actor to play an aging British secret agent.

"How good it is to see you Zack. Just catching a wink or two. Be careful, not to trip over my valises, old boy."

Zack picked his way through a maze of suitcases.

"As usual, I see you're traveling light," he quipped. "But I don't see your tennis racquet or golf sticks. Ash said something about you catching one?"

Winstanly, still grasping Zack's hand said, "Just a minor scratch. But I must have a talk with Ashleigh. I particularly asked him not to mention my inconvenience. Didn't want to alarm you."

"Am I alarmed? No—disappointed? Hell, yes. I was looking forward to whipping your butt in tennis or golf this afternoon. I assume you recall the sound thrashing I gave you the last time we played."

"Thrashing? Now listen here, my good man," Winstanly protested—his face catching a bit of color. "Oh damn. Zack, you are jolly well spoofing me."

Zack said added a bear hug to their greeting. "Seriously now—tell me what happened."

"It was a bloody-hell accident, that's what it was. Never should have happened. Someone took a shot at the Prime Minister! Must have missed him by a mile, thank God. A totally inept shooter, I might add. Makes one wonder about the quality of today's young assassins. Anyway, one of the bloody rounds ricocheted twice, the last time off the limo's blasted wheel cover. Damn thing caught me in the foot."

"How bad is it?"

"Doctor says I need one more week in this God-awful cast before I'm right as rain once again. But now good friend, we have a number of items to go over. I spoke with the President about them two hours ago. In another hour and a half I'll catch a flight to Washington to deliver them personally."

"So why do you need me?"

"In the event something happens to me, dear boy," Winstanley huffed. "The President wants you fully briefed and carrying back-up copies if I fail to arrive in one piece." He reached across the table and picked up a thick Manila envelope marked TOP SECRET. "This is your set. Now let's sit down over here and begin. But first, be a good chap and close the drapes."

"Is your room secured?"

"Most definitely. It is swept electronically every three hours as well as four of our other rooms—the ones on either side and those directly above and below. The sweeps will continue for the duration of your stay here."

"Me? In your suite?"

"Of course. That's the first bit of news. You're to stay on and unwind a bit."

"Unwind?"

"Yes, my boy. That comes straight from the President."

Zack smiled as he sank into the overstuffed chair at the far end of a heavy oak table. "I never argue about getting time off. So fill me in."

Winstanly poured two oversized drinks and brought them to the table. "The Agency is in a sorry state of affairs. I've lost four agents in the past five days from bombs, shootings and poisonings?"

"Jesus, Win. Who's behind all this?"

"Several groups are all claiming credit. The only thing we know for sure is that the events were extremely well orchestrated."

Zack ran his fingers through his hair and let out a sigh. "You must have some clues."

"None. None at all. We have, however, each been issued one of these." He lifted his suit coat and tapped a holstered pistol.

"Welcome to the club," Zack said tapping his waist behind his back.

"Another piece of news, your President was shot around noon today."

Zack leaped out of his seat.

"What! Where?"

Winstanly motioned for him to sit.

"Take a deep breath. It was at a luncheon of the National something-or-other Environmentalist Association. Just a slight flesh wound, I'm led to believe. It nicked her arm and was so minor that the luncheon went on as scheduled once a bandage had been applied."

Zack shook his head in disbelief.

"I understand she received a two minute standing ovation," Winstanley continued. "I'll wager that could tally up to 10,000 more votes for reelection. Let's see where was I? Oh yes, the third news item is…"

"Third?" Zack tapped his glass. "Christ! I'm going to need another drink."

"Over there in the cabinet to the left of the refrigerator. And while you're at it, kindly create another Bloody Mary for me. Never could resist the bloody things. Now, where was I? Oh yes, three. The Soviets seem convinced that your former SDI Star Wars program was just a ruse intended to camouflage some larger project."

"Damn. So it's finally out of the bag."

"The good news is they haven't any information about your Fly Swatter program. However they seem convinced that it is tied indirectly to the refurbishing of the International Space Station."

"Well good for them," Zack said from behind the bar. The President said just last week that it would be impossible to keep Fly Swatter under wraps longer than six weeks—seven at the outside. To tell the truth, I'm surprised we could keep it secret as long as we did. Anyway, here's your drink. Chin-chin Win."

"Yes, bottoms up. Now for event number four. Be a good chap and switch on that projector and insert this." Once the image came into view he said, "Take a look and tell me what you think."

"I heard about this, already. The entrance to Scotland Yard."

"Yes...until some bloody bastards blew ten feet off of the façade and killed six of our blokes. Wounded fifteen, at last count."

"Any idea of who's responsible for this one?"

"No. It's the same story. Everyone wants to take credit for it. Now—are you ready for number five?"

Winstanly took an envelope from an attaché case. "His Majesty has charged me with delivering this letter to the President. Although

I haven't read it, from what I can deduce it spells out why Britain will soon be begging off on future commitment to Fly Swatter. And I must ask you to remember that you did not hear that piece of news from me."

"Mum's the word," Zack said drawing an imaginary zipper across his mouth. "But why would the UK pull out at this stage of the game?"

"The moment the Russians discover we've been engaged in funding American defense systems, we might be asked to resign from the European Union. If that happened, the P.M. feels it may very well put our country into bankruptcy within a year. I just hope your country can muddle along without our support."

"Okay, Win—now I get to provide you with some news that will take the edge off of your dreary list."

"And what might that be?"

"Just promise you'll act surprised if and when the President mentions it."

"I promise," Winstanley chucked, "if only because I need an emotional uplift right about now, tell me your special news. "

"Last Saturday we began initial tests on Fly Swatter."

"My God Zack—that's marvelous. Absolutely marvelous."

"It's true, Win. The project is pretty much a done deal. And the best news is that it actually works!"

"Well then, I propose that we toast the failure of all of the bastards around the bloody planet who've terrorized the rest of us these past few years. Here's to Fly Swatter and to us, the good guys."

"Back at you, Win." They touched glasses. "Of course, I guess it's all relative as to who's wearing the white hats, and who's sporting the black ones."

"Come again, old chap? White and black hats?"

"An old Hollywood gimmick. Before movies had sound, the good guys in western films wore white hats so you could tell them from the bad guys."

"Speaking of cowboys, it looks like the last of your states to ban carrying side arms has finally yielded to the wishes of its citizens."

"Yep—the last one finally got on board."

"I can see it now, Zachary. With all of your citizens bearing side arms strapped on their waist, the country will look like an old time Western in no time."

"Well, thanks to those who are openly packing side arms, there have only been a couple of dozen daytime bank robberies."

"That all sounds rather melodramatic, but apparently the idea has taken hold."

"I hope so, Win. Now give me your thoughts on the King actually taking over the reins of government. I know he was tiring of acting as a figurehead."

"Actually I was in Hong Kong when it all started up, so I could only catch it on like you, on the television news. From what I gather, it all started with the Prime Minister being called up on censure."

"The one who called for a nation-wide ban on smoking?"

"Precisely. He chose to resign before being kicked out of office. Half of London to gather outside Buckingham Palace to celebrate by singing the national anthem. It looked like the rest had gathered outside Parliament, making enough noise to drown out Big Ben."

"Sounds like a modern-day French Revolution."

"It rather does, doesn't it? I imagine the House of Lords was damn well fearful of being dragged out on the street and shot if they didn't come up with an acceptable plan. So, Parliament reinstated the King as supreme ruler in charge of the realm."

"And all this took place because of a smoking ban?"

"Well, not precisely. A fair number of problems had popped up already. The ban on smoking was just the spark that set it off—the straw that broke the camel's back, one might say."

"I thought for sure there was going to be shooting when television showed the military moving in."

"Well, unlike the 1989 uprising in Beijing demonstration, our chaps refused to fire on the citizens. Some even put down their weapons and joined the crowd."

Zack tipped his chair back and shook his head saying, "The Royalists must be happier than a pig in mud."

"That's where you're wrong, old chap. Here, be a good fellow and freshen my drink again—two fingers should suffice nicely. Now let me enlighten you."

Zack returned with two full glasses.

Winstanly continued. "I think you fail to see the bigger picture."

"I think your bigger picture would have the world regressing two hundred years to a form of government that has modern times had left behind."

"Not at all, Zack. Times are changing. You must agree the world seems to be going to hell in a hand basket. And while I grant you that truly democratic governments have provided its citizens more freedom than they've ever enjoyed, the down side is that those governments no longer have a way to make people act responsibly."

Zack shook his head. "Now that's a bit of an exaggeration."

"*Au contraire, mon ami.* How many times have you said that what the country needs is a benevolent dictator? You meant no less than that everyone should take a deep breath and give such a chap five years to clean house. Whereupon, after that, you'd expect to be handed back a healthy country like the one you had before all the do-gooders gave away the store."

"But there's a flaw in your logic, Win. How do you get that dictator to give back the country after they've gotten used to enjoying the fruits of power?"

"Ah yes. And therein lays the predicament. You probably couldn't. That's why monarchies have a chance of succeeding. Think of a monarch as being a benevolent dictator—one that you don't have to do battle with to get your country back. Mark my words, monarchies give us the best chance."

"Perhaps you're right," Zack shrugged. He could feel his drink eroding his republican ideals.

"I'll wager you that Belgium, Denmark, Norway and Sweden will restore their monarchies within a year or two."

"What about Mexico and Spain?"

"They will too. Maybe even China and Japan, as well. Why hell Zach—by this time next year you and I could be Earls or Dukes."

"I've always thought I'd look impressive in a powdered wig," Zack sighed. "But let's get cracking on these papers before you have to leave."

AFTER THE BRIEFING SESSION, Winstanly rose, stretched and snapped shut his brief case. He picked up the phone and summoned the porter for his luggage.

"Oh," he said, before hanging up. "And could you ring me over to the reservations desk?"

Zack stood up and stretched. He went to the window and looked out at the ocean. The seas were calm, and he could see sand pipers being chased by the gentle waves.

"Reservations? This is Winstanly in 110-B. I have already settled my account, but wish to remind you that Dr. Zackary Peters is staying on in this suite for a few days. Would you be a good chap and place all of his charges on my bill and forward it to me in London? Jolly good. Yes, come to think of it, I will need transportation to the airport. I prefer a helio-cab. You will? Thank you."

Zack turned to face his old friend. "Now I see why I was sent here."

"Well , after perusing those documents you can appreciate why we couldn't take the chance of sending them by satellite or video-fax."

"Yes."

"There's just one more consideration, Zachary," Winstanley smiled. "Assuming that I make it to Washington in one tidy piece, your orders are to unwind for a few days."

"I promise. How long will you be in DC?"

"Just long enough to see the President and drop by our embassy."

There was a knock at the door. Winstanly headed over to it saying, "This will be my porter."

Zack stood and said, "I'll walk you down, Win." The phone rang. "Peters here. Yes. Please hold for a moment."

Winstanly waved his hand. "Don't worry about me," As he started out the door he added, "Unpack, unwind and relax. Now take that call. Cheerio."

Zack smiled as the door closed. Just then, he heard his cell phone signal an incoming message:

> ZACK—THERE HAS BEEN A SLIGHT CHANGE OF PLANS. I WILL EXPLAIN WHEN I SEE YOU. OUR ETA IS 1600 TOMORROW. DO NOT COME TO MEET ME. JUST SAVE A SPOT BY THE POOL. LI-HWA.

Walking to the desk, he picked up the hotel phone and pressed Star-6, the speed dial number for the hotel restaurant. A pleasant woman's voice answered; she sounded friendly, and quite young.

"Dining room? This is Zack Peters in 110-B. I want to reserve a nice table tomorrow night for two. The first one available is 8 p.m.? That will be fine. Thank you."

Next, he dialed Star-5. "Room service? This is Zack Peters in 110-B. I'd like a fruit and cheese tray sent to this room tomorrow afternoon at five, along with a bottle of champagne. Preferably a Moet 1991or 1992 if you have it. You have both? Make it the '91. Thank you."

A third call went to beach services, at Star-9. "This is Zack Peters in 110-B. I want to reserve a catamaran for one hour today at 2 p.m. Make it a small one. That's right, Peters in 110-B. Fine. Thanks much." He kicked off his loafers, removed his tie and shirt and stepped out on the balcony with his drink.

Chapter 13

Deep Space (In translation)

"SIR, WELCOME. We have reached the distance you requested from the star and are prepared to commence rotation of your flotilla, Sir."

"Number Two, I remind you that the star does have a name. It is called Sol by the natives, and not using their name for it is inappropriate. What is our distance?"

"Sir, Current distance is 4.5 billion adnaljan from the star, I mean Sol, Sir."

"And the current flotilla configuration?"

"We have completed moving abreast of one another other."

"Separation?"

"Sir, one adnaljan, Sir."

"Excellent work, Number Two. And the flotilla's present velocity?"

"Sir, one-twentieth light speed, Sir."

"How soon can we initiate primary deceleration?"

"Sir, immediately following roll-over maneuver, Sir."

"And the secondary deceleration?"

"Sir, as soon as we slow to one-thirtieth light speed, Sir."

"You may commence rotation on my mark."

"Sir, on your mark, Sir."

"Then roll Alpha on five… four… three… two… one… mark!"

"Sir, Alpha has initiated rotation, Sir."

"Beta on five…four…three…two…one…mark!"

"Sir, Beta has initiated rotation, Sir."

"Roll Gamma on five…four…three…two…one…mark!"

"Sir, Gamma has initiated rotation, Sir."

"You may now roll my vessel on five…four…three…two… one…mark!"

"Sir, Delta has initiated and completed rotation, Sir."

"Will we require any latitude adjustments, Number Two?"

"Sir, No. Alpha reports having attained 180 degrees and is locked. Beta reports having attained 180 degrees and is locked. Gamma reports it had exceeded 180 by five degrees and is now correcting - 184–183–182–181–180. Gamma is locked, Sir.

"Gamma's maneuver was substandard. I want you to speak to its captain in a respectful manner. Remind him that each ship is transporting the most priceless of all cargoes—one billion stasis souls. But right now we need to address the flotilla's shielding before commencing deceleration."

"Sir, All three ships are at full shields. Additionally, each of our back-up systems is on-line, Sir."

"Excellent. You may now increase ship separation from two to three adnaljan. Once the separation is confirmed, commence primary deceleration to one-thirtieth light speed."

"Sir, understood, Sir."

"From this distance the inhabitants of Sol-3 should be unable to detect multiple targets separated by less than 0.02 arc-seconds. Therefore it is essential that the flotilla remains in exact alignment between Sol-3 and our point of departure. I cannot emphasize enough the importance of the overall separation of our flotilla to never exceeding five adnaljan."

"Sir, understood Sir."

"I now return to my quarters. Advise me when we have reached one-thirtieth light speed. All is for Naia, Number Two."

"Sir, yes—All is for Naia.

TWELVE BILLION MILES closer to the Sun, three amateur astronomers had just set up their telescope equipment to observe a newly discovered comet.

"Key West just doesn't get any better than this, Bob. We're blessed with mosquitoes, sand fleas, humidity, stale donuts, warm soda and cold pizza."

"You might want to keep those perks under your hat, Chuck. If word gets out how much fun we're having, everyone will take up our hobby. Especially when they hear about sleeping on the beach after driving twenty-one hours non-stop from Detroit in a nineteen-year-old minivan. A motel break would have been nice," said Chuck. "Even a no-star-motel would be okay. Besides, the drive would only have taken us twenty hours if you-know-who hadn't gotten a ticket outside Cincinnati."

Chuck motioned with his hand. "Hand me Albert's forty-power Erfle. It's on the tray next to the short wave."

"Here you go, but be careful. After plunking down $250 for an eyepiece, he'll stroke out if it gets damaged."

"Just look at that sky, Bob. It sure beats southeastern Michigan this time of year."

"Just check out that Milky Way. I can pick out NGC1261 without binoculars. That is just too cool."

"Yeah, it is great. Say—how the heck long has Albert been gone? I may flat line from hunger if he doesn't get back soon with the hamburgers."

"*Whoa!* Did you see that?" Bob asked.

"See what?"

"The meteorite behind you. It was a really big one and bright enough to be a bolide. It started to the right of Rigel and then ran due east. I can still make out its trail."

"Rats, I missed it. I've only seen a half-dozen or so bolides. Speaking of burgers, what did you think of the kelp burgers at lunch?"

"If I hadn't known what they were, I might have liked them."

"What magnification are you using on the comet?" asked Chuck.

"Sixty, more than enough to resolve the tail into two parts. I think I can even make out a hint of a third."

"I can pick out two of them with a 45-power eyepiece but not the third. Did Albert tell you he called home? Apparently no one up there has been able to pick out the second tail, let alone a third."

"Let's throw on the photometer and get a brightness reading," Bob nodded. "And turn on the short wave so we'll have accurate times with our recordings."

"Did you hear that? It might be Albert. Let's hold off and let him do the photometric scan with the Newtonian."

A voice from the direction of the parking lot called out. "Hey out there. Anybody home? Guys—where are you guys? I can't see diddly-squat."

"Over here Albert. To your right," said Chuck. "It's darker on this side of the trees. And we're ready to pass out from starvation. Did you get everything?"

"As long as you don't mind more of these cruddy seaweed-burgers," Albert laughed. "The folks at the diner said they won't have hamburger for another week or so. Some bone heads tore up the railroad tracks north of Orlando and supplies have to be trucked in for now. On a brighter note, I brought a six-pack to wash down the kelp."

"All is forgiven," Bob said, making the sign of the cross. "Hold the burgers for two minutes until I find that comet again. Ouch!"

"What happened?" asked Chuck.

"I nearly killed an eyeball on the freaking finder scope."

"My bad," Albert winced. "I kicked one of the tripod legs. Here's a beer to ease the pain."

"Great—now the scope's moved off the comet. Where's your right ascension knob? I need to loosen it a tad to search around."

"To the left of the slow motion knob," replied Albert. "Here, I'll get it for you. There, I loosened it just a tad. Try slewing to the west and you should find it."

"Thanks," said Bob. "*Whoa*!"

"Whoa---what?" asked Chuck.

"I was swinging past a dim star and all of a sudden, *whoosh*! It flared up. Must have brightened a whole magnitude."

"Which star?" asked Albert. "Where are you looking?"

"Can't say for sure, but I still have it here in the eye piece. It's already dimmed to its former brightness."

"That sounds fishy," said Chuck. "You still south of Orion?"

"Yeah, and just a little to the west," Bob said. "It's about a magnitude four star, I'd say. If I lose it, I sure I won't be able to find it again."

"Is he in Lepus?" asked Chuck.

"No, further west than that. He's probably in Eridanus."

"Where?" asked Albert.

"The constellation close to Rigel—that's Orion's right knee as we face him. Then it winds down south and ends up at Achernar, the brightest star in Eridanus. Here, I'll show you— "

"Can somebody give me a hand here?" Bob sighed. "If one of you clowns can reach over and tighten the right ascension knob, I'll let go so the clock-drive can kick in and keep the star in the eyepiece field-of-view. Better yet, one of you fools slide in behind me and look through the finder scope to see which star is closest to the cross hairs?"

"I can do that," Albert said. "Just move your butt to the right."

"If I do that I'll end up moving the scope," Bob said. "Gah!"

"What now," asked Albert? "Don't tell me you lost it."

"A quarter-pound mosquito just tried to fly in my ear."

"Albert, you don't have to bother looking through the view finder," Chuck said. "Just tighten the right ascension knob from the other side. Hold on, guys. I'm behind both of you looking up along the outside of the telescope tube. Yup, you're in Eridanus all right."

"Holy cow!" Bob exclaimed. "That son of a gun just flared again. I'd say for at least one whole second!"

"Flared?" Albert said. "That doesn't make sense.

"Okay, the position marker is locked," said Chuck. "You won't lose it now, so you can relax your grip."

"Perfect," Bob said with a sigh of relief. "The star's holding steady in the eyepiece. Can somebody tell me where the heck I'm pointed at and what the name of that star is? And I'll take that beer now."

"I'm looking right at it, but it seems unfamiliar," Albert said. "Let me get the star chart and grab a flashlight."

Bob added, "Grab the one with the red filter. We don't want to lose our night adaptation."

"Right—now just give me a minute with the star atlas...and if I had to guess, you're on Omicron-2. Yup, Omicron-2. Well, maybe 40 Eridani or Keid. Take your pick."

"Can't you make up your mind?" Bob grumbled. "Which is it?"

"All three," shrugged Albert. "It's one of those damn stars with more than one name. Here's your beer and a stopwatch, so you can measure the time between flare-ups. According to this chart there's only one variable star in Eridani—Theta. The constellation's pretty much a loser if you're looking for interesting deep sky objects. If we've discovered a new flare star, it's sure to be big news."

Chuck tuned the short wave to station WWV, easily distinguished by the ticking that marked each passing second.

Bob asked, "Can one of you grab the other scope to measure the brightness of any more flares with the photometer?"

"Give me a second here," Albert replied. "Here it is. Okay, I'm ready. If it flares again, I'll nail it."

"OK," Chuck said. "Everybody hush up. I'm going to start recording."

Bob whispered, "The AAVSO will be excited to hear about this."

"The what?" asked Albert.

"The American Association of Variable Star Observers," Bob whispered.

"Recorder's on," Chuck announced. "I'll log the time first."

A few seconds later the ticking of the radio stopped and a voice proclaimed, "This is London. At the tone the time will be 4 hours, 41 minutes, exactly." Once the tone was heard, the ticking resumed.

Chuck took a deep breath and began. "This is Chuck Halloran, from the Astronomical Society of Michigan recording from Key West State Park, Florida. The date is---"

"Whoa!" Bob yelled. "There she blows! At least one second duration, I'd say. I've started the stop watch."

"I caught it too," Albert said. "It reads exactly magnitude 4.0."

"The date is Saturday, October 9," Chuck continued. "Local time is 11:41 p.m. Eastern Standard, and 0441 hours Universal Time. I am observing Comet 2010-D, commonly known as Comet Jones-Tremonti. With me are Al Kurtyka and Bob Barnes.

"About six minutes ago, Barnes observed a flare from 40 Eridani on a Yakashika, 8-inch, Schmidt Cassegrain telescope, using a 2010mm, f-10, 60-power Erfle eyepiece with a neutral density filter. We've been timing multiple events with two stopwatches and radio station WWV.

"40 Eri has been increasing in brightness to apparent magnitude 3.0 and holding for three seconds before dropping back to its regular magnitude. The readings are being taken with a Kreisner MCX 4000 photometer. So far there have been—how many times has 40 Eri flared Bob?"

"Three."

"We have observed three flares so far and are awaiting a possible fourth."

Kurtyka let out a yell. "Yes! It flared again. Let me check here. There was a 42.1 second interval between events."

Halloran continued the recording, "The interval between the flares has been measured only once. It was 42... what was it?"

Albert responded, "It was 42.14 seconds."

"It was 42.14 seconds. We are continuing our observations to verify the intervals. End recording."

Chuck switched off the recorder. "Gentlemen," he said proudly, "I do believe we are making history."

Chapter 14

ZACK WAS STRETCHED OUT on a poolside chaise lounge grabbing a few rays not too far from the outdoor thatched roof bar where, the night before, he had taken full advantage of a two-for-one special on banana daiquiris.

Slightly hung over, as he drifted in and out of sleep he was enjoying the normal background sounds of resort activity. An ache in his lower back forced him to lift up just enough to slide his hand beneath him to withdraw a pen. Chuckling as he remembered the tale of the "Princess and the Pea', he plopped it into his beach bag and wiggled into a comfortable position.

He savored this all-expense-paid break from his busy schedule. Listening to the waves slapping against the break wall he heard some gulls loudly debating the ownership of a large piece of dried-out toast. And the sun felt so good he didn't give a second thought to whether or not its dangerous ultra-violet rays would be thwarted by the sun screen lotion Winstanley had left him. But to be on the safe side he glanced briefly at the label through eyes that burned from perspiration and lotion. Satisfied, he dropped the tube back in the bag, rolled over to expose his back, and had just adjusted his swim suit for the sake of propriety when a voice came over the public address system.

"Dr. Z. Peters, please call the switch board."

Mumbling some vague obscenities, he lifted himself onto one elbow and fumbled for the hotel's portable phone, supplied as a courtesy to all its guests. Narrowly avoiding letting it drop onto the tile, he flipped it open.

"Peters here."

"Good afternoon, Mr. Peters. I have a collect call to Dr. Zachariah Peters from Dr. Bertram Powell in Arecibo, Puerto Rico. Will you accept the charges?"

"It's Zachary, not Zachariah. And hell no, I will not accept."

A voice from the other end interjected, "That's all right operator. I'll pay on this end."

"Go ahead Dr. Powell. Your party is on the line."

"Zack?"

"Bertie?"

Powell began singing, "*Happy birthday to us....*"

Zack laughed. "Now I know why you're so rich, Bertie. You never pay for phone calls."

"You can't blame a guy for trying old chum."

"Because our birthdays aren't until next Tuesday, I have to ask what the big occasion happens to be, especially since I haven't spoken to you since..."

"Probably since April or May, Zack. But listen up. I have something absolutely incredible to tell you."

"Let me guess; you're either married or going to be because you've gotten an eighteen year-old in the family way."

"I think she's at least nineteen, so give me a break. I've got socks older than that. Though to be perfectly honest I am sort of involved with someone younger who is both beautiful and an excellent cook. Wait a minute, I'm paying for this!"

Zack laughed; Bertie was always easy to distract.

"Let's get down to business," Powell harumphed. "What do you remember about the star 40 Eridani?"

"Okay, I'll play *Bertie's Trivia* as long as I don't have to wake up. Let's see… 40 Eridani also known as 40 Eri and 40 E; about 16 light years away. A run-of-the-mill K1 main sequence...and also called, hmmm, wait for it… Omicron-2, I think it is."

"Very good. So I can assume you haven't heard the news."

"What news?"

"Don't you ever watch TV?"

"Bertie, I'm trying to relax. I haven't picked up a newspaper in two days. Right now I'm lying by the pool trying to recover from last night's failed attempt to drink the hotel's supply of rum. So what's going on?"

"Get ready to have your socks blown off, Laddie. Last night, 40 Eri began to pulse."

"Pulse? No way."

"Way. I said the same thing at first. It began brightening every 42 or so seconds by a factor of three magnitudes. I grant you the media doesn't consider this to be ground breaking news, so they're only mentioning it as filler piece."

Zack sat up, grabbed a towel and wiped his face. "That just shouldn't be. Main sequence stars never pulse. Not unless someone's gone and rewritten stellar evolution."

"I agree with all of that. Don't forget I taught you that at Michigan. Besides, a 42 second pulse rate for 40 Eri is too slow for a standard variable and way too slow for a pulsar."

Zack stood up and scratched his head. "Incredible. Have there been any confirmations?"

"I'm sure you remember Carlos Flusher at Cerro Pachon in Chile. Well he's the only one, from what I can gather. But now that the AAVSO has made an official announcement, everyone will be checking it out."

"Then so far only one optical scope saw it," Zack said. "And there you are sitting on the world's largest radio dish, wishing you had a half-decent optical telescope instead."

"Au contraire. That's the other item I've been anxious to tell you about. I've put together a gadget that will let a radio telescope operate in a quasi-optical mode. As soon as I get the last minute bugs worked out, it will be 90% as efficient a single optical mirror."

"Bertie, if it does what you say it will do, and I don't doubt your word—well, not on something like this, at any rate—you'll be in the history books right alongside of Galileo and Newton. Now, how soon will 40 Eri be high enough off your eastern horizon to get a shot at it?"

"Thirty minutes, more or less. Did I mention that I spoke with Floyd Hutchins in Tidbibbila?"

"No you didn't. That lucky guy has the darkest and the clearest skies in Australia.."

"Yes, and he claims he verified the flashes about 0700 hours local time."

"So old Flush will get credit for the discovery?" asked Zack.

"Negatory, old buddy. It will go to some Michigan amateurs who were visiting the Florida Keys to observe Comet 2013-D. They were the first to file with the AAVSO. And from what I gather, they noticed the pulses entirely by accident."

"The same way Hale and Bopp discovered their comet," Zack said. "It still doesn't make sense, Bertie. What did you say about the length of the pulses and the spacing?"

"Don't quote me, but Hutch claims they came in sets of three bursts spaced evenly for two seconds."

"What was the interval of the pulses?"

"I don't have that in front of me but I think it was on the order of 10 minutes."

"Holy cats!"

"My sentiments exactly. Now let's get down to business. What are the chances of my getting you to fly down here and help me sort through this interesting mess?"

"Is the Pope Catholic?"

"Last time I checked."

"Then count me in. No, wait, I have the hottest of all possible dates in the Western Hemisphere set up for this afternoon."

"Bring her along. As well as her sister for me."

"I'm positive she can't come. She flies for Aeroflot and her schedule won't allow it. So I must reluctantly pass on your invite for at least another day or so."

"My boy, I'm holding two twenty's that say you'll change your mind as soon as I ask you one little question."

"You say $40? You're on. Fire away."

"What if I said I need some input on your specialty at Michigan?"

"It wasn't in variable stars."

"Whoa! Stop right there," Powell jumped in. "You can't answer me directly over the phone. Not unless you can secure the call on your end?"

"No can do. I'm poolside. So what's all the secrecy about?"

"Let me run this by you one more time, and see how quick you are on the uptake. Exactly when was the last time you can remember hearing about main sequence K class stars pulsing?"

"Like I said before, Ks don't pulse."

"So, now can you see why we can't say any more about this until we're on a secured phone line?"

"Bertie, I have no idea what you're driving at. Are you being serious with all this cloak and dagger falderal?"

"Let me emphasize this by saying I am dead serious."

Zack took a deep breath. "Okay, let me try it another way. What does the Hubble team have to say about 40 Eri?"

"I haven't the foggiest. I've urged the President to put a tight lid on this and keep Hubble away from 40 Eri until I can use my 1,000 foot's resolution. Oops. Can you hold a minute? I've got another call coming in."

Zack seemed a bit anxious as he asked, "Wait! Are you saying you've spoken to the White House? What do you need the resolving power of the Big Ear to verify? Christ, Bertie—what the hell is going on?"

"Hold on, Zack. I'm trying to juggle two lines here."

Powell began speaking, "This is Bertram Powell at Arecibo. I have an extremely serious situation going on. It is imperative that I speak to the President's personal aide as soon as possible. Please ask her to return the call on a secured line. Thank you."

"I'm back, Zack. Sorry to be rude. Where was I? Oh, yes. Captain Golightly is going to call any minute so hopefully I will get to speak to the President."

"Priss Golightly? Why the heck are you dragging the White house in on this? What's with all the secrecy? Come on guy, give me a hint."

"Okay, but listen carefully. If I even hear you catch your breath after figuring out what I'm driving at, I'll hang up. Do you understand? Alright then, here we go. How well do you remember your last term at the University of Michigan?"

"Well, it was about the time I discovered women with large breasts were more fun than hitting all the saloons."

"Do you remember some of the papers your roommate turned in?"

"Scooter Gotfredsen? Yes, and well I should. I wrote most of them"

"You think I didn't know that? But do you remember the one he turned in for his pre-doctoral thesis?"

"Sure—'Methods of Terra-forming Exoplanets.'"

"Damn it, Zack—you're not paying attention. This is serious. Keep your answers to a simple yes or no. Now, forget about Scooter's final thesis. I'm talking about his proposal thesis— the one I turned down because you'd already asked me to reserve that topic for you."

"Oh– my–God. You don't possibly mean—"

"Zack!"

"OK. But you have got to be kidding, Bertie. You couldn't possibly mean—no way."

"Zack—careful. Not on the phone."

"Alright, I won't spell it out; but just tell me if you are referring to the paper on Techniques?"

"Bingo!"

Zack paused, and took in a deep breath. "Holy crap, Bertie. If you mean what I think you mean, I think I owe you $40."

"I mean exactly what you're thinking. And do you see why we need to keep a lid on things until we know exactly what's going on?"

"Bertie, I never believed you and I might someday have this conversation."

"So Laddie, would you now consider a visit to Arecibo?"

"Christ! Of course I will."

"Just a moment...I'm expecting a call. Zack, let me put you on hold."

As he waited for Powell to come back on line, Zack could feel his heart thundering in his chest, as hundreds of questions flooded his mind.

"Zack? Sorry for the interruption. I have Priss about to come in on the other line. Remember to play dumb if she gives you a call later on today."

"Dumb is easy Bertie. Numb, I'm not too sure of."

"I'm glad you're getting your sense of humor back. You'll need all of it you can muster in the event a worst case scenario pans out."

"You mean *adios* Homo sapiens?"

"That is definitely in the realm of possibilities. Just remember that you and I did not have this conversation."

After Powell disconnected, Zack still held the phone to his ear. "Yeah, so long Bertie," he said softly,

He dialed the front desk. "This is Zack Peters in 110-B. I'm at pool side using a hotel portable. Is there a way you can patch it into the secured line in my room so I can use it on a call from out here?"

"I'm sorry, Dr. Peters. Our scramblers only work in guest rooms. They have to be attached between the wall receptacle and the phone."

"Thanks, anyway. Oh, are you holding messages for me?"

"I'm afraid not, sir."

"Thanks again."

By now the Sun had shifted enough to have him move his chaise further under the umbrella. As he settled down, a pool steward approached.

"*Que pasa,* Doc?"

"Hi Antonio, are you just starting your shift?"

"Yeah, about ten minutes ago. I'll be here at poolside until seven. Then I move into the main dining room. What time did you call it quits last night?"

"Actually I closed the pool bar."

"Ouch. Would you like me to bring you a Cuba Libre?"

"That sounds good—if you can find any rum at the bar. I think I cleaned them out. No, on second thought make it soda water, ice and lime. A tall one."

"You got it, one aqua pura grande with gas and lime. Here's a newspaper."

"Thanks Antonio."

Zack snapped it open and glanced at the front page. He shook his head and turned the page; page two was just as bad. It was painfully obvious that the world was going to starting to unravel. When the pool steward returned with his drink he gave him the newspaper.

"You can take this paper back. I don't want to read any more about this planet's problems. It's too darn depressing. Instead, I'm going to crash here for a while. Would you do me a favor and wake me at four?"

"Four o'clock. You got it."

It seemed he'd barely closed his eyes when Antonio said, "Dr. Peters, it's four."

"Huh? Oh yes. Thanks. I want to make a call to Aeroflot airlines."

As he started to reach for the phone, Antonio gave out a low, slow whistle. "Doc, would you take one look at that."

"At what?"

"Over there, the drop-dead beauty coming down the steps. I've see lots of fine ladies in magazines and on TV but I never thought they could look that good in real life."

Zack adjusted his sunglasses and squinted. An attractive woman in a flight crew uniform had entered the pool area. With unkempt hair and wearing little or no makeup, she was catching the attention of just about everyone.

Her white uniform shirt was pulled out of black trousers and hung loosely. It was debatable if she'd closed enough buttons to make her street legal, and her sensuous stride was enough to make a man melt. She pulled a rolling suitcase, and a flight bag and jacket were draped over a shoulder.

"Good god, she's coming this way," Antonio said.

"Watch the old master at work," Zack whispered. "I'll wager that after one glimpse at me she'll stop dead in her tracks."

"No offense Doc, but we're talking heavy-duty packaging. She might stop if you were a VIP but not for plain old me and you. No offense. Trust me, she'll walk on by."

"Five bucks says she stops."

"You're covered as long as she does it on her own without your coaxing."

Zack scrunched back down on the chaise and closed his eyes. When she reached the two men, she gave Antonio a warm smile and let her purse drop to the ground. After throwing her jacket and flight bag on the table, she plopped down unceremoniously into a chair and pushed her sunglasses up on her forehead.

Antonio was speechless. He watched in disbelief as Li-Hwa picked up a magazine to fan herself. She puffed a wayward lock of hair from her eyes and said, "Well sailors, who's buying?"

Zack opened his eyes and said calmly, "Antonio, why don't you ask what the lady would like."

Antonio stammered, "Yes, right away. I'll… I'll get it right away."

As he turned to walk away Li-Hwa called to him. "Antonio? Would you like to take my order first?"

He flushed and said. "Yes 'Ma'am. What'll it be?"

"A stiff Bloody Mary. Hold the celery."

He turned to Zack and asked, "And you, Miss?"

Zack shook his head. "Make mine the same."

Li added, "You'd best bring me two of them while you're at it."

Antonio gathered his composure, bowed slightly, took two steps backwards, and nearly stepped into the pool. As he headed for the bar she said, "I guess I haven't lost my touch. So are you or are you not going to tell me how much you've missed me?"

"Very much, But I'm totally confused. The woman at the symphony was cool, aloof, detached and unapproachable. The woman I see now is just the opposite."

"I thought you understood that we women are known for our mystery. At the symphony I wanted to pique your curiosity; and I succeeded. What you see here is as close as you can get to the real me. Well, at least out in public."

"I'm not sure I understand the 'real me' part."

She leaned forward and whispered in his ear, "It's all part of the mystery." Straightening up she said, "Now, wouldn't you like to hear about my flight?"

"I notice you got in early."

"Thanks to a fantastic tail wind, otherwise the trip was boring. Now then, would you like to hear the plans I have for us?"

"I'm all ears."

"After consuming some adult beverages, I was hoping we could take time for some adult interaction."

"Now there's a plan I can go along with."

"Thank you kind sir, but unfortunately there is a caveat to this plan." She fidgeted with the hem of her dress and smoothed her hair before saying, "In other words, bad news."

"Let me guess. You're leaving Aeroflot to spend the rest of your days with me in Bermuda teaching tarot cards and investigating UFOs."

She smiled. "Don't I wish? The truth of the matter is I have to fly out early tomorrow morning."

He placed his hands behind his head and frowned. "The story of my life."

"Mine too." She moved over and got on the chaise with him. Wrapping his arm under her neck, she nestled in close and whispered, "But I will do my very best tonight to make up for our disappointment."

"That sounds promising. Can you tell me in advance how you plan to accomplish that?"

She giggled, "I'm going to allow you to start calling me Li."

"Be still my beating heart."

"The truth of the matter is that my father is seriously ill. It's his heart and I have to get home right away."

"To Beijing?"

"No, Macao. That's where he'll get a transplant Saturday."

"I'm sorry," he said as he began to stroke her hair.

"I have it pretty much planned out. I'll fly out on our JFK Tokyo run and then fly non-revenue from Tokyo to Hong Kong. From there I'll hovercraft over to Macao."

"Try not to worry. Transplants aren't considered a serious operation these days. Is he receiving a donor or a clone?"

"He'll use one of his own clones. He seeded three of them a few years back when he found out about his heart condition. One of them has matured enough for the procedure."

"That was wise of him. I know a few folks who are growing spare organs but the idea isn't catching on very well in the States. It's like younger generations feel immortal."

Zack reveled in the sensation of holding the girl of his dreams in his arms. "Getting back to what you said in DCA about my loving your cooking," he said at last, "do you want to grab something to eat now or start out on one of the tours you suggested?"

"If it's alright with you, I'd rather we go to my uncle's home and grab something out of the freezer. It's only a hop, skip and a jump away on the northeast tip of the island.

"That sounds like a plan."

"I'm anxious for you to see it. But I'm thinking—at the risk of sounding brazen—by the time we get there, open the place up and thaw something, we could just as easily stay here and snuggle in your room."

"Snuggle? Brazen? Do people still use those terms?"

"I still do," she said standing and putting her hair in a bun. "But I'm just an old fashioned girl." She stuck some bobby pins between her teeth and began twisting the longest strands. "Besides, I'm feeling a little naughty. No, scratch that. Make it horny. Guess what I've had on my mind on the flight here."

"A juicy steak and excellent wine, I'd imagine."

She kicked his chaise. "Steak? Am I the only person around here with romance in mind?"

"Well," he smiled, "then I'll torture you with a delicious steak...after I've had my way with you."

"You're on Peters, and I mean that in the literal sense. And then we can tour a bit and go dinner. You're going to fall in love with Bermuda."

By now Li-Hwa had finished with her hair. After stuffing her stockings in a pocket she began hopping from one foot to the other to get her shoes on.

She tossed Zack's shirt at him, grabbed her coat and purse and started to sprint away. "Last one to the elevator buys dinner! And don't forget to bring my travel bag!"

IT WAS HALF-PAST SEVEN by the time they had finished dining in the Somerset Bridge dining room.

"I'm filled right up to here with key lime pie, fortifications and historical markers," he said, pushing his plate forward. "What's more, I've peered down enough cannon barrels and walked enough ramparts to last me a life time."

"I take it you want to skip the other forts. What a wimp. Fort Hamilton has a son-et-lumiere show that is little short of spectacular. That means 'sound and light' to the great unwashed."

"Sorry Li, but I've had it with tours, greens, and fairways. Golf courses must cover one-third of Bermuda."

"It has more courses per square mile than any other place in the world."

"Well, beautiful lady, you've certainly impressed me today."

"You mean my—*ahem*—cooking?"

"Well, that too. Even with everything is closed for Historical Day; I applaud you for being undaunted. A few phone calls and voila, everywhere we went there were cheery faces to open up their place for you. You certainly are a well-connected lady."

"Well, my family is. I spent lots of time here growing up, and still manage to make it back on vacation at least once a year. So, my dear, while we finish our coffee I'll give a pop quiz."

"Be still my beating heart."

"Now then students, I want you to take out a pencil and a blank sheet of paper. Kindly place any books under your chairs."

"That phrase still gives me the chills. Is there a penalty if I choose not to play school with you?"

"Bad sports sleep alone. Come on Zack, we're talking about one of the most beautiful spots on Earth—a pastel paradise is the way they refer to it in travel brochures."

"You sound like a tour guide."

"I was, after graduating. But only part time. Maybe six months total."

"Okay, fire away."

"Good sport. What cargo was the English ship carrying and where was it bound for at the time of its sinking?"

"That's two questions."

"Makes the test go faster."

"All right....the cargo was supplies for the colonists. It was heading for the New Jamestown settlement."

"Excellent. I told you this would be fun. What was the name of the ship and what year was it wrecked?"

"The *Sea Vanguard* in 1709."

"Close enough for government work. It was the *Sea Venture* in 1609. And where did the castaways swim ashore at?"

"Where the Confederate Museum or the Hamilton Princess is currently located? Shoot, I don't remember. I'll go with St. Caroline's Beach."

The waiter approached to set the check on the table. "It was St. Catherine's Beach," he smiled. "Will there be anything else, Miss Zaranova? Coffee?"

"Not for me, Louis. How about you Zack?"

He put a hand over his cup and shook his head. "Are we done with my test yet?"

AN HOUR LATER Li-Hwa walked over to their suite's door wall that lead out to the balcony. She stretched her arms up towards a First Quarter Moon and said, "Have you ever seen anything as gorgeous as that?"

Zack scrunched a pillow behind his head. "Yes, the silhouette of you standing in the moonlight is as delicious as it gets. I'd dearly love a picture of this"

"And lose my reputation of modesty and prudishness?" she answered still facing the Moon. "Not on your life."

Li turned to face him, slowly drawing the sheer curtain across herself. Smiling, she hurried across the room and dove on the bed next to him.

"Delicious, the man says?" She swatted him with a pillow. "Don't you ever think of anything but food?"

She bit his ear. "If you don't feel you're up for Round Three, we could always go out for Key Lime pie and coffee."

"That sounds like a way to recharge the batteries and pull off Three and Four."

"I won't be holding my breath for Four," she laughed. "Now that I've got you where I want you Mister Science Advisor to the President, perhaps you'd be good enough to help me with a rumor our Captain has been passing around."

"What kind of rumor?"

"It has to do with the International Space Station," she said.

Zack wondered what their evening romp could possibly have to do with the ISS.

"The Captain is saying the U.S. has a secret agenda to use it as a weapon." After a few seconds she asked, "So, what do you think?"

"I'm not the one to ask. Besides, if it was true I couldn't say anything about it."

Li-Hwa pulled back a bit and sighed, "You're right. Well, so much for passing my mid-term in the Espionage 101. But I was hoping you could shed some light on it. It's only a matter of time before the other ladies in my flight crew start asking me what my boyfriend does for a living."

Zack kissed her forehead and walked to the bathroom.

"It's only woman talk you know," she raised her voice a bit, calling after him. "Curiosity about my mysterious Mr. Wonderful."

The phone rang. Zack picked up the extension in the bathroom. "Hi Priss," he said. "Well...yes, now that you mention it, I was pleasantly surprised about going an entire day without getting a call from you. Hold on a minute."

He put his hand over the mouthpiece and called out to Li-Hwa, "Do you mind? This won't take long."

"I'll wait on the balcony. Just don't turn the lights on."

He adjusted the scrambler. "Sorry, Priss, but I have company. We're secure now."

"Two items, Zack. The President says that you're to drop everything and fly to San Juan tomorrow morning. The way I understand it, your buddy Bernard Powell at Arecibo NRAO insists that you get there as soon as you can."

"As I recall the President sent me here to bring back copies of Winstanly's documents and enjoy a day off—the operative words being 'day off.'"

"I know Zack, but Winstanly made it here safe and sound with the originals so you're to destroy your copies. As for the rest, Dr. Powell will have you met at the airport and driven out to his facility. I just have to give him your flight arrangements."

"And the other matter?"

"It's the Russians again—or should I say still. There's been a big increase of activity on their secured channels over the last few days."

"Priss, answer me something. Why is it that every time I get away to have some fun, some crisis pops up? I'm not complaining, but this isn't a spy movie and I'm not James Bond. I often wish my salary was commensurate to my air miles and phone calls, rather than for my wit and charm."

"Perhaps the Boss is afraid you'd retire if you become financially independent. But Winstanly is concerned that you-know-who may be getting close to what we're up to. Since your end is secure, I'll patch a recorded message from the President."

"Shoot."

"Here it comes. I'll wait on the line for your answer."

Another voice said, "Hello Zack. It's fair to assume you've agreed to go to Arecibo or you wouldn't be listening to this. Let me thank you in advance. You might want to be sitting down for the following. In a nutshell, Bertram Powell just called me from Arecibo with just about as big a shocker as you and I could imagine.

"He's extremely concerned about the press picking up on an anomalous light source coming from a star in the constellation Eridanus. He thinks that it may not be a natural phenomenon.

"The event, or whatever we decide to call it, was detected last night by amateur astronomers in the Florida Keys. From what I understand, they made an official report to the American Association of Variable Star Observers.

"As is their practice, the AAVSO probably has passed it on to the world's astronomical community as a natural phenomenon. But if Dr. Powell is right, and if that light source turns out to be artificial, we may very well be looking at our first contact with an alien life form.

"Let me be perfectly clear on one point, Zack. You are not under any circumstances to discuss this over the phone with Powell—or anyone else, for that matter. Wait until you arrive and can speak to him personally. Pricilla will send him your flight arrival information and see that you are picked up at the airport. To tell the truth, this whole thing really has my head spinning. As of now only you, Powell, Pricilla, and I know about the situation. As soon as he fills you in and the two of you come up with something, anything, call me. Now—go get 'em tiger."

"Zack, did you get all of that?"

"Loud and clear. Do you have my flight info yet?"

"Yes, it's Atlantic's 103 departing Bermuda at 0930 tomorrow with breakfast. You can pick up your ticket at the Atlantic will-call desk. By the way lover-butt, I want you to know that I get full credit for your being able to stay there tonight—just in case lightning strikes and you actually get lucky."

"Thanks, Priss," Zack sighed. "Keep working on my getting a raise. It's good to hear from you."

"It's good to be heard," she replied.

Chapter 15

COLONEL MIKHAIL KORNIKOV ARRIVED at the top floor of the recently renovated Central Intelligence Service Headquarters, First Directorate, located just outside the Kremlin wall. As he stepped out of the elevator, he smiled at two female Army officers who were about to get on. They gave each other a nod of approval and secretly blew him a kiss, not only because he was handsome: he was also the youngest officer ever appointed commandant of Moscow's CIS, formerly the KGB.

When he entered his suite's outer office, his aide Captain Vasili Rubinsky rose and followed Kornikov into his private office.

"Good morning, Vasili."

"Good morning, Colonel. Your cup is back from the silversmith. Would you care for some tea?"

"Yes, tea might take the bite out of the chill outside." He handed Rubinsky his hat and let him remove the topcoat draped over his shoulders. Settling into a wing-back leather chair, he smiled.

"So what did the repairs cost me this time?"

"I'm happy to report not a single kopek," replied the aide. "Truth be known, the silversmith was apologetic at having to make yet another repair on the handle." He slipped a glass of tea inside an ornate silver sleeve and placed it in front of Kornikov.

"He sent this note and wanted me to mention that he was aware the cup once belonged to your father-in-law, Colonel Federov. He also acknowledged working on the handle more than once."

"It seems there were always repairs being made on this antique. Please, go on with your report." He took a sip as Rubinsky reached across the desk to open files and spread out papers.

"I do appreciate having my cup back," Kornikov smiled, reaching for the briefing papers piled neatly on his desk. He put the unopened note on a corner of his desk and took another sip to his tea. "I'll wager you didn't know this cup is older than you, Vasili. Come to think of it, it could be well older than me."

"I hope you will forgive my calling you at your dacha last night," the captain began. "I was uneasy bothering you, but thought these bombings would be of concern."

"No apology necessary, Vasili. I appreciate your input on matters like these. So fill me in."

"Before I begin—I—I should mention the picture quality on the view-phone is rather inferior."

Kornikov took off his uniform jacket and draped it over the back of his chair. The reports were set out next to some framed pictures. One showed the Colonel standing next to a single-engine fighter. Another was of him with a group of men. The caption read, SOVIET ARMY SERGEANT'S CHORUS - 1977.

On a wall shelf behind the desk was a balalaika propped up between two trophies and more framed photos---one of a younger Kornikov at parachute school, the of him and his old wrestling team.

"There were two explosions that occurred within minutes of each other," Rubinsky began. "One was just inside the Kremlin, and the other was outside this building."

"I saw no sign of damage when I arrived," Kornikov said.

"There wasn't much to speak of. The explosive device had been placed inside the trunk of a taxi. The driver stopped in front of our building and opened the bonnet so it would appear he had engine trouble. He walked away before the detonation. No one was hurt."

"That's good, as is this tea, Vasili. Now tell me about the Kremlin explosion."

"According to the report, a device was placed inside one of the Cathedral Square's rubbish containers by a short, Catholic nun. That blast was the more powerful of the two."

"Left behind by a short nun, you say? Vasili, you do know how to weave an intriguing story. Were there any injuries this time?"

"Fortunately, again there were none."

"And what happened to the short nun?"

"It says she sped away on a large motorcycle."

"So now we have a short nun on a large motorcycle." He shook his head while laughing to himself. "Have any organizations claimed responsibility?"

"None so far, but I expect we'll have a number vying for credit once the story gets into the newspapers."

Kornikov began arranging his files. "This last one appears to be a personnel folder."

"Yes Sir. It belongs to one of our civilian employees who died Saturday night in an accident in Bonn. The details are rather vague."

"Do we know what she was doing there?"

"Apparently, she was on holiday."

"Well, that was unfortunate. Which of our departments was she assigned to?"

"She was in Maintenance, temporarily. Officially, she was employed by the Ministry and on loan to us."

Kornikov drained his glass and motioned for a refill. "You say we had taken her on as a temporary?"

Rubinsky took the glass to a silver teapot on a hot-plate that sat an ornate table by the window.

"She came to us about two weeks ago when several of our people were out sick or on holiday. When her shift here ended Friday, she automatically was back on Ministry's payroll." Returning with the filled cup he handed it back to the Colonel.

"At least that takes the incident out of our hands. Make sure her file gets sent back along with my condolences and any new information that comes in."

"I took the liberty of asking the Bonn authorities to send us a copy when they send their report to the Ministry. But that won't be until they interview the director of the observatory."

"Their hundred-meter radio telescope?"

"From what I could make out, the preliminary report said she was on tour when a terrorist arrived."

"A terrorist, you say? Vasili you have no idea how I look forward to your Monday morning reports. Today I learn about a short nun on a large motorcycle, as well as a poor cleaning lady who died at the hands of a terrorist."

The Colonel slouched back in his chair and lifted his boots up onto the desk. One boot caught the edge of a personnel file and knocked it onto the floor. He reached over and picked it up. "Here, Vasili, don't forget this one."

A photograph had slipped partially out of the folder, just enough to reveal part of a woman's face. Kornikov slid it back into the file.

"That just about wraps it up, Sir. Well, except for something I find rather odd." The young captain looked uncomfortable, but took a deep breath and pressed on.

"According to the authorities, two people were struggling on the observatory's upper balcony. Apparently one was our replacement, the other was the terrorist. From what I read, the two of them went over the railing and fell to the ground ending up in a flash of light. And Sir—only the terrorist's body was recovered."

He reached out to take the file and found Kornikov holding it in a death grip.

"Colonel?"

Kornikov snatched the file back, threw open the cover, and began flipping through it until he came to a page that covered the photograph. Stopping for a moment, he took a deep breath and eased the page to the side.

"Oh my God!" He closed his eyes and took a deep breath. When he looked again he saw that a photo containing the pleasant face of an elderly woman.

"Colonel, you look like you've seen a ghost."

"Vasili—get my wife on the phone. Immediately."

"Colonel....?"

"Immediately!"

As his young aide left to place the call, Kornikov sank back into his chair.

He knew that Tatyana would never belief it. In fact, he couldn't believe it himself.

It could not be, he told himself.

It could never be...but there it was.

The woman in the picture was Maria.

Chapter 16

ON A SCALE OF ONE-TO-TEN, with one being bad and ten good, Zack would have awarded his flight from Bermuda a six. If the award was based solely on air turbulence he might have given it a three. But taking into account the amusement factor of passengers trying desperately to keep their trays from sliding off the drop down tables, it earned a six.

He was dabbing at a coffee stain as the FASTEN SEAT BELT sign lit up. The Captain dutifully announced their estimated arrival time into San Juan and gave an update on the approaching hurricane.

Thanks in part to intervention by the deities, the rest of the flight and subsequent landing at San Juan International went remarkably well. Inside the terminal he saw a dozen or so greeters holding signs bearing names of the person they were meeting.

One particular sign stood out: it was being held upside down. The fact that the bearer was a perky, attractive blonde, bouncing with commendable enthusiasm, made it even better. Working his way through the greeters, he approached her and asked, "By and chance, are you looking for Zack Peters?"

She lowered her sign and put out a hand to greet him. "Yes I am," she panted, slightly out of breath from all that bouncing. "Welcome to San Juan, Dr. Peters. I'm Virginie LaPlage and I'm meeting you on behalf of Dr. Bertram Powell. You can call me Sandy if you like. Just about everyone does."

"And you can call me Zack," he said as he pointed at the sign and giving his index finger a half-turn.

"So, Zack, what do you think of my sign? I hold them that way so I'll stand out among my taller competitors. And please...spare me the blonde jokes."

"The thought never crossed my mind," Zack smiled. "Of course there is one about a blonde who won a gold medal at the Olympics. She was so proud she had it bronzed."

"I have to admit I like that one," she laughed. "You were quite fortunate. Yours will probably be the last flight for a while, due to Hurricane Donald. Did you check through any luggage?"

"Just one piece. In the event it went astray, I threw a pair of socks, a shirt and underwear in this," he said tapping his brief-case. "I hope there no danger of Donald damaging Dr. Powell's telescope."

"The Big Ear, as we like to call it, should survive. The big money around here is on high winds and rain but no real damage. But it could be at risk if the winds are strong enough to move inland from Arecibo. If you follow me, we'll get your bag and hurry out to the parking lot."

Happily, customs was a non-issue. The customs inspector obviously knew Sandy, and gave her a big smile and waved the two of them through. His first step outside was like entering a blast furnace. As they walked to her car he prayed it had air conditioning. He wondered what she was driving. With all of her pep and vitality it could end up being a motorcycle with a sidecar. He was relieved when they approached a garish red sports car.

She moved her hand over the driver's seat and said, "This little darling's a 1980 Triumph Spitfire Mark Four, from the last year it was produced. The passenger roll bar is my only concession to keeping it stock. I added it to the shotgun seat to show that while I may not be the world's safest driver, I like my passengers to stay in one piece."

"Very thoughtful," he nodded.

"I never seem to have enough cash at the end of the month to have it chromed like the driver's bar. So I refer to its aftermarket color as yucky bronze. Do you enjoy fast cars?"

He started to answer, "Well I usually…"

She broke in with, "Me too. I love the wind in my hair. When it's blowing from behind, I can pull 0 to 60 in 14.5 seconds. Admittedly it's not a neck snapper." She stopped talking just long enough to sneeze.

"God bless you. And this is a very nice set of...wheels," he said, cramming his suitcase into the miniscule trunk.

Plopping himself into the passenger seat, he began hunting for a place to put the briefcase. He settled for the floor under his feet.

"I see you're a bit cramped," she said while patting the dashboard with affection. "Sorry about that. But what she lacks in room, she sure makes up in sheer pleasure. I think of her more as a lover than just transportation. The upkeep is expensive, the body is full of dents, and under the new paint there's a ton of plastic fill."

Zack laughed as she gunned the engine and backed out of her parking spot, trusting to God that there was nobody behind her. After she drove through the exit gate and began speeding up, he glanced at his side mirror and saw that a police car was pacing them.

"Not to worry. That's just Julio. He'll leave us alone once we clear the airport property."

"Apparently you have connections with the police."

"Only because I'm here a lot greeting Dr. Powell's guests. Besides, Julio's not a real cop. He works for airport security because he likes the uniform. In his mind it's a status symbol. He thinks it makes him a chick magnet. So he and I play this little game." She sneezed again.

"God bless you," he said, noting that his companion was quite a talker.

"Thanks. As I was saying, Julio likes to pull alongside and shake his finger to scold me. I blow him a kiss and slow down a bit. Then he rolls his eyes and leaves me alone."

Once they were off airport property, she pulled off on the shoulder and turned off the engine.

"I'll drop the top and give you some head room. You might want to take your jacket and tie off because it's about ninety minutes to the town of Arecibo, then another fifteen or so south to the facility."

She stowed the rag top in the boot and took off her jacket and wrap-around skirt, revealing white shorts and a yellow tank top. Donning a pair of white sandals and a white baseball cap with the bill turned backwards, she pushed a stray lock of hair up under it.

"Ready, Dr. Peters?"

"It's still Zack," he replied as she put on her oversized sunglasses and red leather gloves. "And ready for what, exactly?"

She restarted the engine and revved it twice, tapping the tachometer gauge until the needle stopped floating, giving him an inkling of what the next ninety minutes held in store. Glancing over her shoulder, she dropped the car into first gear.

"Hold on!" she shouted.

Zack pulled his seatbelt as tight as it would go, placed his palms on the dashboard, and pushed himself back into the seat.

"Helm, take us to one-quarter light speed," Sandy said, with the calm deliberation of a seasoned starship captain

"Aye, Kepteen," she replied, in a practiced Russian accent. "Von qvarter-light speed ee-tiss."

Great, he thought. My fate lies in the hands of a blonde, female Trekkie.

The clutch popped, the gravel sprayed, and the roadster jumped onto the highway like a terrified rabbit. Zack's anxiety fell a bit as he noticed her skill at double-clutching at precisely the ideal millisecond. The woman is designed for mischief, he thought.

Raising her voice to be heard over the wind, Sandy started a running commentary on their surroundings, reminding him of Li-Hwa describing Bermuda.

"*Déjà vu*---all over again," he murmured.

"The seaside resort of Arecibo lies on the north coast about two hours west of San Juan," she remarked, as the car landed after a small rise in the pavement. "A common misconception is that Arecibo is the location of the world's largest radio telescope. In truth the thousand-foot-wide behemoth is nestled in a natural hollow in the hills nine miles south of the town."

For the next hour or so Zack received a detailed history of the island as well as a topic he was already familiar with—the world's largest, non-steerable radio telescope.

"The telescope dish," she continued, intermittently sounding a tad more like a tour guide than the typical race-car driver, "consists of 38,400 perforated aluminum panels....along the outer walkway....The actual receiver is supported....cables strung from three cement towers placed around the rim...during thunderstorms...then, the receiver takes radio waves that have been reflected up from the giant dish. Not only that, but...."

The whipping wind and roaring engine made Sandy's voice largely indecipherable. He offered the occasional "uh huh" or "That's interesting," trying to portray a rapt attention to the woman who was holding his life in her dare-devil hands while trying his best to relax with his eyes tightly shut. By the end, he'd quite forgotten her last name, but thought he recalled it sounding vaguely French. Once they'd moved off the main highway and started winding their way down a rougher road through a rain forest, he found himself able to pay more attention.

"Some of the tour drivers recount tales from local farmers who claim their cattle have been mutilated with the precision of a surgeon," she ventured, slowing to keep the stress on the car's suspension just under the pelvis-shattering threshold. "I figure it spices up the duller parts of the tours and perhaps increase their gratuities."

"Do they ever report seeing little green men?"

"You mean LGMs? Not really, but I do remember driving by a farm whose scarecrow had been dressed up to look like one of those gray aliens tabloids like to show. By the way, Bertie tells me you two were close buds in Ann Arbor while you were a student and later lecturing at the University. I'd very much like to hear some of your madcap stories."

AS THEY APPROACHED the administration building, Zack spotted Bertram Powell, a Renaissance man of diverse lineage, on the porch waiting to greet them. Though nearing seventy, Powell sprang down the steps toward the car, as agile and lively as a man half his age. Like most good friends, the two men launched into conversation as if they had only been apart a week or so.

"Looks like Sandy got you here in one piece, more or less," Powell laughed.

"I'll tell you one thing Bertie," Zack winked. "In the future I doubt I'll have to worry about passing any depth perception tests."

Carefully unfolding himself from the car, Zack arched his back and embraced Powell with a back slapping hug.

"The flight was bumpy and breakfast was a disaster. More food ended up on laps than in anybody's mouth. If you're as hungry as I am, I'll pop for lunch."

"Thanks, but we're having lunch delivered," Powell grinned. "Come on in and unwind."

As the three of them ambled through the halls of the administration building. Zack marveled at the stunning photos of deep space objects matted and framed on the walls. Finally, they came to a door with a modest sign on the wall beside the carved wooden door:

DIRECTOR OF OPERATIONS

B. G. POWELL PH.D. PHYSICS.

Closing the door behind them, Bernie pointed to the plush-looking chairs set around what looked to be a pressed board coffee table.

"Take a load off and fill me in on the gossip while I build us some drinks."

Zack grimaced as he sat down. His chair looked a lot more comfortable than it felt.

"You okay?" asked Sandy.

"I'm fine. My achy back is acting up."

"I hope the ride didn't cause that," she frowned.

"Don't worry, my dear," Powell said, returning with the drinks. "As the saying goes, they never get all the shrapnel out."

"Were you in one of the Middle East wars, Zack?" she gushed.

"I had the good fortune to skip those pleasantries."

"I'll tell you what the problem is," Bertie said. "It's either sitting in your sardine can or a left over souvenir from Windsor."

"The later," Zack groaned.

"As in Windsor Castle England?" asked Sandy.

"No, my dear. Windsor, Ontario," Powell said. "But that's another story."

Before Powell could explain, the doorbell buzzed.

"It's probably lunch," Sandy said. "I'll get it. And if anyone asks, you charged it with the gratuity included."

As soon as she left the room, Zack turned to his old professor. "All right, three quick questions," he said intensely. "What the hell's going on with 40 E. What's the real story on the gadget you built for the telescope? And what's the scoop on Sandy?"

"As to 40 E, there isn't much I can say until more data becomes available. And I'll tell about my invention and all about Sandy."

Soon, Sandy returned and went about setting the table and opening the packages of food. Zack couldn't stop gaping, marveling at how classy everything looked. "If this is your idea of carry-out, I'm putting in for a transfer," he marveled.

"And unless the boss here is an idiot," Powell grinned, "you'll be hired."

Having laid out the table, Sandy began pointing out some of the highlights. "This is chicken paprikash—and this is the desert, palacsintas. A kind of a crepe filled with walnut paste that is to die for."

Zack's eyes popped. "What a feast."

"And Bertie picked out a super Hungarian wine."

"It's a 1992 Egri Bikaver, Zack. Sandy and I throw it down on a regular basis whenever we can afford one."

"DELICIOUS!"

Zack drained his wine glass and wiped his chin. "Well—now that my hunger has subsided, why don't you tell me about this new damn device."

"Before you two get involved," Sandy interrupted, "I've gotta run. Hope you don't mind if I leave the dishes."

The two men nodded, and she grabbed her sweater, kissed Powell's cheek, and shook Zack's hand.

"The cocktail flag goes up at six, my dear," Powell said.

"Should I find a date for Zack?"

"Thanks, but no," Bertie said. "I can't think of any ladies on the island discrete enough to handle what we'll be discussing. 'Loose lips sink ships', and all that."

"I'm afraid that went right over my head," she said.

"Bertie hasn't used that in years," Zack said, shaking his head. "You know, he's an absolute fount of knowledge on the Second World War?"

"Not a fount, dear boy. Just a pastime. And let's not bring my idiosyncrasies into play."

"Such as the Eisenhower field jacket, the beret, and the kilt?"

"Now wait just a minute. The jacket was fashionable. Well, at least in its day. The others—well, I usually only wore them on the birthday of Robert the Bruce."

"Stop needling one another, you two."

"Truce?" asked Zack.

Powell nodded.

"So, my dear, should we vote on Zack joining our club before you leave?"

"You two are in a club?" asked Zack.

"Not exactly a club," she said. "Just a very exclusive group. Composed entirely of Bertie and We even have a secret handshake."

Zack laughed.

"I'll see you two gentlemen around six."

Zack watched the door close behind her and sighed.

"I HAVE TO SAY these hydrogen-alpha lines are flying off the charts," Zack remarked after spending most of the next hour poring over technical readouts. "Did you consider running them through a color densitometer?"

"Well...."

"No, forget I said that. Interference would probably reveal nothing over these huge distances."

"Maybe now you can see why I wanted to tell you more during our phone chat."

"I have to admit your call had the old adrenaline flowing. The only question now is whether or not this adds up to what you were hinting at."

"It must, my boy. I've gone over the figures a half-dozen times. At the risk of sounding a bit whacky, I think we may be in for a visit by real, live, honest-to-goodness ETs. Or at least their robotic hardware."

"Can you believe it, Bertie? After all these years of wondering, we could actually be getting a visit from extraterrestrials."

"I've been able to think of little else."

"I see now why you were dodging Scooter's thesis yesterday without coming right out and saying anything."

"Precisely. I only risked hinting at Interstellar Vehicle Braking Techniques. But you're excited now, you should have been in on conversations I'm having with the White House. What I wouldn't give to be a little mouse in the corner when the President drops this on the laps of the Joint Chiefs. Speaking of POTUS, I was promised a call from the Oval Office by the end of the day."

"Any possibility that other observatories have picked up on this already?"

"None that I can think of. From what I've been led to believe, the consensus leans towards a flare star. If I was a betting man—especially considering the odds I could probably get—I'd wager those flares can only be high-energy surges from a starship's deceleration maneuver. Remember those first-rate papers of yours on the use of fusion explosions to reduce speed?"

"Unless they're using some technologies unknown to us, at their half way point they'd need to make a 180-degree turn so their ship was approaching backwards," Zack nodded. "Then it's only a matter of firing up their engines to slow down. Or, instead of making a complete-180, they could use a buffer plate at the back of their ship and detonate explosions in front of that plate. Or, I suppose, a more advanced technique could be to use a force field rather than nuts-and-bolts buffer plate technology."

"I quite agree, my boy. In fact, even now we use buffer plate on some jet engines. After landing they close clamshell doors behind the engines so exhaust is deflected forward to slow them."

"Try this one on for size, Bertie. If the ship is still eight light years away, say forty-five trillion miles, it's only half way here from 40 Eri. So they might have to turn the ship so it was traveling backwards and complete the last half of the trip decelerating."

Powell shook his head. "Old technology, my boy. If that's the case we shouldn't expect them to arrive for eight more years; assuming they have no faster-than-light capability. If they have FTL, or their technology allows them to decelerate at the last minute, we may as well roll out the red carpet and put the tea kettle on."

"Maybe our visitors aren't even from an Eri 40 planet. They could be from an even-more distant system, and just positioned themselves between us and 40 Eri to conceal their approach and point of origin. Let's face it Bertie, we need lots more data."

"Fortunately we can do the lion's share of that here at the house. Now, to fill you in on my little invention: I discovered a way to modify a single-dish radio telescope and make it into an almost or 'quasi' reflecting telescope. That gives us the ability to operate it like an optical telescope with all of its advantages.

"I've already sent my specifications to Carlos Flusher in Chile and Floyd Hutchins in Australia. This way, only three telescopes in the world—theirs and mine—will have my system. I made them pledge their first-born child if my idea leaks out before I get a patent."

"That's incredible. I'm really proud of you. But now, as for more important topics—exactly what is going on between you and Sandy?"

"Are you getting romantic ideas of your own?" laughed Powell. "I thought you were trying to start up a relationship with some lovely lady in Bermuda?"

"I am, or have been. And I'm not exactly an alley cat, but I really do find Sandy captivating."

"Well, besides her obvious attributes, she's one of the smartest young women you'll ever find. Gifted in languages, math, politics—and her latest venture, physics and astronomy. But her real talent is journalism—interviewing and reporting. She's a TV reporter working at a station in San Juan and I hear she's a natural."

"About her name. Sandra?"

"No. The family name is LaPlage. That's French for the beach. So, beach—sand—Sandy."

Zack laughed.

"But if you think you have a growing interest now, think of it as a preview, coming soon to a theater near you."

Chapter 17

AFTER DINNER ZACK AND BERTIE were telling tall tales of their days at the university. Sandy dabbed at tears as she waved her hands.

"Stop!" she gasped. "You two have got to stop while I catch my breath. Okay—now I'm under control. So go on Zack. Bertie did what?"

"I swear it's true. We still had twenty minutes left on the clock to finish the exam he gave us and no one had turned theirs in yet. So here's Bertie, sitting at his desk with his nose in a book, pretending not to be ogling a very pretty student sitting in the front row. Turns out she was the first to finish. She stood up, adjusted her sweater and took the exam up to him in a slinky walk— just like this."

He reenacted the walk

"She was not slinking," Bertie huffed. "Sit back down and kindly give me a break."

"Sorry, Bertie, that's exactly how she was walking."

"You've got me hanging here guys. Finish it Zack."

"Bertie is trying to keep his eyes down and focused on his book— "

"Well, It was a bit difficult," Powell admitted

"So she slinks—or walks up to hand him her papers. When he lifted his eyes from the book he apparently only got as far as the pink Angora sweater. He said, 'Well, if it isn't one of my— "

Zack started laughing.

"Damn it!" Sandy interjected. "What—what did he say?"

"...one of my very breast students."

"Oh no, he couldn't. Oh God, Bertie. You didn't, did you?"

Powell nodded sheepishly.

"But the best part of this story is when her sister— "

"No," Sandy said. "Please stop. I'm getting a glitch in my side. You're killing me. You two should be on stage."

"I know. And it leaves in ten minutes," Zack replied. He took his drink out on the porch and Powell followed.

She raised her voice and called after them. "I'll clean up in here so you two relax. And Bertie, here's my joke. What do you call someone who talks a lot but nobody listens? A teacher. "

Zack rolled his eyes. "Now tell the truth Bertie. Are you two an item?"

"You know my feelings on that. A gentleman never tells."

"Come on—as you said earlier, you've got socks older than women her age. You're also the one who claims that old folks shouldn't buy green bananas."

Bertie added, "Don't forget that you had that bumper sticker—LIFE'S UNCERTAIN. EAT DESSERT FIRST.' Did you notice I had one made up for Sandy's car?"

"No, but that doesn't answer my question." Zack stopped short as Sandy came out with fresh coffee.

The phone rang. "I'll get it," she said stepping back inside.

She walked back to the porch, her eyes wide.

"Zack," she whispered, "it's the President's office."

The men returned inside and Zack picked up the phone. "Zack Peters, here," he said. "Oh—thanks much. It was a great trip. No, I'm not sure who has the details. You'd best speak to Dr. Powell."

Powell answered, "Yes? Oh, thank you. We're doing as well as anyone can with this Sword of Damocles hanging over our heads. I'm trying to keep things under wraps as best I can from this end. Hmmm?—well, except for Zack and my staff, the only others who'd know would be Carlos Flusher in Chile at Cerro Panchon and Floyd Hutchins in Australia at Narrabri.

"Floyd has a Compact Array with six, 72-foot dishes. When the six are patched together they act as one large telescope and can pick out galaxies billions of light years away. The beginning of the universe? No, that would be 13.7 billion years ago. If you don't mind my asking, did the Premier give any explanations for their move to DefCon Three? Of course—and we'll do everything we can to keep it under wraps for as long as possible. Yes, we'll wait for a call. Good bye."

Powell turned to Zack, "Did you both hear me mention DefCon Three?

"What's a DefCom?" Sandy asked.

"It's DefCon with an N dear," Powell answered. "It stands for Defense Condition—a gauge of a country's readiness to perceived threats of hostilities."

"And by hostilities, you mean war?" she asked.

"That too," Powell nodded. "There are five levels. The lowest, DefCon Five, is when a country's in a state of defense activities during a time of relative peace."

Zack added, "Four is when there's a general increase in intelligence activity. Three is when the armed forces are on standby waiting orders."

"You often see that in films," Powell said. "When an international situation gets dicey, military leaves are cancelled and troops aren't allowed to leave the base. Two is when the country is ready for combat..."

"And DefCon One means out and out war?" she asked.

"Almost," Zack said. "One is when troops are deployed for combat but haven't started shooting at each other yet."

"Perhaps the Premier moved into Condition Three after finding out about 40 Eri," she said. "I can't imagine our President being able to keep a lid on this with all of the telescopes scattered around the world that could detect it on their own."

"The President's controlling what she can," said Powell, "after browbeating—I mean, convincing some of the staff at the Hubble Space Telescope who are monitoring 40 Eri and then reporting covertly to the White House. They're trying to come up with a way to lock out the star's coordinates so no one can move a telescope to those coordinates."

"I'll bet you dollars to donuts Moscow has broken our Scrambler and has been monitoring Bertie's calls," she said.

The phone rang.

"This is Powell. Yes I'll hold."

He pointed to the telephone mouth piece and whispered, 'the President'.

"Yes. I'm still here. Zack and I were just talking about Scrambler. Yes, I understand: we'll stay off this line for a while. What about Zack? The hurricane has cancelled arriving and outbound flights until tomorrow morning. All right, I'll see that he's on the first one out. I appreciate that. Thank you, Madame President. Good night."

"So much for your vacation, Zack," Powell said. "Looks like you're headed back to Washington for a White House briefing the first thing tomorrow morning, assuming the weather clears. Then it sounds like you'll be heading to London."

Zack mumbled something inaudibly.

"It seems you were right about Scrambler being compromised," Bertie continued. "Orders are we're not to scramble anything or send e-mails until Washington gives us the go ahead. So fill up your glasses my hearties. We've been asked to begin brainstorming scenarios for the White House."

"What if all the countries just tell their people that we have some extra-terrestrials here," Zack wondered, "with the ability to negotiate trips of sixteen light-years as easy as we go to the Moon?"

"Well, if we have ETs are already here and watching us," Sandy puzzled, "shouldn't we have come across them by now?"

"I'd say no, if only because we haven't looking for them," Bertie said. "Even if we were, what would we look for? Who's to say whether or not we'd recognize them?"

"Well," she offered, "we could assume they'd be trying to remain undetected by disguising themselves or by hiding out. And you can bet your socks they'd stay in touch with their home planet. Wow—I just had an alarming thought: what if they've infiltrated our SETI community and are using our telescopes?"

"All this sounds pretty wild," Zack said. "But we do have one thing going for us, and that's the laws of physics. We know they must be bound by the same natural laws of the universe as we are, so they can't travel or transmit faster than the speed of light."

"If that's so," Powell said, "there'd be a thirty-two year time lag between messages. The ETs home world couldn't receive information from Earth for sixteen years due to information traveling at the speed of light...."

"And conversely," Zack said, "an ET living on Earth couldn't get instructions from its home world for another sixteen years."

"Before we start feeling complacent, what if incriminating data was sent to their home world decades ago?" Sandy asked. "They may have already instructed their local people to take action. In fact, one of their spaceships could already be on its way here."

"I think it's a little early for us to suck on a gas pipe," scoffed Bertie.

Zack smiled. "Here's a thought: the ETs wouldn't have to be living on Earth. They could have automatic probes in orbit around the sun. Maybe even buried on the moon."

"You know," Powell chuckled, "that idea was proposed more than fifty years ago by an American astronomer, Robert Bracewell."

"I remember him!" Zack replied. "But we'd have one hell of a job trying to locate one of their devices even if we were looking for it. And we're not."

"Well of all these possibilities," Sandy said, "I like the idea that ETs are not only alive and well on Earth, thank you very much, but they're snitching on us. We should hunt them down, put them in jail, or shoot them."

"That might not be a wise move," Zack sighed. "If we've already done something to antagonize them, killing them might just cook our goose."

Powell nodded.

"If you ask me, our goose is probably already in the oven," she quipped.

"Does the President know if any other telescopes have detected the 40 Eri anomalies and chosen not to announce it?"

"Zack," answered Powell, "that's always a possibility. But I've heard nothing about any strange goings on over at NASA. What I do know is that its BETA-1 telescope can't observe the section of the sky where 40 Eri is located, and BETA-2 will be down for repairs for at least another month."

"So we can safely assume that your thousand-footer is the only radio telescope in on the action."

"I agree," Powell mused. "I just wish we could nail down their distance."

The telephone rang and Sandy answered.

"Dr. Powell's residence. Can you hold please?" She turned to Bertie. "It's Dr. Flusher in Chile."

Powell took the receiver. "Hola Carlos. Say that again? You're sure they're slowing down? Well, that all but confirms it. There were originally tracked at eighty percent light speed; if they keep decelerating steadily we should be able to get a fairly accurate reading on distance, and can probably figure out how soon they'll be on our doorstep."

Another phone rang.

"Hi Perry," Sandy answered. "Yes but he's on another line. Okay—I will. Please hold."

"It's Perry," she whispered. "He's over at the telescope and says it's urgent."

"Carlos, can you hold for just a minute? Perry says there something going on with the telescope."

Powell punched in another line; his face immediately turned grim.

"Yes, I agree," he sighed. "That's just about the last thing we need to hear. Well, keep on it. We'll stay near the phone with the scrambler until its up and running again, then we'll be right over. Do the best you can. Have you tried going off-axis and returning to make sure it isn't something local? How about tweaking the frequency? Good man. If you get calls from anyone just play dumb and pass them over to me.

"And Perry, do me a huge favor. Call Floyd Hutchins at Narrabri and ask if he's been able to grab any data. *Damn*, but I wish we could get a fix on the distance. No, the scrambler's been compromised, but I expect it to come back at any time. Don't say more than you need to. Carlos is on another line. I'll ask him to do the same."

Bertie hung up the phone and turned to face Zack. His face looked drained.

"It was about the light flashes," he whispered. "They just stopped."

Zack hit his leg with a closed fist.

The telephone rang again.

"Good afternoon," Sandy said pleasantly. "Dr. Powell's residence. Hello, Dr. Flusher—can you hold on?"

Pressing the hold button, she motioned to get Bertie's attention. "Dr. Flusher calling back on Line One."

Bernie grabbed the phone. "Flush? Sorry we got cut off. No, I can't scramble. Moscow broke the code, and it hasn't been re-secured. Give me a hint and cross your fingers they aren't listening."

"Well, doesn't that beat all? Did you talk to Washington? What can I tell you? I understand. Scrambler should be reset within the hour. Yes I agree—cat's out of the bag anyway. Just don't say any more than you need to. Hold on a second."

Another incoming call lit up the phone; Sandy picked up the receiver as Powell grabbed Zack by the arm.

"Flush says the inbound light is back on and now reads like a single light," said Powell. "He' suggests that our visitors might be trailing a light sail to help decelerate. And he claims there's evidence of more than a single ship."

"Bertie—," Sandy interrupted. "Priscilla in Washington says Scrambler is back on-line. Our new code is 42 Red Carp. And we can start sending e-mail again."

Powell nodded. "Flush? Sorry about all this. Our phones are going crazy. We just got word that we can start scrambling and using e-mail again— the new code is 42 Red Carp . Let me know as soon as you've analyzed the spectrum. And call Floyd when you get a chance, and say I'd appreciate it if he'd use his array and run a check on everything. There's a chance it's a light sail and the light will likely match the Sun. Thanks."

"Zack, you nailed it again; about their next stage being a light sail or hydrogen ramjet. Sandy, give Perry a jingle. Tell him to forget about calling Floyd. Flush will make the call."

TWO HOURS LATER Floyd Hutchins called with news that a spectrum analysis confirmed that the light from the incoming ships was a dead match to the Sun. This showed that the ships were dragging a sail, and meant that they could not calculate their distance.

"Well Zack," Powell sighed, "I just won five bucks from Floyd about the light sails. Now we need to figure out if they'll be arriving in three months or three weeks."

Zack took a deep breath. "I guess we shouldn't be surprised that they have great technology."

The first thing Powell did was to call the president.

"How did Washington take the news?" Zack asked, as Powell

hung up the phone after a two-hour conference call with the White House.

Powell just shrugged.

"I didn't get a good read on that. But instead of going to Washington, you're now heading to London to meet with Colonel Mikhail Kornikov, Moscow's intelligence honcho."

Zack ran a hand through his hair and shook his head.

"Now that makes absolutely no sense. Lord knows I'm not a bureaucrat. This kind of a trip should be made by the Secretary of State. Even the vice-president would be a better choice."

"They know you have a level head and common sense," Powell replied. "Besides, Kornikov specifically asked for you. I don't want to add to your concern, but you should know you'll be in meetings with all the top dogs from the international security community. On the bright side, you'll get to see your old buddy Winstanly."

"What countries will be there?"

"Russia and Great Britain for sure. Probably France and Germany. From what I gather, they'll be discussing more than the spacecraft from 40 Eri." Powell smiled weakly. "On an up-note, you could end up with a pay raise and a new career as a diplomat."

"In a pig's eye. Besides, what's more important that those starships?"

"For starters, it seems the Russians have a dead alien—or at least the remains of one. They seem convinced that Fly Swatter's a weapon that could be directed anywhere, including Moscow. Their president demands to know if we're in contact with the aliens, even though the White House has flatly denied it. And it looks like our friends could arrive here in as little as six weeks."

"So the Russians know less than we thought they did."

"Next—effective immediately, the National Guard will be assigned to provide security at all of our major observatories."

Zack asked, "Will that include Arecibo?"

"I'm afraid so. We'd better do some house cleaning before they arrive. So ditch all the old wine bottles and make sure your room is shipshape."

Sandy peeked in from the kitchen. "Wine? Did I hear someone mention my favorite word? Oh and Bertie, did you say anything to Zack about…?

"I didn't get to it yet."

"Good. That should be my job anyway."

"Okay," Zack protested, "what did I do now?"

She took one of his hands in hers and gazed into his eyes.

"With you leaving tomorrow," she smiled, "and for who knows how long, tonight may be my only chance to spend some—quality time with you."

"Can I jump in here for just a moment?" Powell interrupted. "Sandy and I discussed this. She's worried about you jumping to any number of wrong conclusions. So no matter what it sounds like, believe me when I say she's the last person in the world interested in what the kids might call 'casual dating.' Under different circumstances you two could have begun a more conventional…oh hell, you explain it to him."

He touched Zack's shoulder as he passed him and said, "I'll let you two sort this out. Personally, I'm heading over to the telescope to see Perry."

"I'd sure like to know why it seems I'm always the last person to know anything," Zack protested. "And sure as hell I'd love to spend some, as you say 'quality time' with you, but as I see it there is only one problem. I've met someone in Washington and— "

"I'd be surprised if you hadn't," she pouted. "Are you engaged?"

"Hell no. Nothing like that."

"How long have you been seeing each other?"

"Less than a month, actually. Come to think of it, we've only been together once or twice."

"In that case, I have an announcement," she said regally. "Let it be known far and wide, that by the powers invested in me by no one in particular, I proclaim and decree this to be an official 'open season' on Zack Peters."

"Does that mean people can shoot me?"

"No you silly man. But all is fair in love and war. I want to be with you tonight. So if you would be kind enough to stop being stuffy and take this altitude-challenged woman in your arms, there is every likelihood that you might get kissed."

He did, and felt her melt into his arms.

"I feel a little off balance here Sandy. Not that I'm…"

She smothered his words with another kiss.

"…complaining, it's just that I…"

She kissed him again, this time more urgently.

"You know, you're really an incredible kisser…"

Touching his lips with her finger to hush him, she kissed him again.

He pulled back momentarily, "Do you promise you'll…"

"…be gentle with you?" she asked raising an eyebrow. "Oh, come now."

"No—but to paraphrase *My Fair Lady*…"

"Yes, I promise to get you to the plane on time."

Chapter 18

AS THE AEROFLOT stretch-Ilyushin 96-300M touched down at London's Heathrow airport, a flight attendant worked his way down the aisle towards Zack, using seatbacks to steady himself. Taking a seat on the armrest across the aisle, he spoke in flawless English without a trace of a Russian accent.

"Welcome to London, Dr. Peters. I hope you did not feel neglected. I've been on the lower level catching up on some paperwork, and since you never activated your call button— "

"Don't worry, Dmitri. I always relish the chance to take an uninterrupted nap."

Well, I imagine you've noticed we were not overbooked on this trip."

Zack smiled, and glanced over his shoulder. The cabin's 306 empty seats made the cabin of the wide-body Ilyushin seem even more cavernous.

"This is definitely the way to travel," Zack smiled. "But I always like sitting in First Class as long as I'm not picking up the tab."

"We were rather surprised when word came to take you to London as our lone passenger. Yesterday, we carried a hundred low-level dignitaries from London to Havana on a charter for some conference or other. On the way back to London yesterday the weather got so bad the pilot chose to lay-over in San Juan and sit it out. As it turns out, you were fortunate. When we got word to bring you to London, no questions asked, we figured you had to be a VIP with contacts in high places."

"I was delighted to get the ride, Dmitri. Do you mind if I ask a question?"

"Go ahead."

"I was just glancing out the windows. Aren't those engines hanging on the wings from Pratt & Whitney? I'm surprised they're not Russian engines."

"You are very observant, Dr. Peters. They're PW2000s. I'm told we still have a few Russian-built engines on selected domestic flights, but I don't recollect their names or designations."

Zack leaned back in his seat. "Aircraft are one of my interests. I even know that Aeroflot had the world's first sustained jet airline service back in 1956. With the Tupolev Tu-104s, I believe."

"You certainly do know your planes, Mr. Peters. But actually, it was the summer of 1955. Well, I placed your bags already up front by the door. The pilot informs me that you're being met at the gate."

"Thank you, Dmitri. My compliments to the crew. It was a great flight."

AS ZACK STEPPED OUT of the boarding tube and into the terminal he was greeted by a Russian Army captain and a sergeant, both replete in spit-and-polish dress uniforms. The captain stepped forward and offered his hand.

"Welcome to London, Dr. Peters," the captain said, his baritone voice thick with a Russian accent. I am Captain Vasili Rubinsky, at your service—Colonel Kornikov's personal aide. If you be so kind to accompany me, I take you to flight lounge, where Colonel Kornikov, he is waiting."

He snapped his fingers in the direction of Zack's suitcases. The sergeant retrieved them and followed the men down the corridor.

"I've been looking forward to meeting the Colonel," Zack said as they stopped at a door with AEROFLOT VIP—MEMBERS ONLY spelled out in black and gold lettering. A handwritten note was taped to the door reading, *Temporarily Closed.*

Rubinsky knocked twice before entering. An Army colonel rose from one of two posh leather chairs and approached, smiling and offering his hand. "I'm Mikhail Kornikov," he said. "Welcome to London, Dr. Peters." He shook Zack's hand with a strong, firm handshake. "I must tell you that your excellent reputation and rumors of a rich and diverse background preceded you."

"Thank you Colonel, and please call me Zack. I've heard glowing reports about you as well. It's a pleasure to be here, especially since it's been so long since I've seen London. I'm looking forward to the visit."

"And you may call me Misha, Zack. I started out my career as a lowly private and try not to forget my roots. Perhaps I will have the chance to show you around London before you head back to the Colonies." A broad smile suggested he had coined that phrase. "I like to think of London as my home away from home. Here, take this seat next to mine."

"I would be uncomfortable using your first name, Colonel," said Zack. "It would show a lack of respect."

"The cure for that is simple. I'm having a Bloody Mary with some special vodka I brought all the way from Moscow. Would you have one?"

"Yes I would, thank you."

Kornikov smiled and gestured to his aide for another round of drinks. Immediately, Zack realized that his stereotype of rigid Russian officers didn't fit this man. He was pleasant and easygoing.

After some small talk the drinks arrived, and Kornikov turned serious.

"I wanted to speak to you privately about something you will want to convey to your president," he said quietly. "I will be holding back on much of it during our group discussions with some European Union security heads, even though I will be requesting complete openness."

Kornikov's brow furrowed, and the lines on his face deepened. "You see Zack; in the brief period since you left Puerto Rico I've had disturbing news that outweighs my original concerns."

"You have my attention, Colonel."

"Your president is aware that— "

He turned to his aide, "Captain, if you please."

Vasili nodded and stepped back to the bar.

"Your president is doubtless aware," he continued, "that we know about your county's Fly Swatter—your secret stealth satellite that leads the orbiting International Space Station by 500 miles and carries a secret weapon. I find it rather strange to believe your president believed we'd somehow overlooked it."

Zack settled deeper into his chair and interlocked his fingers. He looked Kornikov squarely in the eye.

"Actually, Colonel, we'd hoped you had. If you hadn't, we were prepared to explain it away as a storage depot. The President has anguished over this for a long time. He hoped to convince your country that Fly Swatter is only for defense—a long overdue replacement for our earlier misadventure in our 'Star Wars' deployment."

Kornikov smiled. "We often joke about your Star Wars program as your Second Edsel. For ourselves, we are fond of our automobiles even when they aren't commercially successful."

"I like that, Colonel: 'Our second Edsel.' I must find a way to work that into a future conversation."

"Whether Fly Swatter is defensive or offensive is largely a matter of rhetoric," Kornikov said. "But let me put my cards on the table. I will share with you some very hot news; so hot that your president hasn't found out about it yet. A few hours ago, it seems that both the International Space Station and Fly Swatter were compromised."

"Compromised? I don't understand."

"I'm embarrassed to admit that three rogue Russian agents hijacked them both."

Zack eyes widened and he pulled forward in his seat; he took a deep breath to calm himself before speaking.

"Both ISS and Fly Swatter? You can't be serious."

"I'm completely serious."

"Who are they? Are they threatening either of us? And why should I believe they're rogue agents, and not operating on orders of your government?"

"Their motives are unclear, Zack. They claim they have not executed any of the crew yet and will not do so if they're left alone for the next six days. Why that particular number? No one knows, and they are not saying—although I've heard they've been in contact with astronomers at the Russian Academy of Sciences. Specifically, the Pulkovo Observatory."

"Well, I have an idea what this is all about. It's part of the reason I'm here—to lay our cards out on the table and share information. We have indisputable evidence that there is one, perhaps two spacecraft are about to enter the solar system."

Kornikov paused before speaking. "I wasn't prepared for that big a surprise," he said at last. "If it's true—and not that I doubt you, you understand—such ships would be likely headed for Earth, given that we are the only technologically advanced life form in the solar system."

"Agreed, and though only a handful of our people know about them at present, it's only a matter of time until everyone will. But this may have to do with the takeover of ISS and Fly Swatter. I'm thinking your astronomers may have stumbled onto the ships as well, but aren't ready to make the announcement until they're positive about it."

"Great minds think alike, Zack. Yes, the pieces of the puzzle are beginning to fit. But there's something else I need to know. Because we haven't detected a nuclear signature on Fly Swatter, can we safely assume it lacks nuclear weapons?"

"It does not."

Kornikov rose and started to pace around the room. "So this rogue group must have some ties to our astronomers who found out about Fly Swatter. But if it lacks nuclear capability, the one other weaponry I think would be appropriate would be lasers."

"Yes, Colonel. Very powerful lasers, in fact. They are tied into a sophisticated global positioning system. Our military brass brag they could slice the tail off a squirrel sitting on top of the Kremlin wall and never touch a brick."

"Very admirable, Zack. If only our laser program was as successful. Well, we mustn't delay any longer. We should leave for the hotel. On the way there I'll tell you stories about some Little Green Men we've run into over the past twenty years."

Zack's eyebrows shot up. "I can't wait for that," he chuckled. "And I need to contact the White House about the ISS and Swatter takeovers, in case she hasn't received word yet. About those LGMs—I must commend you on keeping them a secret. We haven't heard reputable reports from anywhere lately."

"You may decide, in light of what is happening, the term Little Green Men may not be accurate," replied Kornikov. "Little Old Ladies might be more accurate."

DURING THE DRIVE INTO LONDON, Kornikov told Zack about the intrusions at Green Bank, Moscow, and Bonn.

"I knew your intelligence agencies were excellent, but how did you come up with the story of the West Virginia radio telescope back in the late eighties? After investigating the matter, our people passed it off as urban legend."

Kornikov nodded. "It still would be, except for two law enforcement officers at the telescope. They swore they saw an old woman flash out of existence. They're both retired but keep in contact with each other by e-mail. I'm sure I'm not revealing any state secrets by telling you this, but I make sure my people search the internet regularly for specific words and phrases—including, at times, private emails."

Zack nodded, resolving that he'd never again send an e-mail about anything he wouldn't want the whole world to know about."

"Now," Kornikov continued, " I want to show you something." He opened his briefcase and brought out a small computer screen. Activating the display, he launched a low-quality video; it showed a of a woman on fire in a detention room at Moscow's Annex in1978.

"That's... incredible Colonel. But I can't make out her features very well."

"Practice saying 'Misha,' Zack. Now take a look at this." He handed him a manila folder.

"And this is…?"

"It's a photo of an employee who was on temporary assignment to our department in Moscow—the same woman who supposedly burned up at the Bonn telescope. Do you see any resemblance to the woman on the video?"

Zack took a photograph from the envelope. His eyes popped open and his jaw dropped.

"Good god," he whispered. "She was the night custodian at the Federal Building in Washington when I worked there in 2003.Her name was—Marian? No—I remember now. It was Mary. She was there just before I left the CIA. Now we need to compare it with the woman at Green Bank."

"What the hell is going on, Zack? And these are only three events. Maybe it's just the tip of a larger iceberg."

"How much more will I hear at your meeting?"

"I invited thirteen, and ten accepted. We should have some very interesting information to share. And I'd trade dollars for rubles to know how many aliens are walking around among us at this very minute, and just how long they've been here. And yes I'm willing to come right out and call them aliens."

Rubinsky interrupted, "Excuse me gentlemen but we are arriving at the hotel."

Chapter 19

KORNIKOV'S LIMOUSINE pulled up to the imposing London Waldorf Hilton. Built in the early 1900s with Portland stone and Aberdeen granite, it sat between the Thames River and the financial district, flanked by a pair of West End theaters.

"Someone has got to be kidding," Zack murmured, as he passed the kiosk in the lobby, listing the day's scheduled meetings:

FLAT EARTH SOCIETY OF FINLAND
9 A.M. TO 5 P.M.
FOURTH FLOOR, ROOM B

EUROPEAN UNION ATHEISM ASSOC.
8 A.M. TO 7 P.M.
FOURTH FLOOR, ROOM C

"Are you sure we're in the right place?"

Kornikov nodded. "I assure you we are. My wife Tatyana is in charge of security arrangements, and this was her idea to keep prying eyes from our meeting. You'll see that it isn't listed."

"So those two groups won't be meeting here today?"

"They don't exist."

"So we'll have the entire fourth floor to ourselves. What a great idea! It's not only ingenious—it keeps security costs down to a minimum."

"True, though the money wasn't a major concern. Tatyana figured that fewer security people translates into less attention to our group."

"Any problems with the hotel setting all this up?"

"Actually, they were very cooperative. The moved all their guests from the third, fourth and fifth floors to other floors throughout the building—so we'll have all three floors to ourselves. They also offered them a complimentary night's stay. All at our expense, of course."

The bell chimed and the elevator door opened on five.

Zack was confused. "Aren't the meetings on four?"

"Tatyana set up the elevators to bypass four. We'll get off here and walk down a flight."

Kornikov nodded to the security staff sitting near the elevators in civilian clothes. Rubinsky, his aide, stayed behind to chat with his friends.

ZACK AND KORNIKOV stepped out of the stairwell on four and walked over to an ornately carved wooden door with the name King Arthur Suite in gold leaf lettering.

"Zack," said the Colonel, "before we enter, I want to set you at ease. Don't be intimidated by these people. Even though they are the Crème de la Crème of European Union intelligence, keep in mind they all step into their pants one leg at a time."

"Thanks, Misha. I'll try to hold that image."

"Of course, being from the EU, they often try putting both legs through the same opening."

Zack laughed out loud.

"Another thing, you might think the number of participants is a poor showing considering the size of the EU. But your president and I thought it more useful if our first meeting consisted only of countries sharing well-documented stories about our visitors."

Zack nodded. "So let's go in and get acquainted."

Kornikov motioned for Zack to enter and followed him in.

"Good morning one and all," said the Colonel closing the door behind him. "Let me introduce Dr. Zachary Peters, from the United States. This is first visit to England. Please make him feel at home."

Zack smiled and nodded at the group, his eyes sweeping the room. Langley had trained him well, honing his observational skills. Within a minute he could describe both the room's physical layout and its occupants.

In the center of the room was a wooden, circular conference table with an inlaid surface of English long swords. Their hilts circled the edge and their blades pointed to the center, where the tips touched. Eight chairs were in place; four were unoccupied. Zack knew that two would be for the Colonel and himself. The other two were unknowns.

A glass wall graced the opposite side of the room with two sliding doors opening onto a balcony offering a grand view of the Thames. Against the left wall stood an eight-foot-tall, dark wood armoire, its open doors revealing an assortment of audio-visual equipment.

Centered on the wall to his right was a pull-down projection screen. To the left of the screen was a door, doubtless leading into a room where security personnel were probably reading or playing cards. To the left of the door in the corner a table was covered with white linen and tea and coffee service. To the right of the screen was a table with Danish pastries and finger sandwiches, neatly arranged on a linen-covered dark rolling cart. The wall behind him had a wet bar, with a corridor leading to a dining room where dinner was being prepared, and a second door leading back into the hall. In the corner to his far right a middle-aged, plain featured stenographer sat filing her nails.

Zack nodded as his eyes finally found a familiar face—his old friend J. Winthrop Winstanly. The delegate from the United Kingdom MI-6 was seated next to a remarkably attractive female Russian major who, being roughly Kornikov's age, Zack took to be the Colonel's wife, Tatyana.

Seasoned travelers can often identify a person with distinctive clothing as being from another country, but Zack's training let him pick up on things that were less obvious, such as the way pant cuffs were tailored or the manner in which a fore-in-hand tie was executed. Though his briefing notes didn't include a picture, he surmised that the short balding man in his late fifties sitting next to Tatyana was likely to be Germany's Karl Hoffman from the *Bundesnachrichtendienst*—the BND, or Federal Intelligence Service—that comprised Germany's warning system for overseas threats.

He figured that the BND would probably initiate a new department for interstellar threats—unless it concluded that the assignment posed too great a bureaucratic risk, and decided to drop it into the laps of the German secret military screening service the *Militarischer Abschirmdienst,* their Ministry of Strategic Defense. Zack wondered how the Germans could ever fit all that on a business card.

Red hair was a dead giveaway for the man sitting next to Hoffman—Hamish Larksworth, director of Scotland's defense ministry.

But no one at the table had the Parisian look. That meant the French Sûreté representative, Jacques Puget, was absent.

Each of the delegates rose to greet him with enthusiasm. Winstanly was the first to approach, trying his best to conceal a limp by casually draping a cane over one arm as if it were a fashion statement. He switched it to the other arm and offered his right hand.

"How awfully nice it is to see you Zachary."

"It's always a pleasure seeing you too, Win," Zack smiled. "You're looking top drawer, proving once again that you can't keep a good tennis player down."

Winstanly beamed. "I appreciate the vote of confidence, old man. If I could only deep-six this wretched stick, I'd be right as rain. Yes sir, right as rain. Oh, and lest I forget, Ashleigh sends along his regards. You remember Ash from Hamilton?"

"Of course, he seemed like a fine fellow. Give him my regards."

Zack walked over to Tatyana. "Major Kornikova?"

She rose and extended her hand, which Zack kissed in his most gallant European manner.

"Dr. Peters," she said, with the barest trace of an accent. "I am so pleased finally to have the opportunity to meet you. Your reputation precedes you. I shall let you in on a family secret: Misha has mentioned more than once how he wished your President would trade you for three of our best people. We would even throw one of our—what is your football term? One of our draft choices!"

"If the Colonel's entire department is this charming," Zack grinned, "I'll personally approach the President with that proposal."

Tatyana turned to her husband saying, "Misha, it would appear Dr. Peters would serve us best in our diplomatic areas."

The greetings completed, the group resumed their seats.

"Dr. Puget's arrival will be delayed, due to an unforeseen but urgent matter," Kornikov began. "But before we commence in earnest, I believe that Dr. Peters has some important information to share with us that underscores the reason for this meeting."

"Thank you, Colonel," said Zack, speaking from his chair. "Until last week, our scientists had no explanation for reports of many of the extraordinary events taking place in your countries. A few of them were even inclined to attribute them to an evolutionary leap that was affecting a small segment of the world's population.

"As astonishing as the reports were, they are now seen in a new perspective due to an event—one that is occurring as we speak. There is undeniable evidence that two or more interstellar spacecraft are on a direct course toward the inner solar system."

Eyes widened around the table, and Zack could hear a collective gasp. "Because we've seen no evidence of any other advanced life forms in our solar system," he continued, "it is safe to assume their destination is Earth."

Tatyana was the first to speak. "We had already reached that conclusion, Dr. Peters. After monitoring some messages in the West, our own telescopes were able to verify the existence of those inbound spacecraft."

The Colonel added, "It would seem logical to assume that such a society with a technology to build interstellar vehicles would be—if you would excuse the pun—light years ahead of humans," added Kornikov. "With that in mind, I believe we should discuss our local events."

"If this is true," Hoffman said, "I want to point out something that may be devastating to our egos. Because these beings are technologically superior, it stands to reason they would be far ahead of us in evolution. It could equal or exceed the forty-thousand-year separation between ourselves and our earliest Cro-Magnon ancestors."

"Some of us appear to be getting a bit pale," Winstanley observed.

"I suggest that for the time being we set aside questions that there are no answers to," continued Kornikov, "such as speculations about the purpose for their visit. For the present, let's start around the room so everyone can bring the rest of us up to date with events, from our own countries."

Everyone nodded.

"Tatyana, would you do the honors?"

As the last report had concluded, Kornikov's personal communicator rang.

"Yes," the Colonel said. "Send him in right away."

FROM JACQUES PUGET'S DEMEANOR it was obvious he was disturbed. He greeted everyone in a rush, poured himself a cup of coffee, and sat down. Sweat poured from his brow, and he kept shaking his ashen face. Rumor had it that he was a Pink Panther devotee, sometimes even dressing like the bumbling chief inspector. Zack smiled despite himself, wondering if Puget had ever leaned against a spinning globe or the World, executed a pratfall and leapt to his feet totally unabashed.

"I've received news that is most distressing," he said at last. "Most of you are familiar with our Centre Spatial Guyanais space complex at Kourouas, French East Guiana, *n'est pas*? And how we've operated it since the 1960s? The European Space Agency accepted our offer to share the facility with them in the mid-70s and agreed to help improve the site for Ariane rocket launches. And, of course since then—but—no matter! It pains me to tell you— "

He shook his head and took a deep breath to calm his nerves.

"Early this morning, the facility suffered a terrorist attack. Damage was minimal, but it will delay a few launches. Thank God there were only a handful of injuries but no fatalities."

"We're all sorry to hear that," Kornikov said. "Terrorists are truly a blight upon the civilized world. But when we spoke yesterday, you mentioned a historic announcement. Perhaps you are can share it with us. I can assure nothing will leave this room without your authorization."

"Thank you, Colonel," said the Frenchman; he took another deep breath, and continued. "Until recently, we have successfully kept the project secret. But with this attack, it is only a matter of time until everything becomes known. That being the case, I can now tell you we have completed the preliminary phase of what will make space travel a much less expensive venture. The ground base or tether is complete for the world's first space elevator."

"Did I hear correctly?" Hoffman marveled. "A space elevator?"

Zack shook his head. "That just blows me away. I always felt I was on top of international space community projects; but this one slipped completely by me. Please accept America's heartiest congratulations. It's a monumental accomplishment for future space travel."

Puget bowed his head slightly as he said, "Thank you Dr. Peters, and yes Herr Hoffman, that is exactly what we are building—a space elevator. Until now such a concept was only found in science fiction."

"What a coincidence," Zack said. "Less than a month ago I re-read one of my favorite science fiction novels, *Fountains of Paradise* by Arthur C. Clarke. In it, he introduced the space elevator concept to the masses."

"Correct, Dr. Peters," Puget said. "But did you know that Clarke had other proposals that were prophetic for his time."

"Yes," said Zack. "He proposed instantaneous world-wide communication using three communications satellites in geo-stationary orbits. We use them now and refer to them as being in a Clarke Orbit. He only wished he'd had the foresight to patent the idea."

"All quite interesting, but would you kindly explain all this 'space elevator stuff' to us, old chap?" Winstanley asked from the pastry table, just before stuffing a sweet roll into his mouth.

Puget set his coffee cup down and began, "Simply put, it's the most efficient way to move material into Earth orbit. In time, they will undoubtedly replace present day methods using noisy, polluting, chemical rockets. To build an elevator all that is needed is to construct a sturdy base on the ground that is as close to the equator as possible. The base holds the lower end of a long tether, or cable that stretches up to an orbiting space dock that is in geocentric orbit above the ground base. That is, the space dock must orbit the planet at the same speed as the Earth does at the base's latitude, roughly 25,000 miles an hour. A giant reel that holds the cable is launched up to the space dock and becomes a permanent fixture."

"That cable would have to be extremely long," remarked Kornikov.

"About 26,000 miles long," nodded Puget. "You start by unwinding the cable until it reaches the ground where it can be attached to the base. Then you extend a shorter cable out and away from the space dock to serve as a counter weight, so centrifugal force can keep the elevator cable and space dock from collapsing back to Earth. We chose Kourouas as our site because of its close proximity to the equator, where Earth's rotation is about a thousand miles per hour. That way, any spacecraft leaving the space dock already has a free thousand mile an hour boost."

"Of course," Kornikov smiled, "I'm sure everyone knows that the space elevator concept originated first in Russia."

"That is true, Mikhail," Puget chuckled. "It was your Konstantin Tsiolkovsky—considered the 'father' of space flight due to his many inventions for rockets, including the elevator concept. Less well known is the fact that he also conceptualized the hovercraft."

Puget continued, "The biggest advantage of space elevators is that they are much less expensive than today's chemical rockets that cost $10,000 U.S. to place one pound of payload into orbit."

Zack added, "You can all be assured that elevators won't be limited to use here on Earth. They can be assembled on just about any planet, moon or asteroid except those without solid surfaces like Jupiter and Saturn."

"True," Puget said. "Space elevators will probably open the cosmos to humans in ways we haven't yet imagined."

As the discussion turned to technical matters, the Colonel shook his head. Get too many scientists in a room, he thought, and they get so busy talking about their latest project that trying to discuss anything is nearly impossible. He may as well not even try to fight the inevitable, he chuckled. And perhaps after having something to eat he could turn their attention back to more pressing matters.

"I think dinner is ready," he announced grandly. "I'm told the food is wonderful here—and it should be waiting for us in the other room. Rather than you wandering the streets in search of a good restaurant and possibly being a security risk, my wife took the liberty of making reservations for us in the hotel's Homage Grand Salon. We will have it all to ourselves. And if the Louis the Sixteenth décor fails to win you over, the walk-in wine cabinet should."

"I'll drink to that," Winstanly said with a chortle.

Still busily talking about space elevators, the scientists rose and ambled their way in the general direction of the food. Taking advantage of the break, one of Kornikov's aides approached and bent over to relay a message.

"Excuse please, Colonel," he whispered, "but your party has arrived."

"Thank you. Send her in," Kornikov said.

A female Army officer entered the room in full dress uniform, a garrison cap and dark sunglasses. Kornikov greeted her with an embrace and led her over to Zack.

"My friend, allow me to introduce Captain Li-Hwa Zaranova, Counter Intelligence, Second Directorate. But of course I believe you two are already acquainted so…" Kornikov's phone beeped. He glanced at the read-out. "Excuse me, I must take this call."

Li-Hwa removed her sunglasses, the cap and a pin that let her hair drop down. Cocking her head slightly she offered Zack a disarming smile. She waited for the moment to sink in then lightly kissed his cheek.

"It's good to see you again."

Zack 's befuddlement soon melted into anger. All the while he couldn't help noticing how attractive Li-Hwa was without makeup. It took him a moment to gather his composure.

"It is Zanarova I believe the Colonel said?" he muttered, looking off toward the food table in the next room.

"I suppose I deserved that," she replied mildly.

"So everything that we had and did was pretense?" he hissed.

"No, Zack. You should realize I am a soldier and had been given an assignment. And yes, I admit that part of it was pretense. But you should know that I grew more and more uncomfortable with the deception. I'll rephrase that," she whispered. "It never was deception when we were in bed."

"Nice try. And now that you have lost the innocence you so convincingly displayed, I can tell you, 'that old saw won't play'."

"I never wanted to hurt you. Can't you just think of it as being a pleasant interlude?"

"What about your dog Su Shi?" he said stiffly.

"In my line of work there isn't time for pets or involvements."

He wiped his mouth with one hand, then with a frown added, "In your line of work? You have the gall to stand there and call it work?"

"Let me to turn this around. When you worked for the CIA, which came first: the assignment or romance?"

"You were dishonest, Li."

"The scorned lover act doesn't suit you, Zack. Look at this objectively before you answer. When we were at the symphony, was your first intention to marry me or to bed me?"

"That's not a fair question."

"Not fair, he says. Don't you see what has happened? It is your ego that is injured, not your love life. I very much want to be your friend." She offered a sincere smile while holding out her hand.

"Please."

He took it grudgingly.

"Right. Friends it is."

She stepped closer to hug his arm. "See, that didn't hurt so much. Now if you would please lead me over to the coffee pot, I need some very strong coffee before I can make a coherent report."

On the way to the dining room, Zack and Li-Hwa found Kornikov and Tatyana waiting in the hallway. Smiling, Tatyana handed Li-Hwa a small package she was keeping in her purse. She took it out and handed Li-Hwa a small silver box wrapped with white tissue and a red bow.

"Am I supposed to open this now?"

Kornikov nodded.

As she began to unwrap it she said, "I hope this is a pair of earrings, even if I don't have many opportunities to wear them."

"No need to worry, *Captain*," the Colonel grinned. "You'll find there are many social gatherings in Moscow where you will be wearing civilian clothes."

Li-Hwa slowly lifted the lid. Her eyes opened wide. "Does this mean what I think it does… what I hope it does?"

"It does *Major* Zaranova. Let me be the first to congratulate you. I only have one favor to ask that has no bearing on your promotion. It would please Tatyana and me if you'd accept a transfer and work directly with us."

"Work with you?"

"Yes."

Tatyana whispered to her husband, "Misha, do I sense déjà vu? Remember the pro-motion my uncle gave you forty years ago at the Potemkin Club? Let's hope she doesn't offer a hackneyed toast like you did."

Li-Hwa beamed with pride and winked. "As my first official act as a Major in our glorious army, I shall toast the CIS-KGB!"

Everyone laughed except Zack, who was hopelessly confused.

AFTER DINNER the group gathered in the King Arthur Suite and spoke of the similarities and differences each of their countries was encountering. A common thread was elderly, female custodial workers.

"I have a theory on that," Hoffman said. "Inasmuch as we all have experienced espionage, I ask you: who would have the best chance of infiltrating sensitive areas with complete impunity. The answer I come up with is a kindly, gray-haired old lady with an engaging personality."

"I agree," Winstanly said. "And who else would have that kind of access to strategic areas once the workers had left for home?"

After Kornikov had gone over the events of the day, he closed the proceedings by going around the table and personally thanked each attendee for their participation.

"This is only the first of gatherings we will have during the coming months," he said. "As for tonight, those of you who wish to stay in the hotel are most welcome to do so. But should you decide to start home this evening, we ask that you keep Tatyana advised of your plans. She will assist in making proper security arrangements."

"I believe we are all in agreement," Winstanly said. "If any of us have new events, or come across any new information about the spacecraft and visitors, we must pass it along immediately over secured lines."

Everyone nodded. In agreement

"Two final items," added Kornikov. "Dr. Peters will fly to Washington tomorrow morning with the minutes of our proceedings. And I propose starting the custom of giving a gift to the person who travels farthest to a special gathering. Inasmuch as we didn't have anyone with a sixteen-light-year journey as of yet, Dr. Peters seems to be our first winner."

Tatyana stood, and turned toward Zack. "My husband and I feel it would be fitting to send Dr. Peters home in grand style. And so I've taken the liberty of canceling your commercial flight to Washington tomorrow."

"That's works for me, Major," he said. "I'll send the information to the White House encrypted, and gladly accept your implied offer of a four-day relaxing cruise back home."

"That isn't exactly what we had in mind," she smiled. "But we do have a way to shorten that tedious six-hour commercial flight to one that only takes two hours—our new supersonic Tupelov 244. It was scheduled to make its inaugural flight from Moscow to New York the day after tomorrow. But with some diplomatic schedule tweaking between our respective foreign ministries, the flight will leave Moscow tomorrow morning with two intermediate stops— London, to pick you up, and Washington to set you back down. So with great pleasure I present you with a complimentary first class ticket."

Zack beamed. "Wow! The only thing I can come up with is thank you very much. You've made me one happy camper. Would you believe I have a colored drawing of the T-244 hanging over my desk in Washington?"

"Then you won't miss the shipboard swimming pools and the midnight buffets?" Kornikov asked.

"Not on your life!" Zack laughed. "This is wonderful. Win is the only person who knows that I'm a devotee to jet aircraft. So if you'll indulge me in showing off, the TU-244 is the world's first jet to use cryogenic fuel; meaning its fuel is super-cooled. Its range is 6,000 miles and it can carry 320 souls. It's 290 feet long, with a wingspan of 180 feet, and it can fly at Mach 2.1. That's about 1,350 miles per hour---a little over 2,100 kilometers, for those keeping score."

"I bow to your encyclopedic knowledge of the specifications Zack," chuckled Tatyana, "because only a man would care about such things. You'll leave the hotel at 1100 hours. I'll give you more details later. More good news is that Washington International has granted us a one-time-only landing authorization. That shows you how trifles like interstellar incursions can cut red tape."

"My congratulations old chap," Winstanly said. "But let me ask a personal favor. I'd like you to take along a personal note to your President."

"I'd be happy to, Winn. If anyone else wants to do the same, just drop it off at the front desk by 1030 hours."

"And unless you object, Zack," Tatyana said, "Major Zaranova and I will escort you to the airport."

"Being accompanied by two of your army's most engaging women is too tempting to turn down. And Majors, to boot—how could any man resist? And if the two of you could each take an arm as we walk through the terminal, I'd love to see the looks from all the envious men."

AS EVERYONE WAS SAYING their goodbyes, Li-Hwa cornered Zack.

"Well, Dr. Peters, you've had quite a busy day considering all the various surprises you've had. Do you think you could handle one more?"

"Not unless I won Britain's national lottery. I'll be content to head up to my room, turn on TV and take a long, hot bath—taking full advantage of Misha's complimentary room service."

"That sounds pleasant," she laughed. "But I was thinking more along the lines of sleeping arrangements. How would you like to share your room with a Russian Army Major?"

"Even if Tatyana agreed, her husband would have me taken out and shot."

Li-Hwa punched him in the ribs. "Look at this in a business-like manner. With all the security issues at stake—and given my responsibilities in that area—I'd have to insist on putting a body guard in your room until tomorrow morning."

She took a step closer and began playing with a button half-way down his shirt. "And since I'm trained in hand to hand combat, it seems I would be the perfect choice."

"Believe me when I say I'm there's nothing I'd like better," Zack sighed. "But I have a special relationship starting up in Washington. Otherwise...."

"I can handle rejection, Zack," she said, "but look at it this way: you have a promising future that promises a cozy home, warm fireplace, a wife to grow old with as well as children, grandchildren and a dog or cat.

"But what are the odds are of my having such a future? In the Army, they lie somewhere between poor and nonexistent."

"You have what every woman wants, Li---youth, beauty, and intelligence. You're also hard as nails yet tender. You're a world traveler with a body men would die for. What else could a man want?"

"If memory serves, most men have only one thing on their mind and it isn't intelligence."

"Point taken. Look, I'd be lying through my teeth if I said I hadn't given some thought to our being together tonight, especially with the bonus of my being off the hook with the fireplace and dog thing."

"Okay—here's another less exciting plan. I'll stay in your room and sleep on the couch. You have my word on that. And I promise to be back in my room by 0600 so there is more than enough time for breakfast and getting you to the airport."

"Let me take a guess at where your room is."

"You get one guess."

He raised an eyebrow and pointed. "Straight through that connecting door and in the adjoining room."

"Dr. Peters, you have the makings of a wonderful secret agent."

"Okay...here's the plan. You sleep on the couch and promise to be out no later than six o'clock tomorrow morning. Agreed?"

"Let's shake on it."

She offered her hand, but kept her crossed fingers well-hidden inside her pretty head.

Chapter 20

AS MUCH AS HE APPRECIATED the arrangements to send him off in style, Zack found his supersonic flight to Washington to be disappointing.

Back in the old days at the CIA, Doug Farholm had once told him, "When it comes to SST flights, I find getting on and getting off are the most enjoyable parts of the flight." Zack easily understood the rush of excitement boarding one of those technological marvels, but thought his old friend was surprisingly impressed by the marvel of technology that the supersonic transport represented. But after being cooped up in a 'sardine can' for a couple of hours, he just wanted to get off.

The one saving grace was that the trip was amazingly fast, and he was back in Washington in no time at all. His first order of business was to pick-up Muffins, get a wet face welcome, and unpack. On the Metro ride from the airport the thought even passed his mind to take the phone off the hook. With his luck, it would be an urgent call from Priscilla at the White House begging him accept another exotic assignment.

By the time he arrived home he'd quite forgotten the precaution he'd wanted to take, and as it turned out he was glad it slipped his mind. He would have missed Sandy's call from Puerto Rico telling him how much she missed him, and that she and Bertie were looking forward to hearing all about London. He bemoaned his disappointing flight, discreetly omitting the two stunning Russian Army majors who escorted him to the boarding gate.

Sandy had exciting news to tell him. She'd not only received the Puerto Rico News Broadcaster of the Year award, but San Juan's top TV station had approached her about becoming a news co-anchor. Neither was a big surprise to Zack. Bertie had praised her spectacular two-year career in radio, and she'd already gained a reputation for giving top-notch commentaries.

Their conversation soon moved to more personal things like food likes and dislikes and unforgettable first loves. When Zack's political leanings became apparent, Sandy bet him a night on the town she could win him over to her party before the next election.

After hanging up the phone he glanced at his watch. It was nearly midnight. They'd chatted like teenagers for nearly two hours, and there was no doubt about it. Sandy was a wonderful woman, one of the best things that had happened to him in a long time.

He was half way to the bedroom when he heard a knock at the door. He knew it must be a tenant, since anyone else would have had to buzz from the lobby. He walked over to the door and looked through the peep hole. His first inclination was to throw cold water on his face, since what he saw was impossible. He stood frozen in place until a voice broke the silence.

"Are you just going to stand there with your mouth hanging open, or are you going to open the door and let me in?"

He stepped back and ran his hands through his hair. Then he took a deep breath and opened the door.

Sandy stepped into the room, paused to kiss him on the cheek, and then strode across the room as if intimately familiar with the surroundings. She walked directly to one of the wingback chairs beside the fireplace, draped her jacket across one of them, and sat down. Smoothing her skirt, she crossed her legs in a provocative manner and pursed her lips.

"This isn't right," he said from the doorway. "No—it's damn impossible."

He closed the door and leaned back against it. "Didn't you just call from Arecibo? Didn't we just have a two-hour conversation? Now, wait a minute—admit it. You were here in Washington all along, right?"

She held up a hand and said, "Whoa, big fellow. Let's keep it to one question at a time. I thought you and I agreed we couldn't wait until getting together again? Well, just relax and enjoy the moment. Why not come over and show me how glad you are to see me?"

A dozen thoughts flashed through his mind, most of them revolving around how incredibly attractive she was, even more so than he remembered her. She seemed taller, and walked with the self-assurance of a fashion model. The hair, the makeup, the smile—everything was flawless. Including her sinfully snug-fitting sweater. He walked to the other wingback and plopped himself down. "I'm about as relaxed as possible at this 'moment.'"

"Now Zack, I need you to take a big breath and promise not to be alarmed by what I say or do."

"I can't promise anything until you agree that we ended a lengthy phone conversation less than five minutes ago."

"Yes, we did."

"So you were in town all along?"

She held up her hand. "Before we get into any of that, I should first show you something you will find unnerving. Are you ready for it?"

"Maybe after a stiff drink or two. Would you care for one?"

"Not just now, thanks."

He poured three fingers of bourbon and went back to his chair.

Leaning toward him, she took his hand. "Please concentrate on my eyes."

As he did Sandy's features, clothing, and stature morphed into something completely different.

Phil Macaulay said to him, "Well old buddy, how's it hanging?"

Before he could leap out of his seat, Phil changed back to Sandy.

Zack stammered, "My God, you—you're not human!"

"Well...no, actually I'm not. Not technically, anyway. But I'll keep this image and you can keep calling me Sandy if you like. Our ability to change really isn't very difficult. I just examine your thoughts, find someone you can comfortably relate to, and adjust your perceptions."

"So you're not really changing physically? You just have me imagine you're someone I can be at ease with. That's chilling!"

"Now if you look me over with a critical eye, you'll notice a difference in my appearance by seeing Sandy as being more beautiful, taller, with larger breasts and so on." She morphed once again but only slightly. "This is what the real Sandy in Puerto Rico actually looks like—attractive, but not what one would consider as glamorous. You have a saying: beauty is in the eye of the beholder."

Zack was surprised how quickly he was adjusting to what was the strangest situation any human had ever experienced. "I don't mean to sound harebrained but I'm actually waiting for you to say, 'take me to your leader'."

"A classic science fiction phrase," she said. "I find that humorous."

"It's probably not, really. That's my ill-at-ease humor. More nerves than humor, and funny only by random chance. You did say to call you Sandy?"

"Whatever you're comfortable with. If you prefer, I can become someone else—whoever you'd like."

He shook his head. "No, Sandy is just fine. But you said something about my not being alarmed."

"That's because there's no reason to be alarmed. As I said, just relax and enjoy the moment."

"Okay, but I have a favor to ask. If you choose to return to the real you, please don't be a spider. I don't relate well to spiders."

"I knew that. But we aren't spiders. Do you have questions you'd like answers to?"

"Such as…?"

"Questions you feel are too personal to ask in front of the President tomorrow."

Zack looked surprised. "You know about my meeting?"

"Of course, I'm visiting her in the Oval Office."

"You mean after you leave here or tomorrow morning?"

"I mean now. While I'm here with you, I'm also visiting with her."

"My God, you not only can read minds, you can be in two places at the same time? That borders on the supernatural."

"Even more so than you think. Right now I'm speaking with various heads of state around the planet. This should give you an idea of one of many abilities humans can look forward to."

"Then it's actually you and not others like you that are making those visits."

"That's right. No one else is involved. Just me."

Zack got up and walked to the bar all the while shaking his head. "I need another drink. Is there something I can get you, assuming you drink?

"I would like a glass of Chardonnay."

He returned with two glasses. "Sandy, even though it makes no sense, I'm enjoying this visit. And you're a far cry from the way our movie makers portray aliens. Except maybe for the porno films. But I guess all of those fangs and tentacles they use are just to sell the product."

"I can assure you that any aliens with interstellar travel have long passed through their violent stage. Only primitive cultures use pomposity to project dominance to cover up their many inadequacies. Most humans don't pound their chests and roar like gorillas, but you still enjoy strutting around and parading military equipment whenever the opportunity arises."

"You do have a gift of description, Sandy. I'm glad you'll be joining POTUS and me at our meeting."

"You mean the President of the United States? But why does my being there please you?"

"You can imagine the look she'd give me if I tried to convince her that an alien dropped by my place for a chat. Which brings me to another question—visiting with heads of state makes sense. What I don't get is why you'd take the time to visit me."

"This may come as a surprise, but you and some of your closest friends have an important role to play in our visit. To be truthful, there is something about you I feel drawn to personally. If you were familiar with the Korr, as we call our species, you'd understand how inappropriate it was for me to say that. The Korr find it awkward to think outside our group consciousness, even if it involves something of a personal nature. It's not prohibited, it's just irregular."

When Sandy turned aside for the briefest of moments, he knew he had witnessed something rare. She seemed embarrassed. That was illogical, reeking of Class B science fiction films where the aliens start having feelings for a human. He broke the silence.

"Don't worry Sandy, I promise never, ever to report you to your ethics police."

She smiled, and for the first time he felt less inferior to the Korr than he had previously been. "And I am relieved to know you're not a spider."

She smiled and said, "Well, I had toyed with the thought of displaying eight hairy legs."

"Oh no!" he laughed in mock horror.

"But to be serious, it's important for us to blend in with any species we visit, so we assume various forms. In your case we use a form that suggests a department store mannequin. It provides a perfect scaffolding to camouflage ourselves while engaging in one-on-one encounters."

With that, she morphed into a featureless human without hair or gender. "To get from this to Sandy," she said becoming Sandy again, "we use your mind as a projector, and the form I just showed you becomes our projection screen. It's a simple matter of examining your thoughts to find someone you're comfortable with."

She became Bertram Powell and said, "I'm dying for you to tell me how that meeting in London went and whether or not you got lucky." He winked as he reverted to Sandy.

"This is effortless in a one-on-one situation. It gets a tricky when we're in a group and have to deal with more than one individual at the same time. Still, humans aren't as hard as some species. You all see pretty much what you want to see, and not what is actually there. I'm sure at one time or another you've overlooked a person's imperfections."

"When," Zack asked, "will we be on a par with the Korr and perhaps form an alliance?"

"That will never happen. Too many parts of our consciousness don't translate to human perception. But don't take offense. It's not some kind of flaw on your part, it's just that our brains are too dissimilar. Perhaps some day, when humans travel to the stars, you'll run into life forms that will be impossible to communicate with."

Sandy moved closer and took his hand again. "This conversation you and I are having is between us, and it's private. Not to appear rude, but I need to concentrate on the discussions I'm having with some heads of state. So if I sound repetitive, it's all part of speaking with them at the same time and in different languages." She gave him another smile and his hand a gentle squeeze. "But I promise that you're the only one I'll be holding hands with."

She turned aside and began speaking. "In your travels, humans will meet other intelligent species, and to some extent you'll be able to identify with many of them—but only up to a point. In your attempt to have a meaningful dialog, you'll discover that minds of all species are structured differently than yours. As a result, successful communication will often range anywhere from difficult to impossible.

"But don't be discouraged. Humans are unusually intelligent. At some future point you will be able to understand topics like multiple and parallel dimensions, quantum entanglement, folded time, and more.

"At present, your scientists are puzzled why only six percent of matter in the universe is detectable. They speculate the other ninety-four percent is dark matter—the term they've devised to describe something they don't understand. We suggest they look into neutrinos, black holes, neutron stars, failed stars, extra-solar and rogue planets that float free between the stars.

"For the past two million years your brains have become more complex for one purpose only—survival in an environment where predators could outrun and outswim you. You eventually developed skills unique in the animal kingdom—skills such as cunning, conniving, deceit, thievery and treachery. It is true those talents are nothing to be proud of, but they let you stand toe-to-toe with the worst nature could throw at you.

"Now, however, those roles of prey and predator have turned. You have become the predators, and your predatory skills are no longer needed for your survival. They must be excised from your nature before you can become a truly advanced species. But I must warn you that such a thing is easier said than done.

"Over the centuries we tried to help you by introducing mentors. Among these were Plato, Confucius, Socrates, De Vinci, Copernicus and Newton. More recently you've seen Gandhi, Einstein and Sagan. Though effective to a point, they were unable to show you the ills of war, slavery and corruption.

"You must not blame the Korr for the four major calamities that affected Earth over the eons as some of your scientists suggest. The Deccan Traps volcanic eruptions in what is now northern India, for instance. Or the three recent asteroid impacts, one near the present day Yucatan peninsula, another atop a tectonic plate in the Pacific Ocean, and a third in the Indian Ocean. Although they destroyed more than ninety percent of life forms on Earth, this all happened long before our arrival."

Sandy concluded by saying, "I've enjoyed speaking with you. We will meet again. So depending on which time zone you are in, I wish you either a pleasant day, or a good night."

She focused on Zack. Realizing they were alone once again he said, "You have just earned a listing in the *Guinness Book of Records* for multi-tasking. But you must have a hundred other things you need to take care of."

"Thank you for understanding, Zack. I do. But I can still answer your questions."

"On top of the list would be exactly why you came to Earth."

"Two reasons. We will put humans on trial for their stewardship of their planet and each other. We are also busy locating a species to help us with a task we cannot accomplish on our own, something that would allow whatever species we select to share with us in the greatest adventure of all time."

"Considering your abilities and technology, wouldn't it be easier to just change us into whatever you need to accomplish your mission?"

"Yes, we could change any species we choose to. But eventually that species must be able to function on its own, free from outside influence. Try to wrap your mind around the Korr needing assistance to transfer completely out of this universe."

"You can't be serious. Such a thing is—well, it's impossible. There isn't any place else you could transfer to. Beyond the universe lies non-existence."

Sandy shook her head. "There is an infinite array of universes that exist beyond this one. When we have successfully departed, whatever species assisted us will be free to make a similar transfer."

Zack was taken aback. Learning about advanced technologies was one thing, but what Sandy proposed flew in the face of logic. "Why do I get the impression that Earth is in for a disaster or some sort?" he asked warily. "If it is, can you say what it is, and why you require an assisting species?"

"A disaster of the greatest proportions is coming. I'll explain the details as soon as you come to grips with what I've said so far. I can say that there are numerous species with equal technology that are making similar searches throughout the Milky Way. This particular section was allocated to the Korr."

Zack paused for a moment, to collect his thoughts. "Whatever your reason for coming now, my only concern is what happens to us with a guilty verdict?"

"That decision is not entirely ours to make. We will make recommendations, of course. But your fate, along with other species in your situation, lies in the hands of higher authority.

"In your case we might replace humans with a life form orbiting a dying sun. Or we could continue the experiment with other sentient life forms here on Earth."

Zack wrinkled his nose. It seemed that answering one question, she seemed to bring up at least two more. "When you say other sentient life forms, do you mean you've done this already?"

"Yes, we have already made a replacement here on Earth. The first time we let Neanderthals move forward, leaving their Cro-Magnons cousins behind."

"Are you telling me you interfered by holding us back us so the Neanderthals could advance? What happened to them?"

Sandy shrugged. "The study failed. Although the Neanderthals with their larger brains reached your level of technology two thousand years faster than you could manage, they proved far less aggressive in temperament, and never developed the skills needed to manipulate their environment successfully. They lacked a fighting spirit and the ability to make split-second decisions. In short, they were of no use to us. We ended the experiment, backtracked to the Neanderthal-Cro-Magnon split, and let you develop. Fortunately, you hadn't been wiped out by then. The Neanderthals were too mild-mannered—too 'civilized'—to exterminate a species they could tell was intelligent, even one not quite as intelligent as they were."

Zack shook his head. "It's rather demoralizing to find out that we were only second choice. And all because Neanderthals couldn't quite cut it."

Sandy shrugged.

"Can you imagine what that will do to our ego? Some of us believe we killed off the Neanderthals. All the evidence says they disappeared without a trace over a very short period of time."

"Actually, the keener skills of the Cro-Magnon simply let them out-hunt and out-fish the Neanderthals during a particularly harsh time on your planet. You were too busy finding food, building shelters, and evading predators to add genocide to your to-do list. Now if you don't mind, I will leave you. When we meet in the Oval Office tomorrow you will discover we have more important things to discuss than the Stone Age."

Sandy kissed his cheek and asked, "Was that appropriate?"

"That was nice but I'm wondering if anything else is going to happen."

"I know what you mean Zack. That is for you and Sandy to work on."

And then she was gone.

Chapter 21

THE VISITOR HAD NO DIFFICULTY getting through the White House front gate security, and walked unchallenged into the anteroom of the Oval Office.

"The Secretary of State is here to see you, Madam President," an aide announced. "I'm afraid I failed to put him on your schedule."

"That's alright," answered Jordis Brandstadt. "Send him right in." She wheeled around from behind her desk to greet the party she knew would not be the Secretary.

"Thank you for seeing me on such short notice," said the visitor. "I hope our meeting last night wasn't too unnerving."

"No, except for lying awake half the night after meeting my first extra-terrestrial in my night clothes, I'd say I did pretty well. But I guess the dignity train had already left the station."

"Will Dr. Peters be attending?"

"Yes, I expect him momentarily. I didn't know how long your visit would last, so I cleared my schedule for the rest of the morning. Please sit down. We can talk until he arrives."

"May I ask how long you have been using a wheelchair?"

"A few years ago, when I was the vice-president I arrived in in Windsor, Ontario to sign a treaty with the Mexican president and the Canadian Prime Minister on behalf of the United States. The moment I stepped down from my helicopter the shooting broke out, and I found myself in the middle of a firefight. A bullet struck me, and the rest is history."

The intercom buzzed. "Madam President, Dr. Peters just arrived. Would you like him to wait while you're with the Secretary?"

"No—send him right in. And hold all of my calls."

Zack stepped in, nodded to the visitor and said, "Good morning Madam President. Sorry I'm late."

"No problem. Make yourself comfortable. I understand you and our special guest already have met."

"Yes, we have."

The visitor nodded to Zack and turned to address the President.

"As I explained to you and other heads of state last night, we are visitors from another star system. The reason for those multiple meetings was because our message is not for any single nation, but for everyone."

"Are there any limits or guidelines governing what we can or can't ask you?" asked Brandstadt.

"No. I'll answer most any question," the visitor replied. "But let me say from the start that we are neither missionaries nor explorers. To verify my credentials you need only listen to a message that is being transmitted from space."

It handed the president a sheet of paper. "These are the coordinates on the celestial sphere indicating the location of a fleet of spacecraft, as well as the radio frequency that telescopes can monitor."

"You have more than one ship?" Zack interjected. "We were able to confirm only one, though we thought there was the possibility of a second."

"There are three."

"If you don't mind, I need to call the Russian president."

"Of course," the visitor nodded.

The president handed Zack the sheet of paper and pointed to a telephone on her desk.

"Zack, while I'm doing that, I want you to call Bertram Powell at Arecibo. Use line two or three, and give him this information. When he determines which telescopes can observe the location, have him contact those observatories, record what they hear, and have the results sent to here as soon as possible."

*****

UPON ENDING her conversation with the Russian president, Brandstadt turned to Zack and their otherworldly guest, who were sitting on two facing couches in front of her desk.

"President Primakov said his telescopes need a bit longer before the targets rise above their horizon. He also said that the Kornikov's were both there, and wanted to send their regards."

One of her private lines rang, and she activated the headset. "Bertie? Yes, it's good to hear from you too. You have? Wonderful—just give me a second to turn on the speaker before you pipe it through."

She pressed a button, and a burst of static filled the room. "Bertie—are you still there?"

"Yes I am," Powell replied. "Now—I'll play the recording of what we picked up. So far nobody's been able to make heads or tails of it."

"*Al ciuj nacioj sur la planedo Tero. Saluton de la Korranoj. Ciu nacio cesigu ciujn agojn de milita kaj politika agreso. Ciuj militistaroj kaj politikistaroj en eksterlando tuj revenu al sia hejmlando. Kiu nacio ne obeos, tiu atendu tujan reagon. Ni alvenos post ok semajnoj.*"

"What in the world is that mish-mash?" the president asked. "It sounds a little like Portuguese. Or maybe something Scandinavian."

The visitor said, "Let me explain. We didn't want to appear to be showing favoritism, so we thought it inappropriate to use one language alone. And because the message is intended for the entire world, we chose one that is known by a segment of every country's population."

"I think I know what it is," Zack said. "It's Esperanto."

"That's very good, Zack. At first we found it surprising that your world has never felt the need to have effective communication between its people. But I'm sure you've surmised the reason. Some governments simply don't want its citizens being exposed to outside philosophies."

The visitor placed a device on the president's desk and said, "This will provide you with a translation of that message."

The message repeated, this time in English: 'To all nations on planet Earth, the Korr send you greetings. From this moment forward you will cease all political aggression and military activities. All deployed military and political personnel must immediately return to their country of origin. Any nation not complying will meet with the harshest of consequences. We will arrive in eight weeks.'

The visitor added, "The term political aggression includes political prisoners," the visitor added. "Every person being detained for anything other than a violent criminal act must be released within twenty-four hours, and be immediately returned to their country of origin, while suffering no additional harm. All costs related to such releases and transfers are to be borne by the country detaining them.

"All military and civilian hardware, supplies, and currency being held and-or located in another country must be left there and not returned to the country of origin. The only exception is the equipment needed to return military and civilian personnel to their place of origin."

"That sounds all well and good," Zack said at last. "But realistically it would take months to pull something like that off."

"Under normal circumstances you would be correct," replied the visitor. "But the moment we carry out a first retribution for an infringement you will be amazed at just how fast the task will be accomplished."

"I'm sure there will be attacks on some troops and civilians the moment they begin leaving," Zack protested. "We experience this whenever we begin withdrawing our forces from a country."

"I assure you anyone taking part in any such action will be not present a problem. One more item that was not in the transmission is that every head of state will make a radio or television broadcast to their citizens on June 21st at Noon, local time. The broadcast will include all of the information given to you today and the translated message from space, and no political, religious, or social commentaries may be included in those broadcasts. Finally, you will meet all of these conditions within thirty days of the broadcasts."

"Are we expected to read one of your statements or will be allowed to write our own?" Brandstadt said stiffly. "And do you have any suggestions on dealing with those who choose not to believe the message and simply ignore it?"

"You may adjust the content as you like," replied the visitor, "so long as you include the all of following:

"First, the purpose of our visit is to put humanity on trial for its stewardship of the planet and to each other. Second, the trial will begin eight weeks after the broadcasts, at a location yet to be determined. Third, if found innocent the Korr will depart and leave you to your own affairs. If found guilty, humans will be eliminated. Fourth— "

"Hold on there just a minute," Brandstadt snapped." Did I hear you correctly? If you find us guilty you'll get rid of all of us?"

"Well...yes."

"And just what gives you the authority to stick your nose in our affairs, order us around, and put us on trial?"

"We do so because we are able to do so. Quoting a popular human expression, 'might makes right'. To continue—Fourth, the verdict will be without appeal. Fifth, denial and resistance by individuals or countries is of no consequence."

Brandstadt covered her face with her hands, took a deep breath and massaged her temples with her fingertips. "All this has the earmarks of a bad dream," she muttered. "A nightmare."

"Do you have a name or a title we should use in addressing you?" asked Zack. "Saying that you are merely a guest or a visitor seems—well, it seems so impolite and impersonal."

"It makes no difference to us. Most languages have problems pronouncing our name, so choose any name you wish. The closest sound to it for your tongue would be *Korr* with a quavered 'R'. And Madam President, in regard to your bad dreams and referring to our arrival as a nightmare, I would just point out that humans have had 25,000 years to wake up from your early misconceptions and primitive ways. I assure you that there are numerous inhabited planets that, unlike yours, chose the sensible path of discarding barbarism."

"As a scientist, I'm extremely curious in knowing how many of those planets have technologically advanced societies," Zack said.

"In your galaxy, perhaps one hundred million," the visitor said. "Curiously, until now we had invariably found that aggressive species like yours would have driven themselves to extinction by the time they have attained your level."

"Then I'll take that as a positive," Brandstadt said. "The fact that we're still alive and kicking is an indication of our redeeming qualities."

"Actually, nothing could be further from the truth," the visitor said blandly. "You have survived this long only because you've remained uncritical of the occult, mysticism, and superstition."

"And just where is that line of reasoning heading?" Brandstadt demanded.

The visitor continued, "It is common for emerging societies to explain away the mysteries of nature, especially birth and death, through superstition and the occult. What we find rare are societies that continue on with them once science has explained the natural world. By integrating superstition into your society you have for the present delayed extinction."

"Just one moment," Brandstadt bristled. "This is still my office and you are still my guest. If your reasoning is headed in the direction I think it is you can stop right now. Your innuendoes are impolite and distasteful."

"We have no reason to insult you, Madam President. But may I ask a question? Would you feel the need to apologize to a culture that still believed the world is flat? Of course not—they have only made assumptions based on their own limited observations. But if you are displeased with our interpretation of a similar conviction, or are annoyed by our visit, I cannot give you solace."

"Your callousness is irritating and infuriating," Brandstadt steamed. "I would think a technologically superior society that has mastered space travel would spend time developing a more sympathetic nature. Do you have any more demands to issue today?"

"There is another item with regard to your television announcement. We suggest that Dr. Peters offer the media a briefing just before you go on the air. His scientific background makes him a splendid candidate."

"Zack?"

"Sure. I'll be *happy* to do it."

He turned to the visitor, "I'll need some background information before I respond. The media will have lots of whos, whats, whens, wheres, and whys."

"And as you can see, I've been jotting down a number of questions of my own," the president snarled. "Would it be acceptable for me to record your answers?"

"That would be acceptable."

Brandstadt continued, "Personal feelings aside, I feel ethically bound to voice concerns about your safety. There are those who will hold you responsible for the crisis you are causing, who may make attempts on your life."

"I appreciate the warning, but your concern is unnecessary. Should my present physical form be damaged or destroyed, I myself would not be injured."

"And why is that?" Zack asked.

"You can no more harm us than someone on television can be killed by destroying a television set. But should it happen—though I can't envision how—I would be unaffected. Are we immortal? To your way of thinking we probably are."

"Would you run that by us one more time," Zack asked. "You mean the creature we see is not immortal, but the entity we are in the room with might be?"

"Perhaps I can clarify things by making a transformation," said the visitor. It morphed from the Secretary of State into a naked, sexless, and featureless humanoid.

"What you see here is an entity we call a klatt. As you can see, it is bland and lacks any distinguishing characteristics. But this is a life form we create to foster better communication with the species we visit."

"So on a planet whose inhabitants have a different shape than us, a klatt would be created to match those life forms?"

"Yes. On Earth, we appear as bipedal, standing upright, having binocular vision and opposable thumbs. Actually, in addition we also have a hidden marsupial-like pouch."

The visitor slipped a hand inside a barely visible opening below its navel, removed a golf-ball-sized object, and held it out for inspection.

"I assume that is a device to gather, analyze and store data," Zack said.

"Not at all. We have a physical body as you do, but it's different in size and shape."

The visitor returned the object to its pouch.

"Then where is the real you?" the President asked.

"For now that question must go unanswered."

"So it's fair to say you read our minds," she said.

"Not exactly, although there are sentient beings with that ability. Most can only read the minds of its own species, however." The visitor began to morph again.

"Perhaps you will be more comfortable with the image I appeared to you in last evening."

"That would be fine," Brandstadt said. Jack nodded in agreement.

"I'd like to begin by asking questions and jotting down answers," she said.

*****

FOR THE NEXT HOUR the visitor freely answered the President's questions. Then, suddenly, it stood to leave.

"I will be in contact with you over the coming weeks," the visitor said, walking toward the door. It pointed to the device on the President's desk. "That will enable you to summon me. You will need only to depress the two bars simultaneously."

"I'm sure Zack or I will have any number of questions. But right now," said the president, hoping to salvage something from the visit, "I apologize for being abrupt with you. Knowing us as you do, you must understand how overwhelming your visit is, as well as the challenges you present to many of our belief systems. As to your living arrangements, I can assist you in finding a safe place."

"You needn't be concerned. I can always find a place." It turned to Zack and said, "I recall another of your sayings: Where does a four-hundred pound gorilla sleep?"

Despite himself, Zack found himself smiling. "Anywhere it wants," he nodded.

"Thank you for your concerns. I bid you both good day."

And in a flash, the visitor was gone.

For a moment the two stared at the door, which was still closed. She was the first to speak. "Aside from being put on edge, I admit he made me feel somewhat at ease."

"Excuse me but would you say that again?" he asked.

"You mean about his making me feel at ease?"

"He? I saw a woman."

Zack shook his head and exhaled very slowly.

"That means the Korr can make us see whatever they want us to see," he said at last. "Talk about a perfect disguise."

"In a group of people I assume everyone would see him differently," the president nodded. "They'd be able to come and go as they please, with nobody being the wiser. In your press briefing and in my address, I see no need to hold back anything. Especially their ability to disguise themselves."

"One other thing," said Zack. "I'd feel uncomfortable mentioning the International Space Station situation. Well, that and the dismissive references to any of our beliefs. It might push some people over the edge, and maybe cause others to attack anyone who seemed to be different, or acting strange."

"Lord knows we have enough strange people around. The last thing we need is a modern-day Salem witch trial. Not when we're on trial for our very existence, ourselves. And I agree about ISS. There are too many questions and not enough answers. Besides, Primakov urged me to keep the ISS situation under wraps for now. It would be in his best interest, especially since the hijackers seem to be Russian."

"I can't think of any way to avoid the hijacking if someone brings it up," Zack protested.

"I can't imagine any of them have heard about it yet. But if someone puts you on the spot, just say it's an ongoing investigation and you can't comment."

"What about getting a hand-out or pamphlet printed to distribute at my briefing? With everything bouncing around inside my head, I'll never have time to cover everything before your address."

"If you jot down some info I'll take care of the brochures. And if anyone asks about the trial, just say the date and venue are not firm yet."

"Well I guess that's all we can do for now."

Brandstadt sighed. "I want to start throwing some notes together for me. If you need anything call me on the private line."

"Thanks, I will."

As he started for the door she placed a hand on his arm. "One more thing," she said, smiling sheepishly. "Try to find some new television personality—someone sharp and intelligent, warm and fuzzy. We need someone people can relate to as we get closer to our trial. Assuming, of course, that we're allowed to have media coverage."

"I doubt we'll have a swarm of people vying to be put on the spot like that."

"Precisely. I don't want one of our standard commentators reporting on this. They couldn't help but drag their own personal baggage into it, not to mention their personal spin."

Zack nodded.

"When last I spoke to Bertie," the president continued, "he mentioned an outstanding young lady in San Juan; Virginia something-or-other. She might be perfect for the job. He also said you and she had started up a relationship. Maybe the two you can convince her to come to Washington for an interview."

"That would be Virginie LaPlage. And I agree with Bertie. She's a fine young woman."

"If she works out she'll be our exclusive TV representative, with her own news show from now through the trial."

"I'll give her a call and get things started."

"Let her know that we'll cover any travel expenses. And we'll double her present salary and toss in any benefits she can think of."

"And before you go, please take a minute to explain that 13th zodiac constellation. Just give me your word you'll keep my interest under your hat. The last thing I need is for the opposition to discover I'm an astrology nut."

"It's really not complicated. From our viewpoint the Sun and planets appear to drift through the 12 classic zodiac constellations over the course of a year. That's just one misperception. Most of those bodies actually move through a 13th constellation astrologers probably wish they didn't. That's because 12 constellations fit so comfortably into our 12-month calendar, and so an astrologer will always find the Sun in one of them. But with that 13th constellation muddying up the waters, fortune tellers wish it wasn't so."

"What's the other misconception?"

The Sun doesn't spend 30 days in each zodiac constellation as horoscopes show. That's because the constellations aren't the same size. While the Sun usually spends only three days in Scorpio, it can take up to forty-four days to get through Virgo."

"That is an eye opener. So, what's the name of this troublesome constellation?"

"Ophiuchus."

"And when is the Sun in Ophee…what-ever-you-call-it?"

"From November 30th through December 17th. And it's pronounced oh'-fee-you-cuss. In mythology Ophiuchus was a healer and sometimes thought of being the very first physician."

"This gets better by the minute. With my birthday being on the first of December, I should be an Ophiuchan when all along I thought I was a Scorpio."

Zack nodded adding, "Here's an off-the-wall idea. Why not have a bumper sticker made up for your limo reading 'Ophiuchan and Proud.' Just don't tell anyone I gave you the idea. I'm supposed to be a scientist."

Brandstadt replied, "That's one hell of an idea; but I'm thinking along the lines of having three printed up; one for the limo and the other two for Marine One and Air Force One."

Chapter 22

ZACK SAT IN THE MAIN LOBBY of Washington International Airport working a crossword puzzle and waiting for Sandy's arrival from Puerto Rico. He'd purposely left the condo early to get there an hour before Sandy's flight in case he was delayed in traffic or trying to find a parking spot.

He passed the time by the world's least expensive amusement, people watching. Over the years he found most air travelers fell into clear-cut groups. The most obvious were vacationers, or military personnel going home with a smile or returning to their unit with a frown. The easiest were old men with young women who were probably not their secretaries.

Then there were some visiting a seriously ill friend or family member; perhaps one who was dying. They usually sat alone, dressed in fairly subdued attire and wearing a somber expression., occasionally looking up to check on their departure time. It was always the same: they lacked books, newspapers, computer tablets or anything to detract from the seriousness of their journey.

Newlyweds on a honeymoon were easiest, with their new clothes and pieces of confetti lingering on a shoulder or in their hair. Trying their best not to stand out, they would try not to blush or offer playful elbows jabs, doing their best to act like old married couples.

Then there were those entering the service carrying duffle bags and sporting close a cut haircut in the hope of avoiding the inevitable from boot camp barbers. They often held hands with a lover whose eyes were red from tears.

He put down the puzzle when his communicator rang.

"Peters."

"Greetings old buddy. It's Bertie."

"Well this certainly is a first—calling me without trying to reverse the charges. Where are you and how are you and what are you up to that is street legal?"

"I'm standing in the telescope control room and doing as well as can be expected for an old fart. Did you make it to the airport yet?"

"I'm here right now, waiting for Sandy's flight to get in. I got here early in case they picked up a hefty tail wind. Thankfully, the airline predicts an on-time arrival."

"Good thinking. After we got to San Juan and found that her flight was on time she wanted to be dropped off at departures on a slow roll so we could high-tail it back to Arecibo."

"Why the rush? You expecting anything special?"

"That we are. We're waiting for a call from Carlos Flusher at Cerro Pachon."

"Déjà vu! I've been wondering if his new Chilean tech crew was still complaining about the long trek up the mountain to the telescopes. Be sure to say hello for me the next time you two speak."

"I always do. When he and I spoke last night it was obvious he was really pumped after getting a Telex from the Gamma Ray Orbiting Observatory reporting a heftier than usual Gamma ray burst. He wants to tune it in when it clears his eastern horizon. At that altitude, it could be any time now."

"So why all the fuss? All GRBs are huge and outshine the Sun by a million-fold. I'm sure the gang over at GROO is reporting at least one a month."

"He swears this one may be registering a billion times solar."

"That's one hell of a bright puppy. I trust you have its sky coordinates?"

"Yes and you may want to be sitting down when I give them to you."

"Come on Bertie, give me a break. How come every time you and Flusher get talking it ends up being about some Earth-shattering event like finding out Dark Matter is made of dark chocolate? Don't you guys ever have a normal observing session?"

"Very funny—but you'll probably need a handkerchief as I let you in on a sinus-clearing set of coordinates. Grab a pencil and here goes, Right Ascension of 4 hours, 15 minutes, 16 seconds; declination is minus 7 degrees, 39 minutes, 10 seconds. Are they starting to drain yet?"

"Hold on a minute—that's the location of 40 Eridani. Can you tell me anything else?"

"I would if I could but Carlos and I have to wait until 40 Eri rises above our eastern horizons."

"With the difference in longitude, won't you pick it up first?"

"No---he's on top of a mountain and will pick it up the moment it clears the horizon. That's a good hour before I can—for the most part, our telescope points straight up with just a little wiggle room. But our thousand-foot wide dish will give us a lot more detail."

"Bertie, even though I know the answer I still want to run it by you. What are the odds of that GRB, the incoming spacecraft and 40 Eri sitting in almost the same spot in the sky?"

"Probably a bazillion to one. But for now, I have to get my rear in gear. I'll give you a ring once I've heard from Flush."

"Before you run Bertie, thanks for talking Sandy into coming up here for the interview."

"No problem. Once Jordis explained why she needed her, I—"

"Just a second. How long have you and the leader of the free world been on a first name basis? Is there something you should be telling me, my friend?"

"Buddy boy, what goes on in Washington *stays* in Washington. Can I help it if I'm a chick magnet? Oh, and have you picked up Sandy's gift yet?"

"I got it an hour ago and can't wait to see the look on her face when she sees it. I also told her a job in DC would certainly sweeten her portfolio."

"Absolutely. But I'm sure it was the personal call from the White House that cinched the deal. We'll, I have to scramble. I'll catch you on the flip side."

"Will do. Bye-bye, Bertie."

WHEN HE HEARD the announcement for Sandy's flight arrival, Zack walked over to the baggage claim area to see which carousel her bags would be on, and continued to the escalator that brought down the arriving passengers.

As she came into sight he held a sign over his head that read: "Washington Welcomes Virginie LaPlage". It was upside down.

She stepped off the escalator smiling, and shook her head.

"You are a nut," she said, and gave him a kiss and a hug.

"I thought it would be a good way to get your attention. I got the idea from an old girlfriend."

"That better not be old as in age." As they walked to the baggage area she asked, "Can you believe how fast everything is happening? First, I get your call urging me to make an on-the-spot decision to move to Washington in a few days. A half an hour later, after a call from Bertie urging me to do so, I get a personal call from none other than the President of the United States. I have to tell you, that was one hell of a rush."

She pointed out her luggage as it rounded a corner and came into view. "There—the big tan one with wheels and a yellow ribbon on the handle."

"I think the President wanted you to know how important it was to have you here in Washington." Zack grabbed the bag as it was passing by, and the two of them started toward the exit.

"Well, it worked. How many people do you know who could close up an apartment, put their favorite car in the world in storage, and then pack and ship everything in a day and a half? I'm afraid to look in the mirror because I know I grew a grey hair or two. Don't you think it's appropriate that I receive some kind of recognition, maybe an award?"

"Absolutely. I'll make it a point to see that you get it in spades before the day is out."

"I just love it when you talk naughty."

Soon they arrived at the street entrance. "I'll leave you for a couple of minutes and get your wheels," said Zack. "I hope you don't mind if it isn't this year's model."

"You know I'm easy. As long as it has a loud horn and a rear view mirror, I'll be happy."

A few minutes later, Zack pulled up in a 1980 Triumph TR7 1500. Sandy punched the air and shouted.

"Yes!"

He handed her the keys and registration. "It's all yours. If you want it, that is."

"If? Do owls poop through their feathers? Wow! It's really mine?" She hopped again and clasped her face in her hands.

"English racing green with a tan rag top. Now I understand why Bertie told me to ship everything and only bring a small bag. That's all that will fit in it. Oh, Zack, I'm the happiest gal in the whole world."

"It's leased with an option to buy, in the event we talk you into staying here after your assignment is over."

"I have a better idea," she said. "I'll just win the lottery so I can keep this in Washington and mine in San Juan to use on my trips to see Bertie. After all, he's very dear to me and I could never be away from him for long."

Zack put her suitcase in the trunk. "I feel the same way. Seeing him again after so many years only reminded me how much I care for him. Okay—hop in and we'll get going. Do you want me to drive?" he smiled.

"What do you think?" she laughed, scurrying to the driver's side. She paused just long enough to run her hand over the smooth finish on the hood.

"If you didn't eat on the flight we can grab a bite on the way into town."

"With the bumpy weather I had just peanuts and a Bloody Mary or two," she replied. "You know, there is a place in town I want to try out some time. It got a good review in the cabin magazine. It's called Restaurante d'Argentine. Ever hear of it?"

"I've driven by it and promised myself I'd get in there some day. Word has it they serve a mean steak. While you're settling in, I'll call for a reservation for tonight."

"I hope you dance. The article said it's a hot spot for Washingtonians who enjoy great food and Latin-American music."

"An accomplished dancer I am not.

She started the engine. "We'll work on that. Now, give me directions to my new digs."

As they pulled away, Zack took a brochure from his jacket. "Your suite is on the top floor of Watergate II. Let's see what this has to say about it: 'Just thirty minutes from Washington National Airport, you will enjoy sweeping views of the Potomac River. You will luxuriate among antique furnishings and unique amenities that include high definition television, wireless Internet and a marble bath. Relax in either of two fitness centers each with a pool and sauna and be sure to enjoy sophisticated cuisine in our five-star restaurant Le Mediterranean.' "

He pointed to the right. "Follow the freeway signs reading Downtown. Okay, continuing on… 'You are just a few blocks from Kennedy Center, both Bush libraries, and Georgetown.' "

"Sounds awfully pricey."

"Not to worry. The president has a slush fund for contingencies. Just think of it as your tax dollars at work. Which reminds me, she apologized that she couldn't squeeze you into her schedule for a few days. But she gave me time off to be your personal tour guide. I hope you brought your walking shoes."

Chapter 23

BERTRAM POWELL HAD JUST DOZED OFF on his office couch at the Arecibo Radio Astronomical Observatory when his intercom buzzed.

"Powell," he answered.

"It's Dr. Flusher calling from Cerro Pachon on Line Two."

"Thanks, Consuela." He pressed the button on the phone and sat upright, plopping his feet on the cluttered walnut coffee table that sometimes served as his second desk.

"Carlos, my friend? How are things at Gemini South?"

"Hola, Bertie. We're doing just great. Can you hear me alright?"

"Clear as a bell. I wish all of my connections sounded this good. Have you been able to pick up on that new gamma ray burst?

"Not yet. We've been tied up adding software to our 45-foot optical scope and I almost picked up something on 40 Eri."

"And that is…?" Powell picked up his coffee cup from the table and took a sip; finding it cold and bitter, he shuddered briefly, before replacing it on top of the stained report somewhere in the vicinity of a buried coaster.

"I picked up a very small glitch almost touching the star," Flusher said. "At first I thought it was a stellar flare or a prominence, but it wasn't. I even patched-in my new gamma ray bypass filter I affectionately refer to as Opti-Gam in case we'd picked up some odd ball. But it didn't help."

"Why not use your 220-foot radio telescope, Carlos?"

"I did, and that's when things got exciting. I added your flooder to the radio dish. As you predicted, the radio dish did mimic a mirror. And while you said I might obtain ten percent of what a reflecting 'scope would show, it proved to be closer to fifteen. And when we added my Opti-Gam. A bit in tandem with your flooder, we had even better results."

"In tandem you say. Good. I assume the flooder is my device, or are you experimenting with swimming pools?"

"That's just a nickname I came up with."

"I like it. How did you find a processor beefy enough to handle both?"

"I used two processors, one for your flooder and one for my Opti-Gam A bit of tweaking got the effectiveness up to twenty percent. And don't ask me to explain the physics. I'm not sure I understand it yet."

"I'll be able to give you more news in a day or so, soon as I get authorization to give out classified information on 40 Eri."

"Can't wait to get it, Bertie. Now as to what I picked up—the glitch next to the star is increasing in brightness as well as size. It started as a tiny dot, and has now swollen to the size of a pin head held at arm's length. There's also something resembling a spider web spreading out from it, kind of a funnel with the open end facing Earth. You really need to check it out for yourself when 40 Eri is high enough in your sky for the thousand-footer. It should be there in about six hours."

"I'm afraid I won't be able to, Carlos."

"Why?"

"I only have one processor that's operational. I've tried finding a loaner until the other one gets fixed, but the nearest would have to come from the Miami Electronics Institute. To add your Opti-Gam to the mix, I'd need two. I'd have to get one from the Institute and get it flown here and hooked up inside of five hours."

"Is the Miami to San Juan flying time the problem?"

"That, plus the handling time at both airports and the drive time from San Juan. All in all it would take about seven hours, minimum."

"How about chartering a plane help?"

"Wouldn't help. Any way you cut it San Juan International is a two-hour drive, and the Arecibo runway is being re-surfaced."

"Damn—and double damn. Looks like our plans just went south,

Bertie. Wait a minute—couldn't you have Zack pull some strings and get a processor flown down on a military jet out of Naval Air Station Miami?"

"No good. A jet still has to fly into San Juan."

"Not if you got one of those jump jets that take off and land vertically. VTOs they call them. Zack could probably get his hands on one by going through the President."

"Great idea, Carlos! I just have to clear away our picnic tables so the VTO could drop down next to the swimming pool. I'll call Zack right now. Sorry to cut you off, but I need to get hopping on this. I'll get back to you as soon as I can. But before I go, I have a friendly suggestion. When you start writing papers or lecture on our inventions, do try to make them less technical and more audience friendly."

SANDY AND ZACK were just leaving the dance floor of the Argentine Restaurant when his cell phone rang.

"Peters."

"Zack? Bertie. I need you to pull a rabbit out of the hat. Have I caught you at a bad time?"

"Sandy and I are just checking out a restaurant she'd heard about. Would you believe she's teaching me the tango?"

"That's another thing I failed to mention. So far I've been able to thwart her attempts to lure me onto the dance floor. But here's the reason for the call. I desperately need you to get me a VTO jump jet for a couple of hours."

"A jump jet? The ones that go up and down and can land on a quarter?"

"That's the one. I need a computer processor delivered here within five hours—even if you have to get the White House involved. From my two minutes of research, it looks like the Marines have some at the Miami Naval Air Station. They're called AV-8B Harriers."

"I don't suppose you'd settle for something a little more doable?" Zack groaned. "Maybe a two-lane bridge from Miami to San Juan? Anyway hold on a minute, so I can tell Sandy about the problem."

A minute later Zack was back on the line asking for the details.

"I've already left word with the President's aide, but I need you to ride herd of this. It is absolutely imperative I get the processor down here within five hours."

"Consider it done. Is it at NAS Miami?"

"Not yet. I'm having it picked up at the Electronics Institute in Miami and dropped off at the NAS main gate in care of the Duty Officer along with instructions how to get it here."

"Why not use a standard jet from the Arecibo airport? It's less than thirty minutes from you."

"Its runway is being repaved. And using San Juan would take at least seven hours."

"Okay...let's see if I've got this straight. You need a Marine VTO prepped and ready to leave from the Miami Naval Air Station to deliver a processor to you that has yet to be dropped off at the NAS main gate and all within five hours. Is that it?"

"Yes, my friend, that's it."

"Didn't you jump the gun with the President just a bit before you called me?"

"I had to. I knew you could put it all together, Zack. Have it land next to the swimming pool. We'll have every light in the facility turned on as well as headlights of our cars lighting up the landing area."

"What's the crisis Bertie?"

"I got a call from Carlos. He detected a crazy anomaly that is almost touching 40 Eri. His equipment wasn't up to the task but mine is. It's up to me to verify the discovery in case it fades or disappears. That's why I have to observe it tonight when it's in my overhead sky."

"Sounds like you may have hit the jackpot, Bertie. I'll bet you dollars to doughnuts that anomaly is directly tied to the three you-know-what's Mrs. B. will disclose in her address. Am I right?"

"Exactly. I'll get a much better picture than he did using his optical gamma-ray by-pass filter and my flooder – his moniker for my gadget. Each device needs its own processor and I only have one that's working."

Anyway, I'll get back to you as soon as I have the jet's arrival time. And I especially like the part about using car headlights. It has all the earmarks of an espionage war film."

"Thanks, Zack. Tell Sandy the President assures her exclusive trial coverage as well as her very own TV show."

"Speaking of her first show, Sandy wants you and Carlos to be guests. So are you up to prime time TV?"

"I'm ready to start autographing pictures for my soon-to-be admirers."

"I love your modesty, Bertie. Now, go kiss your mirror; you have a big night to get ready for. But first—what's a five-letter word for piebald horse?"

"Pinto."

"You're the man! Sandy and I will be back out there a little later. Bye."

UPON RETURNING to the table, ZACK told Sandy about Powell's dilemma, and his off-the-wall request.

"I'll need to call Bertie back tonight with an ETA," he sighed.

"Well," smiled Sandy, "to commemorate solving of Bertie's dilemma—as well as your accomplishment on the dance floor—I'm ordering two expensive chocolate martinis."

"Thanks. But what are you having?"

"Very funny. In the meantime, while you were gone the President called about my first show and asked if I could be ready for tomorrow night. Of course I said yes. She also said that you'd fill me in on a super-hush-hush story, one that I would be sitting down with a stiff drink."

"I'll start by saying it's the biggest story in history. So big that only a handful of people know about it, including the President, Bertie, Carlos, and me. And now, sooner than you'll find comfortable, you."

"I'm flattered to be such esteemed company, but if I had my druthers I hoped this secluded table was for romantic chit chat."

"You'll have all of your druthers fulfilled later tonight," Zack smiled sadly. "But here's the scoop."

THROUGHOUT ZACK'S DISCOURSE, Sandy just gaped. And when he was finished, it took a few moments before her brain could re-engage her mouth.

"That's the wildest thing I've ever heard. I'm still trying to sort out which is more amazing—their arrival in a few weeks, our being put on trial, or your tête-a-tête with an alien who looked like me."

"Mrs. B is counting on your show being the way to wean the masses off sports, movies and reality shows. We have to get them thinking about the a bigger picture so when she drops the bomb in her address to the nation, the country will only go a little crazy instead of completely bananas. She also suggests you call the show Washington Space Dateline News. She thinks it's a great tie-in with the station's WSDN call letters. What do you think?"

Sandy nodded lamely. "Works for me."

"Have you settled in on a time slot, schedule and topics?"

"It'll be Monday through Friday evenings at six, with a rebroadcast four hours later. Tomorrow I wanted to start off with interviews by Bertie and Carlos to discuss telescopes, how they operate, and what can be seen with them. The three of us will be in front of green screens with color images dubbed in behind us. Bertie will have an air-shot of his telescope, Carlos will have his optical and radio telescopes and I'll be in front of the Capitol Building naked from the waist up."

Zack's eyes popped open.

"Just kidding!"

Zack shook his head. "Well, before deciding on a cosmetic surgeon to perk up your nude shots, you might want to think about speaking with the President on ways to defuse any Space Station rumors. She told me she's thinking along the lines of a communications blackout. But check with her first."

"I will," she said. "Bertie has agreed to discuss his new gadget and how Carlos came up with a great name for it—the flooder."

"You might mention that he's sure to be remembered along with Galileo and Newton, as though his device allows radio telescopes to mimic optical telescopes. Can you imagine what can be seen with one that is ten times wider than a hundred-foot optical 'scope? Bertie is so excited about his new set-up it may be impossible to get him off that topic. Any thoughts on follow up shows?"

"I thought my second show would be on the Search for Extraterrestrial Intelligence, interviewing two experts. I already have Hoshi Watanabe locked in from Greenbank, West Virginia By the way, did you know Hoshi means star in Japanese? How cool is that? So all I need now is to confirm the other guest."

"You have anyone in mind?" Zack smiled warily.

"I'm working on snagging Dr. Zachary Peters."

Zack raised both hands and shook his head.

"Sandy...I know for a fact that he dislikes interviews with their unexpected and uncomfortable questions."

"Aw come on, Zack.

"No."

"Don't be an old stick in the mud."

He kept shaking his head.

"Well, if that's your final word I'll have to give Mrs. B a call. She warned me that you'd be a hard sell and to told me to call her if you balked."

"All right, already. I surrender. Just don't make the call."

"I knew I could browbeat you into it. After we make you a star, I want to follow up with a second SETI show using folks from the Planetary Society and the SETI Institute. You know the more I think about it, the more I'm sure this gig is going to be a blast."

"And that's a good thing. With those kinds of topics and guests you'll stand a better chance of competing with sports and reality shows. In the past I've found astronomy to be tough sells. But spicing it up with the E.T. angle may be the way to go. Did the station manager say when you should arrive at the studio?"

"She told me to be there tomorrow morning by ten o'clock, so we can practice camera angles and lighting, and have a dry run. Lunch is being catered, so I can leave there about noon and have the rest of the afternoon free before returning at five-thirty for the show."

"Would you like me to pick you up at your place at a quarter to ten?"

"I was hoping you'd offer. Oh, and they wanted to know if I had photogenic legs."

"What the hell does that have to do with the price of eggs?"

"She said cameras will be shooting me from all angles, before and at the end of the show. So I have to wear heels and skirt rather than shorts and sandals. It's the biggest downside I can see to the gig."

Sandy noticed the band was returning from its break. "We don't have to start back for another hour, so let's get you out on the dance floor. You're doing just fine as long as you remember the man starts out with his left foot and the woman with her right. And by keeping our bodies close, I'll know what your next move will be."

"We don't need to be dancing for you to figure that out."

Chapter 24

IN THE ROLLING HILLS and steamy lush jungle some nine miles south-west of the coastal resort town of Arecibo, Puerto Rico, the world's largest and most sensitive single-dish radio telescope hung suspended above a natural sinkhole depression.

Operated jointly by Cornel University and the National Astronomy and Ionosphere Center, the thousand-foot-wide dish stood motionless, except for a single moving part, its 900-ton radio receiver suspended five hundred feet above the dish. The receiver allowed a small amount of wiggle room, barely thirty-eight degrees away from straight overhead.

In the Information Center, visitors got to view short films explaining how radio telescopes differ from their optical cousins; the ones that astronomers stare through. Radio allowed researchers to tune in on natural radio emissions from planets and gas clouds in the Milky Way as well as distant galaxies at the edge of the visible universe.

The telescope, often referred to as "The Big Ear," was sensitive enough to detect natural radio emissions from galaxies at the farthest reaches of the visible universe—more than ten billion light years away, which was another way of saying ten billion light years in the past. Dr. Bertram Powell, the facility director, always had a pat answer to questions about the number of miles in a light year.

"One light year is a little less than six trillion miles," he would say. "So for ten billion light years, you simply multiply 10 billion times six trillion and...well, I'll let you do the math."

But today was crunch day, and the facility was closed to visitors. The processor from the Miami Institute had arrived on time and successfully integrated into the system. Powell's team consisted of three astronomers: his personnel aide, Consuela, in charge of visual monitors; Perry, who kept the telescope on target and monitored the numerous devices to make everything work smoothly; and Miguel, the overall supervisor, charged with holding everything together.

"I don't want any of us to feel bad about our first attempt," Powell announced. "We were pretty close to pulling it off. But close only counts in government work and horseshoes, so I have my fingers crossed we'll get it perfect this time. Perry, how much time before the anomaly and 40 Eri drift out of our view?"

"I'd say we have eight or nine minutes," Perry replied.

"We should be able to live with that," Powell replied uneasily. "At the very least we should have time enough for one more try. How's our tracking?"

"We're right on the nose, sir."

"So my friends, it seems we have no way to know how long our scrounged up processor is going to hold up. I suppose as the instructions they sent were next to useless, we shouldn't complain too much. Beggars can't be choosers. Consuela, would you begin the final report?"

"Both recorders are reset. Our desk monitors are clear, but it's anybody's guess how much detail the big wall unit will give us. But please, Dr. Powell—try to relax. You've done everything possible to put this all together."

Powell nodded, and took a deep breath. "Perry, how are things holding up?"

"The Klystron will be at one-hundred percent burst-charge in a few seconds. Once it is, I can throw on the magnetic field attractors until the top and bottom of the dish are aligned. Here comes the Klystron now in three—two—one—and I'm ready to go."

"Thanks Perry. As for me, I show the beryllium and chromium-oxide mix couldn't be in closer balance. So, everyone…stand by as I open the gates of the flooder in three, two, one…now. All fourteen rim emitters are in the green and flooding… damn. Make that thirteen. We just lost one, but we're still within acceptable parameters. So—if everyone is ready to make history, and no one needs to use the rest room, I'd like a final check. Miguel?"

"Ready to go."

"Consuela?"

"I am good to go."

"Perry?"

"I'm good, too."

"And I'm a good too," Powell sighed. "Stand by to throw your switches in three—two—one…now!"

Though they all turned to look out the windows at the steel monolith, the scene was deceiving. They always anticipated some sort of movement, even though they knew there wouldn't be. But one thought haunted the minds of each of them: What if their undertaking had fallen short?

Consuela was the first to speak.

"I'm beginning to get a picture on my screen now," she said breathlessly.

"Put it up on the wall monitor," Powell replied.

Five feet off the floor, a ninety-inch, high definition color monitor snapped into perfect focus, and the three astronomers filled the room with cheers and high-fives.

"There it is team, 40 Eridani," beamed Powell. "See how clearly it shows an orange-red hue, just like our Sun?" He blew it a kiss. "You are not only a beautiful star, you are one of the first of your size to display a visible disk."

"There---down to the lower right," Perry said. "I can make out the red and white dwarf companions, Eri B and Eri C. This is amazing! What power are we at?"

Powell quickly calculated in his head. "We should be pretty close to six thousand. Not too shabby—though I can't quite make out the Carlos anomaly. It could be that we're in too close."

"Other than a hint of blurred lines, I can't make anything out," said Perry. "But can anyone explain those curved, hair-thin lines that seem to start out close—to the left of 40 Eri before running down and off to the left corner of the screen?"

"Hmm," Powell mused. "Consuela—could you reduce the magnification by one thousand. Let's get a bigger over-all view."

The star system retreated slightly and in doing so redefined into a clear picture. And suddenly there it was, filling half the screen: the Carlos anomaly.

"Would you take a look at that?" Miguel whispered. "It looks like we're looking down-stream into an eddy. No, I take that back. It's not an eddy—it looks like a whirlpool. Some kind of vortex or funnel."

Powell tugged at his chin and said, "I agree, Miguel, but there's a bigger overall picture here. I get a sense of being suspended inside of a huge, transparent balloon." He walked to the screen and tapped it with a pointer.

"There—see? You can make out undistorted stars through the balloon's skin. But those thin, curved lines you mentioned that make up the vortex—I can barely make them out."

"There," Miguel said after adjusting two filters. "There they are. See how the lines converge to a single point just southwest of 40 Eri?"

Powell nodded. "I imagine that point is where my hypothetical balloon would be inflated, and then pinched off to keep the contents from escaping. That assumes something or someone outside the balloon wants to keep the contents from escaping."

Consuela had been quietly staring at the image transfixed. After a moment, she stood up and slowly made her way to the wall monitor. She stopped, looked up and nodded her head to the left and to the right. As if a light of clarity had descended upon her, she clasped her hands over her heart in prayer and knelt. She made the sign of the cross and whispered, "*Veo el ombligo de Dios! El ombligo de Dios!*"

"Consuela?" Powell asked. "Is there a problem? What are you doing?"

Miguel walked over and knelt beside her. Placing a hand gently on her shoulder he asked, "In English please. *En ingles por favor.*"

She turned to him, tears filling her eyes.

"It is the navel of God!" she said.

Chapter 25

As Virginie LaPlage sat in the Channel 13 newsroom gathering some last minute thoughts before her first show, she couldn't help but wish somebody had consulted her on the décor. For one thing, she would have opted for less glitz. But they didn't and as a result it had colors no decent rainbow would approve of. As for the garish lighting, it would have been perfect for a political convention.

Sitting in front of a green screen on which a picture of the Capitol dome would be added for the TV audience, a technician clipped a microphone to her blouse lapel.

"Could you say a few words for a sound check?" he asked.

Before she could reply, the director's voice thundered through her ear bud.

"Sorry about that Sandy. How are you doing? Like a long-tail cat in a room full of rocking chairs? Don't fret; you will do a bang up job. Okay—on your toes everyone! We go live in two minutes."

Sandy stood up and stretched. Serving up mini buck-and-wing step—singing "I'm ready yes, I'm ready"—she received a round of laughter and applause from her crew. Glancing up at two flush-mounted monitors on her table top, she could see Bertram Powell in Puerto Rico and Carlos Flusher in Chile. Both smiled and waved. Each had a large telescope projected behind them.

When the one-minute call came, she fluffed her chair and double checked her make-up. "Just for the record," she smiled, "I'd rather be wearing a tank top and flip-flops."

"You look just fine, Sandy," one of two female camera operators said. "But our camera angles keep shifting, so you need to look business-like. Besides girl—you've got fantastic legs."

A voice over the speaker started counting down the seconds to air time:

"Seven, six, cue music, four, three, and two....and we are live."

The background music rose and faded as she began.

"GOOD EVENING AND welcome to Washington Space Dateline News. It's six o'clock and I'm Virginie LaPlage.

"Here, in your nation's capital, our reporters do everything they can to assure you the latest and most thorough news. As part of our coverage, we'll put things into perspective to help you understand how what's going on in space directly affects us here on Earth. And if you miss our live report at 6 o'clock Eastern Time, we re-broadcast each program at 10pm, local time.

"Our first story comes from 239,000 miles away, on the Moon. Scientists from NASA and the European Space Agency announced the completion today of a joint venture, Project Moon Push. The 224 ion engines mounted in one of the Moon's most central craters, Mösting, have passed their final tests. If everything continues as planned, and we don't encounter any unexpected glitches, Moon Push will be underway by the end of the month.

"The purpose of Project Moon Push is to push the Moon's oval-shaped orbit another 1,000 miles or so further away from Earth. This is to move the barycenter, the balance point between the centers of both worlds, into in outer space—rather than keeping it a thousand miles inside Earth's crust, as it does now.

"Now we have all been on a teeter totter at some time growing up. Imagine for me two people—who we will call Anna and Bubba—are on a teeter totter. Because Anna weighs so much less than Bubba does, the balance point needs to be right under Bubba, not someplace further out on the board.

"By mid-2035, Moon Push will have successfully pulled the barycenter from inside of the Earth and moved it out into space. Nearly all our scientists agree that the constant dragging of the barycenter through the Earth causes our tsunamis, earthquakes, and volcanic activity.

"Then there are the naysayers who feel the cost of Moon Push is too great and it should instead be used to stamp out hunger and poor education. But looking at the historical records, the vast majority of the people understand that during the past 500 years more than 615,000 people have been killed as the result of tsunamis. It is believed that number will double when the big one occurs sometime in the next 700 years. By the big one I refer to the Canary Islands Mount Cumbre Vieja in the Atlantic Ocean off the west coast of Africa.

"Scientists predict that mountain will eventually slide into the ocean, sending a 300-foot tsunami in all directions. Its first landfall will be the west coast of Africa. Nine hours later, after crossing the Atlantic, it will strike our eastern seaboard from Boston to Miami and continue 10 miles inland before dissipating. Can you imagine attempting to evacuate the East Coast with less than a nine-hour warning?

"Then there are Earthquakes that have killed nearly a million people since 1970. Add to that the 200,000 that have been killed since 1586 from volcanoes and landslides. By looking at the numbers, the cost to every person on Earth would be only five cents a year to build and support Project Moon Push.

"But enough doom and gloom. Here is an offer I'm sure you'll want to participate in. Three of you out there in TV land are going to win a $2,000 astronomical telescope by correctly answering a question about Project Moon Push. Those 224 ion engines inside lunar crater Mösting will only operate seven out of the twenty-nine days it takes the moon to complete one orbit. We have a hint for you. The firing of the engines will only take place during one of the Moon's phases if that phase coincides when the Moon's is at perigee and apogee or when it is closest and farthest from Earth. Your question is, why?"

Sandy smiled at the camera. "We'll now take a short break before I introduce Dr. Bertram Powell, director of the Arecibo Radio Observatory in Puerto Rico and Dr. Carlos Flusher, director of the Cerro Pachon Observatory in Chile. So don't go away."

The red light from the camera blinked off, and Sandy stood and stretched; Zack approached from off-camera.

"You're doing a fantastic job, Sandy."

"Do you think I put in too much detail about death statistics?"

"Not at all," he said. "It was necessary to support the project's concept."

A disembodied voice called over the speaker: "Ten seconds, Sandy."

"Oh, I spoke to Bertie and Carlos before the show," Zack said. "They say to relax and have fun."

"That's a lot easier said than done. Okay—now scram lover-butt. I have to go to work."

"Cue up music," said the director. "And three, two...and we are live."

"Hello again," Sandy beamed. "Before we hear from our guest astronomers, I need to mention that while we can't accept your telephone calls during broadcasts, you can call the station any other time with your comments. We now go live to Cerro Pachon Observatory in Chile."

The on-air feed split to show the astronomer on the right and Sandy on the left.

"So, Dr. Flusher, how are things with you and the weather?"

"I'm doing well, Sandy. I want to thank you for inviting me on your program. Our weather is great for astronomy. It's cold at 9,000 feet above sea level. This is why optical telescopes are placed on mountains where most of Earth's weather is below them."

"Would you tell us about your telescope?"

"I'm happy to. It is a single lens optical telescope, a little more than twenty-six feet wide and the largest in its class. This is the type that one peers through with an eyepiece at your end to see distant objects whose light has entered the far end."

"I understand your observatory is one of a two-telescope system known as Gemini."

"Yes. We are Gemini South. The other instrument is Gemini North in Hawaii, 14,000 feet up on top of Mauna Kea. Even though each can do individual observing, they also can combine their signals electronically in what's called optical interferometry."

"Can you explain what that is without getting too technical?"

"Sure, Sandy. Each telescope looks at the same object at the same time, with the same magnification, and then we electronically combine the two images. The results are like having one telescope with the width of the distance between them two telescopes. In the case of Gemini, that's thousands of miles."

"So by combining the two, it becomes the largest telescope in the world."

"That's pretty much the idea, Sandy. The results are spectacular, but some astronomers feel interferometry is too specialized, and has only a limited range of use. Nevertheless, we can accurately measure the sizes and positions of objects with great precision."

"I see that you have some telescope models."

"This is a refractor," said Flusher, pointing to one of them.. "It's the kind people most often think of for star gazing. Here at the front of the tube is a large lens that gathers light and sends it down the tube to the low end where you place an eyepiece."

"I believe refractors were invented by Galileo in Italy," Sandy interjected. "I understand he got himself in hot water with the Church by proving the Moon had an uneven surface. This went against church teachings that all heavenly spheres were pristine and perfect."

"That's true Sandy. But the real credit for inventing the refractor telescope goes to Jan Lippershey, a Dutch optical maker in 1608. When word of his instrument reached Italy a year later, Galileo built one and became wealthy selling them to the military. He should be remembered as the first to use a telescope at night for astronomy."

"I had one of those made of cardboard as a youngster," she said. "It was so flimsy it made objects wiggle terribly and I lost interest."

"We call those junk telescopes. They're mass produced with inferior material. On the other hand, a quality telescope that costs a few hundred dollars shouldn't discourage budding star gazers."

"That's good information for adults who want to put a youngster on the road to astronomy," she said. "Now, I notice you have another telescope that looks different."

"Yes. This is a reflecting telescope. It works much on the same principal as the refractor in that it gathers light, bends it and then sends it to the eyepiece at the other end of the telescope. A reflector has a mirror at the bottom end and the eye piece up front whereas a refractor has a lens at the top and the eyepiece at the bottom. Because an observer's head would block incoming light with small reflectors, the eyepiece is placed outside the tube. A small mirror mounted in the center of the tube bounces the image 90 degrees sideways and out a hole in the tube to the eyepiece."

"So which would you recommend for a beginner, a refractor or a reflector?"

"That's always a tough decision Sandy. The first thing you need to determine is your budget. Both types have disadvantages and advantages, so you need to know what kind of objects you prefer observing.

"Stars, the Moon and planets can be seen well in a refractor. Dimmer objects like galaxies and nebulae gas clouds are seen best in a reflector. Size-wise and inch-for-inch, refractors are generally smaller than reflectors. They're also more expensive and gather less light, which means that you won't see dim objects like galaxies and nebulae very well. On the other hand, bright objects like stars and planets are better seen in refractors

"The two designs are a compromise between cost, purpose and performance. While a refractor is maintenance free, a reflector needs to have its reflective surface recoated and its mirror aligned occasionally. But you can buy larger reflectors for the price of smaller refractors."

"Thank you Dr. Flusher."

"Always a pleasure," he smiled.

"Moving now to Puerto Rico, I'd like to introduce Dr. Bertram Powell, director of the Radio Telescope Observatory at Arecibo."

The viewing screen split into three parts with Powell on the left, Flusher on the right, and Sandy in the middle.

"Good evening, Dr. Powell," said Sandy. "May I assume you prefer astronomy on tropical Puerto Rico to a cold mountain top? It would be a no-brainer for this gal. I'll choose the warmer spot every time. I assume Dr. Flusher hasn't convinced you to move to his mountain top, and give up one of the largest, single-dish radio telescopes on the planet."

"Right you are, Sandy. I enjoy all of the amenities here—like as reaching out of my kitchen window and picking a banana off my tree."

"Would you mind explaining how radio telescopes work?" she asked. "The word radio makes me believing I could pick up old-time radio broadcasts like The Lone Ranger."

"I'm afraid you couldn't. Radio telescopes operate in the electromagnetic spectrum, where both natural and man-made radio signals are found. And while it's true the best spot for optical telescopes are on mountain tops high above light pollution and the weather, a radio telescope can be located anywhere, as long as it's shielded from local radio noise. Ours, for instance, sits low to the ground inside a natural depression."

"You mentioned artificial radio transmissions. Does this mean you might be able to pick up a broadcast from across the universe by aliens?"

"If there are aliens out there with radio telescopes powerful enough to send a message to Earth—and if we knew what frequency to listen to—we might be able to hear them. Of course, it would help if they were closer than 250 light years away. With nearly six trillion miles in one light year that might seem far away. Actually that would be in our cosmic back yard, so to speak; nothing like the 150,000-light-year wide Milky Way—not to mention the universe that stretches 90 billion light years across."

"Wow! And as I understand it, radio telescopes can operate both day and night?"

"That's true. No natural disturbance like clouds, snow, rain or sunshine affects radio waves. On the other hand optical telescopes need dark skies and no clouds."

"But both the optical and radio telescopes can detect far distant objects?"

"Yes. You can actually think of all telescopes as time machines. If objects are bright and energetic enough we detect them as they were, billions of years ago. In the case of the universe we see and hear what was happening almost 13 billion years ago only seven million years after the beginning of the universe. But getting back to delayed alien communication, they need to be closer than 250 light years away. Otherwise, with our current technology, any signal would be hidden in the background noise of outer space."

"I can't help but wonder what you and aliens would find to talk about."

"It would be impossible to carry on a conversation, Sandy. If they're 250 light years away it would take 500 years for the round trip needed for a simple question and an answer. And that doesn't include any time for translating the message."

"So much for our getting the cure for the common cold any time soon," Sandy smirked. "But imagine if we waited 500 years only to receive their answer asking us to call back on a clearer frequency."

As the two men stopped laughing, Powell said, "You may be surprised to find out our radio telescopes detect radio noise from right here in the solar system. NASA's Galileo and Cassini spacecraft have detected huge lightning bursts on our biggest planet, Jupiter. Some were a thousand times greater than found on Earth."

"And your radio telescope can detect those kinds of flashes?"

"Yes, and your television set can too. If you can switch to a channel without programing you'll see thousands of flickering dots. Most of them are probably from your refrigerator's motor, but some of those dots come from lightning in Jupiter's atmosphere."

"I learn something new every day. Now tell us more about your radio telescope?"

"It was built in 1963 at a cost of 72 million dollars in today's dollars. The dish is composed of 20,000 three by six-foot aluminum plates, and as big as 26 football fields. The whole dish is suspended by 30 miles of cable. A much smaller receiver is suspended 450 feet above the dish by cables that connect to three towers. The telescope has even starred in movies. Some companies have shot scenes right here—including *Contact* in the 1990s."

"I thoroughly enjoyed that film," Sandy said. "It was a screen adaptation of the only fiction novel written by the late Carl Sagan. But getting back to the telescope, what can you tell us about the message that was once transmitted to alien civilizations?"

"That took place in 1974; November, I think. The signal was part of the celebration of one of the telescope's renovations. Carlos was actually there. Maybe he can fill us in on some of the details. Carlos?"

"Sure," Flusher responded. "But before everyone starts counting years on their fingers, let me just say I was a very young intern back then."

Sandy laughed. "So tell us about it, Dr. Flusher."

"First, remember that in 1974 no planets had been discovered orbiting other stars. We didn't even know for sure if any planets existed, except for those in our solar system. So the question of where to send the message was harder than deciding on its content, and how to make that content understandable to aliens.

"So we had two choices. Either send it to a star like our Sun, or head it off to a cluster of stars. To insure getting more 'bang for the buck' the choice became M13, a cluster of 300,000 or so stars in the Hercules constellation."

"Can you recall anything that was in the message?" she asked.

"Instead of saying 'Greetings from the planet Earth' they chose to send a message encoded in numbers since numbers would be a universal language to an advanced alien species.

"They sent a combination of 1,679 binary digits in ones and zeros, but with M13 being some 25,100 light years from Earth, it won't arrive there until the year AD 27,074. If out of the millions of planets that orbit those stars there are some advanced civilizations that received it and chose to reply, we wouldn't get their response until AD 52,174."

"That's rather discouraging Dr. Flusher," Sandy said. "Do you remember how information was buried in the message?"

"We figured it would be understandable to aliens with knowledge of math and would recognize that 1,679 is the product of the prime numbers 23 and 73. It would form a picture if the numbers were arranged in an image of 23 columns and 73 rows. If it was put in 73 columns and 23 rows, the image would be nonsense. They would have had to record the message because it wasn't repeated."

"So the digits showed an image," Sandy said.

"Yes and because I am often asked about that image I've memorized some of it," he said. "The top line had the numbers one though ten in binary. The second line had numbers one, six, seven and fifteen. Those are the atomic numbers of life's basic building blocks such as hydrogen, carbon, oxygen...

"The third line showed a DNA molecule as a twisted ladder. Another line gave the world population in 1974. Another depicted a naked female and male. There were complaints about that so that was only allowed after we removed one or two short lines, to satisfy the prudish critics."

"That's ridiculous," Sandy said. "If I came across drawings of two naked aliens I doubt if I could tell the differences in sexes, assuming they had them."

"Most people agreed with you. Another line was a representation of the Sun and the known planets as of 1974. That's all I remember, except for the bottom line, which was an image of the telescope."

"It sounds kind of like throwing a bottle in the ocean with a message inside," said Sandy. "It accomplished nothing except to prove we could do it. Well gentlemen, it's time to thank you for appearing this evening and enlightening us about telescopes."

The images of her guests faded, and Sandy's image filled the television feed.

"Tonight's question is an e-mail sent by K.J. in Plymouth, Michigan, who asks about the conflicting reports on what's happening on board the International Space Station—and wonders if we can explain what's up---pun intended I presume, K.J?

"Because we have no specifics," Sandy continued, "I can only read a release from NASA's Office of Public Information. It states that ISS Commander Scottsdale reports everything to be A-OK after an explosion and electrical fire damaged communication systems and both docking hatches last week. The crew is making repairs with materials on hand."

Looking directly into the camera, she continued, "ISS has a three-week food and oxygen supply that will cover the six days or so to make repairs. Until then, all flights to ISS are postponed until there is no danger of static electricity discharges damaging docking supply ships. They are in contact with Houston and Cape Kennedy using Morse code and the assistance of amateur radio operators on the ground."

Sandy sat up straight and smiled.

"Well, that's it from Washington Space Dateline News. Remember our show replays at 10 p.m. Please tune in tomorrow at 6 p.m. Until then, the staff and I wish you all a wonderful evening. I'm Virginie LaPlage."

Chapter 26

GOOD EVENING. It's six o'clock and you are watching Washington Space Dateline News. This Virginie LaPlage.

"Tonight we'll speak with two renowned guests discussing the Search for Extra-Terrestrial Intelligence known by its acronym SETI. They are Dr. Zachary Peters, the President's science advisor, and Dr. Hoshi Watanabe, director of the National Radio Astronomy Observatory at Greenbank, West Virginia.

"Before we hear from our guest astronomers, I must mention that while we can't accept telephone calls during our broadcast, we urge you e-mail us or call the station with questions or comments."

The screen split in two with Zack on the left. "Well, how are you this evening, Dr. Peters?"

"Just fine, thank you, Sandy. I'm delighted to be here. And please call me Zack."

"Thanks, Zack. It's great having you with us. And also here with us is Dr. Hoshi Watanabe from Greenbank, West Virginia, home to the world's largest, fully steerable radio telescope. Welcome, Doctor."

The screen divided into three equal parts with Watanabe on the right, and Sandy in the middle.

"Hello, Sandy, and please call me Hoshi."

"Thank you Hoshi. Let me begin by mentioning that I did a little research and discovered that the word Hoshi translates into 'star' in Japanese. Was that a coincidence or did your parents hope to get you interested in astronomy from an early age?"

"With them both being classical musicians, Sandy, I'm sure hoped I'd become a classical violinist. But my lifelong dream was to be an astronomer."

"I guess that begs the question—did you ever learn to play the violin?"

"I'm afraid not. But I'm told I make a lot of noise with Irish bagpipes."

"Bagpipes, you say. You should have been on our last show with Dr. Bertram Powell who plays Scottish bagpipes. Is there a difference between the two?"

"A bagpiper enthusiast might be able to compare them, Sandy, but not your average John Doe."

"Sandy," Zack chimed in, "I hope you're not about to spark this into an international bagpipe incident."

"Well, getting us back on track," she chuckled, "Zack, would you offer us some background on SETI?"

"Sure. Let's start with a quote from an astronomer whose name I don't remember." He reached into his jacket pocket and removed a piece of paper.

"For the 4.8 billion years Earth has existed," he began reading, "it has spun around the Sun seemingly untouched by the rest of the universe. Since the time humans appeared they have felt pretty much the same way."

"And you believe that way of thinking has changed?" Sandy asked.

"Absolutely. Here we are almost midway through the 21st Century and our cozy bubble of isolation is about to evaporate. We now know of a few thousand extra-solar planets that have been detected—and a good number of those worlds are as large as, or larger than Jupiter the solar system's largest planet."

Sandy looked amazed as she said, "A few thousand? That's a lot of planets, Zack. But Jupiter types aren't hospitable to life as we know it, being gaseous and such. Don't we need to find something smaller—perhaps near-Earth-size planets—in order to find intelligent beings?"

"On the contrary---or '*au contraire*', as Hoshi might put it. We must take into considering how many moons orbit those huge Jupiters. Many of them will be the size of Earth, could obtain heat from their planet, and could easily maintain an atmosphere, the way some larger moons do here, closer to home. That makes those moons excellent candidates for life. The way many see it, there will be billions of habitable planets and moons suitable for life in our galaxy---the Milky Way."

"May I jump in here, Zack?" Hoshi asked. "We now know that 60% of all stars in the Milky Way are dim, red dwarfs. Because we often discover planets a little larger than Earth, we can assume that as many as 95% of all stars have planets. That means we're on the edge of discovering that we share the universe with a huge number of life forms, many of whom should prove to be more or less as intelligent as we are."

"That was well said, Hoshi," Zack nodded. "Dr. Powell uses an analogy that compares our present situation to a band of hominids living 50,000 years ago that had been geographically stranded for generations. They would look out across impassable deserts, mountains or and wonder if there were any beings like themselves living on the other side of those boundaries.

"In our situation, that barrier is interstellar space. This puts us in a rather humbling situation. Humans are isolated on a small planet orbiting an average star on the outskirts of an average-sized galaxy. And we've been able to deduce that there are more than a trillion other galaxies!"

"So, gentlemen, you've convinced me there are plenty of hospitable planets out there. And that brings us back to the question about our being alone in the universe. Zack, please tell us how SETI programs operate, and why scientists do it?"

"Glad to, Sandy," replied Zack. "You see, SETI—which is, of course, the Search for Extra-Terrestrial Intelligence—is our attempt to find out if humans are either alone in the universe, or among millions of other civilizations, many of which are probably asking the same questions of their uniqueness. And if we never find evidence of other cultures, it does not mean they don't exist. Absence of evidence is not evidence of absence.

"Consider that the Milky Way is about 14 billion years old and Earth is about four and a half billion. It's quite likely that humans came along 'late in the game' and that the 'party', so to speak, ended 500 million years ago. It's depressing to consider that we may have missed out on all the fun. Yet we may be able to prove the concept by discovering clues to some previous gala event and finding the rental hall is a total mess and a few party goers are passed out next to a pile of empty beer bottles."

"Zack," laughed Sandy, "I don't think I've heard of such a wild idea described so—eloquently."

"And bear in mind that we are just venturing into space, Just dipping a toe in the cosmic ocean, so to speak. It's much too early to say anything for or against the complex topic of life and its origins. On a positive note, over the centuries we've been enlightened with hundreds of theological explanations of how life began. Every culture has them. On a negative note, humans may be the result of so many accidents, mutational twists, and blind turns on the long road of evolution that even if it started all over they could never be duplicated.

"It's important that we don't think of SETI as a cult, popular mythology, religion, or a wild-eyed UFO investigation. Simply stated, we study SETI in the hope of finding whether or not we have any cousins among the stars."

"It sounds reasonable—even exciting, Zack. Yet I'll bet there is a segment of the population who oppose SETI, and the idea that we are neither alone nor unique."

"That's so true, Sandy. It's not hard to find groups fearing that a SETI discovery will weaken their power base, and influence their constituents. Off the top of my head I would count in any number of political, religious, and social institutions."

"I understand the idea of ETs is not all that new and that it has been bandied about by humans for centuries. Could you elaborate?"

"Throughout history, cultures have believed in the existence of intelligence from the stars," Zack replied. "You can find numerous books on that topic. Let me look for my next quote...here it is. Around 50 BC the Roman poet Lucretius wrote, 'Nature is not unique to the visible world. We must have faith that in other regions of space there exist other Earth's inhabited by other peoples and animals'."

"That's quite prophetic considering that it comes from 20 centuries ago."

Zack nodded. "In 1610, an Italian theologian, Giordanno Bruno, got in very real trouble for teaching the Copernican theory. It stated that Earth was not the center of the universe, and that planets orbit other stars. He taught that those planets might be home to intelligent life. The Church of Rome found him guilty of heresy, and burned him at the stake."

"That's horrible!" Sandy exclaimed. "I'm glad to know that in this day and age we can theorize and speak the truth without fear of that kind of repression. Now, before the show you mentioned there are four ways humans could communicate with an intelligent alien species. Could you elaborate?"

"Well, of course, the first way is that we travel to those worlds. The advantage is that we could step out of the spacecraft, look around, and try to find some way of talking to the aliens. The disadvantage is the cost and time it would take to get there. Let's consider the closest star to our solar system—Alpha Centauri. At the fastest speed we've managed so far, it would take seventy thousand years for a one-way. Even if we increased our speed a thousand times, it would take seventy years—an entire lifetime—just to get there and look around."

"I think we can probably scratch that idea," said Sandy. "What's number two?"

"Just the opposite—the aliens travel here. We see it in film, on TV, and read about it in books. Usually, we find they want to dominate us, steal our resources, or have us for dinner. Perhaps much of the current UFO obsession fit into these kinds of scenarios. But so far there is no real evidence of this happening—with apologies to those who are certain they've had a UFO encounter, been abducted or, in some cases, had intimate relations.

"The third way is for us to send an electromagnetic signal. And by that I mean radio. It's billions of times cheaper and more efficient than space travel. These signals travel at the speed of light and can transmit huge amounts of information. Dr. Powell spoke about that on last night's show with the transmission sent from Arecibo 1974.

"The fourth method allows us to remain on Earth and listen for signals they might send us. And this would be a perfect time for Hoshi to jump in to tell us about the Greenbank experiment that took place at his facility, the National Radio Astronomy Observatory."

"And that we will," Sandy said. "But first I want to take a short break. When we return Dr. Watanabe, director of NRAO at Greenbank, West Virginia will continue. Don't go away."

Sandy and Zack stood up, stretched, and walked off-camera.

"The reason we went on a break so early," Sandy whispered, "is because my director says you have a call from the President. She's on the line holding for you. You can take it over here on this phone."

He walked over and answered. "This is Zack, Madam President."

"I'll make this brief Zack," said the president. "I know you only have a minute or two on the break. Apparently someone in Russia let the proverbial cat out of the bag. Mikhail Kornikov just called to say that one of their tabloids is running a front-page story about a fleet of space ships headed for Earth carrying monsters. The rest of the piece was pretty vague, but he said it was enough to work a lot of people into a tizzy. He thought it would be a wise move if I moved my TV announcement up a day, and I agreed. So, I'll air at 6 p.m. the day after tomorrow rather than Noon the following day. That moves your press briefing up to 5 p.m. Because it will pre-empt Sandy's show, I'd like you to explain and apologize for me."

"I will."

"Also, I want to make sure you have Sandy in on your press briefing."

"Absolutely. Who'll notify the media on the date and time change?"

"I'll handle that from this end. Now you better get back to the show. We'll speak tomorrow. Tell Sandy I'm proud of her and that she's doing a fabulous job. Goodbye for now."

As Zack and Sandy walked back to the set, he filled her in.

The announcer's voice boomed over the speaker. "Cue up music, four, three, two and we are live."

"Hello again," Sandy said. "Before we hear from Dr. Watanabe, let me remind you that we don't accept phone calls here on the set. But you welcome to call the switchboard with any questions and comments. Use the number shown on your screen. And now back to Dr. Hoshi Watanabe."

"Thanks, Sandy. In the spring of 1960, Cornell University astronomer Frank Drake, often referred to as the father of SETI, used a radio telescope in an attempt to detect extra-terrestrial radio signals. The program was given the name Project Ozma, from L. Frank Baum's book *The Emerald City of Oz*, in which radio was similarly used for communication.

"Dr. Drake, using our old 85-foot radio telescope, could only monitor one frequency at a time. He chose 1,420 megahertz. The two stars he monitored were Epsilon Eridani and Tau Ceti, each about 11 light-years away, and very much like our Sun."

"Was there any particular reason to choose that precise frequency?"

"Yes. He surmised that extra-terrestrials interested in using interstellar radio communication would face the same problems he had—choosing which frequency to use. He assumed they'd try to come up with some familiar universal standard—and as it happens, knew that 1.420 megahertz was the wavelength of radiation emitted naturally by the most common interstellar gas—hydrogen. He called that frequency as the water hole because that is where different kinds of animals universally meet for a drink."

"Did he detect anything, Hoshi?"

"Nothing of any real note. In late 1960, he invited a number of leading astronomers, physicists, biologists, social scientists, and industry leaders to meet at Greenbank to discuss the possibilities of detecting extraterrestrials. The participants became known as The Order of the Dolphins. One important outcome of the meeting was the creation of the Drake Equation. Its purpose was to come up with a number of potentially communicable civilizations in space."

"Without making it too complicated for us, Hoshi, could you tell us about it?"

"Sure. It called for multiplying seven factors together to come up with an answer. In the 1960s, we could assume only one of these factors with any degree of accuracy. That was the first one—the average rate of star formation in the Milky Way galaxy.

"The second factor, the fraction of those stars that have planets, is more-or-less known today. With more than three thousand confirmed planets, we think that all stars have at least one planet. As of now, the five other factors are completely conjecture, because astronomers can't come to an agreement on them. But, for what it's worth, here they are. Number three is the average number of those planets that can potentially support life. Four is the fraction of those planets that go on to develop life. Factor number five is the fraction of those that go on to develop intelligent life, followed by six—the fraction of civilizations that develop a technology allowing them to release detectable signs of their existence. And the last one—factor number seven—is the length of time those civilizations release detectable signals into space."

"Just in passing," Zack interrupted, "let's just assure the audience that none that last bit of information will be on the test at the end of this show."

"So, Hoshi," Sandy chuckled, "just what kind of numbers do we see coming out of that complicated formula?"

"It all depends on which astronomer you ask," he smiled. "Some are quite pessimistic and believe that only Earth has intelligent life. Others are more optimistic, and think there could be as many as ten million technologically advanced species in the Milky Way."

"That is amazing," Sandy said. "You make it sound as if we should be hearing from them any moment now."

"Before any SETI enthusiasts get too worked up on us contacting extra-terrestrials, they need to remember just how vast the Milky Way is. Mathematically speaking, if those ten million civilizations were evenly spaced— and of course, they probably wouldn't be—they'd be separated by about 10,000 light years! That would definitely quarantine them from each other."

"As you can see Sandy, there's more to SETI than our just wondering if we are alone. We'd like to know if such ETs out there would want to respond to any messages they'd receive from. Would their interest in us be friendly, hostile, or non-existent? Would their society be curious? Would they be able to understand, reconstruct and copy our technology? Could we do the same with theirs?

"I remember one astronomer, whose name eludes me," Hoshi continued, "once said that if the space telephone ever rings, for God's sake don't answer it!. Of course he was referring to the danger we place ourselves in if we advertise our presence, who we are, and where we live. There's no reason for us to assume predator species are non-exist out there."

"That does make sense, Hoshi," Sandy said. "It's also pretty scary."

"As for me," Zack said, "I think it's too late for us to be concerned. If ETs are out there, and live within two hundred light years of us, they probably know we're here—and here's my reasoning. In a sphere of space surrounding us and four hundred light years in diameter, there are more than three hundred stars. Think of the number of years we've inadvertently announced our presence with radar, television, radio and other types of energy that has leaked away from Earth since the discovery of radio?"

"Now you two are really beginning to scare me," Sandy said. "I've always assumed that civilizations with interstellar travel would probably have advanced socially as well as technologically and rid itself of violence and aggression."

"I don't believe that at all," Zack said. "Just look at us. We're on the verge of interplanetary travel, and we have a pretty good idea of how to build a starship. All you need do is listen to the news broadcasts—filled every day with wars, fighting, deception, aggression and slavery—to realize how little we've matured as a species."

"Amen to that, Zack," Hoshi added. "In addition to the radio noise we've sent out, consider the spacecraft we've launched that carry messages. Voyagers One and Two each carry gold-plated records, a needle and instructions how to build a phonograph. If a space-faring civilization stumbles on either, they could conceivably put together the phonograph and hear hundreds of sounds from Earth that we put on the records including a crying baby, the roar of a rocket, whale songs and a greeting from many of our languages."

"One thing in our favor is that neither Voyager will pass within a trillion miles of any star system in less than one million years," said Zack.

"But don't forget NASA's Pioneer spacecraft," he shook his head. "They carry pictorial information that shows not only the location of our solar system, but the exact planet they were launched from—Earth. Don't rule out the possibility that an alien spacecraft has already intercepted one of the Pioneers and has figured out where we are. I can just hear a commanding officer of such a ship ordering, 'Helm, let's take a closer look at that small yellow star. Have our weapons and tactical officers' report to me in half a glopnik.' "

"Oh, and by the way Sandy," Zack added with a wink, "that translates to a little less than one hour in alien talk."

"Alright, gentlemen," Sandy said. "No more doom and gloom. After listening to you two I may just go home and hide under my bed. Now, has anyone figured out the odds that we'll be as advanced as any ETs we receive a message from?"

"That's easy, Sandy," said Zack. "Our technology will necessarily be less advanced than theirs."

"And why is that?"

"An alien signal reaching us today would have left their home world the same number of years ago as the planet is distant in light-years."

"Come again?"

"Electromagnetic signals, meaning radio or laser, travel at the speed of light. So if their world is 300 light years distant and we receive a message today, they would have been as advanced as we are today 300 years ago...about the same time George Washington was a little boy."

"I think I understand the concept," she said. "So, let's see if I have it straight. If they're 2,000 light years away and we have just received their message, it would have had to have left their planet when the Roman Empire was occupying Judea. So, in other words, it's impossible to carry on a conversation with ETs."

"You have the concept, Sandy," Hoshi said. "We found it a bit awkward carrying on conversations with astronauts on the Moon, where there's only a three-second delay from the time you ask 'How are you?' until you hear 'We are all fine. How are you?' It will be impossible to have a normal conversation with our people when they arrive on Mars next February, where there's a round trip delay of close to an hour."

"So I suppose our radio telescopes are still the best way to go?" asked Sandy.

"No," Hoshi answered. "There's another system that is being used. We call it Optical SETI. We can't see planets orbiting the closest stars with our optical telescopes. That's because they appear too dim compared to the brightness of their star. It would be like trying to see a firefly sitting on the edge of a searchlight.

"Nevertheless, we still use an optical telescope to examine stars in laser frequencies. So if ETs use lasers to send signals, those signals would be as much as 50,000 times brighter than their star."

"One nice thing about SETI, Sandy, is no matter what the outcome, it's a win-win situation,." Zack proclaimed.

"Why is that?"

"We win if we discover intelligent life out there. It would prove a civilization like ours doesn't automatically self-destruct when it reaches its nuclear age. The fact that extra-terrestrials managed to survive their turbulent teens shows us that humans can do it too."

"And just think of the knowledge that would be available from an advanced civilization," added Hoshi. "If they were of a benevolent nature they could be transmitting the sum of all their knowledge in every direction. It would be an Encyclopedia Galactica."

"You said win-win," Sandy said. "How can our not finding ETs out there be a good thing?"

"It would not only show how precious life is, especially intelligent life, but it would demonstrate just how rare it is in the universe," Zack said. "With this realization, it might encourage us to put aside our petty squabbles and unite us all to protect the rare gift of life. And should we find a way to travel to the stars, we'd become the Johnny Appleseed of the Milky Way, spreading life throughout space. That's an ambitious and rewarding project."

Sandy nodded.

"Besides," Zack continued, "absence of proof is not proof of absence. Aliens could well be transmitting on frequencies we don't monitor, or don't even know exist. They might be content with their lifestyle and not interested in contacting others. And as we mentioned earlier, it may well be that intelligent life has already flourished throughout the galaxy, only to die eons ago. It reminds me of arriving late to a party only to find out most, or all of the guests have gone home already.

"It's the height of conceit to believe we're so special that beings from around the galaxy would rush here just to bask in our exalted presence. It would be like every country on Earth having the urge to use up its resources to travel to Podunk Junction, South Dakota, population 12."

"On that encouraging note," said Sandy, "I'm afraid it's time to close down this segment of Washington Space Dateline News. I want to thank doctors Hoshi Watanabe and Zack Peters so very much for being our guests.

The live shot switched to show Sandy on the full screen. She smiled and looked directly into the camera.

"Tomorrow night we will bring you astronomers from the National Institute of SETI Research. I'll be asking them questions you might consider unanswerable—such as what kind of characteristics ETs might have, what their motivation to contact us could be, how they'd appear physically, whether we could converse with them, if they'd bother to come all this way looking for resources, just to explore—even whether they'd want to mate with us."

"So that's it for tonight from all of us at Washington Space Dateline News. Remember that our broadcast repeats at 10 p.m. tonight. So please tune in tomorrow night at six. Good night."

Chapter 27

"GOOD EVENING. It is six o'clock and time for Washington Space Dateline News. I'm Virginie LaPlage."

"Tonight we continue our story The Search for Extra Terrestrial Intelligence. With me live in the studio are two experts in the field—John Lightcap and Meredith Newmeyer from the California International Consortium of SETI Studies, or CICOSS."

"Thank you for inviting us, Sandy," Newmeyer smiled. "We enjoyed the first part and are pleased to be part of that story. And please call us John and Meredith."

"I will, Meredith. It was our good luck that you were in Washington for the SETI symposium this week. It gave us the chance to have you join us in person. Now, you told me earlier that through some joint research projects you knew both Hoshi Watanabe and Zack Peters?"

"That's right," said Newmeyer. "We've been colleagues for some time now. But let me just begin by saying it wasn't too long ago that SETI researchers were considered a bit far out, excuse the pun. So we're happy to be in a field that's grown leaps and bounds over the past twenty years."

"Allow me to play the devil's advocate for a moment," Sandy said. "Is it true that with all of the research and experiments, SETI efforts since beginning in 1960 have failed to produce a single confirmed signal?"

"May I step in on this one, Sandy?" Lightcap chuckled. "Because SETI researchers often get that very same question, we've put together a standard response. Everyone knows that the universe is unbelievably large. So far, our searches have barely scratched the surface. But I can assure you that when we are finally successful, it will be a culture shock for many, and a joyful occasion for us."

"You said when, John, as if you expect success."

"Absolutely—and I'll bet you a bottle of expensive Bordeaux that we'll have positive results within the next twenty years."

"Until then, SETI enthusiasts will have to be content with sci-fi films and books," added Newmeyer.

"And our field is fortunate to have many qualified writers," said Lightcap.

"One of my favorites," said Newmeyer, "is Dr. Seth Shostak at the SETI Institute in Mountain View California. I find him a very easy read—much like the late Carl Sagan. The biggest difference is that Shostak continually breaks me up with his wit and humor. That's why I recommend his book, *Sharing the Universe* and two others he co-authored, *Cosmic Company* and *Life in the Universe*."

"You've convinced me," Sandy said. "I'll look for them at my local book store. But for now, let's move on to use some scientific reasoning to come up with theories on the more personal attributes of beings from technologically advanced civilizations."

"Well Sandy," Lightcap said, "as amazing as it must sound, we actually can make what we believe to be valid assumptions on an extra-terrestrial's appearance, size, sense organs, and whether or not they resemble human beings. We even theorize about ET's emotions, IQ, morals, reproduction, behavior and even spirituality."

"That sounds like one tall order John," Sandy said. "So I'll just sit back and let you both get to it. I warn you, though—I will be asking some of the same questions I think our viewers might have."

"Before I do," he said, "let me take a minute to talk about one of the detection methods Hoshi and Zack touched on yesterday - optical SETI. I'd like to explain how optical searches can be more productive than radio searches.

"First there's the constant question of funding. Optical SETI costs less than two percent of radio SETI. More important, perhaps, is the fact that optical SETI requires the monitoring of just one or two frequencies, while radio SETI requires monitoring millions. And finally, optical SETI is a lot faster, since we can examine a candidate star in minutes."

"Not to mention that millions of target stars require an awful lot of telescope time," added Newmeyer. "One of our solutions is to enlist the aid of amateur astronomers around the world, many of whom already have sophisticated telescopes that would let them to do optical SETI. Of course that would mean acquiring upgrades that can run upwards of fifteen thousand dollars.

"But considering the investment some of them have in their equipment, this is really a doable project," he continued. "They would need electronic add-ons such as photo-multiplier detectors that are readily available on the market. You can imagine the satisfaction they'd have working with professional astronomers towards such a worthy goal."

"If Hoshi and Zack are watching,," Sandy interjected, "they are welcome to chime in with their thoughts on optical SETI and getting the amateur community involved. But let me ask John what the chances are ETs being similar to us?"

"Most researchers think that the chance is exactly zero. After all we would not look the way we do today if the three-billion-year-long story of evolving life on Earth were to replay itself. It's theorized that since it took millions of events occurring in a specific order for life to advance from one-celled organisms to humans, the chances of it happening again in that same exact order are impossible.

"I'll bet that is something most of us haven't considered," Sandy nodded.

"This is not to say that extra-terrestrials wouldn't have many of our characteristics," Newmeyer added. "We just wouldn't look similar with all the time, starts, and failures it took to produce us."

"Still, it's a good bet that attributes that make us successful is occurring on other world," added Lightcap.

"What would they be?" Sandy asked.

"Well, for one, sense organs placed high enough above the ground so our ET could detect a predator and make themselves a more successful predator. I expect we'd find ET with two well-developed eyes rather than many that are less effective."

"Then we need to add scent and sound receptors," Newmeyer said. "But we'd need to know more about the physical characteristics of the planet in question, as well as the type of star it orbits to draw accurate conclusions. And we shouldn't forget that advanced ETs probably must be land organisms, and not aquatic."

"Why is that?" asked Sandy.

"Civilizations would need combustible fuels to forge metals and other materials in order to create advanced societies. And to put it simply, fires can't be built under water."

"Most important, our ET needs to be mobile," said John. "Locomotion allows a life form to adapt to its surroundings, a necessity for growth, adaptability, and survival. Because plants can't move about it has to stay rooted in one spot and take whatever nature throws at it. And odd as it sounds, we've never considered animals with wheels."

"Meaning they must have arms and legs and wings," Sandy said.

"Exactly!" said Newmeyer. "You can see the advantage of using scientific reasoning on topics like this, and not one's gut feelings."

Sandy shook her head. "Gosh, if I ever lose my day job I'll consider applying at CICOSS because it sounds so interesting. Now that you've given us an idea of what we might expect extra-terrestrials to look like, what can you say about its size?"

"We figure if an ET is too large it won't be able to move around easily," Meredith continued. "Too much time would be needed to forage for food to nourish its large body. On the other hand, if it's too small it will need to spend a lot of time simply hiding from critters who want to eat it. Neither of those size extremes would make ET a good candidate for building complex cultures, let alone an advanced civilization. On an Earth-sized planet, that means an ET advanced enough to be sending signals into space will likely be no smaller than a large monkey and no larger than a small elephant. I may be coming across vague, but hopefully you get the general idea."

"We're going to take a short break now before exploring an ET's undetectable qualities—such as its emotions, morals, behavior, and intelligence," Sandy said. "Don't go away, because we'll be right back."

"WELCOME BACK to the last segment of our show today. Our special guests from the International Consortium of SETI Studies in California, Doctors John Lightcap and Meredith Newmeyer are into a most interesting part of our topic, the unseen qualities or ET. So far, they have done something I would have normally thought impossible – how to estimate what communicating ETs might look like. Now, let's delve into areas that seem even more perplexing. What are they really like? What's their motivation and why do they do what they doing? So, John and Meredith, who wants to start things off?"

Lightcap began. "Let me start off by saying that there are huge problems trying to deal with alien motivation. We must compare our ET with the only intelligent beings we know of—us, a sample that's admittedly too small to know whether that option is good or not.

"We must also accept the likelihood that ET will have qualities and attributes that don't translate—like searching for a word in a foreign language only to discover it doesn't have an English equivalent."

"Will an ET's ideas be recognizable to us?" Newmeyer interjected. "Will we have to guess what they mean by comparing them with our ways of thinking? What we have to remember is that there's a good possibility we could never completely understand an ET. The advantage we have here on Earth is that we can be face to face with someone when we communicate. When forced to use standard mail, the time factor alone often causes misinterpretation. But you can just forget communicating by radio, because the time lag between sending information out and getting an answer would take years, decades—even centuries."

"I understood going in that communicating would be difficult," Sandy agreed. "Now that you have explained it in detail, I see why there would be too much room for miscalculation and misinterpretation."

"Next on our list is motivation," Lightcap said. "Just think: why on Earth, if you'll excuse the pun, would an ET want to make a long, challenging journey to Earth when it's easier, safer, and much cheaper to stay home and send out automated probes or use electronic messaging? To put it another way, would you expect billionaire to fly to Miami only to visit the slums? With all due respect, compared to their civilization, Earth would probably be considered a rather dicey part of town."

"So you're implying that they may not be interested in visiting, communicating or studying us," Sandy said.

"Exactly. Naturalists studying animals, reptiles and birds know they won't be in communication with them. Logically, if we assume

ETs are similarly curious, their chief concern would be to make interstellar travel or electronic communication as inexpensive and trouble-free as possible. A positive reason to remaining at home is they could study multiple cultures at the same time."

"We could also ask ourselves if our ET has self-awareness," said Newmeyer. "Can it identify with itself and others? Or would it have a hive-mentality, existing only to serve the queen and the hive?"

"That sounds a bit like science fiction, with creatures that are half human half machine," Sandy said.

"That's true," he replied. "But if that's the situation, our questions about morals and ethics probably won't apply, because ETs might not feel empathy, or distinguish right from wrong the same way we do. On the other hand, we could expect them to be relatively kind and considerate to their own species. After all, here on Earth we have cultures that while highly civilized at home, become barbarous when warring outside their own domestic realm."

"Another possibility is that some ETs might show total indifference to other sentient beings," Lightcap added. "Perhaps their way of thinking wouldn't let them show concern or interest in the universe as a whole. It might not have the same sense of the past, present, and future that we do, existing only in the present. Of course, if that's true we may never hear from them, and never know they even exist."

"One thing for sure," Newmeyer said, "is that our ET must have some way to perpetuate its species. But the question is how? In an extreme scenario living race of extra-terrestrials may have already died off, leaving behind only artificial intelligence as its heirs."

Sandy said, "This is a true learning experience. We should ask you back sometime and do a show on talk artificial intelligence."

"We're all for that," Newmeyer nodded. "But getting back to reproduction—while all of Earth's intelligent species have two sexes, our ET might have three or for genders. They could even be hermaphroditic, with each individual having reproductive organs of all of its sexes. That concept is found here in some of our lower species."

"People are often surprised," Lightcap smiled, "to discover Earth's life forms reproduced without sex during the first three billion years of the planet's history. Considering that sex is a fairly recent occurrence on Earth, we also need to consider the possibility of extra-terrestrials reproducing by budding. We do that all the time with plants, by inserting buds of one species under the bark of another."

"It's pretty much a foregone conclusion that any ETs we hear from by radio or laser will be far ahead of us technologically," said Newmeyer. "In fact, the more distant they are, the farther ahead they'll be."

"We spoke about that the other night." Sandy said. "But I'll ask you to run that by us again for those who might have missed that show."

"We first have to consider how far ET's planet is from Earth," Newmeyer continued. "That tells us how long ago its signal was sent. For instance, if we receive a signal in 2030 that was sent from a star 150 light years away, simple math shows the signal was sent in our year 1880 at a time when we were 150 years before we'd risen to their level of technology.

"And if ET is 1,000 light years away and a message arrives here in AD 2040, it would have left there in AD 1040, right around the times of Macbeth, King of Scotland, and William the Conqueror."

"We can even take that one step further.," added Lightcap. "If ET is still in existence, they would be enjoying technology thousands of years in advance of ours. That being the case, we might as well shut down our radio telescopes and put the tea kettle on. They could be arriving any day now. On the other hand, if ETs are highly ethical, it follows that they may be spiritual. Remember how often religion has been carried to newly discovered areas of the world by our first explorers."

"And if ET has decided to remain at home," said Newmeyer, "the first messages we manage to decipher may be of a religious bent, not unlike our radio and television evangelists."

"So," Sandy smiled, "instead of stepping out of a spaceship and saying, 'Take me to your leader,' they might say, 'Let us tell you about our leader'. Well, the clock is racing and I can't thank you both enough for being here. The information you brought us was thought- provoking, to say the least. Please accept a WSDN coffee mug as a token of your visit. I'd planned on giving you both sports cars, until our accounting department found out about it."

Everybody laughed.

"Tomorrow night the President's address will be covered by every radio and TV station in the country. For that reason our show is being pre-empted. However, we'll be back the following night at the same time and same station. And don't forget to catch our replay tonight at 10 p.m. Until then, I'm Virginie LaPlage for Washington Space Dateline News wishing you all a good night."

Chapter 28

ZACK WASN'T SURPRISED to find it difficult to get to sleep. After all, he thought, how many people in all of history could lay claim to two, count them two visits with an honest-to-goodness extraterrestrial, all within the confines of a week? Even more startling was the fact that one took place in the privacy of his home, while the other was in the presence of the American President. If that wasn't unnerving enough, he'd be giving a briefing to the press corps about the Korr arrival later in the day, just before the President's nationwide address at six o'clock.

Eventually he did fall asleep, and awoke unexpectedly refreshed and ready to go, with plenty of time to get things arranged. Because his briefing had been opened up to include other media types as well, he wasn't surprised to learn that the White House press room couldn't accommodate the expected crowd. It would now be held in the Potomac Suites Hotel Grand Ballroom.

As if the Korr arriving from another star system and the possible consequences of their visit wouldn't be complex enough, the President asked him to include just enough basic astronomy and physics to give people a better sense of what was happening. And if time allowed, he'd answer their personal questions, as well as those submitted in advance by their editors.

Assuming the late afternoon traffic would be hectic and slow, Zack decided to take a taxi. On his arrival at the Potomac Suites, he was pleased to find that its conference and meetings manager had arranged for him to have a small suite next to the ballroom, which would let him unwind and look over his notes. And later, upon entering the ballroom, he was even more pleased to see that it was standing room only. Apparently, word about the topic had leaked, and no reporter worth his or her salt dared to miss it.

"I'd like to welcome each and every one of you to this briefing. I'm Zack Peters, science advisor to the White House." When he saw they were smiling, he knew this might not be difficult at all.

"I'll start by saying that most of the rumors floating around regarding our space visitors are true—except for the one about us being on their dinner menu."

That got a good laugh.

"I can assure you this will be the briefing of the century, one you probably prayed you'd be at should it ever occur. I suspect a team of terrorist commandos couldn't have kept you away."

The nods and smiles were unanimous.

"Journalism doesn't get any better than this. In a little less than thirty minutes the President will make an historic announcement, so I'm going to give you all a heads-up for the stories you'll be writing. I assure you nothing will be held back, since there's no longer any need for secrecy. By the time you leave here you'll know as much as anyone else."

"Here are the ground rules. First: no one gets to leave the room until after the President's talk. So this is your last opportunity to leave before the doors are secured. Do I have any takers? Okay, then—second: if nature calls there are portable lavatories in the back of the room. Tipping is optional. Third: you are encouraged to take notes. You'll find paper and pens on the table for anyone who didn't bring a laptop. Just remember that Wi-Fi here has been temporarily disabled, so you probably don't want to risk having your laptop freeze while trying to connect to the Internet.

"And so you know in advance, you can't use audio, video, or any other type of recording device including cell phones or land-lines. I mention this in case you found a way to slip something through security. This reminds me, hold on to your check stubs. You'll need them to get your items back, unless you don't mind added security checks and a month's worth of paperwork.

"Before you leave, you'll each get an info packet on what we've discussed, as well as a copy of the President's speech. Feel free to ask anything that comes to mind, no matter how weird it seems. I assure you this briefing will be as weird as any you've ever seen. If the answer to your question is in the packet, I'll say so and move on.

"You probably saw scanners, copy machines, and phone links in the hallway. There are also land lines for you. These are for your use exclusively, but only after the President's address, at which time your Wi-Fi connections will become unblocked. So if there are no questions we'll get started."

As Zack looked around the room it felt like every eye was boring into his brain, and he'd never felt quite so alone. He took a deep breath, and began.

"We know now that we are not alone in the universe. The President has evidence that we share the universe with millions, perhaps billions of other intelligent and technological civilizations living on the surface of planets or their moons.

"We have proof that some extra-terrestrials, ETs if you will, have come to Earth and are living among us in fool-proof disguises. I probably know what your immediate reaction is. Until a short time ago, I would have thought anyone promoting these ideas was crazy.

"Needless to say, the 'Joe six-packs' out there already knew they were here because they've been reading about them in the tabloids for years."

After the snickering died down, Zack said, "Our visitors call themselves the Korr—spelled k-o-r-r and pronounced like apple core. If any of you took a language that trills an R, you'll have it down pat."

Nearly every hand went up.

"I'll get to your questions in a moment. The Korr home world is the second planet out from a sun called 40 Eridani. It's located a little more than sixteen light years away; actually sixteen and a half to be exact. But rounding it off to sixteen is close enough for government work.

"The term light year is a measure of distance. Because one light year equals a little less than six trillion miles, this puts the Korr home world ninety nine trillion miles away. If you need metric equivalents you'll find them in your packets.

"Astronomically speaking, 40 Eridani is close so astronomers have studied it for a long time. Some stars have multiple names. True to form this one has four including Keid which translates to Arabic for egg shells. We also use Omicron-2 Eri; 40 Eridani and 40 Eri.

"For Star Trek fans, 40 Eri was supposedly the star orbited by the planet Vulcan, home world to Mr. Spock, the pointy-eared science officer aboard the USS *Enterprise*."

Zack acknowledged a raised hand.

"I'm confused, Zack. Is 40 Eri a star or is it a sun?"

"I use the terms interchangeably for a reason. All stars are suns and all suns are stars."

"So our Sun's a star?" another asked.

"Correct. A common a trick question found on tests by teachers who hate giving out perfect scores asks which star is closest to Earth. The correct answer is the Sun. Astronomy has other quirky rules. For instance, we use an upper case S when referring to our Sun and a lower case s- when referring to other suns. The same goes for the Moon. We use a capital M for our moon and a lower case m- when referring to other moons. Similarly, a capital G is used to refer to our Galaxy, the one we live in, while a lower case g- refers to galaxies in general.

"You might find discovering the similarities between stars and people to be surprising. Stars, like people, come into existence, live out their lives, and die. They also come in different colors, sizes, and shapes. And like people, they exist for different lengths of time. Speaking of size, you'll also find that our Sun is not a large star or even an average one. We generally refer to it as a dwarf star, albeit on the larger side of dwarfish."

"Apparently we got short-changed in the star department," a reporter said. "If anyone knows the address, I'd like to send a letter of complaint."

After some mild laughter another reporter asked, "Is it true that the Sun's a lot bigger than the Earth."

"That's right. It's a little more than one million times bigger. In comparison, the Korr home star, 40 Eri, is a complicated system. The explanation and other data are found in your info packets.

"As the Sun travels through space, it's orbited by about 350 major objects, specifically planets and moons. Together, they make up the solar system. There are also billions of really small objects—asteroids and comets. We won't get into that for our purpose."

"Amen," someone called out.

"We've observed that more than 60 percent of all stars are accompanied by one or more companion stars. So far we haven't discovered a companion for the Sun. We have found many star systems made up of three and four suns orbiting each another. One system easily seen with the unaided eye is the star Castor in the constellation Gemini. Through a telescope we can see that it's made up of three stars, but with special instruments we find each of the three is actually made up of two stars. Another—Alcor, in the handle of the Big Dipper—is actually seven orbiting suns."

"Can you imagine sun bathing on a planet orbiting one of those puppies?" quipped a reporter. "How would you determine what R factor your suntan lotion should be?"

"With that many suns you'd better use R-2000 and wear welder's glasses as sunglasses," Zack replied. "We've known for a long time that 40 Eri was actually made up of three stars called A, B, and C. The biggest and brightest of them---A—can be seen with the naked eye. But B and C orbit each other, and in turn both orbit A at a distance of four hundred times the distance between Earth and the Sun or 37,200,000,000 miles.

"The star Eri B is a white dwarf star a little bigger than Earth with no detected planets. But even if it has planets, they'd have been sterilized when B evolved into a white dwarf star. The third companion, Eri C, is a red dwarf star that's also a little bigger than Earth. Because red dwarfs are known to flare in ultra violet radiation, any planets it might have would be inhospitable to life."

"So what you're saying there are three stars in that system?" a reporter asked.

"Not exactly. According to the alien we've spoken with, it seems they are constructing a fourth star that we will call D."

"That puts Korr technology a little bit ahead of ours," another reporter wisecracked. "But seriously, where can we find these stars at night?"

You'll find them in the constellation Eridanus the River," Zack said. "But remember, of the three, only 40 Eri A can be seen with the naked eye. You can find details in your packets."

"Here's a way to get a feel for the distance to 40 Eri. In one second a beam of light will circle the Earth seven times. Going in a straight line it would get you to the Moon in about one second and 16 years to reach 40 Eri."

A reporter in the front row stood up. "Tom Jason—News International. It looks to me that when we look at 40 Eri, we see how it appeared sixteen years ago and not as it does currently. Is that how long messages to get there?"

"Yes, Tom. We don't see how it looks now, only as it did sixteen years ago. Because radio travel at the speed of light, it would take sixteen years to send a message one way. A live, two-way conversation is impossible, since a round-trip question and answer would take more than thirty-two years...assuming that they were paying attention, and we didn't have to repeat the question.

"All right—any more questions and comments?"

When a dozen hands went up Zack pointed to a woman who asked,

"Stars appear to stand still. But they are moving, aren't they?"

"I'm sorry, and you are?"

"Betty Smith—Religion Today."

"Yes, Betty. Stars do move, and some of them are speeding along at hundreds of miles a second. But because they're so far away, the motion is barely detectable. You'll find that in your packet."

Zack acknowledged another hand.

"Did you say the Korr live on Omnicrom-2's second planet?"

"Yes. But it's pronounced AWM-knee-krawn with just one 'm'," Zack said. "It wasn't until just a few years ago that we discovered it had planets."

"Can we see them?" the reporter asked.

"No. A planet's brightness compared to its star is like trying to spot a firefly sitting on the edge of a lit searchlight."

"So then how do we know they're there?"

"Planets give tiny gravitational tugs to their star while orbiting it. We can detect a star's side-to-side motion as the planet goes around it. But if a star has more than one planet, the tugging motions are complicated and often hard to separate. Images in your packets will show how."

Zack pointed to a man in the fourth row. "Joel Kahn—the *Examiner*. I have two questions. Have the Korr given any indication about what they're doing here? And, how much do we know about them?"

"Those answers, along with others, are in your packets. I'll just say the ability to travel between the stars demonstrates they are hundreds of years ahead of us technically. Some of our estimates put them between 500 and 5,000 years in technology and evolution.

"With regard to their appearance, they can immediately change how you see them, and become someone you know and are comfortable with. From what we understand, it isn't a physical change, just one in your perception. If there are 500 people in a room, they will appear different to each person."

The reporter from *Religion Today* stood and said, "Some of my readers will be very upset with your mention of the word evolution."

"Miss Smith, I believe it is? As for your readers concerns, there is an ongoing debate over the actual process and minutia of evolution, but no debate as to whether it happened and is still taking place. It is a recognized theory as gravity is. But no one in their right mind should leap off a five story building to prove gravity is just a theory. I'll paraphrase what he director of the New York Hayden planetarium once said, 'Science facts are true whether you believe in them or not.'"

"This is as good a time to remember the arrival of the Korr will drag some folks kicking and screaming into the 21st Century. And that closes the book on a number of beliefs including the one claiming we are special and alone."

When the room paused a few seconds to take a deep breath, Zack reminded himself to write those items down to use again some time.

"Moving right along, I ask that you please hold your questions. If anyone cares to stick around after the President speaks, I'll be here to answer whatever I can.

"About the Korr; on a world where they have a problem with mobility they hitch a ride, on a klatt, a life form below them on the evolutionary ladder.

"In order for them to remain undetected on some worlds, they grow a klatt in all shapes and sizes. To you and me a klatt appears human. It's not unlike humans domesticating horses and camels and elephants to give us better mobility.

"The only difference is that the Korr are carried inside a klatt's stomach pouch—like a marsupial."

"So a klatt is alive?" a reporter asked.

"Yes, but without self-awareness or a central nervous system. As offensive as it may seem to you, Korr consider a klatt to be a disposable item."

"Do klatts eat?" the same person asked.

"Not exactly," Zack answered. "Nourishment is obtained from sunlight and soil nutrients because a klatt is made up of sixty percent vegetable matter, twenty-five percent water, ten percent animal protein, and five percent inorganic material. When klatts die on the home world their remains are simply allowed to deteriorate.

"On a planet with high concentrations of nitrogen and oxygen, a dying klatt will flash out of existence and leave only ashes. We don't understand that process."

Zack acknowledged a raised hand.

"Maybe that's the answer to urban legends of humans walking down the street and catching on fire for no apparent reason?"

"I doubt it. A klatt can self-destruct if directed by the resident Korr in its pouch, but never under its own volition. If the need should arise, a Korr has two options before its klatt destructs. It can transfer temporarily to another klatt that already hosts another Korr—a kind of doubling up so to speak. We know nothing about the process, just that the transfer distance can't be more than a few hundred yards. But that's a temporary solution until a host klatt becomes available.

"The second option is for a Korr to transfer back into the Korr group consciousness. Again, we know next to nothing about that concept."

When a question was raised about procreation, Zack said the Korr have three sexes, and the group would have to use their imagination, or read the data in their info packs.

"The number one question on everyone's mind is why did the Korr choose to come here? We're told they are concerned about their fate when the universe ends. For more than 100 years we have known the universe is expanding. Measuring the speed galaxies are moving outwards and knowing their distance from Earth it's just simple math to run those numbers backwards and find out everything began moving from one spot more a little under fourteen billion years ago. That beginning is usually called the Big Bang.

"In theory the expansion will continue for trillion of years in the following order. Sun-like stars will perish in ten billion years followed by small red stars in another ten billion years. Finally the largest stars will run out of fuel and burn themselves out and all molecular activity will grind to a halt. Soon afterwards the universe will consist of nothing but black holes. In another trillion years they will have merged. After a few more quadrillions of years everything will dissolve into nothingness leaving the universe in total darkness.

"But there's another side of that coin. We may have had it wrong. A few of our astronomers have a theory that gravity will cause the universe to slow to a halt and then pull everything to a single point.

They call it the "giB gnaB." That's Big Bang spelled backwards. Who says egg-heads don't have a sense of humor?

"The Korr share at least one human aversion—that of death. While we have no option than to wait for it to happen, the Korr have come up with a plan to beat the dealer, as they say in Las Vegas.

"They plan to move from their physical state into a non-physical state and wait for the universe to bounce back, like a rubber ball and become another expanding universe. Then, when conditions are favorable, they'll reenter that universe and carry on where they left off.

"That's way over my head," someone said. "Can you explain the collapsing universe in lay terms?"

"Sure," said Zack. "As we look out into space we detect that the universe is expanding. All of the billions of galaxies are flying away from each other in all directions. To compute when the universe began, we take the image of what we see and run the motion backwards in a computer. Think of it as watching a movie in reverse.

"When everything reaches a single point, it would have reached the moment of creation—which we call the Big Bang. We can estimate all this by using facts we know—the outward speed of the galaxies and their distance from us.

"Through math, we come to a moment when everything was squeezed together in one spot about the size of a large atom. As I answered before, it works out to be a little less than fourteen billion years ago."

A reporter raised his hand. "I can grasp what you're saying but need to say it aloud a few times before it registers in my Winnie the Pooh-sized brain. If the Big Bang marks the beginning of time when all the matter in the universe was crunched into a tiny spot, where did that spot come from?"

"That question sends scientists into melt-down. They have no idea what caused the Big Bang, or what conditions were like before it. Most believe that the spot was incredibly hot and occupied the tiniest bit of space. But quantum theory says nothing can occupy a point in space that is smaller than the smallest possible piece of space. That's why I've learned to sidestep those questions." Mild chuckles coursed through the room; Zack smiled and continued.

"The Korr's theory may be correct if these two items are also. The first is that the universe is unable to shrink beyond a certain point. The second is that nothing can occur faster than it can during the shortest moment of time. This would mean our universe is the result of an earlier incarnation in the same way as the Phoenix, the mythological bird that rises from its own ashes."

"Okay, let's see if I got this straight," the reported pressed on. "A previous universe ended when it shrunk to a point and hit some kind of a wall you referred to as a quantum something-or-other. When it did so, it bounced back and created the expanding universe we live in today."

"Fantastic—you have it!" Zack said. "It would then have hit a quantum barrier. But possibly putting an end to all this gobbledygook is yet a third possibility—that being something larger than our universe. Imagine an infinite number of universes floating like bubbles in an infinite sized glass of beer. If this is the case, the Korr would be able to move from one universe to another—forever."

The yellow light flashed on the podium. Zack gathered his notes and put them in a pocket. "That light tells me we have to wrap this up. Obviously, it seems the Korr hasn't worked out all the bugs of trying to jump from one universe to the next. The good news is that they're looking for a culture to work with. The bad news is they feel they need to eliminate any intelligent species that they've interviewed before it develops star travel and pollutes any cultures the Korr haven't evaluated yet.

"Unfortunately, humans appear to fall on the line separating candidate species from those they feel to be eliminated. In a nutshell, they're here to decide what to do with us."

A dozen hands shot up just as the red light came on and a voice said, "Ladies and gentlemen, the President of the United States."

Chapter 29

"GOOD EVENING and welcome to Washington Space Dateline News. I'm Virginie LaPlage. It's hard to believe that four days ago world leaders' announced extraterrestrials have been living among us. We'll keep you updated as soon as any information becomes available.

"Tonight we continue with other world news as it unfolds, including communications failure aboard the International Space Station, damage at the site of the world's first space elevator and a new world-wide network of radio telescopes that includes the thousand-foot-wide dish at Arecibo, Puerto Rico.

"But first, a breaking story from news correspondent Vijay Samoothiri reporting live from Sevastopol, site of Russia's Black Sea naval base. Vijay, can you still hear me?"

As the screen split in two, an intense looking young man appeared on the right half, his hair blowing in the wind. "Yes, Sandy, I hear you just fine. I'm sorry for any delays but I'm swamped with updates."

"So, fill us in. I understand we're looking at a mysterious new Russian aircraft carrier. Is this possible?"

"Yes, that's right. If you look over my shoulder you'll see her about a mile out. And you're quite right. Very few people knew much about her until she sailed into port early this morning. So our information is sketchy at best."

"You say this is a new aircraft carrier Vijay? I'm told Russia only had one, the *Nikolai Kuznetsov*. I have a 1995 picture of her on my monitor taken when she was first fully outfitted. I also see she is called the ship of many names. Why is that?"

"All that is true, Sandy, and here's is her background. The *Kuznetsov* was commissioned with the name *Riga*. That name was changed later on to the *Leonid Brezhnev*. Later still it was changed once more. I guess you can understand what happens when politics change or a politician falls out of favor here in Russia."

"Vijay, as I look at the photo I notice something odd. The front end of her flight deck is curved upwards. What's that all about?"

"All flight decks on carriers in that class were built with what they call a ski-jump bow that compensates for design problems the Soviets had with catapults on its carriers. It's similar to an actual ski jump that gives aircraft an added lift when launching."

"I can't detect a name on that ship behind you, Vijay. Are you sure it's not the *Kuznetsov*?"

"That wouldn't be possible, Sandy. As I previously mentioned the *Kuznetsov* is based with the Russian Northern Fleet at Murmansk on the Barents Sea. You might wonder just what a naval base is doing way up North, where waters freeze over in winter. But thanks to the warm North Atlantic Drift, that area of the Barents is ice-free year round."

Samoothiri was handed papers from off-camera. "Sandy, I can now confirm that this is the RFS *Varyag* commanded by Captain Vladimir Volodimirov. It's a sister ship of the *Kuznetsov* and as you can see, she also has a ski-jump flight deck. As to where she came from, I can only tell you that when the Soviet Union dissolved in 1991, construction on the *Varyag* stopped and China bought it and moved it to Dalian, a northern ice-free seaport. My guess is it was either to pay off an old debt or a payment for services to be rendered in the future. One rumor was that she might be turned into a floating casino."

"So OK, Vijay, we understand Russia now has two aircraft carriers. Perhaps they paid China to finish construction and send it back to Russia?"

"That's always a possibility, Sandy. Back to our situation; Volodimirov has been flying aircraft to the naval air station behind me. I'll wager it's his total complement because we counted 10 combat trainers, 10 helicopters and 20 SU-33 Flanker D fighters passing over."

"Vijay, can you help me us out on this? Why is Capt. Volo-whatever still out to sea. He must be aware that the Korr was very specific on all military units returning to their home base of operations."

"It's Vo-lo-di-*mir*-ov, Sandy, and I haven't a clue what's going on. There is one more important item. The local TV news helicopters are reporting the *Varyag*'s bow and stern anchors have been lowered into the sea and set. That tells me Volodimirov plans on remaining out there, at least for the time being. In any event, this is Vijay Samoothiri standing by in Sevastopol."

Sandy turned to the camera. "Our next story concerns the Korr, our uninvited space visitors. With reports coming in from all over about public outcry, you can piece together a fairly accurate picture of the unrest gripping Earth's seven billion inhabitants. A common thread runs through all of this—a feeling of violation. Let me read you one of the emails we've received from one S.W. hailing from Redford Township, Michigan. He writes, 'How come we've been invaded by space aliens who live trillions of miles away? Scientists say it would take our spaceships thousands of years to fly there one way. At the risk of sounding a bit silly but don't the Korr have something better to do to than fly around bullying people? There must be dozens of planets they could pick on that are closer than Earth is.'"

"Well, SW, I don't think you're silly at all. And I couldn't have stated that better. But I don't have an answer for you. We are noticing a calmness settling in after all of the rioting and mayhem. It's as if those people had to blow off steam before grasping the seriousness of our situation.

"With regard to the communication blackout on board the International Space Station, firsts report indicated that a localized explosion caused malfunctions with communications and control mechanisms operating the docking bays. The good news is ground control is receiving information being sent down by ISS radio operators in Morse code. The bad news is ISS apparently can't receive. Our correspondent Clyve Wyckwire reports from ground control in Houston."

The screen switched to a blond-haired man in short sleeves, standing outside the windowed door to a control room.

"Yes, Sandy, I can tell you first hand that ground control was ecstatic when those familiar dots and dashes started coming down.

The lead controller reminded me this isn't the first time Hams, amateur radio operators, have stepped up to the plate in an emergency. He recalls the 2001 attack on New York's Twin Towers when police and fire departments lost all communications due to their headquarters being in the World Trade Center. The Ham community kept them operating until normal communications were reestablished."

"I wasn't aware of that, Clyve. The next time someone is miffed over an antenna on their neighbor's roof they should remember the vital services Hams provide."

"As I mentioned Sandy, within the last hour Houston reestablished voice communications with ISS. Once again, that's the good news—the bad news being that the terrorists, claiming they are patriots, won't let the crew speak to ground control. A list of demands has been sent down with orders to forward them to Moscow. If the demands aren't met, the crew's lives will be in jeopardy."

"So Clyve, do we know who these so-called patriots are, where they're from, and if those demands will be made public? Also, how did they ever get on board?"

"The only thing we're told is their allegiance is to one of the former Russian territories with broken ties to Moscow. So far, ground control hasn't made the demands public. We do know there can't be more than four of them. That's the capacity of the Russian supply ship used to get up there."

"I would venture to say that sooner or later their demands will be made public. So as soon as you hear anything at all, please get back to us Clyve."

"I will, Sandy. This is ISS ground control in Houston; Clyve Wyckwire reporting."

"It's been more than ten years since the introduction of radio interferometry was introduced," Sandy continued. "This lets us link two or more radio telescopes at separate locations electronically, producing a huge and invisible telescope, as big as the size equal to the miles between them.

"One of the world's largest single dish radio telescopes is found at Arecibo in Puerto Rico measuring a thousand feet in diameter. It's my pleasure to welcome back for his visit to our show the facility's director and a personal friend—Dr. Bertram Powell."

The screen split in two with Sandy on the left and Powell on the right. Behind him was a photograph of the Arecibo telescope.

"Thank you for the kind introduction, Sandy. It's a pleasure to be back."

"I understand your telescope has been designated a co-anchor of a new astronomy project headquartered in Holland and named e-VLBI—an acronym for Very Long Baseline Interferometry."

"That's right, Sandy. We're very proud to play a role in the project."

"I can understand how exciting that must be especially with you chosen to be co-director. We'd like you tell us about the project if you promise not to make it too technical."

"As you most aptly put it, interferometry uses two or more telescopes and with atomic clocks links them all electronically. The result is roughly our using a telescope as wide as the distance between them."

"So telescopes separated by a mile would operate as a one-mile-wide telescope?"

"Essentially, yes. It offers an incredible savings over what it would cost to build a telescope that large—if it was even possible to do so. In the early days, combining two telescopes was never very effective. But we've refined the process to the point that the more telescopes we connect, the better the results."

"Where did the concept of interferometry come from?"

"The idea came from France in the 1870s, but it took more than a century before our technology caught up with our ideas, and made it a reality. I'm sure some of your audience has seen pictures of the Very Large Array near Socorro, New Mexico. It's made up of twenty-seven, 85-foot-wide radio telescopes arranged in large Y formation."

"I've seen them in science fiction films. The two that come to mind are Contact and Independence Day. What else can you tell us about this new e-VLBI?"

"It stands for electronic-Very-Long-Base-Interferometry and consists of a few dozen radio telescopes in five countries. When completed, their separation will be nearly 7,000 miles. And that will give us 100 times the resolution of any current optical telescope."

"As I understand it, your thousand-foot telescope will be e-VLBI's western anchor?"

"Yes, and all of the observational data will be stored at Puerto Rico and Holland."

"It certainly sounds like astronomy will be getting a great device. Thanks for coming on our show, Dr. Powell. I hope you'll let us call on you again."

"Anytime, Sandy. It's always a pleasure."

"Our last news item has to do with the attack on the space elevator under construction in French East Guiana. A space elevator is a bit like the elevators we use here on Earth. In our buildings a cable both pulls the car up and lowers it. With space elevators the cable is motionless and the cars slide up and down it. The bottom of the space elevator is attached to the ground and the top is fastened to a satellite orbiting Earth at the same speed the planet revolves—roughly 25,000 miles an hour. That way the cable stands still pointing up into space.

"Now, just add two cable cars, one at the top in space and the other at the bottom on the ground—and would you believe both cable cars travel for free? While the top car is descending it produces enough energy to lift the bottom car up to the satellite. Unless you're the technical type that loves math and physics minutia, you and I will find the length of the cable fascinating—26,000 miles!

"Well, it turns out that the cable needs to be a little longer than that. It has to extend past the satellite to add centrifugal force and keep gravity from pulling everything down. Aren't you glad we won't be having a 'pop' quiz on space elevators?

"Getting back to Earth, the base tether at Kourouas suffered only minor damage in the attack that won't interfere with work on the elevator."

Sandy's director spoke through her ear bud; she paused for a moment, trying not to appear startled and, without missing a beat, glanced at her monitor and continued.

"Something important is happening at the Sevastopol naval base. Our correspondent Vijay Samoothiri will give us an update. Vijay, are you there?"

Samoothiri appeared on the monitor with a handful of notes. He just finished speaking to someone off camera before turning to the camera. "Yes, Sandy, I'm here. And I have to say things are getting a little...well, crazy. I'll try to piece together what has happened since we last spoke."

"This is about the aircraft carrier?" she asked.

"Yes. The *Varyag* is definitely in trouble. Our first indication was when Capt. Volodimirov flew his entire air arm over to the naval air station a mile or so behind me just before we spoke earlier. We just heard some radio traffic that obviously wasn't meant for us and should have gone out on a secured frequency. The Chief of Naval Operations for the Black Sea Fleet has ordered Volodimirov in no uncertain terms to return to port immediately."

"That's incredible Vijay. We're hanging by a thread. Tell us everything you can."

"World War Two enthusiasts will remember the Battle of the Bulge and when the Germans had us surrounded. When they sent the American commanding officer a demand for his unconditional surrender, his answer to them was just one word, 'Nuts'.

"Well it seems Volodimirov has told his superiors pretty much the same in refusing to return to base, despite the Korr's threat of reprisal. Hold on a minute.

Holding his earpiece, Samoothiri appeared to look off into the distance, before nodding and returning his focus to the camera.

"Okay, I'm back Sandy. We're told Volodimirov has given the order to abandon ship. You should be able to see the crew jumping into the water. Am I getting through Sandy? It seems we're breaking up."

"You're coming through loud and clear, Vijay."

Reading from his notes, Samoothiri continued. "Temperatures onboard the *Varyag* are increasing by—just give me a moment to convert to Fahrenheit in my head, here—by almost ten degrees an hour. If this keeps up, conditions will become impossible and the Varyag will literally melt and sink. It's like we're witnessing another Hindenburg airship disaster way back in 1937."

Samoothiri's audio began breaking up and the picture went black. Her program director caught Sandy's eye, shook her head and pointed to the clock.

Sandy looked directly into the main studio camera. "As you can see we've not only lost our connection to Vijay," she said, "we've also run out of time. I invite you to stay tuned for news updates throughout the evening. Reminding you that this program will replay at 10 p.m., this is Virginie LaPlage for Washington Space Dateline News, wishing you all a goodnight."

Chapter 30

IT WAS JUST PAST TWELVE-THIRTY when Zack arrived at the White House. He went directly to the Intelligence Center, more often referred to as the Situation Room, located on the lower level of the West Wing. Bertram Powell had already arrived and was in the reception area chatting up a presidential aide. He excused himself and went over to greet Zack.

"Hi Zacker. I've been wondering why we were invited to show up"

"I'd imagine it has something to do with the visitor," Zack replied. "The message said to be here by 1 p.m., so here I am."

A second aide entered the room. "You may go right in gentlemen," he said pointing to a set of double doors. He gestured for them to enter and remained outside.

At some time or another, on television or in a movie, most people get to see the Situation Room—or, at the least, some director's version of what a proper Situation Room would look like. Even so, Zack and Bertie found that being there for the first time and taking stock of its 5,000 square-foot expanse to be rather exciting.

Zack poked Bertram's ribs. "I'll bet if we found the right switch to pull we could start a war," he whispered.

A dozen black leather chairs were arranged around a long conference table. In front of each was a leather place mat bearing the presidential seal and set tidily with pens, paper, and water glasses placed on white linen napkins embroidered in gold.

"Just like we have at Arecibo, more or less," Bertram jibbed.

On one wall, two tiers of monitors gathered data from around the world. Six monitors, each with a secured link to Air Force One, helped facilitate video-conferencing. A lead-lined cabinet was employed to store visitor's personal communicator devices.

A dozen chairs lined two of the walls, placed to accommodate less essential VIPs and their aides. During its last renovation, the original mahogany-paneled walls had been replaced by high technology whisper walls to reduce extraneous sound.

"Welcome to what we call the woodshed," President Brandstadt announced from the far end of the room. She stood next to a podium alongside the visitor, and gestured across the whole area. "You might be interested to know this room was originally the Truman-era bowling alley. Now, please come over here and meet our guest."

Standing completely nude, the visitor's appearance was bizarre. If standing motionless it would have looked like a department store manikin. It turned, smiled pleasantly, and extended a hand in greeting to the approaching men. Zack and Bertie were relieved to see that it bore no trace of gender.

The visitor was the first to speak. "It's a privilege to meet you, Dr. Powell. The President tells me you are an outstanding scientist as well as a valued friend."

Powell extended his hand cautiously and said, "This is an exciting moment for me and an honor to make your acquaintance after years of interest in SETI."

"I can understand how this would be a most satisfying moment," said the visitor.

"From what I've been told," Powell added, "your many abilities include allowing one to see you as someone they know or have known who would ensure confidence and respect. I'm anxious to find out who you would choose for— " A look of astonishment crossed his face.

"Oh yes," he continued, "my late step-father was a fine and decent person."

"As a matter of interest," said the visitor, "your Mrs. Brandstadt sees her fiancée as he appeared when they attended college together. Unfortunately he perished in an automobile accident shortly after they had become engaged. She too is comfortable with this effect."

"I certainly am," Brandstadt nodded.

"It is also a pleasure to meet you, Zack. After establishing that this would not cause you discomfort, I've assume the likeness of someone you held great affection for."

Lise Danfers took a few steps towards Zack with her arms opened wide. She embraced him saying, "Hi there handsome. Give me a big hug."

Zack followed through without hesitation. He closed his eyes as they embraced and whispered, "Lise," not noticing that the President's eyes were misting.

"This will be just fine," Zack said. "Actually it's wonderful," he added stepping back but continuing to hold Lise's hand.

Though Powell found himself caught up in the warmth spreading through the room, he tried to get everyone back on track. "Wouldn't it be wonderful if all of us shared our visitor's gift?" he smiled. "It would go a long way in fostering better communication."

He turned to the visitor and added without thinking, "I'll bet you could sell me the Golden Gate Bridge." Flushing a bright red, he quickly moved to make amends.

"Excuse me. It just slipped out—no disrespect intended."

Powell's step-father smiled. "None taken. I'll even throw in the Chunnel between France and England to sweeten the deal."

"The three of us are about to witness something unusual," said the president. "As a follow-up to my address yesterday, our guest is about to make a worldwide TV announcement to a number of heads of state. After that we can chat for a bit. Then, if you don't mind I'll ask you two to leave so my guest and I can prepare for a three o'clock staff meeting. It will be standing room only since I invited the Vice President, CIA Director, Homeland and National Security advisors and the Joint Chiefs and their aides. I may end up having to sit on someone's lap."

"And now to business," the visitor said, proceeding to the podium. Almost imperceptibly, its tone changed to one suitable to address international dignitaries.

"I am making this announcement in person to each head of state simultaneously," it said to Powell. "If you're interested, Zack can explain the process to you." It then turned to face the camera, waiting for the cue to begin.

"A television camera will tape the visitor's address," Zack whispered to his friend, "and then Brandstadt will replay it during her meeting. While you and I will see the visitor at the podium, at the same time it will be with heads of state around the world and speaking their language."

A red light appeared on the camera, and the visitor began.

"I want to thank you for meeting with me on such short notice. I have two announcements to make. The first is that you will be required to pass on to your citizens what I have to say using the media of your choice. The information must be complete, accurate, and released within twenty-four hours. No exceptions. And this is not a request."

The visitor glanced at a timepiece, and continued.

"Regarding the second item, six hours ago, nuclear missiles were launched from four countries with the intent of intercepting and destroying the three spacecraft that are on a course to Earth. It is important to add that each craft is carrying thousands of living, sentient beings.

"Because the missiles were launched simultaneously from North Korea, China, Iran and two former Russian states, it is safe to assume it was a coordinated attack. Bearing in mind the gravitational effects of your sun, its planets and the speed of the missiles, they will reach the spacecraft in seven days.

"In each of those countries, one city with a population of more than 50,000 persons will be destroyed in four days at twelve noon, local time. The cities have been identified to permit the inhabitants to take whatever precautionary actions they choose.

"If another aggressive act takes place, an unspecified number of large cities in the countries involved will be destroyed without warning. A further consequence of this attack is moving your trial date to thirty days from today."

"I was afraid something like this might happen," Zack whispered.

"Me, too," replied Powell, "but it still takes me by surprise."

The visitor continued. "The trial will take place in the Cultural Arts Complex in Washington, DC. Because there was some question as to which were sovereign nations would be represented, the attendance will be based on those 197 countries recognized by the United Nations.

"Further instructions will be provided within two days. And in closing, I will now attempt to imitate your humor. From this moment on the term normal will apply only to clothes and dish washers."

The visitor left the podium and walked over to Brandstadt, Powell and Zack, with an air of nonchalance and a broad grin.

"Well," it said, "I hope you'll agree that went rather well."

Chapter 31

LI-HWA LUGGED HER GROCERY BAGS up the steps of the officer's living quarters in downtown Moscow and offered a retinal scan inside the foyer to unlock the double glass doors leading into the lobby. Smiling as she entered, she greeted the corporal at the security desk. Just a wisp of a thing, with red hair and freckles looking making her look more like girl of fifteen rather than a twenty-five year old young woman, Li-Hwa often wondered how she had passed the recruiter's physical exam. Smiling as she entered, she greeted the corporal at the security desk.

"I'm afraid I have bad news Major," said the corporal. "The elevator has been up on the fifth floor for the past twenty minutes. A new resident, another major, is moving his furniture and personal belongings. It looks like he's propped the door open."

"Well that's inconsiderate," replied Li-Hwa. "I thought our building rules specified that new residents have to use our freight elevator when they move in."

"I did mention it to him in passing, Major, but our freight elevator isn't working and I'm waiting for the repair department to send a technician. Besides, some officers don't take kindly to young female corporals quoting regulations at them."

"I see your point. So let's give the major the benefit of the doubt this time. But if he continues being a nuisance, this major will have no qualms reaming out his posterior."

"I'll be happy to help you up the stairs with those bags if you'd like."

"No thanks, I'll be perfectly fine. And try not to take the major too seriously. We girls must stick together. So if you get the opportunity, give our new resident a welcoming hug from me."

"I'd prefer not to, Major!" the corporal blushed.

AS LI-HWA ENTERED her apartment, the telephone rang.

"Zaranova," she answered.

"Hello, Major. It's Natasha from Colonel Kornikov's office. My but you sound out of breath."

"I am after carrying two bags of groceries up three flights of stairs because some nitwit tied up the elevator."

"That doesn't sound too good. Did you find any good buys today?"

"You wouldn't believe the sale I found on premium vodka. Just between the two of us, I couldn't resist and picked up five bottles."

"You'll have to tell me more about it later. Right now, the Colonel needs to speak to you." In a whisper she added, "To give you a heads up, he's going to ask you to come in tomorrow evening for a few hours even though he's aware that it's a weekend and your birthday as well."

"Thanks for that, Natasha. You can connect us now."

"Connecting..."

"Yes, Major," Kornikov said. "Let me apologize for bothering you at home."

"That is never a problem, Colonel. How may I help you?"

"I received a call from the President. He has received information from the Korr about that rules and regulations to be adhered to during the trial. I believe that identical information has been sent to all of the world's leaders. He wants me involved."

"Being chosen for such an assignment is a wonderful compliment, Colonel."

"Thank you. He sent a copy of the instructions. I'll read you a small portion of it." Clearing his throat, he began, "'Within twenty-four hours upon receipt, the following is to be made available to the citizens of every country by all available media.'

"Now, the President believes the information contains details that don't affect our average citizen. So he wants his national address to be a shortened version of what he received."

"Do you know when he plans to make the announcement?"

"Tomorrow evening at six. So he will be making the announcement personally by radio, but wants me to give the same address on television."

"I'm sure you will do just fine, Colonel. So what can I do?"

"Because I will need someone to introduce me, Tat and I agree you're the best choice in light of your pleasant voice, poise, and excellent diction. It wouldn't be lengthy, perhaps thirty seconds."

When a second phone rang he answered, "Yes… yes I will…" He ended that conversation and returned to Li-Hwa, "Sorry for the interruption, it was Tat just reminding me that we both should be in dress uniform."

The phone rang again. "Yes, Tat...yes, that's a fine idea. I'll ask her. Goodbye."

"Hello again Major. After the broadcast, Tat and I want would like to take you to the Potemkin Club for dinner and drinks in celebration of your birthday."

"That's a pleasant surprise Colonel. And I'll be pleased to introduce you---but the offer for dinner isn't necessary."

"Unless you have a previous appointment, please join the two of us. I assure you there will not be any surprises like young lieutenants jumping out of your birthday cake in their birthday suits. Anyway, I'm sure you'll find the evening to your liking."

Li-Hwa smiled. "Will you make the broadcast from your office?"

"Yes, so I'd like you to arrive one hour early—say five o'clock." When his phone rang a third time he answered brusquely, "Now what? Yes I will. Goodbye Tat!"

He hung up the other phone and said, "Sorry about that. My wife also wanted me to add that you are welcome to bring along a friend."

"That's very kind, Colonel, but I'm happy to come alone. And yes, I will be in your office at five tomorrow afternoon."

"Thank you for volunteering, Major. After the introduction feel free to come in while I'm speaking. You can stand with Tatyana behind the camera making sure you don't cough or sneeze."

* * * * *

THE FOLLOWING EVENING Li-Hwa stood outside Kornikov's office holding a microphone in front of a TV camera. Her name and rank appeared at the bottom of the screen. Behind her was a closed door with an engraved brass plate reading:

COLONEL MIKHAIL GRIGORYEVICH KORNIKOV
DIRECTOR—CENTRAL INTELLIGENCE SERVICE
KGB/FSB—FIRST DIRECTORATE MOSCOW

Receiving her cue, she nodded and spoke.

"Good evening. I am Major Zaranova, attached to the Central Intelligence Service in Moscow. We ask you to forgive this interruption to your regular programming in order to bring you this special announcement. I am speaking to you from outside the offices and conference rooms of our headquarters. It is now my pleasure to introduce to you the director of Central Intelligence, Colonel Mikhail Kornikov."

Tatyana opened the door from inside the office and motioned Li-Hwa to enter. A finger on her lips indicated they were to be quiet.

Kornikov sat behind an elaborate wood desk with intricately carved patterns. He wore a somber expression, appropriate to the seriousness of his announcement as well as his discomfort in the role of a public speaker. On the wall behind him was a gigantic map of Russia.

"Good evening," he began. "Our Russian Federation President has asked me to speak to you regarding new information from our interstellar visitors, the Korr. They have traveled to Earth from a planet that orbits the star 40 Eridani located 156 trillion kilometers, or 96 trillion miles from Earth.

"The star is known by multiple names including Keid. Coincidentally, that is the star orbited by the imaginary planet Vulcan, home world of Mr. Spock of *Star Trek* fame. In addition to having interstellar travel capabilities, our scientists say the Korr have an average life-span of seven hundred years and have evolved far beyond us—technologically, perhaps by as much as five thousand years.

"The Korr have given us information about the rules and regulations of our forthcoming trial. As you know, this event has occupied our media since the visitor announced it. Because the instructions are long and tedious, I will only mention main items. You will find complete details in your newspapers.

"The trial will be held in the Cultural Arts Complex in Washington, DC. Each of the 197 nations recognized by the United Nations are required to attend, and will represent the total population of Earth. Because of seating limitations, only six delegates per nation will be seated in the auditorium. The two mandatory delegates are the head of state, and a legal advisor. It is suggested three seats be given to a scientist, a historian, and a security advisor, respectively. Our visitors suggest the sixth seat be filled by an educator, military advisor, philosopher, or spiritual leader.

"The trial format will be English Law, with one exception. The defendant, humanity, will be considered guilty unless proven innocent. It is understandable how trying these events are and we share your concerns. But for Mother Russia to survive this ordeal, we ask you to exercise patience and understanding.

"Let me stress the importance of restraint from acts of violence by reminding you of the six cities that were destroyed after the failed attack on the inbound spaceships. Once again, I thank you for your attention and wish you a good night. God bless our Motherland."

Chapter 32

AS THE TAXI WORKED ITS WAY through the streets of Moscow, Tatyana turned to their guest. "Li," she said, "I'm so happy to see you enjoying yourself tonight. And just think the evening is only beginning. I also enjoy seeing another side of you—one more relaxed, less official."

"I look forward to the three of us being out together," Li-Hwa replied. "Actually it's a double treat for me. This will be my first visit to the Potemkin Club. Over the years I've had a few chances to visit it, but something always came up at the last minute and I always had to cancel."

"Well, my dear, short of an asteroid strike or a UFO abduction, you'll finally get your night at the Potemkin," Tatyana said, patting her hand.

"And this is my first taxi ride in a long time," Li-Hwa smiled, looking out the window. "I love seeing the city lit up like tourists do. This is going to be a special evening for me."

"We decided to give Rubinsky the night off so he could go to his brother's birthday party," Tatyana said. "By a strange coincidence, it is also it's being held at the Potemkin!"

"Maybe we will run into him."

"Probably not," said Kornikov. "His party's on the second level. It's exclusively for intermediate line officers—captain and below."

"They even have their own entrance," added Tatyana. "I used to think it bordered on exclusionary, but in the long run it is probably more comfortable for all concerned. Younger officers like bright lights and louder music. We seem to prefer a quieter, less chaotic atmosphere."

"Besides," the Colonel said, "for one reason or another the directors never installed elevators. So everyone's content. Especially the older officers who don't like climbing stairs."

The taxi slowed to a stop at the Potemkin, and a doorman came over and reached for the handle.

"This should be a first for him," Tatyana laughed. "He'll be helping a colonel and two sexy female majors out of an old rusty taxi."

"Just tell him our department is making major cutbacks and chauffeured staff cars took the first hit," said Li-Hwa.

Tatyana was still giggling as the three of them passed through the revolving door. She could tell how impressed Li-Hwa was. Quite aside from the widened eyes and distracted steps, her first words were faint whispers.

"This is even more elegant than I imagined."

Tatyana signed the guestbook as the Colonel took their coats and caps to the cloakroom. Upon his return, he was all smiles and chivalry.

"I'll see about getting us a table for dinner while you ladies check out the bar. I'll meet you there and we'll have a cocktail or 'three'."

"This carpeting is incredible," Li-Hwa said as they crossed the foyer. "It's like walking on a cloud, but I'd have difficulty describing the color."

"You know, there's a story behind the unusual color. The club's governing board is made up of Army and Navy officers. So when it was time to choose the carpeting they had to come up with a compromise between Navy blue and Army green. The youngsters upstairs, the junior officers, call it 'bleen'."

"I'll have to remember that, Major. But where I would— "

"Please call me Tatyana when we aren't on duty Li-Hwa. But Misha still prefers to be referred to as 'Colonel.'"

"Thanks—I'll make a note of that. You know, I imagined there would be more marble and granite in the décor. But I find the dark wood paneling very elegant."

"This entire patterned floor is Russian Oak. The upper level is probably more like what you had imagined. It's all glass and marble, so much so that our *maître d'* keeps receiving complaints about the upper level music bouncing off the walls."

"Sounds like they must have a wonderful time up there. I sometimes enjoy that kind of atmosphere. It depends on my mood."

"That makes us kindred souls, Li. Now here's a plan. The next time Misha goes out of town overnight, you and I will dig out our captain's bars, put on dark sunglasses, hike our skirts up a notch or two, slide into three-inch heels, and let our hair down. I'd like to think I still have enough of the old zing to garner some attention."

Li-Hwa laughed.

"And speaking of my lord and master," Tatyana whispered, "here he comes now. Just to let you know, he's on the Club's decorating committee. If given the slightest opening, he tends to numb people's brains with decorating minutia."

"Well ladies, they only have a small table available. The one I preferred won't be ready for another fifteen minutes, so let's wait over there under the oil painting and enjoy our cocktails."

He motioned for a waiter and then held the ladies' chairs.

"You are so gallant, Colonel," Li-Hwa said. "Thank you. I have to say these black leather chairs with gold piping look very distinguished. Your wife tells me you are on the decorating committee."

"Yes, but I'm afraid I can't take credit for the chairs," he said. "I was actually proposing we buy gold chairs with black trim. I lost by a single vote."

"Must have been one of those Navy directors," Li-Hwa grinned.

The Colonel stroked his chin and put his hand on one of Li-Hwa's. "Come to think of it, you are correct, my dear. He was an old salty. But to be perfectly honest, I must admit I like these better."

Tatyana was pleased to see them getting on so well in this casual setting.

Li-Hwa asked if there was a connection between the Club and the painting of the old warship.

"You couldn't have picked a better person to ask, Li. One of Misha's diversions is military history." She turned to him and grinned mischievously. "And darling, please do your best to keep it shorter than *War and Peace* and a bit less convoluted than *The Brothers Karamazov*."

"That's alright, Major," Li-Hwa laughed. "I enjoy Dostoevsky."

"Remember," Tatyana whispered as the waiter came with their drinks. "When we are off duty Li, please call me Tatyana."

The Colonel sat back, straightened in his chair, and squared his drink on its napkin. Li could tell he was comfortable in his role of club historian.

"The *Potemkin*," he began wave a hand to the painting, "was commissioned in 1904. She was not only the flagship of our fleet; she was a prominent symbol of the pre-communist imperialist empire.

"Now, after its humble beginnings early in the Eighteenth Century, by 1914 the Empire had grown to be the fifth largest state in all of Europe. All that came to a sudden end with the glorious Russian Revolution of 1917."

"Just tell us about the ship. dear. Remember—the ship."

"Yes, of course," he harrumphed. "The *Potemkin* was a pre-dreadnought battleship built for the Black Sea Fleet of the Imperial Russian Navy. Barely a year old, she was out on exercises from her home port of Odessa, when she unwittingly became the major event leading up to the minor revolution in 1905, and eventually the great revolution of 1917.

"The ship's enlisted crew was made up of about seven hundred peasants and led by eighteen officers, who came from nobility. As you might imagine, this combination brought the enlisted men much harshness and brutality.

"An interesting side note is that because of their humble beginnings, the enlisted men had been mostly vegetarians. That was the answer to a wager made by the then sitting U.S. President Theodore Roosevelt. As that story unfolds, Roosevelt was drinking heavily one evening when he made a statement about the *Potemkin* crew. He wagered that the reason the crew was known for efficiency was because they were consuming a lot of red meat,"

"Interesting," Li-Hwa said. "What was the outcome?"

"Well the crew heard of the wager and accepted the bet. To prove Roosevelt wrong they gave up eating meat entirely and went back to being vegetarians until, one day when meat provisions were brought on board, they were heavily infested with maggots."

Li-Hwa drew in her chin and pursed her lips. "Ooh, that's terrible."

"It gets worse. The officers ordered the crew to eat the meat, the men refused, and a skirmish broke out. Coincidently, there had been a rash of disciplinary problems throughout the Russian Empire, and the ship's officers had been on the lookout for any such event.

"As a result, a dozen or so agitators in the crew were dragged out on deck and ordered to stand at attention on a large tarpaulin. A number of armed marine-sailors lined up behind them. Fearing for their own lives as well as the crewmates that were about to be killed, the crew mutinied."

"Oh my," Li-Hwa said with a sigh.

"The ensuing melee led to seven officers being killed, including the captain. To make matters worse, the remaining officers were thrown overboard."

"I can see why events like that one sparked the first revolution in 1905," she said. "So what ever happened to the crew and the ship?"

"Like the crew of England's HMS *Bounty*, the *Potemkin* mutineers were forced to sail from port to port for coal and provisions. When no port city would help them, some of the crew surrendered and were executed. The others fled to South America and Europe. Meanwhile, the ship enjoyed a less-than-glorious future. In fact it accidentally sunk one of its own submarines. It was finally decommissioned and dismantled."

The *maître d'* came over to the table. "It will be about five more minutes Colonel."

"That will be fine," Kornikov said.

"And that," Tatyana said dabbing her mouth with a napkin, "will give me just enough time to show Li-Hwa our club's famous collection of glassware over the bar."

AFTER FINDING their seats, Li-Hwa turned to her hosts and sighed.

"I had wanted to ask about those glasses," said Li-Hwa. "There must be a hundred or more."

"More like two hundred," the Colonel replied. "They belong to members who can afford to be extravagant."

"As you can see," explained Tatyana, "the lower three rows are crystal glassware with an etched *Potemkin*'s crest and silver bases and handles."

"Those on the top row are etched with gold inlay," added the Colonel.

"I noticed they looked different. Is there a reason for that?"

"Yes," said Tatyana. "Besides the fact those are the most expensive, they are owned by members who are wealthy, have retired, moved away, or died. They also act as a reminder to everyone to put aside funds for luxuries in our golden years."

Upon receiving a discrete nod from Tatyana, the bartender reached below the counter and brought up a gift box, attractively wrapped with silver ribbon and a bow. He set it down in front of Li-Hwa.

"I believe you'll find it has your name on it, my dear. Misha and I wanted to wish you a happy birthday and hope you will enjoy many years to come."

"What a wonderful surprise. Thank you both very much. It's thoughtful but totally unnecessary."

She began to unwrap it slowly and with care.

"Could someone please explain why women take longer to unwrap gifts than they do to wrap them?" the Colonel asked.

"We call it savoring the moment, dear."

"That's true, Colonel," Li-Hwa smiled. "I want to relish this moment."

The Colonel just sighed.

When she finally removed a silver and crystal cup she was moved to tears. She ran a delicate finger over the initials LHZ on the base. "I'm stunned," she whispered, "and don't know what to say or do. It's one of the most thoughtful gifts I've ever received. If I wasn't in uniform I'd give you both a hug."

The Colonel smiled. "Finding that I receive fewer hugs as each year passes, I encourage you to throw caution to the wind my dear."

With that, Li-Hwa slid off of her chair and embraced them.

"I hope you approve of the monogram," Tatyana said dabbing at a moist eye. "When I found myself unable to discover your middle name I took the liberty of having it engraved LHZ and not just LZ."

"It's perfect. Thank you very much Maj…Tatyana."

"Now if you would cast your eye to the end of the row," the Colonel smiled, "you'll see an empty space reserved for you."

Making a point of looking the full length of the bar, Tatyana turned to the bartender. "Speaking of empty spaces," she said, "I see one where Colonel Pavel Federov, Misha's uncle, should be. I wonder whatever could have happened to it?"

As if on cue, the bartender reached below the counter, brought up a second gift, and handed it to Tatyana. She read the name tag, then turned to look around.

"Does anyone here answer to the name of Mikhail?" she asked.

At first the Colonel looked perplexed, then his face grew quite serious.

"I certainly hope you haven't gone and…"

"Just relax and open it."

When he also removed another cup, one that was etched in gold inlay with two initials MGK & PAF, he choked up slightly and said, "My dear Tanya, I don't know what to think. This belonged to Uncle Pavel."

"Now it belongs to both of you," she said softly. "I know he would have approved. And knowing how frugal you are, I managed to move you to the top row by paying just for the extra engraving. That empty place up there among the K's now belongs to both of you."

When the *maître d'* told them their table was ready, Tatyana suggested pouring the drinks into their new glasses and bringing them along.

On the way, Li-Hwa nodded politely at a young female lieutenant having dinner. Before she could ask why the junior officer wasn't upstairs, Tatyana laughed and explained.

"As you can see," said Tatyana, "she's with a colonel. Perhaps they are having a business meeting or…" At that point the older man took the lieutenant's hand and began stroking it.

Tatyana winked. "Or perhaps something else."

After dinner the Colonel removed three sets of papers from an attaché case. He passed them to the women and kept one for himself.

"These are the parameters for the trial, and I find them to be a strange mix. While most items seem valid, I can see some others posted in a child's day-care center. For instance, number sixteen."

The two women followed along as he read. Before, long, they found their eyes beginning to glaze.

"'The sixth seat assignee may be replaced once a day, but only before the beginning of that morning's proceedings or for a medical emergency.' And let's look at number eighteen: 'The remainder of the auditorium's seats will be used by representatives of the World

Court, translators, building security, invited media and technical personnel.' The next item, nineteen, specifies that other rooms in the Convention Complex will be reserved ...."

Li-Hwa stifled a yawn; Tatyana, having grown accustomed to dealing with her husband's eye for detail, delivered a discreet kick to her shin.

"Okay," the Colonel continued, "now jump to number twenty nine...."

Li-Hwa's eyes widened; when she looked at Tatyana, she saw the latter's glaze disappear into a scowl of warning, and Li-Hwa managed to disguise her yawn as a smile.

"And then we finally arrive at the final item, number forty five: 'Although there will not be scheduled lunch hours, food will be available in the food courts outside the chamber during each of the four intermissions."

"I honestly can't find fault with any of those, Misha," Tatyana said hastily. "Not given the problems of bringing so many cultures together under one roof, if only to be reprimanded. But can you imagine how you would feel if it were up to you to inform a king or queen that they couldn't use the toilet facilities for ten more minutes?"

He and Li-Hwa nodded.

The Colonel continued, "As I said there are twelve of these that any adult would know without having to be told. For example, where is that one? Aha, here it is—number forty eight: 'During the one-hour sessions, there must be no outbursts, disruptions, napping, sleeping, unnecessary talking or use of recording devices.'"

Li-Hwa shook her head, "It still makes me shudder thinking I might have to forbid a VIP the use of the loo."

"Does it say how large the television monitors will be?" Tatyana asked.

The Colonel flipped forward a couple of pages. "Here it is, item number eighty eight: 'There will be seven, twenty-foot-square, screens in the auditorium. Three will be set across the front of the auditorium and two more on each side wall. The middle monitor in front will display whoever is speaking as will one of the two on the side walls. Every sixty seconds the remaining screens will rotate color images of nature scenes taken at random in the countries attending. Topics may include, but not be limited to oceans, seas, sea shores, jungles, woods, meadows, mountains, lakes, rivers, tundra, and deserts. They may display flora and fauna but no humans. No human artifacts or constructions are to be shown.' And it just goes on and on." The Colonel shook his head, flipping through several more pages before dropping his packet on the table.

As Tatyana ordered another round of drinks, the *maître d'* came up.

"Colonel, you have an important long distance call. The manager suggests you take it in his office."

"Thank you." Kornikov pushed his chair back. "If you ladies will excuse me…"

"I'm sure it is good news, Colonel," Li-Hwa said hopefully. "My intuition is whispering that we will soon be calling you 'General.'"

"As much as I like hearing the sound of that, I'm not eligible for advancement for another year. Still, a special promotion would give us another reason to celebrate, and justify ordering the more expensive vodka."

"I'll drink to that my dear," Tatyana laughed.

After Kornikov left, Tatyana slid her chair closer to Li-Hwa. "I think this is as good a time as any for us to have a girl-to-girl talk," she smiled.

"I'm comfortable with 'Li' when it's just the two of us."

"You know, I picked up on the look on Zack's face when you walked into the meeting in London. It was more than his being surprised. He looked stunned, almost wounded. Have the two of you been in touch since we took him to the airport?

"No."

"Come now, Li. I'm entitled to more than that. Remember, Misha and I told you up front that your assignment with him was of great importance to the country. It was crucial to find out what the Americans had discovered and what they were up to. You've never said anything personal about him in your reports. Now then—woman-to-woman—did some kind of 'personal situation' develop between you."

The waiter brought over drinks, set one down in front of Tatyana and emptied the other into Li-Hwa's new glass. Tatyana signed the charge slip.

Li-Hwa sipped her drink. "Yes," she said softly.

"I thought as much."

"You and the Colonel knew I would gladly do whatever was asked of me. But as my mission progressed, I realized the assignment was becoming more and more personal. Not at first, only after we said goodbye in Bermuda. That's when it began to sink in. By that time I was very fond of him. Let me rephrase that. I cared for him. And after I dropped him off at the airport, I knew I had fallen in love."

"Oh my poor girl. I thought as much when our people advised me you spent your last night together in London. Do you think that was wise?"

"Yes—even if Zack only wanted to enjoy the moment. I needed to be close to him and was afraid it could be our last time together."

"You certainly sound like a charter member of the Zack Peters fan club. As to the competition, were you referring to Virginie LaPlage in Washington?"

Li-Hwa wrung her hands as she spoke, "She is an incredible woman."

"How do you know? He surely wouldn't have told you. Did you meet her?"

"No, but I did use our department's resources to research her background."

Tatyana shook her head. "I strongly suggest you mention that to nobody other than me. What did you discover?"

Li-Hwa ran her palms forward and back on her lap and took a deep breath. "Though she's rather short and diminutive, she is attractive, witty, talented, educated, single, and has a striking figure."

Tatyana reached over and touched her hand. "You know, you have all those qualities, and more."

"Like…?"

She leaned closer and said, "Well, to begin with you are just like the girl from Ipanema, tall and tan and young and lovely. So snap out of it. Your eyes are gorgeous with only a slight…what do you call it?"

"Epicanthic fold."

"Yes that's it. Did you know that all babies have those folds when they are in the womb? Most babies lose them but a few don't. Yours make you sexy and mysterious. And if you feel it's such a problem you can always opt for cosmetic surgery."

"Do you really think they're sexy, Tatyana?"

"Yes, I do. And don't worry that you don't share Zack's interest in science. Hell, while Mikhail loves singing and playing his balalaika, I'm so tone-deaf I couldn't carry a tune in silver-plated troika."

Li-Hwa laughed out loud. "So even if I don't know a comet from an asteroid I still have sexy eyes, right?"

"Absolutely."

"But there's more, Tatyana. Sandy was a talented radio and television personality in Puerto Rico before President Brandstadt brought her to Washington to report on the aliens. She's even provided her with her own TV show, Washington Space… something or other."

"Are they living together?"

"No, thank goodness. I guess she's old fashioned and wanted her own place. But her condo in Washington and her car are both paid for by the government. I just don't think I stand much of a chance."

Tatyana shook her head. "That's just not true. Here comes Misha. Let's give him a big smile. From the look on his face, he needs one."

The Colonel plopped into his chair. He looked to be fighting back tears. "Tanya, it was about Boris," he said at last. "He was killed outside our London embassy earlier today by a suicide bomber."

"Oh, no!"

"Did I know him?" asked Li-Hwa.

"No dear. Boris Dmitryevich was one of Uncle Pasha's closest friends."

The Colonel sat down with a sigh. "Describing his life would be like sorting through the history of the KGB, FSB and CIS."

Tatyana said, "Yes, Boris was younger than Uncle, but older than Misha. When he retired from the Army while stationed in London he chose not return to Moscow and give up his lifestyle."

"Don't you mean, give up English women Tanya?" the Colonel smiled sadly.

"Mikhail Grigoryevich!" she admonished gently. "Anyway, as I was saying, Boris thoroughly enjoyed the lifestyle London had to offer. And yes, he had been involved in more than his share of embassy love affairs."

"There, we see eye-to-eye then," the Colonel said. "Boris was extremely fond of the ladies and they reciprocated in kind."

"I have to agree with Misha. He was a charmer."

"That he was," he said. "In any event, his remains are being flown to Moscow next week for a full military funeral."

When the waiter returned to offer the desert menu, there were no takers.

Part 5

Earth is the cradle of humanity, but we cannot live in the cradle forever..

–Konstantin Tsiolkovsky

Chapter 33

WEEKS OF PREPARATION had gone into making this gathering of the leaders of nearly two hundred countries a success. No one could have predicted the chaos that would occur the moment the attendees stepped inside the auditorium of the Washington Cultural Arts Complex. The air itself seemed charged with electricity, and few were surprised when some of the assembled heads of state seized the chance to vent their frustration in public.

Despite non-stop pampering by the coordinators, the frustrated leaders seethed with discontent. Then tension worsened after it became apparent the seating arrangements had been made by a random computer selection, and not by a nation's standing in the world. That was the straw that broke the proverbial camel's back, for many of the nations in conflict around the world found themselves sitting uncomfortably close to their antagonists. The Master-at-Arms needed a full minute of pounding his gavel to bring some semblance of order to the gathering

"In accordance with the procedures that have been set forth," he announced at last, "our first order of business will be oral addresses by any country that requested the chance to speak. As such, a maximum of five minutes will be allowed.

"Each of the twenty microphone podiums placed throughout the auditorium will each have a red and yellow light. After four minutes the yellow light will come on to alert the delegate that one minute remains. When the red light begins to flash, it will indicate that thirty seconds remain. When the flashing stops, it means the microphone will be turned off in ten seconds.

"The prosecution, or if you prefer the Korr, has considered each of the questions that were electronically submitted. Because of the impossibility of answering each question, your particular question may or may not be answered during the trial.

"Following the roll call and the addresses, the next order of business will be a formal reading of the charges leveled against humanity by the Korr. They are identical to the charges given earlier to the heads of state.

"I will now proceed with the roll. When your country is called, its representative will stand and answer 'yea'. If that country is on the prescribed list to speak, the representative will then proceed to the nearest podium and give a statement."

"The Republic of Afghanistan..."

A woman stood and said, "Mr. Chairman, the Republic of Afghanistan offers a yea. We have no statement." She sat down.

"The Republic of Albania..."

"Mr. Chairman, the Republic of Albania offers a yea, and wishes to speak."

"The chair recognizes the representative from Albania."

The delegate walked to a podium. The microphone squealed as he tapped it.

"The Republic of Albania, a nation whose proud citizens trace their lineage back six hundred years to the tribes of Elyria—a country that successfully withstood invasions by the Romans, Slavs, Turks, and Communists—now states categorically that it does *not* recognize the authority of this court. In addition, we— "

The President interrupted. "You sir, are out of order. Return to your seat."

A few representatives began to stamp their feet and pound their hands on the table; in response, the chairman loudly banged his gavel. "This assembly will come to order! Turn off the microphone!" he commanded.

Over the tumult, the Albanian delegate continued in a loud voice. "In addition, we object to a bug-eyed-monster who has the gall to disguise its ugliness by projecting the sacred form of a human being!"

The representative returned to his seat with up-thrust arms and clenched fists, preening amid the isolated but enthusiastic applause from some of the delegates.

Zack turned to Sandy. "If you need a lead-in for your show tonight," he whispered, "it could be you were present when the proverbial shit hit the fan."

She shook her head. "My viewers would take a dim view of your verbiage. Instead of losing my ratings and perhaps my show, a simple, 'when the proverbial wheels fell off the school bus' should do just fine. "

Sandy's computer screen flashed in critical mode. She typed in a coded password and opened a message from her program manager at WSDN. She read it and then turned to Zack with an appearance of urgency.

"Something big is going down. They want me at the station ASAP to go live with a breaking story."

"Will they also have you do the six o'clock show?"

"I think so. By then I'll be able to discuss the trial as well as the new story."

Zack helped her gather her belongings. "Do you want me to come with you?"

"No thanks," she smiled. "I'll just grab a cab. You stay here and enjoy the show. We'll connect later once I figure out the game plan." She gave his hand a squeeze.

"Toodles," she said.

SANDY'S PROGRAM DIRECTOR was waiting at the curb when the taxi pulled up. On the elevator, she briefed her on the news from the International Space Station.

"You won't have time for make-up," she said pushing the studio door open. "But not to worry, you look simply *mahvelous dahling*."

"Forget the marvelous." Sandy said, scurrying towards the news desk. "This is as good as it's going to get. I ran a brush through my hair in the cab. When I flossed, touched up my lipstick and asked the driver to hurry, he thought I was late for hot date."

Sandy was glad to see the camera crew was set and ready to go. They gave her a wave.

"Here's the game plan," the director said. "Streeter Van Allen is standing by and ready to go live in Houston at ISS Mission Control. He'll report on some important event."

"Anything particular you want me to ask him?" Sandy asked, as the technicians adjusted her microphone.

"No—just go with the flow and follow his lead. But feel free to interrupt and ask something you think the audience would want an answer to."

"And when he starts getting too technical?"

"Well, yes...he is a dyed-in-the-wool science guy with a tendency to talk over everyone's head. He's a great guy and excellent reporter, but sometimes needs help translating science to regular folks."

"I know what you mean," she nodded. "Will his story interfere with my regular show at six?"

"Not at all. We'll have both his ISS update and your recap on today's trial."

A voice came over the public address. "Thirty seconds everyone. Cue the music."

Sandy moistened her lips and checked the clock, confirming that it was still morning. When the light on Camera One changed from red to green, a disembodied announcer said, "We interrupt our regular programming for this breaking news story."

The camera zoomed in, and Sandy began.

"Good morning everyone, I'm Sandy LaPlage and this is a Special Report from Washington Space Dateline News."

She smiled, and looked directly into the camera.

"As you know, the opening session of our trial began a few hours ago in the Washington Cultural Arts Complex. Be sure to join me at six for our regular show and my latest updates. But now go to Houston and our science reporter, Streeter Van Allen. He's at the International Space Station Ground Operations with breaking news on an ISS incident. Streeter, are you reading us?"

"Loud and clear, Sandy. Just moments ago I attended a closed briefing by the director of ISS operations regarding an incredible development aboard the space station.

"About six hours ago, the rogue cosmonauts holding the ISS crew hostage left the space station. Let me repeat that: the rogue cosmonauts have left the space station. I can assure you that everyone at Mission Control was taken totally by surprise when that message came down."

"Well, that is truly an unexpected turn of events."

"The good news is that the crew reports everyone in good spirits and first-rate health. And in addition, the cosmonauts left behind two-weeks' worth of food and supplies, which will tide everyone over until the next supply ship arrives."

"What about the station's damaged docking hatches?"

"Apparently, that was just a ploy to keep others from trying to dock. So although this hectic situation seems to have turned out all right, we're still left with any number of questions. Who were the cosmonauts? Why did they take over the station? What about their demands? Why did they leave so abruptly—and where will they land?"

"Let me interrupt, Streeter. If they left some six hours ago wouldn't they have had enough time to land by now?"

"That's the confusing part, Sandy. According to Mission Control, the spacecraft never initiated a deceleration burn—the first step taken to return to Earth, where a vehicle in orbit slows to begin its descent. Instead, their spacecraft started accelerating forward in the same direction as the space station orbits. And they seem to be remaining at the same altitude of ISS."

"Let's see if I understand you, Streeter. The cosmonauts are moving away from ISS in the same direction the space station is moving, and they are maintaining the same altitude."

"That's right Sandy."

"Now, can ground control say where they are now, how fast they're going, and whether their communications can be monitored?"

"Yes. They are now about five hundred miles in front of ISS and moving away from it at two hundred miles per hour. Although ground control is monitoring a bunch of frequencies, no transmitting or receiving has been detected since they left ISS. What I find interesting is how they knew not to point their craft straight ahead when accelerating. That would have put them in a Hohmann transfer trajectory."

"Excuse me, Streeter. What kind of trajectory?"

"A Hohmann trajectory, Sandy. Named after Walter Hohmann, a German scientist who, in 1925…"

Sandy interrupted again. "Streeter, you've just mentioned a term few of us know about. What is a Hohmann transfer trajectory, and what in the world does it do?"

"In a nutshell, when a smaller body is in orbit around a larger body, as ISS is with Earth, any increase in that smaller body's speed will lift it into a higher orbit. That lifting movement is called a Hohmann trajectory. It's often used whenever a spacecraft is being sent farther out into the solar system."

"I think I understand," she said. "So if they wanted to go faster and at the same time stay in the same orbit as ISS, they'd have to aim their ship slightly downwards. Perhaps that could be called a non-Hohmann trajectory."

"Very good Sandy." Van Allen was handed yet another report.

"So when the spacecraft is aimed slightly down," Sandy continued, "it's actually taking a short cut inside the curved path of ISS. Later, when it reaches the ISS orbit it would slow a bit and end up far in front of ISS and at the same altitude. That kind of a maneuver would have had to be worked out by professionals. Do you have any idea why they'd want to be far out in front of ISS?"

"Not off hand, Sandy. And I must congratulate you on nailing that Hohmann maneuver—or as you said a non-Hohmann. I hope you aren't shooting for my job?"

"No," she laughed, "it's not in my cross-hairs, Streeter. I'd rather sit at my nice, cozy desk than live out of a suitcase, traipsing around the world."

"Actually they do allow me to take two bags. But back to our story—I've just been handed another update. We now know that the hijackers seem to have had another goal in mind, not just taking over and leaving the space station."

He held up some sheets.

"Here's the real story right here in this latest report. I might suggest everyone sit down and take deep breath. Those three rogue cosmonauts have docked with one of our top secret satellites called Fly Swatter. It orbits five hundred miles in front of ISS. It was launched by our Defense Department, which has successfully kept its existence under wraps until now."

"But that makes no sense, Streeter. When you consider the transparency of our space program and the extensive media coverage of manned launches, how could any agency come up with a way to sneak anything into orbit?"

"Those were my thoughts earlier today, until I took a few minutes to surf the Internet."

"Did you find out anything?

"I certainly did, and very easily too."

"Let's make something clear here. Before our viewers get the idea you're leaking sensitive data, you did say this information is on the Internet, correct Streeter?"

"That's right, Sandy. It's available to anyone who wants to look it up. Hold on a minute. Major Rodd is walking our way and may have new information. I'll try to get him to say a few words to your viewers."

Sandy spent a few minutes recapping events while Van Allen hurried Major Rodd toward the camera, vamping seamlessly while the news crew got the new arrival miked and ready for the camera.

"And now," she said at last, "let's return to Streeter Van Allen in Houston. Are you still with us, Streeter?"

"Yes I am, Sandy, and I'd like to introduce Air Force Major Ramsey Rodd, military liaison for the International Space Station."

"You can call me Ram if you like, Miss LaPlage," the major said.

"Roger—wilco, Ram...and please call me Sandy. Now, what can you tell us about this mystery satellite, Major?"

"Now that our highly classified project is rapidly become public domain, I've been given authorization to reveal some of its details. The Fly Swatter is a military satellite measuring twelve by thirty feet. It is cone shaped, with the pointed end aimed at Earth and its base pointing into space. And I can confirm that an unauthorized spacecraft just docked with Fly Swatter, and one or two people have entered it."

"Just for clarification, Ram, has it been determined yet if they had to break into Fly Swatter, or did they somehow get the key?" Sandy asked.

Major Rodd smiled and shook his head. "I'm afraid there are no keys in space, Sandy. It hasn't been very crowded out there, so up to now there hasn't been a reason to install locks. But after this event, where one nation has illegally entered another nation's property, I imagine we'll be rethinking the policy of not locking the door."

"Is there a life support system inside Fly Swatter?" asked Van Allen.

"No, Streeter. Anyone entering would need a space suit. And any such visit would be considered an EVA—an extra vehicular activity."

"From the size you described," said Sandy, "I'd imagine those inside would find it to be close quarters. Am I correct?"

"Definitely," replied Rodd. "It can barely hold two people. Three would be a very tight fit, unless they were all midgets. I should add that Mission Control is trying to abort any activation commands that could be triggered on Fly Swatter. So far, we've been unsuccessful."

She looked startled. "But up until now you've been successful in hiding that satellite, Ram. Am I right? And given all the secrecy, can you explain how this event could occur?"

"While specific details must remain classified, Sandy, it would not be an exaggeration to say that we were able to produce a stealth satellite. It all has to do with Fly Swatter's exterior. Rather than being perfectly smooth, it has a complex texture. That, along with the addition of special coatings, reflects both light and radar away from it."

"Can you telling us anything about Fly Swatter's mission, Ram?"

"Yes I can. It's one and only mission is to protect the U.S. from aggressors."

"But how could Fly Swatter protect us if neither we nor an aggressor knew it's up there?"

"I'll try to answer that one Sandy," Van Allen interrupted, "since I suspect the full answer may be classified. My take is that it's a weapon designed to protect us from a preemptive strike."

"Forgive me if I sound picky, Street," Sandy said, "but I understand the accepted definition of a preemptive strike to be one implemented by a country that believes another country is about to strike it. So for your term to be accurate, another nation would launch missiles at the U.S. only after determining we were planning to attack it."

"You are both correct, up to a point," Major Rodd said. "It is a weapon as Streeter surmised, but not one for countering a preemptive strike. Fly Swatter is our 'ace-in-the-hole' should any nation be about to strike, or if it's already launched an attack against us."

"It sounds to me, Major, that this all boils down to semantics." Sandy said. "Can you to tell us what kinds of weapons we have up there?"

"I can say, within the confines of confidentiality," he answered, "that Fly Swatter carries a bank of laser cannons accurate enough to be used on both static ground targets as well as rapidly moving objects, such as guided missiles."

"I am truly impressed Ram," she said. "Would it be reasonable for us to assume that since the first Space Shuttle flight in 1977, the long list of defense projects we had on the drawing boards was just a cover-up to keep the Soviet Union at bay and allow funds to be diverted to Fly Swatter?

"I can neither confirm nor deny that, Sandy."

"I'll take that as a 'yes'."

"That's your prerogative. But with regard to the first space shuttle, OV-101 Enterprise X, I'm sure you know that it never actually flew in space. But many remember the event with great enthusiasm inasmuch as it was named after the starship in the old Star Trek television series."

"I did know about the Star Trek connection," she said, "but didn't know it never make it into space."

"Good point," Van Allen commented. "*Enterprise* wasn't built to orbit, although her designation suggested it might since OV stands for Orbiter Vehicle. Was that because she lacked engines Ram?"

"That's right—no engines and no heat shields. Her mission was just launch, glide through the atmosphere, and make a dead stick landing."

"Ram," interjected Sandy, "can you tell us why Enterprise wasn't ever refitted with engines and heat shield so she could actually make it to space?"

"Between the time *Enterprise* was designed, and then built and flown, specifications for the shuttle fleet changed dramatically. To become operational she would have had to be disassembled and sent back to the sub-contractors for refitting—which would have been a very expensive proposition, even for the Government."

"Major," said Sandy, "I think our viewers might be interesting in hearing about some of our defense programs that almost became operational but didn't. Could you shed a little light on that?"

"Certainly," Rodd smiled. "During the 1960s our entire national missile defense program was built around ground launched missiles like the Sentinel program. However Sentinel was never deployed.

"A few of those ground launched missile programs were ERINT, FLAGE, HOW and ERIS. Then in later years we had AEGIS, BMD, MKV, THAAD and PAC-3. But in 1983, with the threat of intercontinental missiles, President Ronald Reagan initiated a space-based defense system called Strategic Defense Initiative, or SDI. It was commonly referred to as Star Wars, from the film of the same name. Then in 1991 SDI was renamed Ballistic Missile Defense Organization, or BMDO. Still later it was renamed a third time as Missile Defense Agency—or MDA."

"My apologies to the audience," Sandy laughed. "I am sure opened up a can of acronyms for our viewers with all those names. But since you've taken us this far down the road, can you take us a step further? If I'm hearing you correctly, did any of these programs actually get off the drawing board?"

"Absolutely, but even though some of our anti-ballistic missile projects were developed, the majority weren't."

"Let me toss in my two cents here," Van Allen said. "It wasn't so much that there was a lot of wasteful spending going on or that we didn't have clear set goals. You have to realize the Soviets hadn't been standing still all this time. They were constantly upgrading their systems, trying to match and surpass our latest programs."

"That's true, Street," Rodd nodded. "Eventually the U.S. researched both X-ray and chemical lasers with various levels of success. Those systems were called HPTE, MIRACL, THEL, BEAR, RME and LACE."

"I appreciate using only initials for those systems, Major. But I suspect we've gone well past the amount of minutia our audience wants to hear."

"I tend to agree," Major Rodd smiled politely. "Let me just say that each of those systems—and others I haven't mentioned—all had advocates as well as opponents."

"Thank you, Major Rodd for giving us a perspective on defense systems leading up to Fly Swatter. And thank you Streeter for another comprehensive report."

"Always a pleasure to be on WSDN," Van Allen said. "If anything breaks at this end I'll get back to you."

"And that wraps up our breaking news story from Houston. I invite you to join me tonight at six for our regular broadcast of Washington Space Dateline News. I'm Sandy LaPlage."

Chapter 34

As SHE RECEIVED HER CUE from the director, Sandy took a deep breath. She had no idea how her audience would react to the evening's show; in fact, she wasn't sure how to react herself. But she had too much professional pride to let it show. And she was grateful that Zack would be there tonight, to help her through any rough spots.

"Good evening," Sandy began. "We have three guests making up our panel to discuss today's trial proceedings and the President's address that was aired three hours ago.

"Two of my guests are representatives from the Russian delegation here in Washington. They are Colonel Mikhail Kornikov, Director of Internal and External Intelligence in Moscow and his wife Major Tatyana Kornikova attached to the Moscow Security Agency.

"My third guest is no stranger to us here at WSDN. Dr. Zack Peters, formerly with the Central Intelligence Agency and now science advisor to the President, will be with us to help sort through the day's events.

"But first, the main news story of the day—the first day of Humanity's trial. It was an extraordinary event that I witnessed this morning at the Cultural Arts Complex. For the first time in history, the leaders of 197 nations were gathered in one room and under one roof.

"The first order of business was a roll call. It took two hours because a few delegates had asked to make oral statements. Those who did speak were of a common mind, expressing outrage at being placed on trial like common criminals.

"But it was the Albanian delegate who would have easily been the poster child for the day's 'most angry award.' After his allotted five minutes were up he refused to stop speaking—or, to put it bluntly, to stop yelling. His microphone was eventually disconnected, once it became apparent that he had no intention of being held to the clock,

"In the end, he was escorted to his seat, his arms thrust upwards like a prize fighter. The audience reaction was a mixture of heckling and applause, which faded after several minutes of gavel-pounding by the presiding officer.

"The ensuing calm became a dead silence when the Chairman of the Assembly announced that the next order of business would be an introductory statement and a list of charges by the prosecution—the representative from the star Epsilon Eridani.

"However, in the end it was the Assembly Chairman who read a statement on the Visitor's behalf. We will show a video of both the introduction and charges for those of you who may have missed the broadcast."

Sandy's image faded as the video began; the camera panned over the audience before stopping to show the chairman of the assembly standing at a lectern, banging a gavel to call the meeting to order.

> "In a moment our visiting guest will speak to you in a somewhat amazing fashion," said the Chairman. "So amazing I might add, that your initial reactions may be that you're witnessing an illusion or a deception. Be assured that neither is the case.
>
> "One of our prolific authors, Arthur C. Clarke, suggested that if humans ever come across the technology by an advanced civilization, it will appear to us as magic. In keeping with that premise, the visitor will address us in a manner that will be the least provocative, noting the diversity of our culture, language and ethnicity. As you can imagine, it wouldn't be possible for our guest to be seen and heard in one form that would evoke universal confidence. Therefore, our visitor will be seen only on your personal monitors and not at the podium or on the auditorium screens. Translations won't be necessary given that our guest will speak to you in your language."

The video paused, and Sandy's her image appeared in the upper corner of the screen. "At this point," she said, "everyone in the auditorium, including me, was astonished to see displayed on their monitor a person, living or dead, that they had always held in high esteem. The effect was even more stunning in that image on the screen appeared in differently to everyone in the room, in varying but always modes of dress and speaking in normal speech patterns simultaneously in whatever language the listener was most comfortable hearing.

"We've transcribed what was heard. But because the speaker was unique to each viewer in the auditorium, we can't show the image or hear the words. Instead, we will show background images taken in the auditorium, adding the Visitor's statement as subtitles in your own language."

The recording resumed, and as the camera panned the audience, the Visitor's words appeared in printed captions across the bottom of the television screen.

> "Citizens of Earth, we bring you sincere greetings. From your expressions, it is apparent you are irritated at being required to attend these proceedings and for that I apologize. Let us first address what appears to be a common concern. What gives the Korr the right to intervene in human affairs? The answer is because we are able to.
>
> "Over the millennia most of your countries involved themselves in expansion and colonialism. In doing so, you unhesitatingly forced your culture, mores, politics and religion upon those populations.
>
> "Getting back to our interference, I ask you to imagine what responses the leaders of empires such as the Arab, Greek, Mongol, Ottoman and Roman would have given to the inhabitants of those countries being colonizing if asked why the empire was intervening in their affairs. My guess is that those who demanded a reason would have been executed.
>
> "In more recent times, I want you to consider the colonial aspirations of Great Britain in India; Germany in Africa; France in Indo-China; Europeans in Japan; Japan in

China; China in Eastern Europe; Spain in Central America; Portugal in South America and the United States in Hawaii, Puerto Rico and the Philippines. Did any of these expansionist countries feel any obligation to apologize or defend their actions?

"But that was then, this is now. Be assured the Korr is neither expanding its sphere of influence nor colonizing Earth. By way of this trial though, we will provide evidence that your species has always been defective and irreversibly flawed.

"To those of you who have raised children, do you remember their stern expression when being scolded? You could almost hear them say sarcastically, 'Who died and left you the boss?'"

"Because of the twenty-five years or so difference in your ages, you were content that your authority came from years of experience.

Sandy took advantage of a short break in the statement. "You might notice," she said in a voice-over, "that some of the delegates are nodding in agreement."

"You can see then how comfortable the Korr is in the knowledge that our civilization is thousands of years in advanced of yours.

"Our initial conclusion with humanity has not wavered. You lack the judgment to handle your affairs. Consider how many of your countries have nuclear weapons. Would a wise species allow such a situation to exist when two of those countries alone had in excess of twenty-thousand such weapons? If they were ever to be deployed, the human species would become extinct. It is distressing to find such a promising civilization as yours teetering on the brink of self-annihilation.

"I will now present the schedule for the next five days. Each day the Korr will present one of five charges followed by sixteen ten-minute oral rebuttals from randomly selected countries that have asked to be heard.

"Today, Monday, the charge against you is 'your predisposition for aggression, crime and war.' On Tuesday the charge will be 'your stewardship of Earth's oceans, lakes and rivers.' Wednesday's charge will be 'your stewardship of Earth's atmosphere.' On Thursday the charge will be 'your stewardship to the land.' Friday's charge will be 'your stewardship to one another.' Because there will not be a session on Saturday or Sunday, you will be free to pursue your own interests.

"The following Monday, the court will hear the defense summation. As before, sixteen countries will be given the opportunity to make an 'oral summation' after being chosen from the electronic summations each country was required to submit by midnight the previous day. On the ninth day, Tuesday, the prosecution will offer its summation followed by a three-hour recess. When you return the verdict will be given.

"If you are found innocent the proceedings will be at an end. All delegates will be dismissed and the Korr will depart from the Earth. If found guilty, your sentence will be pronounced as well as the time of its implementation."

The video ended and Sandy reappeared on camera. "In a few minutes our panel will offer their views on today's events," she said. "But before they do, we take you to the White House for an announcement by the Press Secretary.

A glitzy WSDN logo appeared with upbeat music and a moving ticker tape repeating SPECIAL REPORT. The Press Secretary stepped up to the podium, greeted the media representatives and began.

"Let me preface the following announcement," he began, "by saying I will not be taking any questions." After a few moments the audible grumblings subsided, and he continued.

"A hand-out will be distributed to you with further details as you leave this briefing.

"Late this afternoon, President Brandstadt received a disturbing report from the International Space Station Mission Control in Houston. She will disclose more details in an address to the nation later this evening. Two hours ago, a secret and unmanned defense satellite of the United States, code name Fly Swatter, was illegally boarded by the Russian cosmonauts that had held the ISS crew hostage. This defense satellite is orbiting five hundred miles ahead of the space station and in its 350-mile-high orbit. Until today the satellite's existence had been top secret.

"The rogue cosmonauts entered Fly Swatter Sunday night at 11:15 p.m. Coordinated Universal Time. Since then, without the knowledge or authorization of Mission Control, Fly Swatter has been activated and become fully operational.

"All attempts to regain control have been unsuccessful. As reported yesterday, the cosmonauts had originally boarded ISS after stowing away in a commandeered automated Russian supply vessel that was carrying provisions to ISS.

"As you can imagine, this is both a local and international concern, now that it has been revealed that Fly Swatter is outfitted with missiles. That is all I can tell you at this time. Be sure to pick up your information packets at the door."

The Secretary thanked the stunned press corps and left the podium, leaving behind a growing torrent of questions.

SANDY FINISHED briefing her guests just as the Press Secretary disappeared behind the door to the Briefing Room.

"How soon do we go live?" she asked.

"Right now," came the answer through her ear-bud. You're coming up on Camera Two in three...two...one...."

"Welcome back," she said, looking directly at the camera. Her assembled guests sat with her at a round table. A microphone, laptop computer, and water glass or coffee mug adorned each position.

"Earlier this morning I reported an important development regarding a previously unknown American secret satellite at the same altitude as the International Space Station and positioned five hundred miles in front of it. According to the press briefing we've just seen, the satellite called Fly Swatter has been boarded by the cosmonauts who had recently commandeered ISS.

"My three guests this evening all attended today's opening session of the trial. Let me introduce two of Russia's trial delegates—Army Colonel Mikhail Kornikov, Director of Internal and External Intelligence in Moscow and his wife Army Major Tatyana Kornikova, vice-chair of Foreign Affairs Directorate also in Moscow. Coincidentally, she is also a trained cosmonaut.

"Last but certainly not least, with us is Dr. Zack Peters, science advisor to the President and formerly with the Central Intelligence Agency. Dr. Peters was recently on our program discussing the search for extraterrestrial intelligence.

"I thank the three of you for being her and taking time out of your hectic schedules at the Cultural Arts Complex."

Her guests smiled and nodded; Zack and Kornikov sipped coffee.

"First, I'd like to have your thoughts on this illegal boarding of Fly Swatter and a report claiming it has just become operational. Colonel, may I begin with you?"

As the Colonel formed his thoughts, Zack said, "Excuse me, Sandy but before the Colonel responds, there's something I feel needs saying. As the intruders are members of the Russian cosmonaut corps, some may jump to unhelpful assumptions about Fly Swatter and the earlier hijacking of the International Space Station, thinking that there's a compelling case to portray all Russians doing nothing but causing problems. But we should all take note that without Russia as an ally in World War II in the 1940s, winning that war would surely have been impossible, or at best extremely costly in lives and materials.

"I am the first to admit that our two countries have had their fair share of hot, cold and tepid periods over the years. But the fact remains that today Russia is our friend."

Tatyana leaned over and hugged Zack. "I haven't been this nervous and as close to tears since I found out Grandfather Frost wasn't real," she said, turning back to face the camera.

"Grandfather Frost is the Russian version of Santa Claus," said Kornikov. "And I also appreciate your kind words. But that doesn't get our nation off the hook for the actions of those three cosmonauts. I assure you we are as surprised and shocked as the rest of the world must is."

"That's true Sandy," Tatyana said. "The moment ISS was boarded we began looked into the backgrounds of these rogue intruders, their history as cosmonauts and personal files. To our surprise absolutely nothing showed up out of the ordinary. All three have exemplary records, and were in the top five percent of their graduating classes."

"We've all read and seen enough espionage stories to know that a spy, or mole often will go under the radar—drop out of sight—and lead a perfectly normal life for years until they are given an assignment and reappear," said Sandy.

"Off the top of my head," Zack interjected, "I could name at least ten moles working for foreign governments who, in the past had successfully infiltrated sensitive areas of our government and military undetected."

"Can you add anything Colonel," Sandy asked?

"Only that two of the cosmonauts are married, have families, and participate in all of the regular things that all parents do—being involved in school programs, interacting with their children's teachers, and the like."

"It sounds like the storybook lifestyle of a successful double agent and mole," said Zack."

Tatyana turned toward her husband. "Perhaps you might recount what we discussed on the way to the studio. About the possible reason for commanding the ISS.

"It was just a passing thought Tatyana, and may not warrant any consideration."

"I disagree, Misha. Please repeat what you told me."

"Very well," Kornikov sighed; he paused a moment before continuing.

"What if their plan all along was to hijack ISS just to get attention? The world would then be focused on the safety of the ISS crew as well as the demands of the Russian separatist territories, or the fear that they would destroy the space station in a suicide pact.

"With that kind of a distraction, they could take time to work out the fastest route to Fly Swatter, travel there, and board it before Mission Control could place it in a lock-down mode."

"I think the Colonel may have something," Zack said. "Once the cosmonauts gained control of Fly Swatter, they'd have the leverage to get a host of demands met. They could threaten to destroy ISS, and from Fly Swatter they could target any place on the planet."

"I'll wager that future radio transmissions from Fly Swatter will soon confirm this theory," the Colonel said.

Sandy took a sip of coffee and spilled some on her sweater. Zack offered a handkerchief and she dabbed at the spots. "That wasn't very professional of me. Remind me not to attempt brain surgeries today.

"But moving right along, I'd like to get back to evaluating the trial. Who wants to start? Dr. Peters?"

"Two things stand out in my mind, both concerning the emotional state of the delegation. On one hand they appeared to swagger and bluster, as if their overconfidence could somehow make the trial go away. At the same time I sensed an underlying fear and dread. I found myself imagining them wringing their hands like a kid who's been caught with his hand in a cookie jar. Did anyone else sense that?"

Tatyana nodded, "I was thinking along those very same lines, Dr. Peters," Tatyana nodded. "You must be a psychic."

"It's 'Zack'," he smiled. "Please call me Zack."

"Yes, Zack — it was like they knew they had been caught doing something wrong. At the same time I was impressed with the serenity of the prosecution. He or she, depending on who you perceived, was disarmingly casual. Rather than pontificating, he read the charges so casually he sounded like a sommelier in a three-star restaurant going over the wine list."

"I agree with my wife," the Colonel said. "I saw the visitor as a female and completely at ease while reading the war and aggression charge. If that attitude was a strategy to keep the delegates focused, I'd say she pulled it off quite well."

Sandy searched though pages in her hand and asked, "Does anyone happen to have their list of charges? I seem to have misplaced mine."

The Colonel held up his list for all to see.

"Would you read them for us, Colonel?" Sandy asked.

"Certainly," he said grimly. "This is her definition of war."

"After extensive research," Kornikov began, reading from a display on the laptop in front of him, "we have formed this description of what you mean by 'war.' It requires two or more nations, countries, states, groups, or citizens of one country who organize themselves in violent conflict with each other using physical force, weapons, and military techniques. You employ these to confiscate by lethal means the other's property, land, cities, population, aircraft, ships, and weapons, and this continues until the process comes to an end, either by surrender or the destruction of one of the entities.

"Upon discovering how deeply the concept of war permeates your culture, we were confused by your expressed abhorrence of it. You celebrate it with national holidays and embrace it in literature and song. You award citations and medals to some, while others you reward using veteran's organizations, military museums, special cemeteries—even your entertainment industry. All things considered, our first charge in these proceedings will be Humanity's Propensity to Wage War."

Kornikov looked up and gazed into the camera. "There are several pages of data, outlining human history and demonstrating that there has never been a period in recorded history when there hasn't been a major war going on, somewhere in the world."

"In fact," added Tatyana, "her account of human history shows that there have been occasions where as many as thirteen lesser conflicts were taking place in the same time frame."

"According to the prosecution's account," Kornikov continued, "there have been a total of a hundred million military and civilian deaths. World War I alone brought about death and injury to thirty million people."

"And what astonished me," said Tatyana, "was his reference to the millions tortured, murdered, and maimed in any number of religious wars."

Sandy was about to remind the viewers that the Visitor could appear to two different people simultaneously as either male or female when a message appeared on her personal monitor.

> THE PRESIDENT ENTERED THE BUILDING A MINUTE AGO. SHE IS NOW IN THE ELEVATOR HEADING UP TO THE STUDIO. SHE HAS ASKED TO SIT IN ON THE PANEL SO YOU NEED TO MAKE SPACE FOR HER WHEELCHAIR AND BEGIN GATHERING YOUR THOUGHTS. DO YOU WANT THE PANELISTS TO READ THIS?

Sandy typed "YES", and then broke in to the conversation on religious warfare. "I have just learned that we will have a surprise guest joining us momentarily," she said. "Someone who won't need an introduction."

A technician with head phones draped around her neck scurried out to place a water glass between Zack and Kornikov, who were already in the process of moving their chairs to make room. The moment Brandstadt came on to the set the studio crew began applauding. She gave Sandy and Tatyana a hug and shook hands with the Colonel and Zack. Before setting her hand brakes she gave a wave to the cameras while a sound technician attached a lapel microphone to her jacket. Taking a deep breath, she smiled at the camera and began to speak.

"I want to thank all of you for allowing me to barge in on you like this. I was home getting ready to watch your show when I had a surprise visit from the Visitor. Even though the news I was given will be broadcast later this evening, I thought it important enough to visit your show and break the news right now."

"We are delighted to have you here, Madam President. My station manager is undoubtedly rubbing his hands with glee, imagining the boost it will give our ratings."

"I scribbled some notes on the way over," Brandstadt said absently, rummaging through the briefcase attached to the side of her wheelchair. "Given that it's only a matter of time before Fly Swatter's weapons capability is made public, so I can safely tell you that it does not carry nuclear weapons. It's armed with lasers, but not the kind lecturers use during a presentation. They could more accurately be described as cannons—very powerful laser cannons."

Sandy and the panel exchanged looks of bewilderment and surprise. Finding what she was looking for, the president turned and gazed directly into the camera.

"Our strategy has always been to use Fly Swatter as a last resort," she continued, "and only if a nuclear attack on the United States. seemed imminent."

"Over the past year, however, we made some modifications that would let those cannons point out into space. Dr. Peters was part of a small group outside government circles who knew about this refit, which was designed to use Fly Swatter to defend our planet against threats from space—even though we never anticipated threats coming from other life forms."

Turning to Zack, she made eye contact with her old friend and sighed. "Would you fill us all in on NEOs and the dangers they pose?"

"Certainly, Madam President. NEO—an acronym that stands for Near Earth Object—refers to asteroids and comets that occasionally cross Earth's orbit during their journey around the Sun. I can assure everyone that it would be a disaster if a half-mile wide Near Earth Object and Earth ever showed up at the same place at the same time.

"Until now we had no way to defend ourselves against them. Thankfully, Fly Swatter is a workable weapon against NEOs, even though there is no guarantee how well it would work—or even if it would work at all."

Sandy asked, "How many of them are there out there and what are the odds of one hitting Earth? And if one does, what kind of damage can we expect?"

"So far," replied Zack, "we've discovered close to 6,000 NEOs out of the 165,000 or so that we've catalogued orbiting the Sun in the Asteroid Belt located between Mars and Jupiter. That's roughly 350 million miles further from the Sun than we are. But we don't have any idea how many undiscovered asteroids are NEOs. There could be millions.

"As for the potential damage—some NEOs travel 26,000 miles an hour and measure miles across. Depending on its composition, one of them a half-mile wide can weigh four-hundred billion pounds, more or less.

"But you asked about the odds of an impact. Although scientists have their own estimates, we can say that on average, about two thousand large ones will hit us within the next five hundred million years. Historically it appears that we get hit by mountain-size NEOs every million years or so."

"A million years?" Tatyana asked. "Then I won't lose any sleep over it."

"Well, the operative words here are 'on average.' We're as likely to get hit in the next five years as we are in the next million years."

"It sounds like you are saying it's not a question of if the Earth will be hit," Tatyana said, "but when."

"Oh yes. And to see evidence of past collisions one can look around the planet. You'll discover about 180 impact craters—each one all the result of asteroids and comets."

"Do you know if any of the NEOs have our name on it?" Sandy asked.

"Not exactly. We do know of three formidable ones. that include On Oct. 26, 2028, one of them—Asteroid 1997XF11—will miss Earth by about 600,000 miles—just over twice the distance from here to the Moon. We like to call that a bullet burn.

"Six months later another asteroid, Apophis by name, will miss us by just twenty thousand miles. If that one doesn't clear everyone's sinuses, you might want to consider Asteroid 1950D. On March 16, 2880, several astronomers believe it has a one in three-hundred chance of hitting the Earth. As we get closer to the date, those odds will surely to change—for the better or for the worse."

"In fact," offered Kornikov, "wasn't it an asteroid hitting Central America that caused the extinction of the dinosaurs about sixty-five million years ago?"

Zack nodded.

"Do we know how large that one was, Zack?" Sandy asked.

"We named that asteroid, Chicxulub. Judging from the 150-foot-wide crater it left on the coast of the Yucatan peninsula, it was probably about six miles wide, and struck with two million times the power of the largest nuclear bomb ever detonated. Some suggest that a two-mile-wide NEO would bring us close to extinction. There's also some scientific controversy on whether the dinosaurs were killed off by Chicxulub alone, or by a combination of events occurring at roughly the same time. One possibility is the million-year-long period of volcanic activity taking place at the same time in Northern India called the Deccan Event."

Brandstadt said, "And now the reason for my visit," Brandstadt said grimly. "Something I'll announce in more detail on radio and TV later this evening. ISS Mission Control has confirmed that two hours ago, Fly Swatter fired at the incoming spaceships."

Chapter 35

AFTER A PAINFUL SILENCE, Brandstadt continued. "When I received the first call from Mission Control about Fly Swatter, and how they hadn't been able to do anything about it, my first reaction was that its laser cannons could be fired.

"I asked the Joint Chiefs for options but they had none. They couldn't launch a missile because we had nothing accurate enough to get to Fly Swatter. I thought my last option was to contact our guest from 40 Eridani."

"And how were you able to accomplish that, Madam President?" the Colonel asked.

"The visitor left me a communication device during its last visit to the White House."

"Were you successful in reaching it?" Sandy asked adding, "I know it sounds awkward but I never know how to refer to the visitor."

"Yes I was. It confirmed that the lasers had fired at the incoming space ships and that nothing could be done about it."

The Colonel asked, "Am I to understand there wasn't a way to send some kind of warning message?"

"Not unless you can change the laws of physics, Colonel," Zack replied. "Lasers and radio signals both travel at the speed of light. Even if a warning been sent the instant the lasers were fired, the warning and the lasers would arrive simultaneously, which would have been less than helpful."

"That reminds me of the saying about a bullet that is fired at you," Tatyana added grimly. "Because bullets can travel near the speed of sound, you never hear the one that gets you."

"How long before we find out about what the result was?" Zack asked.

"We won't have to wait Zack," Brandstadt said. "The visitor said the lasers missed the ships by five hundred miles due to their inability to hit fast-moving targets at a distance of a half-billion miles."

Sandy added, "I'd say it also tells us to stick to doing what we do best," Sandy observed. "Destroying targets and killing people right here on Earth. I'm sorry. I realize that retort was uncalled for and I apologize."

"But that wasn't even the biggest surprise," the President said. "I was informed that the three alien ships are not headed for Earth, and are not carrying Korr from 40 Eridani."

Zack threw his arms up in frustration and placed his hands behind his head with interlocked fingers. "Okay, folks," he said, tipping his chair back. "That just about does it for me. I say we turn off this stupid soap opera and switch to a county music station.

"Be sure to tune in tomorrow," he continued, imitating a broadcast announcer, "and find out if Dr. John will break his engagement to Penelope after discovering she's his step-sister and dying from an incurable disease caused by a pygmy blow-gun in the wilds of East Africa."

"You missed your calling, Zack," the President smiled.

"I'm afraid I have to side with Zack," said Kornikov. "Who are they? Where are they coming from? And where the hell are they going?"

Tatyana touched his arm and gave her husband "the look."

"They're called Naians and originate from a star system that is more than 200 light years beyond 40 Eridani, or about 219 light years from Earth," said the President. "To make sense out of the path they are taking, I was told to imagine a crooked yard stick.

"Put the Naian home star on one end of it, at the one inch mark and their actual destination at the 36-inch mark. Now put 40 Eri at 18 inches from the first inch and our Sun at 27 inches. That way you can best see the path they are traveling; 1 to 18 to 27 and finally to 36. To be truly accurate, of course, you'd have to add two more stars between their home star and 40 Eri.

"For them to undertake a journey of that magnitude," said the Colonel, "I guess we are safe in assuming Naian technology is comparable to that of the Korr."

"Not at all," answered Brandstadt. "The Naians fastest travel speed is still below the speed of light. It takes them hundreds of years to complete such a journey, in vessels called 'generation ships.' Both those who began the journey as well as their children will grow old and die along the way. Their descendants will be the ones arriving at their final destination."

"Were you told what that destination is?" asked Sandy.

"It's a sun very much like ours with two habitable worlds. Because it doesn't have a name we would be familiar with, I copied down its coordinates in the sky: five hours, thirty two minutes, fifty five seconds in Right Ascension; plus nine degrees, twenty seven minutes, thirty-two seconds in Declination."

"Oh—that one," Tatyana joked. "Seriously, why are they taking a slightly jagged route rather travel in a straight line?"

Brandstadt explained, "It has to do the usage of stars along their route to accelerate their spacecraft to greater speeds. Later, when the ships are about half-way to their destination, they reverse the process and decelerate by stealing momentum from stars along their route. Would you care to step in and help me out, Zack?"

"Sure," he nodded. "You need to understand that stars themselves travel at hundreds of miles a second and are millions of time more massive than any spacecraft. If you cross a star's orbit directly behind it, your craft accelerates and gains speed. Cross a star's path directly in front of the star, and gravity makes you decelerate—or, in other words, you slow down.

"But besides affecting the speed of a spacecraft, you can also use a star's gravity to change your direction. And because the stars don't have to be lined up perfectly from your origination point to your destination, you have some wiggle room."

"Thank you Zack," the President said. "By the time the Naians arrived at 40 Eridani and got a speed boost and slight change of direction, they had already made two similar maneuvers at two other stars along the way. Our Sun is just the next star along the way. It was our own ego and self-importance that led us to assume they were coming to visit us."

"I have a question," the Colonel said. "By stealing some of a star's momentum to accelerate or slow down the ship, wouldn't you change the star's movement and speed?"

Zack shook his head. "There is no effect at all on a star," he said. "Our calculations show that when our Pioneer and Voyager space probes stole momentum from Jupiter and Saturn in order to get a speed boost as well as a slight direction change on their way to the outer solar system, they did slow down Jupiter and Saturn. But the amount was so insignificant that a million years from now those planets will only be two inches short of where they would have been had they not been robbed of momentum."

"What about that message the Oval Office received from the Korr about their three ships arriving here in eight weeks?" Sandy asked.

"We were led to believe that was the situation," the president said. "The Visitor made arrangements for the message to be sent to us from the Naian ships because the Korr were curious to see what our reaction would be. As they surmised, our response was aggressive. As a side note, the Visitor says it is common practice for cultures beginning interstellar flight to steal momentum from stars until they develop more efficient means of propulsion."

"So it was all a ruse," Zack said. "And to think that we might never have known about the ships flying by Earth towards the Sun if it hadn't been for those amateur astronomers in Key West. It's almost inconceivable that they were observing a miniscule spot in the sky at just the right moment. What are the odds, a trillion to one?"

"I would assume," said Kornikov, "that all space travelers would seek permission to borrow momentum from a star that hosts planets harboring civilizations with interstellar capability. Because no damage would be done, it would only be a matter of courtesy."

"They could be asking for safety reasons," Tatyana guessed, "even if the odds of hitting a local spaceship would be remote."

"It still seems like a terrible waste of resources to go to all that trouble of building three starships just to go exploring," said Sandy.

"In this particular case, the Naians are not exploring," Brandstadt said. "They are migrating to a new and permanent home once they discovered that changes in the life cycle of their star would make life impossible within the next five hundred years. For them to survive, they had to migrate. And that's where the Korr comes into the picture.

"The Korr had found a suitable star with two planets out of seven similar to those the Naians had to abandon. The three ships we discovered were the last of ten that had been constructed. Seven are already under way to their new homes. These, the last three will be traveling for another ninety years before reaching their home."

The President leaned back and smiled. "Well Sandy," she said, "I've enjoyed my visit but now I must get back to work with only three hours to prepare for my television address. Thanks for letting me barge in on you so unexpectedly."

"It was an honor and an unexpected pleasure, Madam President."

Brandstadt left, and the panel got back to discussing the events of the day. Tatyana was first to speak.

"I find it interesting," she said, "that we haven't heard a thing from the United Nations. Why wouldn't they want to be involved? But I haven't heard any UN delegate proposed a single resolution since the Korr arrived."

"I'm not surprised," said her husband. "The UN is only effective as an international sounding board to bring world attention to a cause. In other words they throw an idea up on the wall to see if it sticks.

"In the late 1970s," he continued, "Grenada's Prime Minister sponsored Dr. J. Allen Hynek, the father of serious UFO investigation, to propose that the General Assembly create a permanent panel to investigate UFOs on an international basis. A few years later, Gordon Cooper, one of the original astronauts petitioned the UN to investigate UFOs based on experiences of he and his fellow astronauts."

"If you hadn't guessed already," Tatyana said directly to the camera, "my husband is also a flying saucer enthusiast."

"Not just UFOs," Kornikov shook his head. "In 2008, a group of scientists and astronauts from the International Panel on Asteroid Threat Mitigation proposed that the UN make a contingency plan for the destruction that would occur in the wake of a devastating impact by an asteroid or comet. As in the cases of Hynek and Cooper, the proposal went nowhere. The panel received a lukewarm reception by some delegates and a flat-out rejection by the rest."

"Can anyone explain why such good proposals receive such poor responses from the UN?" asked Sandy.

"Personally, I think it's similar to the story of Pandora's Box," said Zack. "Once she opened it, she found it impossible to put everything back inside. Remember, the UN was never designed to be democratic in nature. The only way it could get up and running was give veto rights to the five super powers at that time, China, France, the USSR, the United Kingdom and the United States. Any one of those five was allowed to quash the adoption of any proposal, even if all of the other nations voted in favor."

"That sure sounds stupid," Sandy said.

"You're not the first to voice that criticism," replied Zack.

"Well, tomorrow brings us to the second day of our trial," Sandy said, moving to wind up the broadcast. "The second charge against humanity explores our stewardship of Earth's water resources. Let's pray we fare better than we did today on aggression and warring."

She turned to the camera.

"And that wraps up today's edition of Washington Space Dateline News. Thank you for joining us. We look forward to visiting with you tomorrow evening. And remember—this evening's program will repeat at 10 p.m. on this station. Goodnight to all of you. I'm Virginie LaPlage."

Once the cameras were turned off, the panel sat back and began to unwind. Kornikov got up to stretch, and Zack offered to top off anyone's coffee.

Sandy gathered her stack of notes. As she was putting them away, her director walked over with a perplexed expression. He pulled his cell phone away from his face; wide-eyed, he shook his head.

"There must be a dozen Government agents swarming around the building and in the lobby," he said. "In fact, they've sealed off our building."

Bewildered, Sandy stood up.

"Say that again? Who is doing what?"

Just then her cell phone vibrated. "Yes?" she answered

"Sandy? It's Jordis Brandstadt."

"Oh yes, Madam President. Did you leave something behind?"

"No," the President said. "I'm here in the White House Situation Room with the Joint Chiefs, watching your show with a bizarre mixture of amusement and concern."

"Well, I'm not sure— "

"Please tell me who that impersonator was. Quite aside from her perfect imitation of me, we need to find out where and how she obtained all of that highly classified information."

Chapter 36

ONE OF THE CULTURAL ARTS COMPLEX courtesy limousines pulled up to the entrance of Peter the Great restaurant.

"Sorry but I'm afraid I won't be able to pick you up after dinner, Dr. Peters," said the driver, turning to lean over the back seat so he could talk to his passengers. "It's going to be a hectic night with so many delegates having places to go. We only have so many limos and drivers."

"I understand," Zack replied. "We'll grab a cab later. Thanks for the ride."

The doorman, sporting a Cossack uniform and an accent thicker than cold pig fat, opened the limo door and helped them out. "Welcome to PETER THE GREAT," he said with a flourish.

Zack checked their coats, and advised the *maître d'* they were with the Kornikov party, but not before Sandy had already spotted them.

"There," she said. "Over in the booth by the fireplace."

Kornikov stood up and waved as they approached the table. "Hello you two," he said. "Li-Hwa and I have already started with drinks. Let's get you one." He summoned the waiter.

"Hello Colonel," Sandy gushed. "And Li-Hwa—it's really great good to see you! I didn't know you were back in town already."

"My flight arrived a couple hours ago," replied Li-Hwa. "The Colonel had a car meet me at the airport to bring me right here. I'm afraid I may look a bit frazzled. I didn't have a chance to change clothes or work on this mop I like to call my hair."

"You're beautiful as ever," Zack smiled. Li-Hwa winked back, as she and Kornikov slid further into the booth. Sandy sat next to her; Zack scooched in next to Kornikov.

"This is my first visit here," Zack said, looking around. "It's quite a restaurant."

"Tat and I really like it," Kornikov replied. "Many of our consulate people come here. And please call me Misha.."

"I noticed many are speaking Russian," Sandy said. "But I don't see Tatyana. Is she in the powder room?"

"She stayed back at the consulate with a headache," laughed Li-Hwa "I'm afraid the Colonel is stuck with me tonight. How about Dr. Powell? I'd hoped he might be joining us."

"He was," Sandy said, "but he's visiting at a clinic for a minor medical procedure."

"Nothing serious, I hope," said the Colonel.

"I don't think so," she replied, "But knowing Bertie, he's very private about things like that. He did send his regards and suggested that Zack should pick up everyone's bar tab."

"It's an on-going joke between us," Zack laughed. "I'm used to it."

The waiter came and took their drink order. Two rounds later, he took their order for dinner.

"Let's toast the planners of this impromptu dinner," Zack said, as the waiter left the table. "Tatyana and Sandy."

"After today's trial session," said Li-Hwa, "I imagine your show tonight will discuss the charge of the mess we've made of oceans, lakes and rivers. Do you have any special time to arrive at the station?"

"Yes by quarter-to-six, because I won't need to prepare. Tonight, the director's letting people call in to voice their opinions. My job tonight will be to keep them on track and away from philosophy or politicizing. "

"The doorman is wearing an impressive Cossack uniform complete with one of those wool fur hats," Zack said to the Colonel.

"It's meant to impress tourists," Kornikov replied, "even though it's really not accurate for an Imperial Russia Cossacks. In the days of Peter the Great—but there I go boring you with details. It's my curse as a military enthusiast and historian. I enjoy delving into minutia whenever the opportunity arises."

"Not at all," said Zack. "I do the same with astronomy. It seems that when the public sees the image of an object with craters, they always assume it's our Moon, when it could be any one of dozens of moons and planets throughout the solar system. So I launch into a mini-lecture on moons and they all go to sleep."

The two men clinked glasses in an unspoken toast.

"So," Kornikov slurred, "how many moons do we have in the damn solar system?"

"Colonel," Li-Hwa interrupted, "that man standing at the bar with the Russian Deputy Trade Representative. Isn't that your Vice-Consul? And do you see who's approaching them."

The Colonel sighed harshly.

"Damn!" he grimaced. "It's Hilda something-or-other, the society editor for the *News Herald.* My Vice-Consul can't stand her. Grab your drink Zack, we're going over. We'll not only make points with the Vice-Consul, we'll save him from embarrassing Mother Russia when he accidentally spills a drink into her décolleté."

"Her what?" Zack asked.

"Her low-cut neckline," Sandy whispered.

"Been there—and done that," he whispered back.

"Well," he announced, "I'm all up for a rescue mission. Let's go Misha. If you lovely ladies will hold down the fort, we'll see if we can get into some trouble over at the bar."

Li-Hwa gave Zack a knowing smile, recalling her own décolleté situation.

"I love seeing those two in action," Sandy said. "If I believed in reincarnation I'd say they once were brothers. But I thought you once mentioned the Colonel and Vice-Counsel were always at odds with one another about something?"

"They are Sandy, but at Tatyana's suggestion I needed an excuse to get the Colonel and Zack to leave us alone so you and I could have a private girl talk."

"Sounds intriguing. So what's up?"

"It's not gossip, Sandy. It's about Zack—specifically, you and Zack. I need to know where things are between the two of you and what your feelings are. You see, I've grown very fond of him. Oh—hell with that. I've fallen in love."

"And Tatyana knows about this? I must be the only one in the dark about this."

"I assure you—neither Zack nor the Colonel knows about this,"

Li-Hwa answered. "And I admit to crying on Tatyana's shoulder more than once."

"Whatever it is, I can ease your pain, because I have a few romantic problems of my own. Bertie's flying to San Juan tomorrow so he can get back to Arecibo and his telescope for whatever time he has left."

"I'm so sorry, Sandy. Do you know what the condition is or how much time he has?"

"He's too stubborn to tell me. He said only that the doctors assured him he has at least one good year left. Two, with any luck. It depends on how well he responds to treatment. I've also given my notice to the station and the President. Bertie and I will fly back together on Friday after the end of the trial."

"I imagine Zack will want to be with you in San Juan, won't he?"

"If he does, I'll talk him out of it. He'll take it like a trooper, after I explain the situation. Over the years I believed I loved that wonderful old guy as a father, but it's more than that. I plan to move in with him for until…well, for as long as we have. And I have come to grips with the fact he may never marry me. In that case, I'll be content to be a friend with benefits."

Li-Hwa reached over and took her hand.

"I'm speechless," she said. "But here is the real story about Zack and me, one he already knows. I'm embarrassed to admit that our meeting and the romance were planned in advance as part of my assignment in Washington and Bermuda.

"I felt I had complete control of my emotions and could treat the situation as a means to an end. But by our third meeting, I knew I'd fallen in love and was too shy or maybe too reserved to say or do anything. Especially once I discovered you two had become involved."

"Well Li, I can't put off telling him any longer so I'll do it tonight." She squeezed Li's hand.

"If you truly love him," she added, "I insist you jump right in and tell him, so because I plan to be out of the picture before the night is over."

Li-Hwa glanced away.

"Here they come," she said, dabbing her eyes. "Time to put on our happy faces."

*****

WHEN DINNER WAS OVER Zack glanced at his watch. "We better get a move on if you want to get to the studio on time," he said to Sandy. "I'll grab our coats and meet you up front."

"We had a wonderful time," Sandy said to Li-Hwa and Mikhail. As she gathered her things she added, "My show tonight will only be a rehash of today's water pollution charge and viewer call-ins. Forgive us for leaving early and missing out on the entertainment."

"The Colonel and I will be just fine," Li-Hwa said. "I'll take another glance at the desert menu—that double chocolate cake does look tempting. I also plan on buying the Colonel another martini as part of my master plan to get him out on the dance floor."

"I doubt you'll succeed, Li, but that martini might give you your best chance. It was wonderful getting together. I know Tatyana will be sorry that she missed the party. We'll see you both tomorrow."

As they moved through the restaurant, Sandy noticed that many of the patrons had gathered by the television sets. When Zack approached with their coats he noticed the same thing.

"Let's go see what the big to-do was all about," he suggested.

As they neared the screen, they saw fire and smoke; through a momentary clearing of the smoke, a few details became visible.

"Oh my God," Sandy gasped. "It's our building! Someone just blew up the station!"

Chapter 37

HAD THE WEDNESDAY MORNING EXPLOSION in the entranceway to the Washington Cultural Arts Complex been less destructive—once the flames were out, the smoke dissipated, and the major pieces of debris cleared away—one could have admired the planning that had gone into it. The only problem would have been piecing together the events leading up to it. But eventually a chain of events emerged, letting the Capitol Police and government investigators piece together a rough sketch of what had happened.

An hour before the delegates arrived at the Arts Complex, what seemed to be a routine traffic event was taking place two miles to the east. Witnesses saw two police cars chasing a white van that was speeding westbound on Arts Boulevard, the street the Arts Complex was located on.

At the same time, two miles to the west of the Complex, an identical situation was taking place: another white van was being pursued eastbound by two police cars.

By the time the six converging vehicles were within a block of the Complex, the flashing lights and sirens had drawn the attention of pedestrians, as well as the other drivers, who had all slowed and moved to the curb. With perfect timing, all six of the cars and vans arrived in front of the Arts Complex at the same time.

The two vans turned off Arts Boulevard and headed up the circular drive to the front entrance of the Complex. Meanwhile, the four pursuing police cars continued past each other at high speed, continuing on in opposite directions. Distracted by the lights and sirens, security personnel in the booths at either side of the circle drive were caught off guard as the vans raced past them and accelerated up to the building entrance.

The resulting explosion rocked buildings across the street and shattered windows for a block in all directions. Fortunately, when the emergency vehicles and teams arrived, they discovered that the only fatalities had been the two the van drivers.

"I'M JASON HURN and this is a WSDN-TV special report. Late last night, the Washington Cultural Arts Complex was the target of a terrorist bombing. We take you live to Virginie LaPlage at the scene."

Sandy was standing in front of police barriers on the circle drive. Behind her was the twisted wreckage of the two vans.

"As you can see, Jason, the scene is under control and relatively quiet, considering what occurred here just a few hours ago. Except for these burned out vans that carried the explosives, the lion's share of the debris has been cleared away. It would appear the police have completed investigating the vans and tow trucks are backing in to take them away.

"We also have a good handle on the events leading up to this disaster. One would wonder how the vans made it to the entrance of the Complex without having been overtaken and stopped. D'Arcy James, a favorite on-scene reporter for WSDN, was already here when I arrived."

James moved on camera, to stand next to Sandy. In his hands he held a microphone and a few notes scribbled on scraps of paper

"D'Arcy, please fill us in on what you've been able to find out."

"I've spoken to several witnesses, enough to paint a pretty fair picture of what went down," said James, looking grim and businesslike. "What emerges is a simple yet elaborate plan, requiring six dedicated drivers in two vans and four sedans. The vans were totally nondescript, with no exterior markings. On the other hand, and to embellish on the charade, the four black and white sedans looked to all the world like police cars, with lights flashing and sirens wailing."

"Were those the police cars witnesses reported earlier?"

"Sandy, as it turns out, the drivers weren't even wearing police uniforms. They had on dark blue shirts and military-style hats—the kind with a hard, black visor. And get this Sandy; those cars were two-door sedans. The norm for police patrol cars is four doors. And police dispatchers have confirmed that no officers reported engaging in a chase anywhere near the scene of the incident."

"That seems to validate what psychiatrists tell us—that our brains let us see what we expect to see, which is not always what's actually there."

"Now if you'll excuse me, Sandy, I have people piling up behind me that I need to talk to."

As James walked off-camera, Sandy continued.

On a special note," she said, "Today's trial proceedings at the Arts Center have been cancelled. While it hasn't been confirmed yet, it's safe to assume today's charge—stewardship of Earth's atmosphere—will pick up first thing tomorrow morning. We will have to wait to discover if the prosecution will present two charges on the same day, atmosphere and land.

"So, until tonight at six, when I'm sure I will be able to announce tomorrow's trial schedule and offer an update on the overnight bombing I'm Sandy LaPlage. This has been a Special Report for Washington Space Dateline News."

Chapter 38

THE PRESIDENT OF THE ASSEMBLY tapped the podium microphone.

"Good morning, delegates," he began, adjusting the volume to eliminate the ear-piercing squeal. "I hope you enjoyed yesterday's one-day vacation—though I am sure we all regret the destructive event that enabled you to have it. You all probably experienced traffic problems this morning on Arts Boulevard, now that it has been blocked off to most vehicles. We trust that the problem will ease tomorrow as local residents find alternate routes to their destinations.

"Today's first order of business today concerns some housekeeping matters. Many have mentioned that the auditorium seemed uncomfortably warm. I trust today you will find it cooler.

"Another common complaint was frustration at being unable to ask the prosecution questions. The reason is two-fold. Certain questions would only be a ruse to make a political statement. In addition, the prosecution believes that time taken for such questions would cut into that day's schedule. As a result, you are encouraged to direct your questions for the prosecution electronically. I've been led to believe that you will receive your answers promptly

"Moving on to the day's agenda, in order to get back on schedule after losing the whole of yesterday, we will address two topics today. This morning will be dedicated to 'Stewardship of the Atmosphere'. This afternoon will pursue 'Stewardship of the Land.' Each session will be followed by oral rebuttals. But, due to the limitation of time, some delegates will be unable to voice a rebuttal. They may do so electronically, with the Prosecutor's assurance that special attention will be given to them.

"Now, it is my pleasure to reintroduce our distinguished host and prosecutor."

In the silence that followed, the Visitor took the podium in as many guises as there were delegates viewing it.

"To begin," it began, in a chameleon voice as varied as its appearance, "I would remind you of a minor difference in the way the Korr legal system operates. At the beginning of a trial the accused is deemed guilty until proven innocent. There is one more point we want to make perfectly clear, before you respond to a charge. You may be assured that the only evidence we use is from your own official records, and not from sources known only to the Korr."

The prosecutor reached beneath the podium and withdrew a large globe of the Earth.

"We know how much easier it is for you to understand things intellectually if you have a visual representation. A globe like this is readily available for your inspection in schools and libraries, throughout your world. You understand that your planet's atmosphere does not extend out forever through space. Instead, it is an extremely thin layer of gas bound to the surface of this planet by gravity.

"If you were estimate the thickness of the atmosphere in relation to this globe, it would be roughly the thickness of the lacquer a manufacturer sprays on globes to protect them." Tapping the globe it added, "In this particular case, humans can breathe only the lowest 10% of the thickness of the lacquer. If for any reason it becomes lost or impure you will all die.

"By the beginning of the 21st Century, more than a hundred million people were living in countries with air pollution levels far exceeding standards set by your own National Ambient Air Quality Standards Organization. Those pollutants are nitrogen oxide, carbon monoxide and sulfur dioxide. During the last ten years of the 20th Century, countries that were major contributors of carbon dioxide emissions alone were China, Japan, Russia and the United States. In that same period of time, each of the four countries emitted between one and six billion metric tons of carbon dioxide.

"By the end of that century Russia had not only doubled its

emissions, a fifth country—India—joined the four by emitting six billion metric tons. Ironically, Russia deserves your praise for having cut its emissions by nearly one-fifth."

The Russian delegates were grinning and nodding their heads; members of the other four were squirming in their seats.

"The World Health Organization has reported the greatest air contamination today is found in Asia, where almost 1.5 million people die each year as a result. You may recall Tuesday's discussion when we quoted reports from WHO pointing out that a half-million Asians die each year from the consequences of water pollution alone.

"Please note on your personal monitor a very long display of your own sources by which the Korr receives its data. Others will be added from time to time. Our list is in flux because some organizations change their names, and others have been closing their doors."

The sources displayed ranged from the American Lung Association, through the International Environmental Bureau, to the World Meteorological Organization, including bureaus and agencies from nearly every country in the world.

"Because we Korr are objective observers, we have the luxury of evaluating facts without the weight of personal interest. And our conclusion is that human refusal to recognize human responsibility for poisoning so much of your planet in is due to the roles played by economics and politics.

"Now, before you begin your lunch break, I want to offer you some charts and video clips...."

DURING THE INTERMISSION between the day's sessions, Kornikov found Zack at a local sushi bar and sat down in the seat across the table.

"My President has asked me to put together ideas he can add to a proposed list of concessions," said the Colonel. "These will be discussed Saturday during a private meeting by the heads of state and later offered to the Korr."

"Let me guess," Zack said, swallowing his tilapia. "This has the hallmarks of you doing the work and your President taking the credit."

"I'm sure that's the case," the Colonel chuckled. "I know I'm asking a lot from you on short notice, but if you could stop by the embassy tonight and help come up with some ideas I'd appreciate it."

"Sure," Zack sighed. "I'll be happy to come by. Li said the ladies are having dinner tonight, so this will give me something to do in addition to enjoying the company. What time do you want me there?"

"If you can make it at six, I'll buy dinner."

"You know, Misha, the more I think of it, the more I'm convinced that the Heads-of-State meeting won't stay confidential for very long. But I think it's a good idea to offer the prosecution some kind of proposal in the event the trial goes south."

A bell chimed the hour, and the Colonel rose from his seat. "You're right," he said. "That is the plan. Now, we'd best get back. We don't want to miss out on us getting our collective asses kicked for the way we've taken care of the land."

"I HOPE YOU ENJOYED your break," the Visitor said from the dais, as the delegates wandered back to their seats. "There are five items regarding your land stewardship that I will bring to your attention. The first is your mounds of refuse plastic that is guaranteed to endure longer than the five-thousand-year old pyramids in Egypt.

"The second is the amount of chemical fertilizer used in agriculture so you can sustain nine billion people, and how it is directly linked to soil degradation and subsequent water run-off. We will save speaking about your excessive population until tomorrow.

"Three: there is a limit to the amount of food humans can grow in the foreseeable future, despite any advances you may achieve in agricultural methods. As your birth rate continues to grow exponentially with no sign of abating, I must remind you of what happened to Old Mother Hubbard: when she eventually went to the cupboard, she found bare.

"With regard to nursery rhymes and fairy tales, the Korr found them in virtually every culture we have examined. Inevitably, they are written for children, but we find that adults often fail to make the connection to the underlying reality they represent. But I digress.

"Returning to item three; your current situation is like giving a late-night party and discovering you have more guests than you invited. Not only do you find yourself running out of food and refreshments, but you find all the grocery stores have closed. In essence, this is what is happening to you, here. Your run-away birth rate is taxing your ability to produce the food necessary to sustain today's population, and you are making no provision for the future.

"Four: methane gas has forty times the capacity to generate greenhouse gasses than anything commonly produced by humans and nature. We find that methane is currently being released into the environment at an alarming rate from lakes of permafrost in the Arctic. Permafrost covers more than twenty-four percent of your planet's land mass, yet you have paid it little attention amid your decades-long controversies on climate change.

"And, as if that isn't bad enough, the warming of the atmosphere brought on by Arctic methane will release a second source of this gas, one locked up in carbon that was produced millions of years ago by animal and plant decay and now located deeper than surface permafrost. It is just waiting to be invited to the warming festivities.

"Five: seventy-percent of all the fresh water available on this planet is now used in the production of food. Do any of you realize that it requires fifteen pounds of grain to produce a single pound of consumable meat—not including the fresh water needed to produce the grain. And from what we can see of human nature, it is unlikely you will ever change to a healthier, non-meat diet.

"To sum up, there are three options open to you. You can continue with unrestricted birthrates that will result in the deaths of hundreds of millions from famine, you can legalize mandated euthanasia, or you can embark on decades of wars resulting in the death of hundreds of millions as nations roam the planet attempting to steal the final vestiges of food.

"I continue to find the use of quotes effective in making a point. The American agronomist and humanitarian, Norman E. Borlang was a 1970 Nobel Peace Prize winner who probably saved millions from hunger. He said, 'There can be no permanent progress in the battle against hunger until the agencies that fight for increased food production and those who fight for population control are able to unite in a common effort.'

"Let me take you back more than sixty years to a time when humans made their first venture to other worlds. American astronaut Michal Collins prophetically said after observing the fragility of Earth, 'I hope the space programs of all nations will allow everyone to look at the Earth from afar and realize what a wonderful planet this is—one that should not be befouled.'

"Let me paraphrase Collins' words. He also said how lucky you were to have clean air to breathe and clean oceans to place your hands into and pour over your heads. And he observed what a tragedy it would be to allow filth and pollution to contaminate your planet, Earth.

"The intermission will now begin followed by your rebuttals."

Chapter 39

FRIDAY MORNING ARRIVED. It was to be the final day of charges followed by oral and written rebuttals by the defense.

After welcoming the delegates, the assembly President announced a private conference to be held Saturday for delegation leaders only. Although the topic went unmentioned, rumor had it they would be putting together a list of concessions the countries would offer in the event their rebuttals proved inadequate, and sentencing seemed inevitable.

The prosecution took the podium and greeted the President and delegates. "Before we address your stewardship to each other, I wish to mention something in line with the topic—something we have found both entertaining and absurd. We were amazed that you have such a wide range of terms contradicting your claim to being civilized.

"This makes you rather unique among other worlds we have interviewed so far. I ask you to note on your personal monitors the terms that you use to describe human inadequacies.

"We ask you to place each of these words at the end of the question, 'Why are humans so: abusive, aggressive, antagonistic, argumentative, arrogant, autocratic, belligerent, bigoted, brutal, callous, cantankerous, coldblooded, coldhearted, condescending, confrontational...."

Zack looked around, and noticed that many of the delegates had started shifting uncomfortably in their seats.

"....loathsome, malevolent, malicious, mean...."

Kornikov signed harshly, wondering how long this portion of the monologue would continue.

"....pitiless, pompous, prejudiced, pretentious...."

Zack checked his watch. If he had to do it over, he thought, he'd probably set the stopwatch function to see how long it took to come up with so many different ways to say asshole.

"....rude, ruthless, sadistic, self-absorbed, self-centered, selfish, self-righteous, self-seeking..."

The Colonel turned to the row behind him where Zack was seated in the U.S. delegation. Once they had made contact the two men rolled their eyes and offered looks of sympathetic monotony.

"I believe I've made my point," said the visitor. "Because your history is rife with a passion to subjugate others, the topics this morning will be bigotry, caste systems, racism and slavery. We are aware of your plethora of excuses for these despicable actions, which begin with your need for inexpensive labor and females for breeding stock to increase your populations. You also feel the need to enrich and widen your assets by the taking of lands and property of others through war. However, you are reminded that this topic was addressed last Monday.

"Some 200,000 years ago, when you were hunter-gatherers, it was prudent and necessary for groups of hominids to avoid contact with other groups. Without the language skills that could have permitted you meaningful dialogue, it was impossible to understand why such encounters occurred. So, you feared the worst. At best, such a meeting would conclude with food being stolen or one group being driven from its hunting areas and water holes. At worst it meant females and children were taken prisoner and the males killed.

"Let us first consider your treatment of the females of your species. Because written records first appear only 5,000 years ago, there is no account of 9,000 years ago when the first permanent communities formed at Hacilar and Catalhoyuk in Neolithic Turkey. But beginning with your earliest records, we find that in addition to ubiquitous warring, the conditions being endured by females were deplorable...."

Throughout the morning and afternoon, the prosecution built its case against humanity's predilection to slavery, caste systems, and the inequitable distribution of resources and wealth. And when it was time for rebuttals, or to make a defense, not a single representative rose to offer one.

* * *

"GOOD EVENING, ladies and gentlemen. It's six o'clock and time for Washington Space Dateline News. I'm Virginie LaPlage.

"This will be my final appearance on WSDN. Following the defense summation on Monday, I will be flying back to San Juan, Puerto Rico to resume a career in radio and television. Because I've never been at ease with farewells, let me simply offer my heartfelt thanks for being invited into your homes.

"Our panelists this evening are doctors Hoshi Watanabe and Ralph Pendleton. Good evening to both of you gentlemen and welcome to the show."

"Good evening, Sandy," they responded.

"I'd like to begin with you, Dr. Watanabe. You are the director of the National Radio Astronomy Observatory at Green Bank, West Virginia. I also see that you are about to travel to Puerto Rico to be interviewed for directorship of the thousand-foot radio telescope at Arecibo. You mentioned before the show that you have had a longtime interest in working with the largest, single-aperture telescope ever built."

"That's right, Sandy," Watanabe replied. "I'm lucky to have known the facility's outgoing director Bertram Powel for many years. But because I'll be going up against some stiff competition with a lady from the Mauna Kea Observatory in Hawaii and a gentleman from the Cerro Tololo Observatory in Chile, I decided not to order new business cards until it's a done deal."

"Well good luck to you Dr. Watanabe. And now Dr. Pendleton, I see that you're currently the assistant director of the World Health Organization regional office in Washington. Can you tell our viewers a little about WHO?"

"Thanks Sandy. We are the health arm of the United Nations and our responsibilities include monitoring health trends, outbreak of disease and setting models and standards. We also offer technical support to countries by reviewing and evaluating their health care."

"It's easy to see the need for the UN to have centralized authority to oversee global health," said Sandy. "This raises some questions I've heard bantered around here about assuring our ongoing encounter with the Korr. Is there any possibility they may have inadvertently brought with them one or more diseases that could be dangerous, even deadly? Another thing I'm curious about is how WHO would respond to such dire prospect?"

"I agree this ET encounter is a valid concern, Sandy. We decided early on that it would be irresponsible for us to add fuel to the fire by admitting we had some genuine worries about alien pathogens. But while we've discovered a few abnormal health problems occurring since their arrival, I can assure everyone that we've found no direct connections to the visitor from 40 Eridani. I say 'the' visitor because there hasn't been a confirmation of how many of them came to Earth."

"Come to think of it, I don't recall that question having been posed to the prosecutor, Dr. Pendleton. I'd now like to ask you gentlemen to comment on the trial, especially on the merits of today's charge—our stewardship to one another. Can we begin with you Dr. Watanabe?"

"I don't think that particular charge brought any surprises, Sandy. Anyone familiar with conditions in the world already knows how poorly we've treated each other. With few exceptions, we've largely turned a blind eye to our misbehavior. It's bad enough to mistreat our planet, but the mistreatment of fellow humans is inexcusable and indefensible."

"What exceptions are you referring to?"

"I think of the dedicated individuals and organizations that devote so much time and energy combatting crimes against humanity. Dozens of alliances, institutes, and societies come to mind—so it would be a disservice to mention some and omit others."

"I understand your caution, Dr. Watanabe. But with all of the challenges over the years, how would you evaluate the results?"

"I'd be dishonest to claim that results have been more than minimal. Because their goals are so overwhelming, we can't expect anyone to change human nature. If I was to single out the worst problems it would be worldwide child prostitution. The numbers quoted by the prosecution were staggering. It was sickening to hear that the amount of such hapless youngsters could range upwards of ten million. That's why I feel we're fighting a losing battle."

"As in Don Quixote's, 'to fight the unbeatable foe'?"

"Yes, it takes a true hero to not become discouraged when trying to right unrightable wrongs. Otherwise, our most dedicated humanitarians would just give up."

"That is truly introspective, Dr. Watanabe. How about you, Dr. Pendleton? Will you share your thoughts on the charge and our rebuttals?"

"I agree with Dr. Watanabe, Sandy. With due respect to our delegates, it's sad and bitterly amusing to hear them wax so eloquently during their rebuttals. And it's been going on all week. They may rightfully praise some strides we've made to clean up our madness, but when all is said and done, humans will continue with business as usual. I'd almost say it's in our genes—so much so that we not only keep fouling our planet, but enjoy making a profit while doing so."

"Ralph's right," Watanabe sighed. "This brings me to another thought. Even if it's true for the Korr to say their race possesses intelligence far ahead of ours, I don't understand why we can't sit down with them and carry on a meaningful dialogue with them."

"And that, good friend, brings us to the real nature of the Korr," said Pendleton. "For the past few days the Visitor acknowledges receiving electronic messages from delegates asking for answers about inconsistencies in the information they've been given about actions that might be taken against us."

"Can you expand on that Dr. Pendleton?" asked Sandy.

"Let me read to you just a couple of questions that have been posed to the Prosecutor and not answered. Why did the Korr sink a huge warship and destroy three cities because one or more persons refused to obey a single directive, then disregard other things we've said and done? I sometimes wonder if they might be a strange breed of biological robots. Or some other totally unknown type of living entity."

"And what exactly do you mean by biological robots?"

"Could the Korr representatives be mindless life-forms, operating on programmed instructions with no will of their own?" Ralph asked. "And that's just one of many questions I have. Are from this universe, or some parallel universe? Do they come from the future? And if they are, wouldn't they already know the outcome of events they seem so desperate to change? Do they use conventional space vehicles?"

"I particularly liked that last question," added Watanabe. "Especially in light of the fact that our fastest spaceships would take 85,000 years to travel one way to Alpha Centauri, the closest star system and 200,000 years to travel to the Korr home world. How do we know there is a Korr home world? Are there other Korr individuals anywhere at all? Is their total population just the few we've had interaction with?"

"Or," Sandy offered, "could they be holographic projections?"

"I don't give much credence to that notion—though I have heard others wonder about that, as well. Images shouldn't be able to break the laws of physics by traveling faster than the speed of light. And it would mean instructions from their home world would be take decades to arrive to Earth."

Sandy glanced at her monitor. "Let's pause for a moment. I'm told that demonstrators are now gathering outside the trial auditorium, demanding passes for Monday's proceedings, claiming to be religious groups that believe the prosecutor is the Second Coming."

"Talk about déjà vu," Watanabe said. "Ralph and I were just discussing that very same thing back in the green room and wondering how long it would take before some groups came up with a cockamamie idea like that. If you'll allow me to get back to the idea of inconsistencies, I'd particularly like to know why the original story we were given about them arriving in a few weeks, was either a mistake or an out-and-out lie.

"And now even that story has changed," he continued. "It's the Naians who are heading this way, not the Korr. And they aren't even coming to Earth. We're being told that these Naians are just passing the Sun while on a journey to some far distant star."

Pendleton nodded. "Exactly—and then we were told how humans would pose a threat to any less advanced civilizations after developing interstellar capabilities. What was it the prosecutor said? I wrote it down somewhere…here it is. I quote, 'Because of your aggressive nature, you would pollute such civilizations by interrupting their natural development.' Give me a break. That idea is totally hypocritical considering how the Korr interrupted our own natural development."

"That's the perfect word—hypocritical," Sandy said. She searched through some papers. "Our viewers will recall that they've been invited to send comments and questions to the station. This one fits right into our topic. Rich from Fort Worth asks, 'Just how many of them alien critters do we have here? A whole bunch, a few or just one? If there are just a few of them, I'd be happy to show them good old Texas hospitality by driving to Washington City and shooting their sorry…' " Sandy blushed and stopped reading..

"And how does everyone feel about the rumor that the Korr have used other humans to spy on us over the years?" asked Watanabe. "I really find that rather unreal."

"You're not alone in that regard, Hoshi," interjected Sandy. "I imagine most of us share your feelings. And while I'd love to delve into that a little more, our time is flying and we must tie up some loose ends. Considering the inconsistencies, it's evident that nothing is crystal-clear regarding the Korr. No one can say where they're from, who they are, or the reason for their visit. We can only say for sure that they have us on trial, they apparently have extraordinary technology, and are blatantly inconsistent."

"Well I refuse to accept the idea that we misinterpret what they say because our brains are not as evolved as theirs are," Pendleton bristled. "Hell—for all we know the Korr are just a bunch of teenage hoodlums running wild among the stars. If that's so, I'd appreciate it if some interstellar cops would show up and throw their petty asses in jail!"

Sandy laughed. "Gee, Dr. Pendleton, why don't you just tell us how you really feel?"

"I'm sorry. That was totally unhelpful."

"No apology needed. In fact, it helped spice up my show." She glanced at her monitor again. "Well it's confirmed. The delegations have been formally asked by the President of the Assembly to submit suggestions for a list of concessions to be submitted to the Korr. It's also been decided that only countries with a population greater than 500,000 will vote on the final document. This seems to be a last ditch attempt to show our good intent, and gain a reprieve if the verdict goes against us.

"Well Dr. Watanabe, Dr. Pendleton, I'm afraid our time is up. Thank you for being with us tonight. And to all of my loyal viewers, I offer you one final adieu. This is Virginie LaPlage saying goodnight and goodbye."

* * * * *

ZACK MET WITH Mikhail Kornikov for dinner that evening at the Russian embassy. After their second glass of wine, the two of them worked on some additional concessions for the Colonel to add to the list before giving them to the Russian President to include in the official document to submit the following day.

After they'd finished, Zack took the elevator down to the garage. As he pulled past the security booth at the street entrance, one of the uniformed guards stepped out and directed him to a parking space. Walking to the passenger side, the guard motioned for Zack to lower the window.

"I hope you're not going to give me another speeding ticket," Zack smiled.

Bending over to lean into the window, the guard morphed into Lise Danfers.

"That's a pretty spiffy car you're driving," she said. "Mind if I hop in for a moment? We need to talk."

"Of course," Zack answered, knowing full well he was talking to the Visitor. "Hop in. It's good to see you."

"And it's good to be seen," she replied, as she opened the door and slid in alongside of him. "Don't be concerned about that other guard in the booth. He thinks he's working alone. And he isn't even aware that you're parked here."

Zack scratched his head. "I wasn't sure if we'd get the chance to see each other again. But for the record, I'm happy we're having this meeting."

She slid closer.

"As a scientist, and from what you know about our two species, we are incapable of having a sexual relation considering how physically dissimilar we are. We also lack the ability to show warmth or be approachable. In fact those words— friendly and approachable—just aren't found in our dictionaries. Or would be, if we had dictionaries. I just want you to know that I am sad this is the last time we will meet in private. I will miss you.

"I will miss you, too."

"Getting back to business," she said, turning away, "I've tried to explain that we came to Earth to see if there was any way that humans and the Korr could become partners and as such get out of this universe before the catastrophe occurs. But before I leave, I think you deserve to know what that cataclysm is."

"So, at long last you are finally going to explain it?"

"No," she sighed. "It will be better if you see it with your own eyes. It will be easier for you to observe what's in store for humans through my eyes. I'll do the travelling and just tag along. Okay?"

"So you do all the work, and I get to stay here comfy and cozy while observing through your mind?"

"That's not completely accurate," she said. "Try imagining you're in a theater with a wrap-around screen that allows you to see in all directions including up and down."

"I can handle that."

"So Zack, through the years you've viewed the universe through optical telescopes and heard it with radio telescopes. But their imagery was muddied by Earth's dusty and humid atmosphere, as well as the dust and gas between the stars. Certainly your space telescopes were a fantastic improvement, but they are still inadequate. How often have you dreamed about a perfect viewing location with totally clear skies?"

"Every time I'm out star gazing."

"How would you like to have such a location six trillion miles away?"

"That would certainly be on my bucket list, Lise."

"My bucket list would be for us to always be at each other's side."

Zack smiled at hearing the first thing the Visitor said that was passably romantic.

"But before we start Zack, you will probably find this adventure unnerving, especially with your dislike of great heights. I'm going to put one arm around you snugly and ask you to clasp my hand."

Zack did as he was told.

"Now, close your eyes. I'll tell you when you can open them."

"You sound like one of the ghosts from Dickens' 'Christmas Carol.' "

She put her mouth to his ear.

"*Boo*," she whispered. Zack found himself aroused by her warm breath in his ear and the hint of fragrance, and tried his best to dismiss the feeling.

"Okay," she said at last. "We've arrived at our destination. You may find this overwhelming at first, so take a deep breath and slowly open your eyes."

"Oh, my God!" he gasped.

"I fail to see the religious significance," she said gently. "But I agree that being in deep space is truly breath-taking. I never grow tired of it."

Slowly, he looked around, in all directions. Suspended in space, and in the darkest location imaginable, the sight was so stunning he forgot to be afraid. He was out among the stars and lost amid their vivid colors. As the euphoria passed, he felt his heart racing.

The visitor sensed his anxiety and squeezed his hand tighter to offer assurance. "Don't worry," she said pulling him closer. "I've got you."

"That's all very reassuring, but who's holding you?"

"I hope you're enjoying this," she said. "But to make the scene truly realistic, I'll add the nebulae and galaxies and speed up the passing of time. You will be seeing the motion in the galaxies so brace yourself."

The stars blurred for a moment and when they refocused, thousands of galaxies of every type, shape, size and color came into view. What he found most extraordinary was how the galaxies were slowly converging on one particular location in space—and the location was him. He cried out again, "Oh my God. The universe truly is collapsing on itself. We call this theory the Big Crunch."

"So what do you think?"

"I see what you meant by the big picture—the real picture. So this is what's really going on. Yet for the past century we've seen that the universe is expanding. Why couldn't we detect this?"

Lise turned his chin so he faced her. "This is what we do with societies that we think might help us. By disguising the universe as moving away, we were shielding you from the realizing that Earth, the planets, the Sun, everything in the solar system and in the universe itself was coming to an end. In your case, we've enclosed your solar system in a bubble that extends out to the orbit of the dwarf planet Eris."

"The list of questions I had for you just tripled. In effect the Korr have hidden the real universe from us."

"Yes. And now I'll let you observe the bubble."

Once again the stars and galaxies blurred and refocused. Zack now could make out a transparent shape surrounding the solar system—a giant sphere with the universe as we see it projected somehow on the inside. But it wasn't a perfect sphere. Zack pointed at a slight pucker on the area that faced Eridanus.

"This is probably what Consuela from Bertie's team saw and attempted to describe—a converging vortex where the bubble puckered in the direction of 40 Eri. It had been a fleeting impression when she referred to it as the navel of God.

"I can see now why you want to find a life-form to help you escape the Big Crunch."

"I vaguely remember you alluding to that in the President's office. I didn't fully grasp the situation until now."

"Well, my dear, I'm having difficulty maintaining this little excursion of ours. I am going to have to return to Earth. Close your eyes and hold on."

In an instant, they were back in the front seat of Zack's car.

"That was amazing," Zack panted. "Words can't describe it. But it's a destination that's much easier to return from than to get to."

"Sooner or later, all civilizations come to realize they are just microbes clinging to a tiny planet," said Lise, "orbiting an unremarkable star, one of 400 billion in the Milky Way. And this galaxy is only one of a trillion others in a seemingly endless universe. Add to that the possibility that their universe may only be one of an infinite number of universes and it's no wonder that knowledgeable societies feel so insignificant upon discovering that everything they know is facing destruction. In our case, we chose to do something about it rather than go down without a fight."

"The problem is enough to drive a man to drink," Zack sighed.

"I do understand why you find these concepts, especially the trial, distressing. But humans are flawed. Your flaws, combined with the fact that you've attained such a high level of technology, makes you too dangerous to be left to your own devices.

"Humanity's greatest shortcoming is your lack of discipline in action and thought. You would be amazed to know how close you are to achieving interstellar travel. With that capability you'd have the power to disrupt societies only a few light years away. Before long you'd realize that faster-than-light travel is just a small step from interstellar travel.."

"These concepts are more than most of us can visualize, let alone act upon," replied Zack. "In our present state of affairs, that kind of knowledge is like handing a child a loaded gun. But what do you do with societies that clean up their act?"

"As soon as a species becomes capable of running their affairs without supervision, we remove the bubble and let them see the real universe. Then, if they are no threat to others, we leave them alone unhindered."

Zack shut his eyes to think; a moment later, he reopened them. "So why did you rush us into this trial?"

"Time is growing short. We may not be able to maintain Earth's bubble much longer. It all has to do with the buildup of interstellar matter following the mingling of dark energy and dark matter—something I couldn't explain to you even if I had the time.

Another problem we have is the lack of time to replace you with another species."

"Why is that?" he asked. "While I hate to admit it, the idea sounds extremely compassionate."

"We don't know of a species that is in immediate need of a planet with Earth-like conditions. Neither can we return to your past and allow another hominid group to evolve. We did it once and let the Neanderthals develop. When that proved unsuccessful we went back a second time and allowed your ancestors, the Cro-Magnon, to advance. As you can see, that didn't work out either. So with no more hominids to experiment with, and time running out, the Korr is out of options."

Zack took a deep breath and took a moment to think. "After the trial," he said at last, "what will happen to you? Will you return to 40 Eri or continue searching?"

"Neither is possible. I can stay on Earth for the rest of my existence, or I can reenter our group consciousness. I don't find that appealing because it's easier to get in than it is to get out. This has always been a one-way trip for me."

"Then it's a no-brainer. I vote you to stay here, travel around until you find the perfect location to settle down—and perhaps choose a companion to share your life with."

"Today, I'd pick either be Switzerland or the Canadian Rockies."

"They both sound pleasant," Zack said "And to keep busy, considering the journey you took me on, you could produce planetarium shows."

She wrinkled her nose. "That sounds too much like I would be stuck inside all day."

"Well, if you have an inclination to do good you could go around stopping evil. Given time, you could clean up the whole world—perhaps as a superhero. You could call yourself Eridani Man or Eridani Woman. Wearing a flashy costume would be optional. And with your longevity you could have dozens of other avocations."

She opened the door and got out.

"Sadly, I feel this will be our last time together."

Leaning through the open window she added, "I've enjoyed your acquaintance, Zack."

He could see tears starting to form in her eyes.

"I wish you good fortune and much happiness."

"The same to— " he began.

She was gone before he could finish.

Part 6

Extinction is the rule. Survival is the exception.

—Carl Sagan

Chapter 40

ON MONDAY, for all intents and purposes the trial was over. The prosecution had presented their five charges and each charge had been followed by oral rebuttals with speakers from the nations that were representing humanity.

Today the defense would present its summation using three speakers selected from among those delegates who had proven themselves to be the most eloquent and articulate.

The previous day being a non-event day, the delegates had met to prepare for the worst. Although their summation would undoubtedly be well-crafted and persuasive—at least, to themselves—most had the gnawing thought that the prosecution had presented an airtight case. On the bright side, however, few delegates had found fault with the food or its attractive presentation in the food court area of the auditorium foyer.

THE COLONEL AND Zack were grazing at a table in the Asian food area on one of the breaks shortly after noon when Zack happened to look up from his crab leg. "Look who's headed our way," he said, pointing toward the approaching form of J. Winthrop Winstanly, Great Britain's M-6 director.

"We might end up with a family reunion," replied the Colonel, pointing in the opposite direction. "Here comes Larksworth too."

"Greetings and bon appetite," Zack said. "I haven't seen you since London. How are things at the Ministry, Hamish?"

"Not as well as I'd like," Larksworth replied, his Scottish brogue muffled by a mouthful of hot dog. Wiping mustard from his red moustache, he added, "Just the same, it's nice to run into you Zack. And Colonel Kornikov, how are things with you and the bonnie Tatyana?"

"Well enough, all things considered. Thank you for asking."

After exchanging a few more pleasantries, and sharing their displeasure with the morning's summations, Winstanly's eyes lost their twinkle, and his face clouded with purpose. "What say I bring you up to speed on our Project Noah?" he said, lowering his voice as he took a seat.

"Thanks," replied Zack. "I'd appreciate it. While privy to the overall picture, I really haven't gotten any of the details."

"I find myself in the same boat," Kornikov added. "But I'll bet my last Euro that Tatyana and I won't be found on any of the passenger lists. Have any of you received such an invitation?"

They all shook their heads

"I must say there is an interesting spin to the program," said Winstanley. "At the last minute, all of the Royal family's senior members publicly declined to leave, choosing to remain behind with the rest of their citizenry. That allowed their 10 billets to be available to the grandchildren who will be chosen by seniority."

"I am impressed," the Colonel replied. "From what I've heard, three of the nine nations with nuclear subs want their VIPs to escape and to hell with the hoi polloi."

Winstanley shook his head. "That is terrible, to say the least. From what I understand, the Royals flew up to Faslane this morning. That's home port for the Vanguard and Astute class submarines."

"I'm not up-to-speed on those boats Win," Zack said. "Can you fill us in?"

"Both of the classes are nuclear powered, but only the Astute class carries nuclear weapons. The Vanguards still have conventional missiles. Presently, there are only four Astute in the water, *Audacious*, *Artful*, *Ambush*, and the *Astute* herself. She was the first to be launched and the class designee."

"With Scotland being the home base for nuclear subs," the Colonel offered, "I'd have thought it would have been more convenient to sail down to London to pick up the Royals."

"It all has to do with time, old chap," Winstanly answered. "They all need extensive refitting to accommodate civilians. Even after the missiles, torpedoes, launch and surveillance equipment are removed to create more comfortable living spaces, it's taking far longer than planned. They also had to build storage and refrigeration for the bread and beans to feed everyone, no matter how long they stay submerged."

"Tell me Win, is there any truth to the story about the Brits taking a few, how should I put this, selected males as well as a dozen or so artificially impregnated females disguised as crew members and government aides?" the Colonel asked.

"I won't comment on it officially," Winstanly said. "But you can understand how that would be an excellent way to jump-start the human race, should the need arise."

"Sounds like you are describing a Garden of Eden reboot, in case the rest of us meet our maker following the trial," Zack smirked. "But if what you say is true, I'd be willing to bite the bullet and volunteer as one of those selected males."

The men at the table all laughed.

"Well, remember that aside from the need to rotate its crew and take on provisions, nuclear subs can remain underwater for the entire lifespan of their nuclear reactors," Winstanly said. "At least in theory. And that would be around twenty-five years, now that we've refined generating air and drinking water from salt water."

"It's not only Great Britain," Larksworth added. "At least eight of the countries with nuclear subs are known to have their own Noah programs, including China. They have at least two submersibles."

Zack's communicator pulsed. He looked at the readout, and a puzzled look crossed his face.

"It's Sandy, Misha."

"I thought she and Hoshi flew to San Juan today. Could they have already gotten there?"

"Hello, Sandy," Zack said into his phone.

"Hi, Zack," came the reply. "Well, as fate would have it our flight had a mechanical and the earliest we can leave is 10:30 tonight."

"I'm sorry about that. Do you want us to get you passes for the rest of today's sessions?"

"No thanks. The airline gave us a couple of day-rooms at the airport hotel, so we've decided to stay here and watch the festivities on TV. In the meantime, Hoshi has come up with a super idea. He'll be a happy camper if we let him buy the two of us dinner. And we get to choose the restaurant. How does that sound?"

"It sounds great. Let me put you on hold for a second."

He turned to the Colonel and said, "Their flight was cancelled and they're booked on a 10:30 flight tonight. Hoshi wants to treat Sandy and me to dinner. Would it be okay with you to invite them to join our party?"

"Absolutely. Have them meet us at six. While you're at it, ask Sandy if she's gotten word whether Hoshi is getting Powell's job at Arecibo."

"Sandy? We have a better plan. The Colonel, Tat, hopefully Li-Hwa and I will be at Peter the Great for dinner. What about the two of you joining us at six? Great—we'll keep an eye out for you. Oh, and did Hoshi get the job? Well, ninety-five percent sounds very promising. Have you heard anything about Bertie's condition? Well...let's hope he'll perk up once the two of you are back together."

"Mention the traffic," the Colonel whispered.

"Sandy? The Colonel wants to remind you about the lousy traffic so allow yourselves plenty of time getting here. And just tell the maître d' that you're with the Kornikov party. We look forward to seeing you. Bye for now."

THE TAXI DRIVER turned to Sandy and shook his head. "This traffic and the crowds are unbelievable. And look over there. Some are carrying booze around and drinking right out in the open?"

"It has the flavor of New Orleans at during Mardi Gras," she replied.

"When I was down there a couple of years ago it was amazing to see all of the drive-through bars," Hosni nodded. " It was a real hoot to drive up and say, 'One scotch and water to go'."

"Wouldn't the cops down there have frowned on that?" she asked.

"Not at all. When I mentioned the very same thing to one of the officers, she said they have fewer disorderly conduct arrests during Mardi Gras than any other time of the year."

The driver honked and politely waved two women aside who stood in front of the taxicab. One of them giggled, and walked over to Sandy's window and tapped on the glass.

"Hi there," she giggled. "We just wanted to ask you if that good looking gentleman in there was your husband."

Sandy shook her head and started raising the window.

"Because if he isn't," the woman added, "we'd like to rent him for an hour or so."

The driver laughed. "I wish they'd asked me. They actually look almost classy. Not like the other kind, if you know what I mean."

Sandy inched forward on her seat and pointed out the windshield. "There—that's our restaurant. Half-way down the block on the right. It's the one with the green awning extending out to the curb."

"Miss, with that crowd I don't think there's any way I can make it past this intersection. Would you mind terribly if I dropped you off here so I can turn at the corner?"

"Sure," Hoshi said. "The meter shows $35. Take this and keep the change."

"There's no way I can accept a fifty, sir."

"You've earned it. Just remember to pass it forward."

Once inside they found the lobby stuffed with patrons waiting for tables. They inched their way over to the *maître d'* and asked about the Kornikov party. As he went over his list, Tatyana walked up and embraced Sandy and then offered Hoshi her hand.

"Dr. Watanabe, I'm Tatyana Kornikov. I'm so glad to have the chance to meet you. Just grab my sleeve and I'll plow us through the crowd."

Slowly, they inched their way through the mass of bodies.

"We settled for a table in the bar," Tatyana shouted over her shoulder, "because dining room tables are as scarce as hen's teeth."

She held up a pack of cigarettes and made a face as they walked. "Can you believe what these are going for? Twelve Ameros! I don't know what the conversion rate is, but it's probably enough to convince any sane person to take the cure."

Zack and the Colonel stood when they arrived at the booth.

Tatyana said, "Except for Dr. Watanabe, everyone should know everybody. This distinguished gentleman over here is my husband, Mikhail."

As Hoshi and the Colonel shook hands, she slipped the cigarette packs discretely into her husband's pocket.

"Hi Hoshi," Zack said offering a handshake and a pat on the back.

"Hi Zack. It's great to see you."

"Hosni, this is Major Li-Hwa Zaranova. She's with the Colonel's Moscow Security Division."

"Please call me Li, Hoshi."

Tatyana smiled and motioned for him to slide in next to Li-Hwa. She followed behind adding, "Li and I want this good looking man sitting between us, isn't that right?"

"I wouldn't have it any other way," Li-Hwa laughed, patting the bench next to her.

"Sandy, you sit next to me," Tatyana added, "and Misha, you can slide in on the end next to Li."

After all of the commotion, Zack found himself standing in the aisle.

"Oops. Sorry about that old friend," the Colonel said. "See if you can borrow a chair from another table."

Zack thanked the couple at the next table and pulled a chair over to sit half-way into the aisle.

"So Li—you look out of place, being the only one in uniform," teased Sandy.

"I was on courier duty today and had to make a speed-run across the pond to London. The Colonel was kind enough to have me met at the airport when I returned. Actually, I just got here a few minutes ago. That's my excuse for looking bedraggled in a wrinkled uniform and disheveled hair."

"Don't give it a second thought," Sandy said. "You always look great."

"And, Colonel," Li-Hwa commented, "I have to say you are definitely looking very slim and trim. Is it your mufti or has Tatyana been watching your diet?"

"Mufti?" Hoshi whispered to Tatyana.

"It's a military term meaning civilian clothes," she answered subtly.

"I'm afraid my husband's idea of a balanced diet is a glass of vodka in each hand," Tatyana smiled.

After staring at the dance floor for some time, Zack turned to his companions. "You know, I'm not exactly a prude, but I can't help noticing that all of the couples are dancing rather—well, let's call it 'intimately.' Is it just my imagination?"

"No love, you're right. There's a lot of coziness going on out there," Li-Hwa said. "If I had to guess, it's the realization that we could be coming to the end of normalcy, something nobody wants to talk about."

The Colonel's communicator vibrated.

"Viktor's in the lobby with a copy of the concessions," he told Tatyana. "I'll have the manager make us some copies. It won't take long."

"Should I order for you if we find a waiter?"

"Not quite yet. The evening's just getting started and I want to buy some more drinks."

As he walked away, a puzzled Hoshi turned to Tatyana.

"Concessions?"

"Over the weekend, each delegation leader met to create a secret list of items that everyone could vow would be followed to the letter. If the trial looks to be going badly, then at some point we'd give the concessions would to the prosecutor to consider.

"I see," said Hoshi.

"Since the Korr seemed to consider us guilty from the onset, this seemed to be our last chance to influence their decision."

"So then they haven't been given to the prosecutor yet?"

"As Misha understands, they will be given to the prosecutor later this evening."

"With so much emphasis on secrecy," said Hoshi, "I'm impressed that the Colonel managed to get a copy."

"You'd be amazed at the number of IOUs Mikhail has amassed over the years. We like to think of them as perks that go along with his title, one known for its low compensation and few rewards. And speak of the devil—here he comes now."

Chapter 41

KORNIKOV LOOKED ANYTHING BUT CHEERFUL as he approached the table. He dropped the photocopies on the table and slid back into the booth.

"Well dear, aren't you going to pass them around?" Tatyana asked with a look of anticipation.

"Yes—yes of course. Here Li—take one and please pass them down."

"Of course."

"The list takes up six pages," he said, holding up his set. "But before we start I'd like to say it's an impressive piece of work. I also think it will be a cold day in hell before every nation agrees to follow it to the letter."

"Why do you say that?" Tatyana asked, before glancing at the first page. "Oh… I think I know what you mean."

For the longest time all was quiet. The only sound was the rustling of flipping pages. Finally, Zack broke the silence.

"I have to say these appear to be pretty forward ideas," he said. "To say the least."

"Does anyone believe these are realistic and doable?" asked Sandy.

"It has more to do with intent," muttered Kornikov. "This document was put together by people who realize tomorrow will be the most decisive day in the history of this planet."

Tatyana shook her head. "I'm sorry, but I refuse to go down the doom and gloom pathway. Let's be optimistic. I believe the visitors will strongly censure us, and then give suggestions on how to change our ways. On top of that, we'll probably be given a deadline once their proposals are set in place."

"I agree," Hoshi nodded. "No matter what they have implied, we'll receive a slap on the wrist and a stern warning to shape up as our wake-up call."

"I guess that puts me smack in the middle," Sandy said. "While I go along with Tatyana and Hoshi insofar as our being given a stern scolding, I'll take it a step farther. I think we'll be given probation and if we don't shape up, we can expect the worst."

"Me?" said Zack. "I'm a born-again pessimist. We're going to get axed. Have any of you been following the odds makers in Las Vegas. This morning they were giving 12 to 1for annihilation. What's your take, Colonel?"

Kornikov looked down and swirled his drink. "I agree with Zack. They wouldn't come all this way, study us for more than a century, and go through the charade of a trial only to tell us to play nicely from now on and not make them come back here."

"What's my take?" He tossed back his drink. "By this time tomorrow human beings will be extinct. The Naians might even be invited to take a one-eighty turn return here to settle. On a more hopeful note, let's read through the list. Tatyana, my dear—would you begin?"

"It appears I have by far the longest," she grimaced. "So here goes: WORLD FEDERAL GOVERNMENT, or 'WFG.'

Shaking her head at the length of the section, she continued undaunted.

"The 195 nations currently recognized by the United Nations pledge to relinquish individual sovereignty and become individual states of a World Federal Government. They will relinquish self-rule, their currency and present laws. They will participate in a Federal Congress to enact judicial and economic laws for the WFG. To prevent future wars, they will dissolve their military, relinquish all large scale weaponry and maintain a small peacekeeping militia for themselves that is comparable to the other 194 states, making it as impossible to wage war with one another as it would be for the German states of Baden-Wurttemberg and Lower Saxony, the Canadian provinces of Nova Scotia and Manitoba, or the American states of Ohio and Florida.

"While we provide no specific blueprint for the organization of the WFG, it is suggested, it would follow democratic principles allowing every citizen to have equal input into the governing of its state and the WFG. However, member states may no longer govern themselves by any existing system including, but not limited to: anarchy, authoritarianism, autocracy, aristocratic, communism, corporatic, despotic, diarchy, dictatorship, ethnocratic, feudalist, gerontocracy, kleptocracy, kratocracy, militaristic, magocracy, monarchy, ochlocracy, plutocracy, socialistic, stratocracy, theocracy, timocracy, totalitarianism and tribalism."

Tatyana shook her head. "I have absolutely no idea what some of those systems are, how to pronounce them, or where they are currently practiced. With such a high percentage of countries run by totalitarian governments, it's amazing this item ever got on the list. Frankly, I think this idea is impossible."

"I think I can top that," Hoshi sighed. Item Two: GENDER AUTHORITY. Women shall hold all positions of authority whether appointed, elected or assigned from president of the WFG down to military and local police. Men will continue to administer, coordinate, control, direct, manage, organize, and supervise areas of public and commercial endeavor."

"You have got to be kidding," Zack muttered. "What moron came up with that one?"

"You sir, are a flaming chauvinist," Sandy bristled.

"Do I detect feminism raising its ugly head?" he mocked.

"All right you two—stop it!" Kornikov snapped. "These points were drawn up by the heads of state, not by us. Li-Hwa, would you read number three?"

"I think I'm getting off easy," she said. "Item Three: A SINGLE WORLD CURRENCY. Well...that doesn't seem to require an explanation. Sandy?"

"I've always felt this would be a good thing," Sandy said. "Item Four: A WORLD LANGUAGE. Every adult shall become fluent in two languages: that of their own country, and a yet-to-be-determined world language. Individuals shall be free to learn and speak as many languages as they wish, in addition to the required two."

"Zack?"

"Item Five: EDUCATION ," said Zack. "Each citizen with normal mental ability and aptitude will complete a minimum of twelve years of schooling. The curriculum must include, but not be limited to, art, anthropology, biology, chemistry, economics, geography, geology, history, mathematics, music, physics and astronomy, sociology and psychology. Mathematics must include algebra and geometry. No state will be allowed to sanitize its history, or sanction home or parochial schooling."

"That brings it back to me," said the Colonel. "Item Six: A WORLD COURT. This court will consist of judges chosen from an unspecified number of states. Each state will maintain lower courts that adhere to agreed-upon principals, statutes and laws. And we are back to you Tatyana."

"Seven: MEDICAL CARE. Every citizen will be provided with a lifelong universal standard of quality medical care, details prescribed at a later date. When a person reaches eighteen years of age, they will execute a document acknowledging that they understand they will be denied medical care and or welfare if it is determined that any future afflictions and disease were the result of their own unhealthy life style."

"So in other words," Hoshi said, "if anyone chooses to abuse their body and becomes ill from the abuse, they won't be eligible for aid."

"Hoshi you're next."

"Eight: POPULATION. Within thirty years, all states will have decreased its population to a number set by a world commission. That organization will decide the number of citizens that each state can sustain using its own natural resources. The manner of population reduction must be approved by the World Court.

"In states with inadequate natural resources, the population limit will be determined by the state's ability to generate an economy through tourism, food production, manufacturing, and providing educational and research facilities to other states as well as hosting prisons for world criminals."

Li-Hwa said, "Item Nine is short: CHURCH AND STATE: All governments will be free from the impact, influence, or effects of any theological institution. Next?"

"Another long one," Sandy groaned. "Item Ten—SPORTS: To wean human nature from violence, all combative sports will be prohibited including, but not limited to, boxing, fencing, sport hunting of any living creatures, wrestling, and American football.

"Non-combative sports will be allowed and promoted. They

include, but are not limited to—aquatics, archery, baseball, basketball, boating, cricket, curling, cycling, equestrian events, fishing, golf, gymnastics, handball, hang gliding, supervised ice hockey, orienteering, and parachuting—gosh, give me a second to take a breath—supervised horse and greyhound racing, racquet sports, supervised rodeo events, rowing, soccer, softball, sport shooting, tennis, volleyball, weightlifting, winter sports including bobsled, luge, sledding, skating, skiing, and land-water-air vehicle racing."

"Oh, for crying out loud," Zack sighed. "Moving on to Item Eleven: NATIONAL BOUNDARIES. Most existing national boundaries will remain intact. Some will be adjusted to more accurately take into account topography, natural resources and ethnicity."

"Item Twelve: SPACE EXPLORATION," began the Colonel. "Both crewed and non-crewed exploration will be allowed between the Sun and the edge of the Kuiper Belt. All research into propulsion systems that would allow interstellar travel or the testing thereof is prohibited."

"Item Thirteen, INCARCERATION," said Tatyana. "There will be two categories of facilities housing prisoners. Those serving life sentences with no parole will be confined in states other than the state where the crime was committed. There will be no visitation. Criminals not serving life sentences will be confined within the state the act was committed and will be allowed visitation."

"Just three left," said Hoshi. "Item Fourteen— CAPITAL PUNISHMENT: Execution and mutilation are prohibited with one exception. If convicted of a murder, a prisoner may opt for immediate and humane execution at any time while serving a life sentence.

"Those serving life sentences with no parole will be housed in a humane facility, but without entertainment amenities. As mentioned in number eight, such facilities will be established in states with high poverty or few natural resources.

"Item Fifteen," Li-Hwa said. "PARENTING. To eliminate the causes of Xenophobia; the procreation of children will be allowed only to legally married individuals from dissimilar races originating from any of these subdivisions: (1) Africa; (2) the Caribbean, including Central America and Mexico; (3) North America; (4) South America; (5) Asia, including Central, East, North, South, Southeast and Southwest regions; (6) Circumpolar North; (7) Europe; (8)

Australia; and (9) Polynesia, including Melanesia, Micronesia, and any regions not previously mentioned. Married persons who choose not to have children may be of the same race and gender."

"And finally," Sandy said with a sign of relief. "Item Sixteen: GUN CONTROL. A private citizen may not own or possess a weapon with lethal capability. Only non-lethal devices that temporarily incapacitate will be allowed."

"I have my own idea on how to make those items with regard to crime work better," said Li-Hwa, stacking her pages.

"Let's hear it, Li," Zack said.

"I'd call it 'Lie Detection.' To reduce crime, the Korr will provide humans with a foolproof lie-detecting device. This is because today's criminals know in advance that even when apprehended and tried, they won't necessarily receive jail time. "

"A capital idea," the Colonel said. "In order to reduce crime, a suspect could no longer rely on using a false alibi or a bogus witness. All individuals suspected of a crime would take the lie detector test. If they passed they would be exonerated. If they failed they'd be sentenced. Additionally, those who are currently incarcerated would be examined. If shown to be innocent they would be released."

"Another advantage would be that we'd never have criminals released because a judge or prosecutor made a procedural error," added Sandy. "Trials, attorneys and jury systems would be eliminated. I have another suggestion. This would be Number Eighteen—'Entertainment.' We'd place greater restraints on the film, music, print and television industries."

"Enough of this," sighed Tatyana. "Time for food, dancing and joviality. Let's celebrate what may prove to be our final get-together. And please—help me convince our shy and retiring Colonel to join me on stage when Karaoke begins. I promise you some fantastic Russian folk songs and harmony."

"This you will not want to miss," Li-Hwa laughed. "They are fantastic."

When Sandy began to show concern about missing their flight, the Colonel told them not to worry. He had arranged for Viktor to drive them to the airport in the embassy car with lights flashing and embassy flags fluttering.

"Does anyone have special plans for tomorrow's recess?" Tatyana asked.

"I believe I own bragging rights," Zack said. "POTUS has made arrangements for Li and me to take Marine One and fly off to a mystery destination and lunch."

"POTUS?" Hoshi asked. "I assume that is political-ese for President of the United States. I know that Air Force One is the president's large plane and Air Force Two is the vice president's. But who flies in Marine One?"

"Marine One is a helicopter," Kornikov began dryly, "The VH-60N to be precise. It transports the president on short trips when a motorcade would be too time-consuming and the use of Air Force One would be overkill. And here's one very interesting point—rather than regulation flight suits, the crew wears dress blue uniforms on Marine One. In addition...."

"Please darling, less minutia," Tatyana laughed. "Calling it the President's helicopter would have been enough."

"Well," the Colonel continued, "I hope that you two don't enjoy yourselves too much in Puerto Rico. We don't want you to forget coming back for visits. And before I forget, I have some wonderful news. Tatyana and I just found out our application for adoption has been approved. With a little luck, we'll soon have twins—two beautiful three-year-old boys."

Li-Hwa hugged Tatyana warmly. "Congratulations," she said. "That announcement gives me the perfect time to say that in two days, Zack and I will begin our own personal, three-day project."

"That's so exciting, Li," Sandy gushed. "Best of luck."

Zack was talking to Hoshi and had only heard part of Li's comment. "Slow down Li. Before you get me hooked on one of your home projects, I'm not a handy man. Never was, never will be."

"You better check the batteries on your Stupid-O-Meter," Sandy whispered. "You will definitely not see Li hiring a handy man for her project."

"I do believe the man is blushing," Tatyana said.

A FEW HOURS LATER, they gathered outside the restaurant to offer final goodbyes. Viktor pulled up in the Ziv, with diplomatic flags unfurled. He held an exterior green light up high, and caught the Colonel's eye. Kornikov nodded, and Viktor placed it on the roof above the windshield.

Tatyana handed Sandy a basket. "We just couldn't let you leave empty handed, so we put in fruit and sandwiches for the flight. My husband added a personal touch with caviar. My contribution is a bottle of champagne."

Thank you very much," Hoshi said. "Though we feel we couldn't eat another bite, I'm sure we'll find room enough to enjoy the champagne."

"You know," added Sandy, "we really should have been allowed to pay our share of dinner."

The Colonel replied with a wave of his hand. "Don't give it a second thought," he said. "I used Zack's credit card."

Zack patted his pants pocket. "I knew I should have left that puppy at home," he winked.

"Well, we need to get going," Sandy said. "If we miss this flight we'll be back here looking for a couch to sleep on."

Sandy's communicator buzzed. She glanced at the readout and her face brightened. "Talk about déjà vu," she beamed. "It's Bertie."

Moments later, she turned to the others with a smile that knew no bounds. "Bertie just heard that his new meds have taken hold with a vengeance," she said. "The doctors all think he'll have at least two more good years, as long as things keep progressing."

Everyone was elated at the news.

"Colonel," asked Viktor, "should I call you when I am leaving the airport?"

"That won't be necessary," Kornikov replied. "You can return to the Embassy. My wife and I will find a ride home."

Before climbing into the limousine, Sandy handed Li-Hwa a gift. "I already have one of these at home," she said. "I wanted you to have this extra one."

"Thanks Sandy. But I'm uncomfortable accepting a gift when I don't have one for you."

Sandy stepped into the Ziv. "Don't give it a second thought. If you like it, let me know. If you don't, Zack knows where to return it. Goodbye everybody. We love you all."

RETURNING TO their table, Li-Hwa tore open the gift with relish.

"It looks big enough to be some kind of a fur," Zack said. "You know, she has one in San Juan for those cool evenings when she wants to look her best."

Finally, the gift was unwrapped. As she pulled out two large bath towels, Li-Hwa tried not to show disappointment.

"Bath towels?"

Zack pointed inside the box. "Dig a little deeper," he said. I think there's an envelope peeking out at you."

Li-Hwa found the envelope, and let the contents slide out on the table: an insurance card and registration, a set of keys, and a photograph of a Triumph TR7 1500.

"Oh-my-God," she squealed. "She left me her car!"

"That's right," Zack laughed. "English racing green with a tan rag top. But if you don't want it, Winstanly or Larksworth will gladly take it."

"Are you crazy?"

On the dance floor, the band leader took the microphone. "Let's have everyone who isn't falling asleep come up here for our version of American line dancing," he announced. "Get ready for the Hopak!"

The Colonel turned to Tatyana. "Slip me a couple of your pain pills. I may need some reinforcement with these old knees."

Zack asked, "What the heck is the Hopak?"

"It's actually a Ukrainian dance," Tatyana explained while digging through her purse, "but we like to pretend it's Russian. You start out squatting, with your arms extended forward or your hands on your hips. Then you hop back and forth on one foot while kicking straight out the opposite leg. Mikhail and I were great as a team twenty years ago. But tonight, I'm not too sure."

After washing the tablets down with vodka, the Kornikov stood, stretched, squatted twice, and offered Tatyana his hand. Before she could take it, Li-Hwa reached and took it for herself.

"Would you consider accepting me as a partner, Colonel?"

"I'd be delighted, Li."

Tatyana rose and took Zack's hand in hers. "Well handsome, that leaves just you and me. What do you say? Shall we sit here and enjoy the show or head out there on the dance floor?"

When the vote was taken, the result was unanimous.

They stayed at the table.

Chapter 42

IT WAS Tuesday morning and time for the prosecution's summary. Tension crackled throughout the auditorium. Everyone hoped their four-hour intermission would be a relief from what they feared would be a disaster—the Prosecutor's summary.

As Zack and Li-Hwa were settling into their seats he said, "I can't remember seeing everyone so quiet."

"It's not so surprising," she responded. "The reality of the situation is starting to kick in. And after listening to our lackluster summation yesterday, I think our only hope of pulling us out of the loo will be the concessions. I pray they have enough substance to tip the scales in our favor. On a brighter note, have you heard any more about Sandy's special report this evening? Giving her a live link to the proceedings from San Juan should make her broadcast as effective as if she were in Washington."

"I spoke to Bertie earlier. He said word is already out about her return to San Juan as well as her looking for a permanent job, there. Some radio and TV stations have already made lucrative offers. Let's hope her only problem will be to decide which one to accept."

"That's fantastic and an example of how some people can get on with their lives in spite of the trial," Li said.

"It also may be a coping mechanism. Something humans are good at."

"Well here comes the feature attraction—Mister Warm-and-Fuzzy himself, along with the Chairman. Things should start heating up any minute now."

The Chairman and Visitor stepped to the podium. The assembly hushed as the Chairman adjusted the microphone

"Good morning," he said. "Rather than recap the events of the past week, I believe we can just get with our next order of business, the Prosecution's summation. After that, we will adjourn for four hours before returning here to find out the decision." He stepped back and took a seat.

The Visitor began.

"As the assembly president suggests, it would be redundant for me to go over what took place last week with our charges. This summation will prove beyond all doubt that your problems and lack of effective action are indefensible.

"None of the information I will present is new. Coming from your own records, it has always been available if you had taken the time to seek it out. Your foremost problem is the exponential growth of your population, a subject you continue to debate but never come to an agreement on.

"Over the years that growth has occasionally come to a halt, but not because of your coming to your senses. The respites were due to war, disease, and natural disasters. This proves that those pauses in growth were only temporary.

"Other problems of lesser consequence include toxic waste, fossil fuel depletion, deforestation, carbon emissions, soil erosion, rising sea levels, and the overall degradation of your planet's atmosphere, land, and oceans. Add to that food and topsoil are less available to you, and the result is obvious: you have ever-more mouths to feed and less food to do it with. Though the solution to these issues is not complicated, they will remain unresolved as long as your political and theological communities persist in encouraging an increased population.

"And why is that, may you ask? Governments require more and more people to support their needs through taxation. Faith-based organizations need more followers to promote their beliefs and to proselytize. And countries need citizens to produce materials for their economy, and to maintain your various military establishments.

"Eventually your land, a non-renewable resource, will become overtaxed to the point where it can no longer provide for the growing population. That result is mathematically calculable. Within eighty years you will be so burdened with famine, disease and malnutrition, that war will be your only solution to reduce your population, one way or another.

"While each of you can recite the name of a favorite television program, motion picture, vacation spot or a restaurant, how many can discuss the 1987 Montreal Protocol, the 1989 Hague Declaration and the 1992 Kyoto Protocol or the findings of subsequent conferences on your failure to end world poverty and address issues of climatic change?

"Consider your feeble attempts to produce environmentally sustainable and stable societies without depleting resources and adding pollution. The basic cause of these problems is your throw-away addiction. You refuse to recycle your own human sewage to let you live in a world without dependence on coal, oil, or gas. You also will not agree on which alternative energy sources to pursue such as solar, wind, nuclear, or marine tides.

"Consider three facts. First, you are attempting to feed ten billion people with one billion less acres of trees and one trillion less tons of topsoil compared to what you had fifty years ago.

"Second, you use one-third of your supply of food grain to feed livestock, to enable you to continue consuming animal flesh.

"And third, your worldwide military spending budget is one and a half trillion dollars each year. Is that because your military leaders convince you they need weapons in the event a war breaks out? Or, in the event peace should break out, are those leaders doubtful they could find employment in the civilian sector that would offer them the perks now enjoyed in the military?

"Do you actually believe it is possible to change human nature to stop measuring your success by wealth and possessions? The Korr does not believe so. We think your materialistic nature and consumeristic addictions are permanent aspects of your character preventing the changes needed to maintain a sustainably habitable planet. Without these changes, you rob natural resources from your descendants, and burden them with devastating debt.

"You have turned a blind eye to your faults for so long you can no longer see them or admit to them. Through rationalization your feeble excuses have become: no one is perfect or it's just human nature or one must survive or everyone else does it.

"This requires a dispassionate observer to identify and evaluate your most significant failures; inadequate stewardship to the planet and to each other. We find it inconceivable that any civilization that is required to live in a closed environmental would keep fouling its nest.

"There are, of course, explanations for your foolhardiness. To survive while migrating out of Africa 250,000 thousand years ago, your ancestors had to develop the necessary skills to be aggressive, deceitful, dishonest, and treacherous. The reason is simple. They had neither fangs nor wings to out-fight, out-swim, or out-run the predators for whom humans were a tasty and easily attainable food source.

"Fortunately, humans acquired a complex brain and a strong sense of self. So when your population occasionally dropped to the near-extinction levels of 20,000 or fewer individuals, you managed to persist and endure. For this you earned our respect. But that was then, this is now. Why do you continue to retain almost all of those ancient survival techniques when they are no longer necessary? The answer is that they have become second nature to you, and if not permanently discarded will become implanted in your genes.

"Had these techniques been only temporary, they could have been overlooked in the same manner you do when your warriors returned from war. You usually gave them time to ease their way back into society, discovering that most eventually do, even as others become the flotsam and jetsam of your society, living lives of dependency and indolence.

"Your history as a species demonstrates the strong likelihood that you will fail to make those changes. Normally, these failings would pose no threat to other civilizations in the nearby star systems. But your rapidly advancing technology makes it inevitable that you will venture into space, along with your nuclear and biological weapons. I'm sure you can see the threat this would pose to still-developing worlds.

"Because they would be unable to defend themselves, we cannot allow Humans to become a threat to them. Of the many civilizations we have examined, yours is vastly superior in the speed with which you resolve challenges that would overwhelm most other species.

"This past weekend, your heads of state presented us with a list of concessions in which you pledged to abide by should your guilt remain unchanged. You hoped this list, along with items we might add to it, could allow you to escape extermination. Our question to you is whether you could be trusted to follow through on those proposed items? Or, in your own colloquial idiom, are you only trying to buy time by blowing smoke up our collective asses—assuming we had them, which we don't.

"Because of the many the factors in this case, as well as new items that have surfaced in the past few days, we have found ourselves unable to reach a consensus. We will discuss this later in the day. At this time, I invite everyone to take your first recess."

ZACK WAS MUNCHING on octopus at one of the Asian buffet stations when he heard his name called. He turned to see Hamish Larksworth, director of Scotland's Ministry of Strategic Defense, approaching his table.

"Good morning Zack," Larksworth said, wiping mustard from his mouth and switching his half-eaten hot dog to the other hand. As he reached out to shake hands he grimaced saying, "Aye, and what is that repugnant item you are consuming? Good God man, are those wee legs I see sprouting out from your lips?"

Zack nodded while dabbing his chin with a napkin. "Not legs, Hamish. Tentacles. And yes, I'm happy to see you too. Is that a new red beard you have there?"

"Aye. I do na' think there's anither way to camouflage my extra chins."

"Don't worry about it, Hamish," grinned Zack. "The beard makes you look almost distinguished."

Larksworth roared with laughter. "And where be the big guy?"

"Kornikov? Behind the ice sculpture with Winstanly and Puget."

"I'll wager they be telling each ither wild tales about encounters with bonnie lassies. There, I think I just caught their attention. Here comes that big laddie now."

Kornikov waved and walked over, his two companions in tow.

"Tell me gentlemen," said Larksworth, "how are things at the Surety and M-6?"

"Just splendid," Winstanley replied. "How is your own Ministry holding up?"

"We be holding up as best we can. I hope none of you are gonna consume one of those leggy creatures that Zack has. I canna trust me stomach to see anither one a-slitherin' doon."

The Colonel chuckled as he placed his hand on Larksworth's shoulder. "I might do just that Hamish if just for the chance to see you lose your lunch."

Larksworth gave out with a hearty laugh as he stuck his chin forward and said, "Ye be a cruel, cruel man, Kornikov. Nae, I do na' think I'll offer ye such satisfaction."

"Have any of you noticed something out of the ordinary with our visitor?" he asked. "The Colonel and I think it's becoming repetitive, and expressing disconnected thoughts."

"I tend to agree," Puget replied, "though I haven't voiced a concern. But she is definitely repeating herself. Each time it happens I glance around and what do I see? Any number of furrowed brows telling me others are finding it odd, as well."

Winstanly nodded. "I agree, too. He doesn't seem to be his usual overbearing, condescending self. He keeps repeating himself, and then skips to any number of different topics."

Puget shook his head. "A psychotic prosecutor is something we do not need at this point."

"Zack," the Colonel asked, "do you mind if I mention your garage incident?"

Zack shook his head as he bit into a California roll sushi.

"The other night Zack came by our embassy for dinner and to help me with a project. Afterwards, as he was getting into his car in our parking garage, the Visitor showed up dressed as a uniformed female security guard. She said this would be the last time they'd meet and that she was going to miss meeting with him. Also, she'd be staying on Earth for some reason or another, because she wasn't able to return home."

"So that be a good sign, nae?" Larksworth asked. "Perhaps things will go back to the way they were before they arrived."

"No," Zack replied. "that's no guarantee we won't be dispensed with. I've been told the Korr don't require food, drink or companionship, so if we were to disappear, they could live anywhere—in an empty house, mansion, palace...anywhere."

"But that's when it got truly strange," the Colonel continued. "While she was explaining all of this to him, he says her moistened and tears formed. And that gentlemen, is completely out of character."

"I grant you none of that makes any sense," Winstanly said. "But to get us off such a dull and depressing subject, let's compare what we'll be doing on the four-hour break. I, for one, will enjoy a leisurely meal in a magnificent restaurant along with Jacques and his wife. Then we'll watch the world soccer match on the telly and enjoy a few bottles of ale. You're all welcome to join us."

"Tatyana already made plans for the two of us," the Colonel said. "I have no idea what it will be, but I plan on being surprised. And speaking of surprises, our comrade here," motioning to Zack, "will be surpassing all of our plans. The President made arrangements for Li-Hwa and him to spend a few private hours at a New England Inn."

"New England you say," Puget commented. "And just how, may I ask do they plan pulling that off; with, a bullet train?"

"Something better," Kornikov answered. "The President's is loaning them Marine One for the afternoon."

Larksworth looked puzzled. "Di you no mean Air Force One Mikhail?"

Delighted with an opportunity to expound on Military trivia in the absence of his deflating wife, Kornikov launched enthusiastically into an expansive history of Air Force One, Marine One, and a host of other aircraft and naval vessels, especially with Tatyana not being there to curb his enthusiasm. When it became apparent that they could stand it no longer, Winstanley took it upon himself to come to the group's rescue

"So Zack," he asked, "are you to be picked up on the south lawn of the White House as you wave insincerely to the bloody press corps as you climb aboard?"

"Actually Marine One is sitting up on our roof as we speak," he grinned, pointing overhead. "But it isn't all cake and ice cream, fellows. Li and I will have to climb a flight of stairs because there isn't an elevator to the roof."

"I knew it sounded too good to be true," the Colonel chuckled. "And with that, gentlemen, I believe our break is over. It's time to go back and hear even more reasons why we are a complete and utter disappointment to our visitors."

RETURNING TO THE AUDITORIUM, Zack was pleased to discover a new seat had been saved for him, one row in from of the Americans, and directly behind the Russians. He thanked the members and sat down, all the while thinking they probably were getting tired of passing notes to and from the Colonel.

The Chairman called the delegates to order, and soon their prosecutor resumed his lecture.

"Over the past few weeks," said the Visitor, "we have visited most of your heads of state, as well as a select number of individuals to discuss the purpose of our visit."

Kornikov leaned back in his seat and turned his head toward Zack. "This is the third time we've heard this crap," he whispered.

"To some," it continued, "my explanations could seem redundant. Others seemed to be hearing it for the first time. For some reason—whether political, religious or societal—some leaders failed to pass on my information to their populations as I requested. Perhaps the fault is mine, in that I failed to disclose all of our reasons. I will do so now."

Zack leaned forward. "Wake me when this part is over," he whispered to the Colonel.

"Our original mission," it continued, "was to protect immature societies from harming themselves, as many have in the past. On some occasions we came across societies with capabilities they didn't know they possessed. On rare occasions, this included the ability to alter their past by merely wishing certain events had not occurred.

"Obviously, such powers could affect other societies on the verge of attaining star travel—perhaps even some already able to do so. We realized that it could also alter the normal maturation of any such societies in nearby solar systems.

"Though some who studied psychology or paranormal activities were confident they had found such powers in isolated cases, humans failed to recognize they had that ability. Obviously you did not realize the impact on their society if a large number of individuals ever focused those changes at the same time.

"We had been here on Earth for a few hundred years because we considered you a potential partner with us. But recently, we discovered the bubble we had surrounded your solar system needed readjustment. We have since discovered that it was prematurely weakened by your testing of nuclear bombs following your Second World War.

"Eventually we concluded that partnership with us would be unwise, given your proclivity for war and lack of proper stewardship over this planet, and towards one another."

The visitor stopped speaking and stood motionless as it starred off into space. About ten seconds later, it resumed speaking.

"You are now on the verge of discovering technologies that will allow interstellar travel. That was the tipping point that made you a candidate for elimination. That is just one of the reasons for this proceeding.

"Our second goal was to seek out candidate species to partner with the Korr to accomplish the goal of leaving this universe before it collapses onto itself.

"Such collaborating partners would also be called upon to help us position protective bubbles around the solar systems of other candidate partners, to let us investigate them before the imminent end of the universe caused them to lose their focus. These partners would help us relocating doomed societies to a new solar system should its star become unstable. They would also assist in preventing aggressive species with new interstellar capability from contaminating other worlds.

"When I say the true nature of the universe, I refer to the fact that it has ceased expanding. Its trillion galaxies are currently falling inward to a point of incredibly high temperature and density that rival those found in the proximity of a black hole.

"Two terms your scientists have used to describe a collapsing universe are 'Big Crunch' and gnaB giB—the latter being'Big Bang' spelled in reverse. We shielded humans from this knowledge by a protective bubble acting as a camouflage provided by a science that is thousands of years ahead yours. But I am getting ahead of myself."

Zack sighed in irritation.

"You may be asking yourselves why, with all of the millions of night sky images taken by professional and amateur astronomers, none have detected your bubble. We believe it was because no one was looking for it.

"But beyond this, the first photograph of a night sky object, the Moon, wasn't taken until 1826. Third, the imaging of more distant, hence dimmer objects like the great nebula in the constellation Orion didn't occur for another thirty-four years. And the first photograph of Earth taken from space wasn't obtained until 1946. Simply put, you have had little time to discover the truth for yourselves.

"In a short period of time, cosmologically speaking, the physical changes taking place in the collapsing universe will raise temperatures to such a point that life will not be able to exist here or anywhere else. Fortunately, the Korr has determined that once the universe collapses into an ultimate crushed state of matter, not unlike a black hole, it will rebound again as it did with the last Big Bang marking the beginning of this universe 13.8 billion years ago. If you do not believe me, it has all been confirmed by your own data, gathered by NASA's Wilkinson Microwave Anisotropy Probe."

Most delegates were shifting in their seats, and shaking their heads in frustration. But because no one dared to provoke the visitor, everyone sat in silence.

"We believe that a rebound will produce another expanding universe. Being optimists, we hope it will be like the one we live in now, though we cannot be certain. Or, if we are unlucky, this current expansion and collapse will prove to be a one-time event. We hope, of course, that it is just one of an infinite number of occurrences. We won't know in advance, however, because all evidence about what has happened before was erased at the moment of the last Big Bang."

"This fruitcake is starting to lose it," Zack whispered to Kornikov.

"You may be asking," the Prosecutor continued, "if it would have been more expedient simply to transform an existing species into one that we could use, considering our capability of building star ships, traveling in time, manipulating thoughts and more. The answer to that supposition is no. The species we will choose to be our partner must be able to initiate action on its own and be independent to outside influences.

"In theory, our plan is simple. The concept of removing our race from this universe, keeping it in hibernation and then reinserting it into a new universe may sound to you like fantasy. But we have no doubts it can be done. The last piece of the puzzle is to find a partner to help facilitate our plan.

The prosecutor began to speak hesitatingly. "That's why Earth...was placed in a bubble and put in a holding pattern...not unlike airport controllers temporarily delaying aircraft from landing or taking of...or freight trains being taken off of a main track and placed on a siding so that a faster or a more important train can pass."

The Colonel let out a loud sigh, and one of his companions nudged him. He turned in his to face Zack.

"I won't be able to stand much more of this" he said aloud. "What is that idiot talking about? I've heard this story so many times I could make its summation."

Zack leaned forward. "Me too. What do you think would happen if we just slipped out of here and headed to the bar?"

Suddenly, the Visitor stopped speaking and stood motionless, staring out into the auditorium.

Zack's eyes popped wide, and he froze in place. "I hope *la merde* didn't just hit the fan," he said.

After a long, painful silence, the Chairman rose from his chair and walked to the podium. He asked the Visitor if it was feeling unwell. When it continued to be unresponsive, he returned uneasily to his seat.

Moments later the Visitor began speaking as if nothing happened.

"When a civilization becomes capable of acting independently and without restrictions, its bubble is removed. It is then allowed to interact with and contribute to the welfare of other civilized worlds.

"An important reason for this trial is that you are running out of time, maturing and we cannot maintain Earth's off-line pattern much longer. Our powers seem to be diminishing, perhaps due to the increased buildup of mass and heat from the collapsing universe.

"And did I mention you have been living under a misconception? Rather than being descendants of the Cro-Magnon line of early hominids, your ancestors were actually the Neanderthals. We know this because we traveled back some thirty thousand years and instituted the change.

"When the Korr first arrived on your planet, the species we found were successors to the Cro-Magnon line of hominids. While their technology was more advanced than yours is today, the Neanderthals of the day lacked the ability you have to analyze and solve problems quickly."

The Colonel turned to Zack. Without lowering his voice he said, "This guy is totally nuts! He is saying the opposite of what he's been claiming all along and what we know. I can't be the only one picking up on this. Ask your president."

Zack looked down the row and caught the eye of President Brandstadt. She looked back and shook her head.

"Worlds like this planet are actually quite common. There are few that don't have advanced civilizations. When we realized that Cro-Magnon were not the solution, we thought about bringing a needy civilization from another star system and let it develop here. Of the two, we decided to discontinue the Cro-Magnon line and allow a different indigenous hominid species to develop—namely the Neanderthals.

"To accomplish this we traveled back to the near limit of our capabilities, about 30,000 years—the time of the Neanderthal and Cro-Magnon divergence. We let your predecessors, the Neanderthals, develop. That is why you are here."

The prosecution stopped to adjust its microphone. The Colonel took advantage of the pause and turned to Zack. "What kind of bull shit is this? We're descendants from the Cro-Magnon, not Neanderthal. I think this nut case must have flunked Anthropology 101."

Zack nodded, and the visitor continued its summation.

"By the time that experiment came to a conclusion, if was apparent humans could never partner with the Korr. That being so, we were left with the least disruptive option, for us to return once again to the Neanderthal-Cro-Magnon split and try something else. This time, rather than eliminating one, we allowed both species to survive by interbreeding. That is the reason why three percent of your DNA is Neanderthal.

"For us to announce that decision to you would be of no consequence. The instant we made the adjustment, this time line would disappear, having never taken place, at least this time."

The Visitor froze again, this time for a minute before resuming.

"Please don't despair to realize that humans are merely unimportant microbes clinging to a dust mote that orbits a..."

Again there was an uncomfortable pause. It wasn't a technical glitch. The Visitor appeared to have frozen in place, much like a video after clicking the pause button. After another minute, as it had done previously, it began to speak again

"And as if this wasn't bad enough, you have an inexcusable record of wars in the name of religion during which millions of men, women and children were tortured, maimed, murdered..."

Once more the prosecutor froze. This time it was for a full two minutes before it began speaking.

"Some members of the Korr suggest it would be impossible to get humans to fulfill the concessions and we should depart after leaving behind enforcers to dispose of those of you who chose to subvert..."

"That's all I can take," Zack said out loud. "Look around. Some delegates are already walking out. I think our Korr buddy up there is about to stroke-out."

The Visitor began once more and carefully enunciated its words. "Given the choice...humans have always preferred mystery over reality...You seem to desire something greater than you by attaching yourselves...to objects believed to have supernatural powers such as amulets, bones...crystals, and jewelry.

"This concludes our summation. Because I am concluding one hour earlier than planned, you may add that hour to your recess and return at 4 p.m."

Chapter 43

LESS THAN AN HOUR after Marine One had left the Complex, Li-Hwa and Zack were relaxed and enjoying tea at a country inn owned and managed by Anna Kingswood, a lifelong friend of the President.

As Zack Peters took his first sip of tea he realized that the Earl Grey in front of him was not to his liking, and worried that it would make him an outcast among the world's dyed-in-the-wool tea lovers. Across the table his attractive companion, a woman in her thirties, was in mid-sentence.

"—so as far as I'm concerned—"

Realizing that he'd drifted from their conversation, he tried very hard to refocus.

"—a pile of dog poop. This whole business is so maddening, so insane—"

He nodded, absently noting that his being inattentive was entirely excusable, considering everything that's happened since their uninvited guest arrived. Damn, he thought—he was one lucky guy. She was beautiful inside and out. He wondered if they'd met at a different time or place, whether they'd have the relationship they had have now.

"So as far as I'm concerned," Li-Hwa continued, "the visitor, or whatever cutesy name we're using for it, her, or him this week, can just go and—"

Zack kept nodding. It was the little things about her that

fascinated him the most. Who else would dare wear a dark jacket without concerns about dandruff?

"—up a God damn rope!"

She'd said something about insane, he noticed. If he could just slide back into the conversation letting her realize he'd been daydreaming.

"What's so insane?" he asked.

"What's so insane?" she repeated. "This whole crappy situation. Let me rephrase that—this rotten situation. That's what's insane. And then when you throw in the intimidation during the trial—oh well, you know what I mean," she waved her hand in frustration. "It's just everything. And, look at me. I'm feeling guilty enjoying our tea and crumpets and munching on this whatchamacallit while the rest of the world's going crazy."

"Scone—that's a scone."

"Scone, shmone whatever."

She waved it around and let it drop on her plate. "You know something? Any normal person would figure with the end of civilization just around the corner, so to speak, that we should—"

"Now hold on just a minute," he ventured. "Nothing is etched in stone about this being the end of anything. At most we might find ourselves forced into changing the way we go about our daily business. But even that's not certain."

"Don't play word games with me, Zachary O. Peters. You are definitely the world's worst understater. Oh, did I just invent a word?" She tapped her spoon to her lips in a pensive manner and then pointed it at him saying, "By the way, and for the hundredth time, what does the initial O stand for? Ornery?"

Zack was pleased that he could still distract with the best of them. "I thought I made it clear," he said without missing a beat, "that until I'm in my honeymoon or death bed—hopefully in that order—I'm not discussing the 'O' word."

"Okay, let me rephrase that—the 'possible' end of civilization. Anyway, an event like that should have more fanfare. Trumpets blasting from on high, lightning flashing, choirs singing—you know, all that kind of stuff."

Her words trailed off as she pulled a wisp of hair away from her eye. She turned to the window next to the table and looked outside through the white lace curtains.

Beyond the glass panes that had celebrated at least one hundred birthdays sat the Montezuma Marine One, squatted on a wide expanse of freshly mowed lawn. Its rotor blades drooped after the flight from the nation's capital. Amid such serenity, the behemoth with its military markings seemed completely out of place.

Beyond the window a myriad of trees awash with a rainbow of autumn hues blanketed the rolling hills, their greenness stripped away by the photons emanating from Earth's daytime star. To the north a white steeple from the nearby village poked through the vivid colors.

Li-Hwa returned her gaze to the room. She began drawing figure eights with her spoon on the tablecloth, all the while muttering, "Damn the Visitor, and damn us too." She took the floral print napkin from her lap, dabbed her lips and lowered her chin to one side to dab at a tear.

He took a handkerchief from a jacket pocket, leaned across the table and dabbed at one she had missed. She managed a half-hearted smile, and she leaned forward to caress his cheek with the back of her hand. She folded her napkin with precision and placed it on the table next to the vase of flowers.

Pushing back her chair she stood up, straightened her skirt, and walked past the stone fireplace and over to the Dutch door leading out to the Montezuma. She unlatched the top half and pulled it back against the wall. Leaning on the ledge of the lower door, she closed her eyes and let the sun wash her face.

Zack got up and moved next to her.

"You know something?" he sighed. "This is not only one of the most beautiful locations to be found anywhere, I find myself standing by one of the most beautiful women in the Orion arm of the Milky Way galaxy."

"You mean in just the one cruddy arm and not the whole Milky Way? And that's supposed to be a compliment? *Harrumph.*"

Zack moved behind her. As their bodies touched, he slipped his arms around her waist and lowered his chin to her shoulder. He kissed the nape of her neck and whispered: "I think I am falling in love."

She turned into him to meet his kiss. "I knew you would," she smiled. "We better find Mrs. Kingswood and thank her for opening up for us."

"You're right. Without her hospitality I wouldn't have had the chance to enjoy my very first high tea."

"Sorry to break the illusion, Zack," she laughed, "but you only had a low tea." She pulled him closer to dab at a piece of torte on his chin and to adjust his tie. "One must have finger sandwiches and meats before it qualifies as a high tea."

They turned back to the doorway to take in the scenery.

"Not to change the subject," he said, "but this doesn't really mean the end. I have a hunch our visitor might be receptive to some kind of counter-proposal."

"You're joking aren't you? It sounds like you slept through most of the trial. Remember the prosecution's closing statement? From where I sat, it sounded like we were only allowed this trial as a courtesy."

"Well, I disagree."

"Well, I'm not going to argue about it. It doesn't take a quantum physicist to predict what the verdict will be."

"I'm not too concerned," he said nonchalantly. "That's because I already know that this story will have a happy ending."

"And how, may I ask do you know all this?"

"Because you're in it."

At that moment a voice crackled through his communicator. "Dr. Peters? It's Hayes."

Zack walked to the table and took a phone from his jacket. She followed him back to the table, sat down and pulled aside the curtain. Two men were standing next to the Montezuma, one with a headset pressed to his ear. At the same time he raised the palm of his hand towards the inn as if he was being distracted.

"Go ahead, Hayes."

"Sorry about that, Dr. Peters. Captain Golightly was just calling from the Oval Office. They need us to start back."

"Did she say if the jury had returned with a verdict?"

"She just said for us to high-tail it back—ASAP."

"We'll be with you in a few minutes. Go ahead and fire her up."

Hayes moved to the front of the helicopter. After catching the pilot's attention, he began to make slow circles in the air with an upraised index finger—a universal engine startup command. A moment later, the first of its two jets hummed into life. Zack closed his phone and returned it to his pocket.

"Do I have time to powder my nose?"

"Sure. I'll get our check."

He walked to the cash register and kindly, gray-haired woman came into the room.

"Looks like the two of you are about to leave me."

"I'm afraid so, Mrs. Kingswood. You'll never know what all this has meant to us. We really needed a couple of hours of R & R. I wish we could have stayed for a few more days."

"You certainly would have been welcome. I've been glued to the television throughout the trial, Zack. For whatever my humble opinion is worth, you have done a superb job."

"I wish I felt that way," he smiled weakly.

Li-Hwa returned to the room and met them at the cash register.

"I was just telling Zack what a fine job he was doing," said the innkeeper. "I'm sure the whole world is impressed with him, also. And you know something else? He's better looking in real life than on television."

"Amen to that!" Li-Hwa laughed. She put an arm around Zack's waist and gave it a tug. "One day he'll make make some lucky lady a very happy camper."

"So what's the damage, Mrs. Kingswood?" he asked.

"Don't even think about it. I opened up for you as a personal favor to the President. I don't know if she told you, but the two of us were as thick as thieves back in our university days. She and I would like you both to view this afternoon as a personal thank you."

"I hope we can come back some day and enjoy a high tea," he said.

The words caught in her throat as she said, "Yes that would be very nice if the two of you—"

The engines outside drowned out the rest of her words.

Zack's phone vibrated. He reached into his pocket and pulled it out. "Yes, Hayes. We're on the way."

The couple started for the door, stopping only to turn and wave to their host as they stepped outside.

"Bless you both," Anna Kingswood whispered, her eyes glistening.

They two raced hand-in-hand across the lawn as Hayes beckoned them on. Nearing the helicopter, they bent forward, even though the rotors cycled a good seven feet above them. Once on board, the other crew member removed the lock-down pin from the landing gear and followed them in. Hayes spoke briefly into his communicator, made a last visual sweep of the area, and stepped on board. Moments later, the giant helicopter began its slow climb.

Anna Kingswood locked the door and lowered the window blind, revealing the word CLOSED. Turning off the lights, she walked to the counter, unfolded a newspaper and glanced at the headline.

GUILTY VERDICT INEVITABLE

ODDS-MAKERS PLACE HUMAN ANNIHILATION AT 9:1

She opened the cash register and reached to the back of the drawer. She kept reading as she took out her small handgun. The metal felt cold against her temple.

Chapter 44

IT FINALLY CAME TIME for Humanity to receive the verdict.

The heads of state and their various entourages were all dragging their feet as they entered the Complex auditorium. For the first time since the initial roll call a week earlier, they were close to becoming unruly.

Eventually, most settled into their seats; a few remained in the aisles, conversing. They all had reached the end of their patience with the Visitor as well as the proceedings. Sensing their mood, rather than pounding the gavel impatiently the Assembly President politely asked them to come to order. It wasn't until it became clear that attempts at being polite would be useless that he reverted to his gavel. Eventually, the assembly settled down.

Even those with no psychic ability were well aware of the questions that still needed to be answered. Had all of the points the defense needed to make been made? Had they been successful in proving Humanity's innocence? Did the concessions carry any weight in the reaching of a verdict? And why, after 200,000 years of existence, had aliens chosen this particular moment in time to sit in judgement?

The Visitor entered and moved directly to the podium. With chilling nonchalance, it slowly looked from one side of the auditorium to the other before speaking.

"Actually," it said, matter-of-factly, "we are as yet undecided if you were successful in disproving guilt. We will reach our decision tonight, by midnight, before any sentence is carried out."

Without so much as a word of goodbye or farewell, the Visitor turned and retreated behind the curtain, never to be seen again.

The delegates were dazed. The Assembly President had to take a moment to grasp what he had just heard. He approached the podium and banged his gavel firmly three times.

"Ladies and gentlemen," he said, "I now declare these proceedings to be at an end. You are dismissed."

At a a loss as to what they should say or do, most delegates simply gathered up their belongings and filed out in silence. Only a few stayed to argue, deliberate, and discuss.

Albania's lead delegate—unquestionably the unruliest of the Assembly—stood on his desk and unleashed a tirade of insults directed at the Visitor.

Results of the trial flew around the globe at the speed of light. How much time the citizens of Earth had to prepare for midnight depended on where they lived.

Chapter 45

FROM HIS HOME in Arlington Heights, Ralph Pendleton had always enjoyed an easy commute into downtown Washington and his office as Deputy Director of the World Health Organization.

He and his wife Krista had already decided how they would spend the last hours of this final day. It couldn't be referred to as an historic day because there might never be a future to look back from.

They chose to stay home with their eight-year-old twin daughters. Whether just a "wife thing" or a way to keep busy, Krista decided to deep clean the house, while Ralph mowed and edged the lawn, trimmed the shrubs, and washed the windows. The twins had been talked into polishing the silver with a promise of all the ice cream they could eat after dinner.

Some of the neighbors at the intersection of Nottingham Boulevard and Barrington Road had planned house parties. Others decided on a fireworks display. Others in a more reflective mood chose to attend worship services at the new church on the site of the old Prosser mansion.

The girls were happy to go to bed at ten after enjoying a treat of ice cream, chocolate chip cookies and a glass of warm chocolate milk that had been surreptitiously laced with a sedative. In addition to normal sedatives, many local pharmacies had doled out much stronger palliatives without prescriptions, the kind from which you never awoke.

While Ralph showered and shaved, Krista fixed her hair and

applied makeup. She laid out the same clothes they'd worn the week before, at the American College of Obstetrics and Gynecology dinner dance.

After making phone calls for a last goodbye to their closest relatives, and making sure the twins were sound asleep, Krista and Ralph took a folding table and two chairs out to the end of the driveway. The bucket he'd previously used to wash the windows was now a bucket of ice cubes, replete with a special and expensive bottle of Cuvee des Moines Brut.

At eleven-thirty, Ralph opened the champagne that they'd kept for a special occasion. Krista commented, "Darling, I guess tonight's about as special as it's ever going to get. Oops, I forgot the glasses. Do you want regular glasses or the engraved flutes?"

"Engraved flutes for sure," he said. "And please don't dilly-dally. I might start the party without you."

"Don't you dare, Ralph Pendleton," she said over her shoulder as she scurried up the drive with her long party dress hiked up to her knees.

At five minutes to midnight they held hands, sadly reminiscing about their happy marriage and the wonderful girls they'd been blessed with, and enjoying the soft music wafting through the air from the church down the street.

As had been announced by local authorities, at five minutes to midnight a siren wailed a ten-second long warning.

They stood and walked to the center of the street hand in hand. Many of the neighbors did so, too. Nobody felt like sitting down to take whatever the Korr had in store for them.

All too soon it was midnight. As the church bells began tolling twelve, the couple held each other as close as possible, closed their eyes and whispered in unison, "I love you."

Except for the chirping of a few crickets, the world was dead silent. After a minute or two had passed, they carefully opened their eyes. When a few more minutes had gone by uneventfully they began to relax. Then they decided to finish off the last dregs in the bottle.

"Nothing has happened," said Krista. "Everything is as it was before. Did the Korr change their mind?"

Neighbors in the street started wandering about, whispering to one another. Some looked up at the sky, since everyone knew that was where bad things come from. By half-past midnight everyone was back inside their homes to retire for the night.

Chapter 46

THERE WAS NO NEED FOR AN ALARM CLOCK. By the time it would have gone off, Krista and Ralph were already up. Not only had they survived an unknown fate, the world seemed back in perfect order.

"You know," Krista said lightheartedly, "I wish the Korr would drop by more often. It gives me a reason to clean house."

For some strange reason, the morning news seemed to gloss over the fact that nothing had taken place the previous night. Many failed to mention the trial, or speculate on the whereabouts of the Visitor.

Feeling refreshed after their second cup of coffee, the couple sprang into action . Krista started a load of wash and made breakfast while Ralph resumed his routine by humming and whistling Man of La Mancha tunes, having forgotten most of the lyrics.

Even though this would just be another school day, the twins were as perky as they could manage, though feeling the slight effects of the previous night's sleep aids.

The family planned out the day over breakfast. The very first piece of business would be to catch up paying the monthly big items such as car notes, insurance, mortgage, and any other items that had been put off in the belief that in the future there might not be anyone to send out dunning notices.

The girls were delighted to find out school was closed until the following day: the cafeteria needed restocking, much like the Pendleton's own pantry. Krista and the girls planned to go shopping, and Ralph's car was overdue for an oil change.

*****

ON HIS WAY to the garage, Ralph decided that he could put off car maintenance for another day. But he chose not to go directly to the office. Kathleen, his office manager, had proven herself more than capable of keeping things running smoothly. So smoothly, in fact, that she often suggested that for the price of giving her a hefty raise she could make sure he could work half-days whenever he wished. Sensing the weight that had been lifted from Humanity's shoulders, he decided to celebrate by playing hooky for a while, and took the scenic route to work, lowering the windows and savoring the nice weather. He knew it was probably his imagination, but it seemed to him that the sun was brighter, and the sky bluer, than he could remember.

A tourist at heart, Ralph enjoyed casual drives through the nation's capital. Sometimes, he'd even fall in behind sightseeing buses, to tour monuments he'd neglected. He was pleasantly surprised to see that streets in front of the federal buildings were again open to traffic. After being blocked off for security reasons, it seemed just one more sign of normalcy settling in.

It was just after ten o'clock when he strolled into the WHO District Office on Twenty-Third Street. Kathleen offered only a harsh sigh, and shook her head. That was her way of letting him know she was being swamped with telephone calls. She paused from answering one just long enough to motion to the credenza just outside his private office.

"There's your paper," she said, "and a not very warm coffee. Sorry about the coffee." She put an incoming call on hold.

"Need I say these phones are driving me insane? And don't be too shocked by the stack of messages on your spindle. A couple of them are from Dr. Phelps in Atlanta."

As he picked up the coffee and paper she handed him two more messages. "And I have Dr. Barringer holding on Line Two."

"Thanks. I'll grab it inside."

Another line rang. Kathleen sighed, and took a moment to recover her cheerful, peppy voice before picking up the phone.

"Good morning. World Health Organization, Deputy Director Pendleton's office. This is Kathleen."

A cheerful voice greeted her.

"And an extra special good morning to you, Kathy. It's Tom Phillips your across-the-street-and-one-floor-up secret admirer. If you glance out the window, I'll blow you a kiss on behalf of the American College of Obstetrics and Gynecology."

Kathleen laughed.

"A simple wave will do nicely, Tom. But I'll take a rain check on the kiss in case you ever get the urge to buy me lunch. And you're right. It is an extra-super morning. I suppose you'd like to speak to old what's-his-name?"

"Yes. I'm having a weird situation going on here, and I think I need his input."

"Well you're in luck, Tom—he just got in. I'll put you on hold and see if I can dig him out from under his stack of phone messages."

"Thanks. And you might mention that it's rather urgent."

Pendleton interrupted his conversation to answer the intercom. "Yes Kath?"

"I have Tom from ACOG on Line One. He says it's urgent."

Ralph sighed and shook his head.

"I'll take it right now. In the meantime, pop onto Line Two and give my apologies to Dr. Barringer. Tell her I'll get back to her as soon as I can, and ask for her new direct line."

"I'm on it."

Ralph took a deep breath and opened Line One.

"Morning Tom. Kath tells me you've got something going on. If it's anything like this stack of phone messages I've been going over, they all refer to stillborn babies."

" I wish it was just one incident," Tom answered, 'but it seems to be every birth since eight this morning. At least that's what I'm getting from the hospitals that are calling in—including big ones like George Washington and Georgetown University."

"Were they just reporting or did they want your advice."

"No, they definitely were not just notifying me," said Tom. "They asked if I thought transferring expectant mothers to other facilities might help. If there's a nasty bug floating around out there, we could be in for a real headache."

"That transfer idea might help ease the problem," said Ralph. "In fact, I'll probably be suggesting the same thing."

"There's just one catch Ralph. Most of our area hospitals are in the same boat. What are your thoughts of moving the pregnant moms out of town? Or at least to the suburbs?"

Ralph thought for a moment.

"I'll have to give that some thought. From what I gather, births happening before eight all seemed normal. It might just be a coincidence, but you know my feelings on coincidences."

"I have come up with something that's a little off-the-wall."

"Hey, at this point, I'm open to off-the-wall," Tom replied.

"Okay then. Because Washington is on Eastern Time, I figure 8 a.m. here in DC is Noon Greenwich Mean Time in England. You can see I'm still old-school and say GMT for what's now Universal Time."

Pendleton's intercom buzzed. "Hold on a minute," he groaned, depressing the intercom button. "Yes Kathy?"

"Sorry to interrupt, but Dr. Phelps in Atlanta is calling again on Line Four. She insists on speaking to you."

"Sheesh—I should have stayed in bed," muttered Ralph. " Okay, I'll take it."

"Remember—Line Four."

"Tom. Can you stay on the line? I have to take a call from our director in Atlanta at WHO."

"Sure. I have nowhere else to go."

Ralph sipped his coffee, cleared his throat and switched lines. "Good morning, Dr. Phelps."

The voice he heard was somber. "Good morning, Ralph. Have you had many stillbirths in your area this morning? We're being deluged with them in Atlanta."

"Same here. And for the most part, they all appear to have occurred after eight this morning."

"Our situation's similar, Ralph. Apparently births before eight were all normal. What's more, similar reports are coming in from California to Nova Scotia. But, there's one fly in the ointment. The times don't seem to coincide."

"I'm afraid I don't follow you."

"Give me a moment to find something in this rat's nest I refer to as a desk top—here it is! Let's see now...San Francisco claims stillborn started at five this morning, those in Halifax began at nine. I can't make head or tails out of that. In any event, I'd appreciate you getting back to me before Noon with your take on this, along with anything new that crops up. I'm arranging a teleconference at Noon and would love to sound like I know what I'm talking about."

"I'll give you a jingle as soon as I can, Dr. Phelps."

He set the phone down and stared into space. His eyes picked up on a photograph on his desk. He pursed his lips and went back in on Phillip's line.

"Are you still there, Tom?"

"Yup, I'm hanging. So what's the good word from Dr. Peach Tree?"

"This whole thing seems weirder by the minute. Janet Phelps said she's getting calls from all over the place about stillbirths. But these events aren't happening at the same time. And there's something bouncing around in my brain you mentioned earlier."

"You mean where the day begins—Universal Time in Greenwich?"

"That's the one, except that Greenwich is the place the world links its clocks to. Wait a minute—oh, crap. I lost it again. Let me chew on this a bit. Can you hang on?"

"Be my guest. I'm working on a crossword puzzle, anyway."

Ralph eyes drifted to a photograph on his desk. It was taken years ago on a cruise he and Krista had taken with Tom and his wife. It showed them in wacky native costumes including grass skirts and leis as part of an initiation for shellbacks—first timers—into King Neptune's Court.

Unlike tougher rites of passage sailors had to endure in navies around the world, cruise lines had a milder version of initiating passengers making their first crossing over the International Date Line in the Pacific Ocean.

Ralph felt a chill grip his spine.

"Tom," he said, "do you remember the cruise the four of us took that crossed the International Dateline and we had to go through all of that King Neptune shtick?"

"Will I ever forget that scratchy coconut bra? Like never."

"I was just looking at this photo we had taken, and before I start to panic, I want to check something.

"Ralphie...you're starting to scare me."

"When it's five a.m. in San Francisco, eight a.m. in DC and nine a.m. in Halifax, what time is it in Greenwich?"

"Well, if you figure in the time zone differences it would be eleven—no, twelve noon."

"And if it's noon in Greenwich, what time is it on the International Date Line?"

"It's on the opposite side of the planet, so you just add or subtract twelve hours. That would make it midnight."

"When did the prosecution say our sentence might begin? Midnight! So that's the answer to our mystery. Throughout the world, still births started taking place at midnight!"

"Sweet Jesus," Tom sputtered. "Those rat bastards…dear God, they wouldn't…"

"Bingo."

Pendleton punched his intercom.

"Kathy—in here! Now!"

She rushed in with her notepad, and gasped.

"Ralph, what's the matter? You look like you're in shock."

"Listen carefully," he said, as calmly as he could. "In this order, I need to speak to President Brandstadt, the Director General of WHO in Geneva, and Janet Phelps in Atlanta."

"Ralph— "

"STAT!"

ABOUT THE AUTHOR

A retired *Detroit News* staff writer, television host, public lecturer, and lifelong astronomy enthusiast, Navy veteran Mike Best managed to visit 31 countries during a 20-year tour of duty in the travel industry. In his novel *The Navel of God*, Mike offers an intriguing answer to a question posed by the late and great astronomer Carl Sagan: what would a dispassionate observer think of our stewardship of our planet, and each other? Mike lives in Westland, Michigan with Kathy, his wife of 46 years, along with Lily, their dog, and a cat named Fruitcake.

76009931R10257

Made in the USA
Columbia, SC
01 September 2017